LOVE'S FURY—PASSION'S RAGE

Victor stared into her deep, determined eyes. Was it possible Paris didn't know the things her grandmother had done? The full picture of the West Coast's first lady had slowly emerged in his investigation, and it wasn't pretty.

"Let's talk about it tomorrow. You haven't forgotten we have an appointment in the morning?"

Paris refused to be sidetracked. "I want to know now."

"Darling—"

She shook her head, her honey-gold hair glinting on her pink sweater in the glow of the candles like burnished copper. "Don't patronize me!"

Exasperated, he said, "What the hell do you want me to do?! One minute we're lovers and the next you're carving up every word I say and spitting the pieces back at me! Is this a business discussion or a personal one?"

Paris pushed away from the table, too upset to control her temper. "Is there a difference?" She glared. "Don't you find me much easier to convince after you've taken me to bed? Isn't that why you set out to romance me . . . ?"

PARIS

by Christina Carroll

*A glittering, irresistible novel
about women in the fast lane*

PARIS

CHRISTINA CARROLL

CHARTER BOOKS, NEW YORK

PARIS

A Charter Book/published by arrangement with
the author

PRINTING HISTORY
Charter edition/October 1986

ISBN: 0-441-65023-6

Charter Books are published by The Berkley Publishing Group,
200 Madison Avenue, New York, New York 10016.
PRINTED IN THE UNITED STATES OF AMERICA

To Gayle and Clancy,
for the good times . . .

Author's Acknowledgments

Ocean Beach is, of course, Long Beach, California. The historical background is easily recognizable, but the characters are purely fictitious, as are their experiences and actions. No similarity to persons living or dead is intended.

I would like to thank a number of people who shared their knowledge and memories of Long Beach and made the writing of this book possible: Jeanne and Ken Kopp, Roberta Bemis, Gayle Colden, Clarence Petty, Evelyn Kopp, Sue and John Sperry. And a very special thank you to Dan Marlowe, who was willing to share quite a different experience.

RACHEL

❧ Prologue ❧

FOG LINGERED IN the early morning quiet. The street lamps, which had not yet been extinguished, shimmered in rainbow halos. A faint sound, indistinguishable at first, roared closer until the distinct clatter of car engines and honking horns could be heard. The fog took on a pink cast as headlights winked at the end of the street. Voices and laughter rang out as a caravan of cars careened around the corner and pulled into Union Station. The lead car, a shining black Reo, pulled up before the columned entrance in a screeching halt. Half a dozen young people spilled out before the driver had braked completely.

"Hey! You can't park there!" A uniformed railroad employee tried to wave them off. A tall, dark-haired youth flung his arm across the man's shoulders and drew him along with the laughing group. The man looked back helplessly as three more cars cut their engines and disgorged passengers.

In the last car, Rachel Grant drew the collar of the Nearseal coat around her neck as damp, cold air filled the car when the driver opened the door. She had long, luscious brunette hair and a slender neck that gracefully curved into an oval face graced by high cheekbones and violet eyes. She had the air of a woman unaware of her own beauty, though her glowing eyes hinted of an acute intelligence that absorbed and assembled

3

the events unfolding now. The man beside her, fair and lanky, was not her equal in looks or acuity, but he did possess a rambunctious eagerness that was helpful at the least, if lacking in the elegance to be tagged "gentlemanly." He scrambled for the latch, jumped out ahead of the party, and turned to help Rachel from the vehicle. But as she put her gloved hand in his, Amelia Bixton pushed impatiently past her.

"Oh, do hurry—the train will be leaving!" she cried, and tumbled forward in her haste. Elliot Maveen released Rachel's hand to grab the other woman and help her out.

"There's plenty of time," he said, laughing in a musically deep voice. "I'm not in that much of a rush to be off to war."

Amelia giggled. When she tried to cling to him, Elliot adroitly freed himself and handed her over to Nat Sherman, who had climbed down from the front seat and waited. Then he turned back to Rachel and offered his arm. Rachel took it as they followed the boisterous, laughing crowd into the station.

Ahead, the others clustered around handsome Josh Fantazia, the girls fawning and the boys full of colorful camaraderie. With animated, striking features that bespoke both strength and elegance, a firm body that tapered from his broad shoulders, Josh bore his ancestry in uniform well. He had an animal magnetism, yet a refinement that showed in the graceful way he carried himself. Josh still had his arm around the station man's shoulders as Rachel and Elliot walked up, including him in the revelry as though he'd driven from Ocean Beach with them. The man had forgotten the illegally parked cars and was relishing the festivities. Rachel wondered if they'd passed him the bottle. She'd been the only one to decline it in the Buick. Even Elliot had taken a grudging sip since, like Josh, he was a guest of honor and it was expected of him. Ocean Beach was giving a gala send-off to two of its finest, both going off to war. She shivered inwardly, not realizing she hugged Elliot's arm until he smiled. *How young they are to be going off to fight and kill,* she thought. It was difficult to imagine the sound of gunfire or shells exploding, even more impossible to visualize trenches and mud and wounded men—and death. She shuddered again, and this time Elliot squeezed her gloved hand. She smiled up at him, in acknowledgment.

Why had she come? She'd be branded Elliot's girl, even

though their dates had been limited and confined to groups. But everyone had been caught up in the war fever. Young enlistees were heroes to be feted and sent off boisterously to the war so that only happy memories lingered with them. How could she refuse to be part of it? She would have preferred an invitation from sexy Josh Fantazia, but he seemed not to know she existed—at the moment. Usually women swarmed around him and diverted any attention he cast her way. Although she had only been out with Elliot twice, she had scarcely exchanged more than a few words with Josh, who was older by two years, and a student at Stanford. When they passed on the street, or when they were in high school together, his eyes had glowed as they took her in, and he had acted as though he knew who she was. Certainly her last few years had seen her blossom into what the town considered a beauty, and she was known to be gifted; however, a senior paying attention to an underclasswoman, much less someone ranked lower on Ocean Beach's social scale, was unheard of. Yet, he had seemed several times, in their confrontations, ready to take her arm and escort her aside. No full-fledged conversation developed, because if he paused and said hello, he'd soon be surrounded by his clique—women his age, and his endless male companions, all from Ocean Beach's wealthiest.

Elliot, on the other hand, had gone directly from graduation at Ocean Beach High School to work in his father's profitable auto livery business. He'd been an honor student, and possessed extraordinary promise as a tenor in the church choir —to the extent that many encouraged him to go to Hollywood. But so far he seemed content to stay attached to Ocean Beach. His beautiful voice would most likely only grace the heights of the church's rafters, but with the war ahead, anything might change, including Elliot's heart.

Elliot and Josh were as different as night and day. Physically, Josh was classically handsome and dark, and athletic, while Elliot was light, and almost willowy in appearance. Fantazias, too, were old blood. They didn't toil for a living, they simply lived. A great-grandfather had married into a Spanish land-grant family. The descendants were in land management, finance, and politics. Old money gave them rights and privileges. It could have gotten Josh out of going into service. Her father had said it was common for wealthy young men to buy their deferments. Why hadn't Josh?

The crowd had moved onto the platform, and girls and boys alike jostled to be close to Josh. He held court, his dark gaze touching momentarily on each to impart a special good-bye. Elliot stopped on the fringe, taking Rachel's hand and looking into her amethyst eyes.

"Will you write, Rachel? I have no one but my family to keep in touch with. I would enjoy hearing from you." His pale face was solemn.

She smiled. "As soon as you send an address. I shall keep you informed of everything that happens in Ocean Beach, though I daresay you'll find chitchat dull when you have too much to think about."

He raked his fingers through his sandy-red hair awkwardly. "I wish I had taken along my father's Kodak when we went on that picnic." His face reddened. "Will you—could you possibly send me a snapshot of you?"

She nodded hesitantly. It wasn't right to encourage him, but she didn't have the heart to refuse.

The train whistle shrieked. Laughing, Rachel covered her ears.

"All aboard—!!" A bell clattered.

The crowd broke into excited and tearful good-byes. Rachel lost sight of Josh as his friends surged to say their last farewells and bestow handshakes and kisses. For a moment his eyes seemed to search her out of the crowd and linger on hers.

But Elliot took her hands again. "Rachel . . ."

He looked so somber, so concerned. Impulsively she stood on tiptoes. "I'm told it's customary to kiss the boys good-bye, Elliot. Josh has more than his fair share. . . ." She put her lips on his boldly. Startled, he took her in his arms to return the kiss. When he released her, she studied his glowing pink face.

"All aboard—!!"

Suddenly the other women in the party noticed Rachel's action and mirrored her attentions. Amelia and a dark-haired girl who'd ridden in the Buick with them crowded against Elliot. Amelia flung her arms about him and gave him a resounding kiss on the mouth, holding him so long he finally disentangled himself breathlessly.

"I know you're going to be a brave soldier!" Amelia clung to him, posing her head on his shoulder as though for a portrait. The dark-haired girl took Elliot's face between her hands and pressed her lips to his with a loud smacking sound. His color deepened. Josh, meanwhile, was still occupied by others not more than ten feet away. But with the crowd so thick, it could have been fifty.

"You're both so wonderful—you and Josh—I can't bear to see you off to this terrible war. . . ." Tears spilled over the dark-haired girl's long, dark lashes.

Rachel smothered a smile. Elliot hadn't even met the girl before this morning, when, disappointed at not being able to ride in the Reo with Josh's immediate court, she'd been relegated to the Buick.

"All aboard!!!"

Elliot looked at Rachel. She hid her hands in her muff.

"Good-bye, Elliot—"

"Hey, we're off, fella." Josh pushed toward them. Clamping Elliot's arm, he fended off the two girls as he gazed at Rachel. It was another one of those brazen looks that she could never quite interpret.

"I don't believe we've kissed," he said with a grin. "You can't send me off to fight for my country without a talisman, can you, Rachel?"

Astonished to hear him use her name for the first time, she shook her head. "Of course not. That would be unpatriotic."

He closed the space between them in a stride, sweeping her into his arms and bending her off balance as he claimed his due. His lips were warm and hard against hers, and for an instant she felt the wet heat of his tongue. He released her mouth but kept his arm about her waist and gave her a quick squeeze. She swallowed hard and tried to catch her breath.

"I'm told you will undoubtedly be valedictorian of the Class of '18," he said with a grin, still holding her as though he had a proprietary interest. His warm embrace sent a flush through her cheeks. "I expect you to mention the brave lads of Ocean Beach who are saving the world to make it safe for democracy." He tilted his fedora at a rakish angle. "And I expect you to be here to greet me when I return the conquering hero." He brushed her lips affectionately, then grabbed Elliot's arm, not knowing how stunned she was by his recognition, nor how her heart raced.

"Over there—over there . . ." He sang in a deep baritone, two-stepping to match his stride to Elliot's, then affecting a military march. At the steps of the Pullman he solemnly shook the conductor's hand before climbing aboard. He and Elliot stood on the car platform and surveyed the farewell party, waving. Josh blew kisses from the tips of his fingers, which the girls eagerly returned amid shouts and cries. For a moment Josh's eyes caught Rachel's, and her heart pounded harder. Down the station, the engine chugged and clouds of steam billowed into the chilly gray morning.

Rachel was caught up with the group of boisterous young people as they followed along the platform until the train picked up speed, then ran as they chanted the refrain Josh had begun.

"And we won't come back 'til it's over, over there!" A few of the more athletic boys raced the train until they reached the end of the platform. The whistle blasted a last echo. . . . The train grew smaller in the distance, but Rachel imagined she could see Josh and Elliot waving. And both to her.

Could she be so self-centered? Yes, Josh must have been waving at the cluster of them on the platform, not at her in particular. Yet the way he had kissed her lingered in her mind. . . .

The ride back to Ocean Beach was more subdued than the trip up. There was speculation about what Josh and Elliot would encounter when they reached French soil. Was it true that the Germans had stopped the allies at Ypres? War gossip, gleaned from the newspapers, fed imaginations and stirred lively discussion. Rachel scarcely heard. Huddled in a corner, she could no longer repress thoughts of Josh's kiss. She recognized how it had unsettled her and left her with a strange excitement. She'd thought Josh was unaware of her presence, especially today with so many of his friends around. The farewell caravan to the train had been his idea, shared with Elliot with *bonhomie* because the two would soldier together. His largess had included a casual remark that if Elliot had anyone who wanted to see him off, "bring them along." And so her invitation had come from Elliot, not the host.

Yet as she remembered the sequence of events, she recalled that Josh had known her name—and his kiss had drawn her into his charmed circle. She felt an inner tremor, like the faint aftershock of an earthquake. Josh Fantazia, who had always seemed so remote from her life, someone to be worshipped from afar in the small society of Ocean Beach, had sought her out. She was now certain of it. Her life had shifted in that moment as surely as if the earth had moved. She had felt Josh's power fuse with her own. She had glimpsed vistas beyond the limits she had been willing to envision until now.

When the war was over. . . . She knew she would have him when he came back. The glow in his eyes had been the glow of desire.

❧ One ❧

SHE RUSHED UP the steep road, heedless of the loose gravel under her white cabretta boots that threatened to pitch her headlong. An angry pulse thundered in her ears, and her face was damp with perspiration from the glaring sun, giving her beauty a flushed glow. She raised the confining hem of the silk georgette crepe, not caring if any of the neighbors saw her exposed calves. She would be the talk of the Hill soon enough. Let them have their malicious pleasure. She lifted her face to the waxing breeze and inhaled sharply.

The war, the war! Incessant talk of the war sickened her. The Armistice had been signed months ago. It was over. She would not think about it anymore. One would think Father had served in the front lines, when he'd actually been no more involved than she! California was a continent and ocean apart from the action. The way Father talked, the Western Front might have been just beyond Darien Hill.

She slowed as her anger began to dissipate, vented on her father instead of where it belonged—squarely on her. She had done nothing to encourage her parents' belief that she was waiting patiently and hopefully for Elliot Maveen's return from France, nor had she uttered a word to discourage it. But now that he was here, she would not be swept into resumption of the courting he'd begun before he left.

She turned onto the east road at the fork, away from the Maveen house. She didn't want to encounter any of Elliot's family when they would be bubbling with news of his homecoming. Her father heard it this morning at the Farmers' Market. Word of Elliot's return had eclipsed talk of crops and prices. The Maveens had received a telegram saying he would arrive soon. No day or time, but it wouldn't be long. The city was already planning a hero's welcome for the first Ocean Beach veteran. Everyone knew that Elliot had been awarded the Distinguished Service Cross, even though that, too, was shrouded in mystery. His family did not know the details of the action that had brought him glory. Nevertheless, he would be welcomed with pomp and ceremony. The city and high school bands would be dispatched as soon as the time of Elliot's arrival was known. There would be banners, a photographer from each of the newspapers, a speech by the mayor, and a ticker-tape parade, tape compliments of Hirsh & Lowen Brokerage. Of course, Elliot's family would greet him first, her father informed her, but she would then claim her rightful second place in the welcoming line.

Impatiently she brushed back a chestnut wave that had strayed from her marcel, remembering the cold morning in Los Angeles when she'd seen Elliot off. Her violet eyes gazed into the distance, dancing with the memory. His memory had been almost totally eclipsed by Josh Fantazia's kiss. If only Josh were coming home. . . .

Forcing her thoughts to Elliot, she tried to recall his face and voice. She'd promised to write, nothing more, and that only because he'd asked so hopefully. He'd asked for a snapshot as well, but she'd never sent it. She had penned several chatty letters detailing news of the Hill and her graduation speech, but she had refrained from giving any hint of romantic promise. She'd received only one letter in return, stiff and awkward and smeared with brown mud he'd tried to wipe away. It had been written at the front, though he rarely made a reference to the war except to say that he hoped it would end soon. She assumed action on the front was the reason he ended their correspondence so abruptly. Her answer to that single letter had been the last of her letters.

She had written long intimate letters to Josh, but she had never mailed them.

She was glad Elliot was coming home, of course, but she

wasn't waiting for him in the sense her father supposed. She was no longer the schoolgirl who had kissed Elliot good-bye at the train station. She was a woman, and she knew she did not want to spend the rest of her life with him.

She slowed as she passed the Fantazia house near the crest of the Hill. She had not heard from Josh at all, but she knew through mutual acquaintances that he had fared well in France; and since she kept up with the long published lists of war dead, she knew he would eventually return, healthy and in one piece. With the war having ended six months ago, he'd return home soon. She felt a flush that was not caused by her exertion. He would find her changed, she hoped. She smiled, thinking of his astonishment when he discovered she had matured so much. Since graduation, she had devoted herself to learning all she could about the world the Fantazias knew. A course at Miss Dalton's Business College taught her fundamentals that enabled her to understand the financial pages of the newspapers and in-depth articles of magazines like *Forbes;* she paid more attention to fashion, both her own and interior decoration; and she had sharpened her administrative skills by working mornings at McCutcheon's Real Estate, where she could immerse herself in the world of land speculation and financing. She became versed in the business, even astonishing her father when she engaged him in conversation he usually found only at the Mecca, where he discussed business with other merchants. "A head for business," he'd said, and she knew he was pleased. Josh would be, too. She'd never settle for the dull existence of a housewife who spawned annual babies so her husband could prove his manhood. Times were changing. A woman could have more. A woman could have a strong man to love and share his interests. A woman— *she* could have Josh Fantazia! Wasn't she considered attractive and—yes—gifted? Surely she could satisfy such a desirable, demanding man, Ocean Beach's finest?

She brushed a sleeve across her face. Summer had come early and hot. The hills were baked brown, the lush winter green parched by the relentless sun. Darien Hill always enjoyed a breeze, but today it was little more than a ripple that had a dry bite. Panting, she reached the knoll and sank beneath a misshapen oak, her back against the rough bark. She gazed down the road, where the dust she'd raised was settling. Soon these roads would be paved. The Hill would be part of the city, no longer a secluded enclave for a cross section of Ocean Beach families. Ocean Beach was going to grow, she sensed it deep inside, as though the seed for growth were within her. She was part of it. She belonged here. She felt a sense of destiny, a feeling that often welled in her. She had felt "special" since a young girl.

She sighed a moment. Why did she feel she had to settle the future here and now, map it carefully so nothing was left to chance? She knew that wasn't possible, or even desirable. Life was filled with surprises, the unexpected. The trick was to take them in stride, good or bad, and make the most of them.

She squinted skyward as she heard the roar of an airplane, then jumped to her feet and scanned the burnished sky. In the distance toward American Avenue, she saw the wavering speck of the Jenny. Clasping her hands, she watched Earl Dougherty's biplane move like a laden honeybee to the hive. She shaded her eyes as the descending plane blended into the skyline, then vanished against the background of trees and buildings.

She smiled as she thought of how Earl used to launch his homemade gliders from the top of the Hill. She and the other children would race along beside him as he ran to gain speed, then stare in awe as the big wings caught the updraft and carried him aloft. She'd begged him to allow her a try, as some of the boys had done, but Earl gave her a doleful look and shook his head.

"Your pa would kill me for sure, Rachel, and I don't have a hankering to end my life just yet. Someday you'll fly. Wait and see."

She was aware of a movement behind her and turned to find a tall, slender, ruggedly handsome man starring toward the distant spot where the plane landed. One hand rested on the trunk of the oak, but there was no relaxation in his tense stance. He seemed unaware of her.

His hair was wheat-colored, his face tanned, and his features sharp. The soft lines around his mouth indicated he knew how to laugh. His eyes were an electric blue that rivaled the sky.

His gaze lowered and settled on her. "I'm sorry, I didn't mean to intrude. I heard the plane—"

"Please, don't apologize," she said quickly. "I find airplanes exciting. I admire Earl Dougherty's courage to follow his dream." He looked puzzled, and his brow furrowed. She pointed in the direction of American Avenue. "His airstrip."

"Ah." He nodded.

He was a stranger. No one from Ocean Beach had to be told who Dougherty was. Strangers on Darien Hill were even more of a novelty than airplanes in the sky. She studied the good-looking man with interest, searching for some family resemblance that would identify him as a visiting relative to one of the Hill families.

"I believe the airplane is the transportation of the future, Mr.—?" She waited expectantly.

"Hillary Upfield. What is the excitement an airplane stirs in you, Miss—?" He smiled engagingly, countering her game.

"Grant—Rachel." She returned his smile and moved toward the grassy spot where she'd been sitting earlier. He gazed down, then crouched a few feet from her, tugging a blade of dry grass and pulling it through his fingers.

She pondered the question. "The freedom," she answered at last. "Unlimited horizons and choice of direction."

His smile widened. "You can have that without an airplane."

"I suppose. Perhaps it's a symbol that brings it together succinctly and glamorizes it."

"Do you always glamorize things?"

"On the contrary. I am very practical, but even the most practical persons can enjoy excitement and glamour." She glanced at a small cloud scudding over the clear horizon where the mounds of Catalina Island appeared a dusky purple. "Think of the good that can come of air transport. People and goods—"

"And the evil." His tone was so intense, she looked back abruptly. His smile had vanished and the lines deepened in his brow. His blue gaze penetrated her, and she felt her cheeks flush. "I have seen destruction from those machines you think glamorous. Guns blazing death when a man had no chance to escape."

Her breath tightened. "You were in the war," she said softly.

He nodded, his gaze still fixed on her almost hypnotically. "The sound of an airplane sent us diving for cover more often than not." He looked away suddenly as though he realized he was staring. "I confess my heart quickened when I heard that Jenny a few minutes ago."

"Have you been back long?"

"Not long enough." He looked at her and grinned. "I'm afraid war tends to uncivilize men. I'm forgetting my manners, blathering on about things best forgotten. Forgive me." He sank onto the grass and stretched out his long legs.

"I've lived on the Hill all my life, and I have never seen you here before," Rachel said.

"I have never been here before. I accompanied a wounded California soldier home from the East Coast."

"You're a doctor?"

"No, just a friend." Pain flashed through his eyes.

The import of what he was saying struck her. "Someone from the Hill was wounded . . . ?"

"Elliot Maveen. Do you know him?" He watched her closely, his voice matching the concerned look on his rugged features.

How had she not heard? His parents had said nothing—did they know? She tried to collect her thoughts. "Yes, I know him. The Hill is a very small place, where everyone knows everyone else—and his business, though I confess I had not heard that Elliot was wounded. Does his family know—I mean, did they before he returned?"

Hillary shook his head. "He refused to let them be notified."

"But he is all right? His wounds are not serious?"

His eyes took on a faraway look and it was several moments before he answered. "He's lost a leg."

"My God!" she cried and clamped a hand over her mouth as shock swept her. She imagined his tall form, sandy-red locks, and "academic" look—a man somewhat delicate but vital. How would he manage without a leg?

"The physical wounds are healing, but he'll carry mental scars a long time. I've seen men refuse to return to their families at all under similar strain. They feel too apart from the natural order of things to go back."

She was aware of the dry breeze against her face and the shrill sound of cicadas in the heat. "And Elliot?" she whispered.

He hunched his shoulders. "He wanted to come back. His life is here, he's never known any other. It will take time for him to adjust. He's withdrawn from—" He looked at her intently. "From everything he knew. His friends on the Hill will find him greatly changed."

She felt uncomfortable under his steady blue gaze, but she could not look away. Nor could she find words for the questions that crowded her mind. She wondered at the peculiar lack of emotion the news of Elliot's injury stirred in her. Was she heartless? Uncaring? She felt only pity, and she was ashamed.

"You will find him changed, Rachel," Hillary said softly.

She scowled, not sure she wanted to pursue the track of the conversation. It had become highly personalized, as if—

"He asked me to convey his regrets that he won't be calling on you," Hillary said.

He knew—he'd known all along. The meeting was not the chance meeting he pretended. He'd sought her out, as Elliot's emissary. She accused him with a glance, and he lowered his gaze momentarily, then looked back at her.

"He saw you pass the fork in the road and asked me to come after you," Hillary explained. "He wanted you to know. Perhaps in a few months he'll be more comfortable about it and will want to see you, but for now it will help if you respect his desire not to be disturbed."

She realized her breathing had become shallow, and she forced herself to gulp some air. "It's not healthy for the mind to retreat from reality."

Upfield, pensive though still handsome, rubbed his cheek in a thoughtful gesture. "Can any of us say what's right for another? I'd like to encourage him to come out of the shell and put his life back together. I'll do anything I can to help him. But even the doctors agree he needs time more than anything else right now. So that's what I'm giving him, and what I'm asking you to give him."

She moistened her lips, not knowing how sensuous she looked. "I'll respect his wishes." How could she tell him that she was relieved? How could she tell anyone? She needed time as much as Elliot. Time would soften the truth when it had to be spoken. If it had to be spoken. . . . She felt a surge of hope that Elliot had not framed any illusory expectations of her. "Thank you, Hillary," she said with a smile. "Elliot is very fortunate to have a friend like you." She smoothed the silken georgette skirt, brushing off a leaf that had drifted from the oak. More questions shot through her mind. "Did you serve with Elliot at the front?"

"We were together more than a year," he said, his rugged face clouding. "I guess I'm like Elliot, though for different reasons. I prefer to forget all about the damned war. It took two years from my life, and it's time to put it behind me. I'm not one to sit around reminiscing." He laughed abruptly, the lines in his face forming into pleasing proportions. "Sorry, I warned you about my lack of manners."

"I find you refreshingly honest." She smiled. "We won't talk about the war. I, too, am sick of it. Tell me about yourself. Where is your home? What did you do before the service? How long are you staying on Darien Hill?"

He propped himself comfortably on an elbow, beaming those electric blue eyes at her and chatting as easily as though they had been lifelong friends. He revealed that he was from New York City, where, before going in the service, he'd helped his parents operate a small Coney Island hotel. He was considering a university degree now that the war was over, but it seemed a waste of time when he could be applying himself to making a fortune. He didn't intend to work for his parents all his life, or for anyone else for that matter. He wanted to be the sculptor of his own destiny, and the only business he knew was hotels. He'd seen fancy spas and resorts in Europe that grossed a thousand times more than his parents did. One day he'd have one that surpassed them all. He planned to stay in California only a few weeks to nurse Elliot through this critical time, unless he found the magnificent climate irresistible. Resort hotels did well in Ocean Beach. People of northern climates longed for winter sun and those from the East and the Midwest sought cool ocean breezes in summer. Ocean Beach had everything anyone could ask for. He smiled sheepishly at the end of his long recitation, as though she had coaxed deep secrets from his most private soul. He didn't ask about her, and she was relieved he didn't force her to parry questions about her relationship with Elliot.

When at last she said she had to go, he sprang to his feet and offered his hand. She got up, brushing her skirt. He gazed into her violet eyes earnestly.

"Will you do me the honor of showing me some of your beautiful city?" he asked. "I'll be spending as much time as possible with Elliot, but he rests for several hours in the early afternoon. It would be a favor to both of us if you would help me bring him news to rekindle his interest in the world."

She hesitated, then agreed. It would be interesting to see Ocean Beach through the eyes of a stranger. She smiled at Hillary, whose fair good looks once again creased into a smile. No, she could not think of him as a stranger. How fortunate Elliot was to have him as a friend.

Rachel tilted the gaudy parasol to shield her face. Parasols were an affectation she rarely indulged in, but then, so was strolling the Pike in midday. She hadn't done it since she was ten, when her father had shepherded her to the brand-new Looff carousel, and watched her ride, shouting encouragement all the while. Her joy had soared that day. But he had never bought her an oiled paper parasol painted with lotus blossoms and pagodas.

She twirled the wooden handle and watched the rainbow of colors flicker. A thought flashed across her mind that perhaps she was becoming stodgy, and she laughed silently. If she were, Hillary Upfield was a certain cure for it.

In the past three weeks they'd walked, ridden, and driven a thousand miles! She'd seen places she hadn't visited for years and some that she had never seen before. His eagerness to absorb Ocean Beach had opened doors of her memory to places long forgotten. They explored residential neighborhoods, parks, shopping streets, the Farmers' Market. They strolled the length of Seaside Walk, from Pine to Belmont Pier, where, exhausted, they had hired a cab to take them back. They rode the Pacific Electric cars, whose rails followed Pine Avenue and spilled onto Seventh Street, then returned to American. Hillary often refused to drive the Buick Maveen's Livery loaned to him. He could not pay attention to driving and view things of interest at the same time, he claimed. When he discovered that Rachel had not yet learned to drive, he insisted she learn; he found deserted roads beyond Anaheim, where she took the wheel and practiced shifting, steering, and braking.

Hillary was good company and she enjoyed being away from her mother's afternoon teas and incessant house cleaning. She had a sense of freedom she'd never known, like a fledgling at last freed from the nest.

Hillary paused in front of the Art Theater to watch a barker tantalize the crowd with the performance of half a dozen fleas cavorting in a small box.

"Look at that," Hillary said, shaking his head. "Did you ever see the beat?"

She laughed. "Don't tell me you want to go in and see the show! We'd be booked for the rest of the day."

He squeezed her arm as they turned away. "It wouldn't live up to the teaser," he said with a grin. "The Pike isn't any different from the Boardwalk back home. The come-on is always the best part of the show, but it makes the barkers feel good to hear someone in the crowd give them a boost." He ducked under the parasol and winked. "When I was a kid, I earned nickels by shilling on the midway. I'd join the crowd around a booth and feed the pitchman lines. 'What are you doing there, Mister?' 'I'm getting ready for the next show.' 'What's the box for?' 'For the frogs.' 'Are they trained frogs?' 'No, they ain't trained, kid. Why don't you go ride the merry-go-round?' 'If they can't do tricks, what do they do?' 'They get eaten by the Snake Lady. Now beat it, kid, I got work to do. Here y' go, folks, step right up. See Ophidia, the only living gen-u-ine Snake Lady. She walks! She talks! She crawls on her belly like a reptile!' "

Rachel laughed until tears streamed down her cheeks. "Did you really?"

"Sure did. All this makes me nostalgic." His face sobered and he looked at her solemnly. "I've done a lot of thinking these past few weeks," he said. "I haven't talked to Elliot about it, Rachel. I want you to know first. I've decided to stay in Ocean Beach. It'll take me longer to get going here, not knowing people or having roots, but I'm going to open a hotel. Right along the beach. It'll have to be small at first. Army pay didn't let me save much, but I have a few dollars set aside. When I find the right place, I'll get a bank loan. I'll turn it into the finest hotel Ocean Beach has ever seen—better than the Virginia!" He was watching her, studying her reaction.

"That's wonderful, Hillary! I know you can do it—and why not here?" she said encouragingly. "More vacationers come to California than to Coney Island!" She expected him to laugh, but his face was somber, his eyes questioning.

"Is that the only reason you'd be glad to have me stay?"

It caught her off guard. She'd thoroughly enjoyed the past

few weeks, but she'd thought of Hillary as a pleasant companion and Elliot's friend. She glanced away from his direct blue gaze. He looked handsome in his white jacket, pale blue shirt, and dark blue tie.

Hillary clasped her hand. "Don't answer that," he said quickly. "I shouldn't have asked. What do you say we go down to the Virginia Hotel? I've been studying how they operate and the tricks they've used to decorate."

"Hillary—"

He shook his head. "It's forgotten. Let's go along the beach. It's cooler." He guided her onto West Seaside Boulevard, remarking on mundane things as though they deserved his complete attention.

Guilt seeped into her conscience. Had she led Hillary to believe she felt more than friendship toward him? No, he'd misread her willingness to devote herself to being a tour guide and friend. He'd given no indication he considered her anything but Elliot's girl, temporarily available because of Elliot's wounds and self-imposed isolation. She'd found him attractive, and might have flirted with him—as he had with her. But it had been to keep things light in somber times on her part. Any romantic notions he had were of his own making.

At the Virginia they walked slowly through the lobby, stood at the doorway of the dining room as though deciding whether or not to enter, then climbed the magnificent marble stairway to the mezzanine to gaze over the railing at the graceful crystal chandeliers below.

"I'm inclined to favor one large central chandelier and smaller wall lamps for softer lighting. What do you think?" Hillary asked.

"It would depend on the size of the lobby," she said. "In one this big, a single fixture would be lost."

"I hadn't thought of that," he said, smiling. "When I have my hotel, will you advise me? I think women have a natural instinct for good decorating. My mother never lacked ideas on how to brighten a wall or make the dining room sparkle."

"I'll be delighted." She'd never thought herself talented along lines that hinted of domesticity, but when she thought of it, she could imagine hundredfold ways to improve the decor. Ideas blossomed in her mind.

"Well, then, let's have a cup of tea in the dining room. The maître d' needs reassurance that we haven't found him lacking." He offered an arm as they turned to descend, then drew back abruptly as they nearly collided with a couple coming along the hall.

"Excuse me," Hillary said with a slight bow to the beautiful dark-haired woman who barely reached his shoulder.

"Oui, m'sieur." She smiled prettily. She was dressed in an exquisite afternoon dress of pearl-gray embroidered Canton silk, with fine lace inserts and a collar of a delicate pink. She resembled a porcelain doll.

Rachel flashed her a faint smile as she became aware that the woman's escort stared at her. She shifted her gaze and her mouth opened in speechlessness. His gaze absorbed all of her, sending a ripple up her spine, then he smiled.

"Rachel? Yes, Rachel Grant!" He reached for her hand and held it between his in an affectionate gesture.

"I didn't know you were home, Josh." Her voice sounded distant, though her pulse thundered in her ears.

"I haven't been very long. Four days. Make that five if you count the night the train came in." He peered at her waggishly. There he was—tall, dark, and elegant—not much changed since the day he waved good-bye on a train platform, only he seemed tanner. "As I recall, you were supposed to be there to welcome home the hero."

She felt Hillary's quick glance, and color rose in her cheeks. "I didn't think you'd remember. Had I known of your arrival, I would have met the train just to show you I can be depended upon."

"Would you, now?" he said very softly. His eyes met hers and they glowed· in that way that seemed specially directed toward her. Or did he affect all women that way, making them feel special? He was certainly a charmer.

"Josh, this is Hillary Upfield. He was in the same company as Elliot and returned to California with him."

Josh extended a hand. "It was hell over there, wasn't it, buddy? How is Elliot? I haven't seen him since we left. Is he back?"

Hillary nodded. "And not as lucky as we. He lost a leg."

Josh looked shocked. "Poor devil!" he swore, and the girl on his arm shuddered. He petted her delicate white hand comfortingly. It took him a moment to recall he had not introduced her. She looked nervous, uncomfortable, though Rachel suspected her fragile beauty heightened this effect.

"This is Collette, my sweet little bride," he said proudly, his soft dark eyes looking down at her very protectively and sparkling.

Rachel's smile froze. Numbness swept down her throat, paralyzing it, and to her heart, where the impact took her breath away. She was aware of Hillary congratulating them, asking where Collette had lived in France. The words were a jumbled roar inside Rachel's head, a painful sound that left her skull throbbing. Bride! Sweet little bride! He sounded like a four-year-old showing off a new toy!

"Aren't you going to congratulate us, Rachel?" Josh's dark gaze shifted to her, and the protective look he had cast to Collette turned to that glow she was all too familiar with.

She forced a smile. "I know you'll be very happy in Ocean Beach," she said to Collette. "Josh knows all the best places and people. You'll never lack for amusement."

Collette's doll face lit ecstatically as she clung to Josh's arm, her smile answering along with a murmur of French.

"Collette hasn't learned much English yet, but she's working on it," Josh explained.

"Will you be living on the Hill?" Rachel asked, focusing again on him. A thought pierced her: How could she watch him pass every day? His presence would mock all her foolish dreams and plans.

"We're staying here at the Virginia for a few weeks, sort of a second honeymoon." He squeezed Collette's hand, but looked intently into Rachel's eyes. "We didn't have time for much of a first one. I want Collette to get used to the ocean. The DeWitt house is for sale down near Naples."

Rachel was familiar with the grand Victorian mansion that stood like a sentinel on a bluff, standing in magnificent splendor overlooking the ocean. Her composure returned, the numbness eased. "I'm sure she'll love it," she murmured.

Josh shrugged his broad, well-tailored shoulders. "The ocean scares her." He smiled indulgently at Collette.

Collette plucked at his coat sleeve, eager to get away. Josh glanced at her with an adoring look, then said, "Nice to see you again, Rachel. Nice to meet you, Hillary. Say hello to Elliot for me. Now, if you'll excuse us?" He bestowed a genial smile as he led his petite French bride down the marble stairs. Rachel watched as they crossed the lobby and breezed out the main doors, then stood under the high columns a moment before vanishing from view.

Hillary sensed the change from the moment Rachel had recognized Josh. She'd gone from an explosion of magnetic energy to shooting sparks, to smoldering embers.

"Let's have that cup of tea," he suggested. He made no attempt to take her arm as they descended the stairs.

❧ Two ❧

THE WEDDING TOOK place in early November, when a steady dry breeze blew over the Hill, making it yearn for winter rains. Rachel's mother marshaled an army of caterers who erected a white awning to screen guests from the acres of fields, barren after the harvest. Bowers of fresh flowers, which her father had ordered directly from a grower in San Joaquin, were strung between the eucalyptus trees, trumpeting a burst of color. Potted palms and roses lined the altar and guest section, and a white carpet, laced with pale yellow rose-buds, filled the aisle.

More than a hundred invitations had been sent, and Rachel personally drew up the list of acceptances as they flooded in. Mr. and Mrs. Joshua Fantazia did not even bother to send regrets.

Her parents' wedding gifts to their daughter and her husband were generous: to Rachel a large lot on the southeast slope of Darien Hill for a future home; to Hillary the Oceanside Hotel, a modest, middle-class establishment on the bluff at the end of Cherry Avenue. Mills Grant, who'd made a modest fortune in his real estate and vegetable business, considered both gifts an investment in the young couple's future.

After a brief honeymoon in Palm Springs, Rachel and Hillary returned to take up residence in the hotel. It would be awhile before they could build on the Hill lot, until they could afford the kind of house Rachel envisioned. Privately, Mills offered to lend Rachel the money to build the house immediately, but Rachel refused. She felt it more practical to live at the hotel to make sure it got off to a good start. When it began to show a profit, plans for the house could get underway.

Mills Grant was pleased with his daughter's choice of a husband. At first he'd been uncomfortable about Elliot Maveen, but Elliot had not emerged from his self-imposed isolation, and likely never would. For five months Elliot had been locked away, refusing to see people. There was some speculation that the injury had affected his mind, but it was just talk. No one but the Maveen family and Hillary ever saw Elliot, and they didn't discuss the matter. The best Mills ever got out of Hillary was a staunch "He's doing well."

Mills understood why his daughter had succumbed so quickly to Hillary's charm. He was friendly and outgoing, and handsome, if not in a classical way, and always eager to make friends. In the hotel business it was an asset to be able to receive people warmly and to remember names and faces. Ocean Beach wasn't like some areas where an outsider was automatically excluded. With so many tourists and people from other states moving to California, being from elsewhere was an advantage. It eliminated the feeling tourists often had that natives considered them outsiders.

The Oceanside was nestled in a block studded with weekly-monthly cottages and apartments. The four-story frame building was somewhat weatherbeaten, but clean and tidy. There were forty guest rooms, plus a small apartment behind the lobby for the owners, a dining room, a kitchen, and a spacious lobby with a sitting room off to a side. It boasted a regular staff of four maids, two cooks and a chef, and three girls to wait tables. One of the aging bellmen doubled as relief desk man. The former owners were content to keep rates low and depend on steady old clientele rather than attract a new, maybe more chic crowd.

Hillary longed to strip all the rooms and start from scratch, but had to content himself with redecorating gradually. During the slack winter months, they could allot half a floor at a time to the workmen without disturbing guests. This would also allow operating profits to cover the cost of renovation. Rachel had insisted.

Hillary sat in the apartment's parlor and pored over sketches and figures, making lists of things that had to be done. He sought Rachel's advice on color schemes, wallpapers, bedding, and carpets. He realized quickly she had an eye for beauty and a knack for choosing good combinations of color and form. He was delighted when, during their first week, she transformed the hotel sitting room into a rather lush oasis. She replaced the antimacassars from chairs and sofas with bright cretonne slipcovers. She raided her mother's attic for a cherrywood table, which she polished to a high gleam and highlighted by bright pyracantha arranged in a *bleu de roi* Sevres vase that had been a wedding gift. She swept the Victorian clutter from the mantel and graced it with a pair of silver candelabra with light, graceful lines. She lit tall tapers in the evening when the shadows began to lengthen, and after the dinner hour a fire blazed cheerfully in the grate. Even the stodgiest guests commented on the cheerful atmosphere and secretly worried that their room rates would go up.

Hillary's handsome features glowed, and he had been effusive in his praise. "You have wrought miracles!" he told her, taking her in his arms when they were alone. He buried his face in the halo of her chestnut hair and inhaled the scent of verbena that lingered on her skin. "I am a lucky man. You have brought me more happiness than any man deserves." He kissed the hollow beneath her ear and caressed the silky curve of her neck. "I still can't believe you're mine. I'm overcome with guilt when I think of poor Elliot's misfortune that made this possible."

"You mustn't think that way!" she cried. She forced herself to banish images of Elliot pining in his solitude, too crippled to move.

"But if he'd come home whole—"

"Don't say it!" Guilt filled her. It was not Elliott she'd waited for, not Elliot who'd smashed her dreams. The specter of Josh Fantazia was impossible to exorcise.

"Darling . . . darling . . . forgive me . . . I love you. It's just when I think how fate managed to bring us together—" He sighed as he tilted her face to his, and bent to kiss her lips.

She enjoyed the sensual pleasure of his touch. She breathed unevenly, closing her eyes as he caressed her back and moved to her breasts, cupping and kneading the heaving mounds with his fingers. He had opened a world of physical pleasure to her.

He was too skilled a lover to be a novice, but she had never asked about the women who must have preceded her. Instead, she reveled in the skills he brought to her and explored the deep well of her passion, which often left her trembling and weak but never dissatisfied.

"I love you," she whispered in return, losing herself in the warm sensations engulfing her. "I love you. . . ."

She offered no objection when he led her to the bedroom, her dress half unfastened, and her heart throbbing in expectation.

She kept her job at McCutcheon's, both for the added income and to keep herself from stagnating in over-domesticity. She truly enjoyed being in touch with what was going on in the city, and although she concentrated on administrative work, she absorbed such a wide knowledge of real estate business, Mr. McCutcheon soon shifted her into part-time sales. Josh Fantazia had not bought the DeWitt house down the beach; instead he had built an impressive home near the crest of Darien Hill. Collette apparently had been quickly caught up in the social whirl of the city's elite, while Josh had plunged into the Fantazia empire of business and high finance.

Rachel had just finished filing the last of the papers from the wire basket on her desk one morning when the bell above the front door chimed. A young couple rushed in, laughing as they struggled to shut the door against the gusty April shower.

"Oh, dear, I'm soaked," the girl complained, shaking her velour coat and stamping her feet encased in French-heeled slippers topped by fawn-colored spats. She pulled off a wide-brimmed hat to brush away moisture that had beaded on the upturned brim, her auburn hair tumbling free to reveal a pretty though not beautiful woman. The man smiled indulgently.

"You'll dry out in no time, love. Excuse me, miss, is Mr. McCutcheon in?"

As Rachel turned, the girl released an astonished cry. "Rachel! My word, I haven't seen you since—" The girl shrugged helplessly, finding the time that had passed too difficult to calculate.

For a moment Rachel couldn't place her face, then she recalled the last time she had seen this woman. "Hello, Amelia. Since Union Station in Los Angeles, two and a half years ago."

"You haven't changed a bit!" Amelia declared. The heavy-set man cleared his throat impatiently, and Amelia giggled. "Oh, Stanley, don't be a bore!" she chided. "This is an old friend, Rachel Grant."

"Upfield now," Rachel corrected.

Amelia's mouth formed an O. "Congratulations, darling. Upfield? I don't recall . . . Someone from Ocean Beach?"

Rachel shook her head but didn't elaborate. She'd read about Amelia's marriage to Stanley Chames in the society pages. There had been a portrait of the bride before the wedding, and the next Sunday a photo from the Virginia Hotel reception. Rachel had recognized several of the dancing people, including Josh and Collette Fantazia.

"I told Mr. McCutcheon we'd be in today," Chames said pointedly.

Rachel said, "I'll tell him you're here." She crossed the office to tap at the glass-paneled door of the president's sanctum.

"Send him in," McCutcheon said quickly when he learned Chames was waiting. McCutcheon jumped up and pulled one of the leather armchairs closer to his desk, an indication the buyer deserved courting.

Amelia pushed her husband off alone. "You don't need me to discuss stuffy business arrangements, darling. Just be sure you don't let him forget he promised us the garden furniture. Go on now. . ." She gave his broad back another ineffective push. "I'm going to say here and talk to Rachel!" She settled into one of the chairs across from Rachel's desk. "Now tell me everything you've been doing!" she cried. "I heard about Elliot coming home crippled. Is it true he's still a recluse? I declare. . . . And where did you meet—what's his name . . . ?"

"Hillary Upfield." The wedding announcement and pictures had also emblazoned the society pages. Rachel was amused by but tolerant of the other girl's uninhibited questions. Rachel answered that Hillary was from the East without explaining the circumstances that had brought him to Ocean Beach. Amelia's interest had already leapt to new vistas.

"We're buying that lovely big house on Juniper Street! I can hardly wait to have the decorators in. I'm having Sloans from Los Angeles. I really think they're the most innovative. Honestly, I just can't abide all that big heavy furniture and dark colors! It would be like living in a mausoleum!"

"It's a lovely home. I'm sure you'll enjoy it." Rachel saw Miss Hollingwood glancing in her direction, but there was no way to cut Amelia off without being rude. It was a McCutcheon rule never to offend a client.

"I'd really like to live up on the Hill," Amelia pouted, "but Stanley doesn't like driving past all those ugly farms." If she realized she had committed a faux pas, she gave no indication. Rachel's expression didn't change as she listened to the empty chatter. "I told him, if people like the Fantazias don't object, why should he? But he's so stubborn. Anyhow, I like this house better. Did you know Josh and Collette are back from France? They say the Riviera is just as gay as it used to be. You'd never know there'd been a war."

When Rachel smiled, Amelia interpreted it as an encouragement.

"Josh is going into politics, can you imagine?! Stanley says it's certain he'll probably be nominated to the city council, though why he wants to bother is beyond me. But I suppose he likes knowing what's going on in town." She shook her head and surveyed the soaked, wilted plume on her damp hat. She tried to comb it with her fingers.

Rachel was relieved to see McCutcheon's door open and the two men emerge. McCutcheon was jovial. He'd apparently closed the sale. Amelia cooed when McCutcheon congratulated her, trumpeting his praises of her choice in a new home, not knowing his words echoed Rachel's of a few moments before. Rachel watched on, amused.

"Now, don't you be such a stranger," Amelia called to Rachel as her husband steered her out the door. "You know where we live!" Giggling, she braced herself behind her husband's shoulder as they went out into the blowing rain and crossed to a new model Reo parked at the curb. A few minutes later the car pulled away in a splash of muddy water.

Such wealth, thought Rachel, for such fools. A new kind of ambition and bitterness began to seep in as she turned away from the window.

Rachel glanced up from the *Tribune* as Hillary entered the kitchen. He hadn't shaved, and his eyes were red-rimmed. The flannel robe she'd given him at Christmas fell open at his chest to expose a thick mat of golden hair. She felt a familiar stirring as he bent to kiss her.

"You were very late last night. You should have slept in this morning," she scolded lovingly. Recently he'd been playing cards with the guests until late in the evening, his hail-fellow good nature hard to repress.

He shrugged as he sat across from her.

"We have to see about that fish order. If we can buy directly from the boat, we can save twenty percent. I've been thinking about having a fish special on the menu every day," she said, trying to get his mind lodged on business.

"We'd need all new menus. Printing costs..." he protested.

She shook her head as he drank the orange juice she put in front of him. "We'll list it as 'Catch of the Day,' and have the waitresses tell people what it is and how it's prepared. Sort of a personalized menu reading. Some of the best places in New York do it, as you know."

Hillary was silent as she cracked two eggs into the skillet and let them sizzle while she set ham and hot muffins on his plate. A tub of sweet creamy butter and a crock of her mother's homemade orange marmalade were on the table; she moved them within Hillary's reach, then slid the eggs onto the plate and brought it.

She had begun to worry that Hillary was not paying as much attention to business as he should. "Father asked me again about a bookkeeper. Have you found one?" she asked, masking her growing consternation.

Hillary buttered a muffin. "I've interviewed a few. The young ones don't have enough experience, and the older ones want to run everything. I'll make a decision soon." He bit off a mouthful of muffin. Butter ran at the corner of his mouth and he wiped it with a linen napkin. To him, it was okay for Rachel to worry about details. She'd already done a splendid job in a few months' time. The lobby and sitting rooms trumpeted an air of sumptuous comfort, and were wreathed in laughter and conversation that rang out throughout the day. The hotel burst with life and color as never before. Hillary had organized an ongoing bridge game three afternoons a week, to cash in on his naturally convivial nature. Though bridge was not his game, he encouraged others and put up a ten-dollar cash prize for the winner at week's end. While the women were thus occupied, he set out cards and chips in the other sitting room so that the men could play poker. There was no house prize, but if Hillary sat in on a game, he opened a bottle of whiskey for the table.

Evenings when Rachel was not delayed by a client or a late showing, she and Hillary ate supper in the apartment and afterward discussed plans for the hotel. Hillary was in favor of enlarging the hotel right away, doubling the number of rooms so they could attract more guests. Rachel said such a plan was too impractical and hasty. First, the slim profit of the hotel would not finance such a scheme. Second, it made better sense to first build a solid clientele of high-caliber people so that when the expansion came, the Oceanside would become a beacon for the rich, who would pay for luxury and a magnificent view of the ocean. If they were to be grander than the Virginia Hotel, every step had to be in the direction of elegance.

Hillary had conceded, and Rachel began decorating for luxury. But what Hillary did resent was Mills Grant's intercessions. Hillary hadn't expected his father-in-law to be a silent partner. Admittedly, he was a good businessman, but running a hotel was different from selling vegetables in a wholesale business.

He liked the old man. Mills didn't put on airs. Mills was a self-made wealthy man who owed no one a penny. He was sharp enough to be admired by his customers and smart enough to listen and learn from them. But Hillary didn't like him butting into the hotel business, suggesting he was squandering money and not paying attention to detail.

Hillary had hinted his irritation to Rachel, but she was touchy on the subject. She and her father thought alike on so many things, any attack on the old man became an automatic challenge. Hillary had learned it was better to leave some things unsaid. The subject of a bookkeeper had come up a few weeks ago when Hillary unexpectedly found Mills in the hotel office looking over the ledgers. He'd listened to Mills's lecture on balance sheets, inventories, and profit-and-loss statements, but it rankled.

The hotel was doing well. After eight months, three quarters of the rooms had been redecorated and they had a steady influx of guests. Most weekends they were filled to capacity; weekdays they were comfortably busy. Mills should praise his achievements instead of harping on sins of omission.

"Good." She settled across from him with part of the morning paper. The other half was already folded next to his plate. It was one of the things he loved about her: she wasn't a chatterer who kept him engaged all the time. She respected comfortable silence.

After a few minutes he heard her sharp intake of surprise. He looked up and saw her beautiful features aglow. "Josh Fantazia has been appointed to the city council," she said.

"Fantazia? I didn't think he was inclined to work very hard at anything." To Hillary, people like Fantazia clipped coupons and stacked money in tall, neat piles. If he was going into politics, it would feather his own nest in some way.

"He's been in his father's management firm since the war," Rachel said thoughtfully. "Knowing what's going on in the council might prove useful."

"There's your answer, then." Hillary finished the last of his breakfast and pushed the plate aside. "Has your father ever considered getting into politics?"

"Father?" She laughed. "He wouldn't have the patience for it."

"The way this city is growing, it may be time to think about putting those fields of his to better use than vegetables. Maybe he could sell them for forty to fifty thousand dollars," Hillary said, smiling. "He talks about retiring, but you know he won't be able to spend his days whittling or fishing."

Her thoughts, which had lingered on Josh Fantazia, caught up with Hillary's. It was the kind of thinking Josh would follow. He couldn't serve the people of Ocean Beach without serving himself and the Fantazias first. But her father would refuse to work for someone else, even to learn a new business. But would he have to? Was building political support any different from selling truckloads of produce? He was well liked and had a reputation for honesty. After two years in Mc-Cutcheon's office, she had considerable knowledge of how the office was run. Maybe they *could* team up in some way.

"You should suggest it to him," Hillary said. "I'm sure he'd develop enough patience to help us pad our nest in some way." When she smiled at his humor, he winked broadly. "Maybe *I* should think about it. Would you like a husband in politics?"

She laughed. "Somewhere I've heard the expression 'Politics makes strange bedfellows.'"

His smile widened to a grin. "Now, that might be interesting to explore. I may go into politics just to see if it alters our
nocturnal adventures in any way, eh?"

She felt a warm rush to her cheeks as he gazed at her
intimately. After all these months he still had the power to
make her go weak with a glance or a touch. She was disappointed when he reached for the coffeepot to refill his cup,
then settled back.

"I've been giving serious consideration to expanding," he
said. "What would you say to making discreet inquiries about
the land adjacent to us?"

She frowned. "The Crescent has been doing well. I doubt
you could convince the owners to sell."

"I was thinking of the other side. Mrs. Johnson is moaning
constantly about the lack of business and how much it costs to
have anything done. She spent a fortune repairing water damage on the top floor when she put off installing a new roof last
year." He shook his head sadly. "The estimates won't be any
lower this year. Frankly, I don't think she has the money. If
she settles for another cheap patch job and we get heavy rains,
she'll be in real trouble. She'll be glad to sell out."

Rachel was quiet. Mrs. Johnson's rooming house was one
of the least attractive buildings on the block; it was shabby
almost to the point of being an eyesore. It had only twelve
rarely occupied guest rooms. Since her husband's death, Mrs.
Johnson had cut corners wherever she could in an effort to
keep expenses low, but her occupancy rate followed suit. A
poor businesswoman. Hillary's logic made sense, but it was
too soon to think of expansion. Without a profit-and-loss
statement for the year, it would be foolhardy to take on an
additional debt. Still, Ocean Beach *was* growing fast. The
population had jumped from seventeen thousand to fifty-five
thousand in less than ten years. Maybe this was the perfect
time to look ahead.

She brought her attention back as she realized Hillary was
still talking.

". . . her daughter in Colorado. She wants to be closer, but
since the girl's husband has a decent job there and doesn't
want to move, it's up to her. She's planning to spend a couple
of weeks with them at Christmas. She says she's going to just
close up the rooming house." He grunted. "Don't blame her.
It doesn't pay her to stay open. She had three guests last

December. Now this year, with us doing so well right next door, she'll be in worse shape. Frankly, we'd be doing the poor soul a favor by buying her out."

"Let's think about it," Rachel said, not wanting to dampen his enthusiasm but knowing the matter would require serious investigation and thought.

"Good enough," he said. He glanced at the banjo clock over the sofa and pulled his napkin through the silver ring engraved with his initials, then pushed back his chair. "You haven't forgotten Teddy is arriving today."

"Teddy?"

"Teddy Reno, my friend from New York. I mentioned his letter saying he was coming out."

"Yes, of course." The visit had completely slipped her mind. Hillary had mentioned Reno's excursion about a month ago. "How long will he be staying?"

"He didn't say." Hillary rose to his feet. "Unless he's changed a lot these few years, it won't be long. Teddy's not one to grow roots." He came around the table and bestowed a kiss on her cheek, lingering there.

"It will be fun to meet an old friend of yours." She gazed at him. "Do you realize this is the first of your friends I'm meeting? I've had you selfishly to myself all these months."

He stroked her hair. "So you have . . . and I have loved every minute of it." He bent and kissed her again, her lips eagerly seeking his before he drew away.

"I'll have the chef prepare something special for dinner. Will seven be all right?"

"Seven's fine."

She watched his lean figure stride from the kitchen and suppressed a sigh. She'd been wishing he would suggest they return to the bedroom together, but he would probably dress and go to the lobby to engage guests in conversation while she prepared for work. She picked up the *Tribune* and reread the article about Josh Fantazia.

She glanced in the pier glass, giving her soft dark waves a final pat. One good thing that had come of the war was bobbed hair. The short wavy style accented the perfect oval of her face, her high cheekbones, and wide violet eyes, and on a practical level, it was infinitely cooler during the summer months. The dress was becoming, too, and she was glad of an occasion to wear it. It had been part of her trousseau, too fancy to wear at home but perfect for entertaining guests in the hotel dining room. The soft taupe put a blush on her skin and colored her eyes a woodland violet. When she was a child, her parents had taken her to Big Bear, a wilderness several hours' drive from the city. Her mother had been terrified of the rustling leaves and soughing wind in the pines, but Rachel had run about discovering the wonders of the high country. She had been enchanted by the tiny purple blossoms that grew in damp places, and had picked a handful, only to cry inconsolably when they wilted before she got home.

The snug-fitting bodice of the dress was accented by twin rows of tiny buttons in a basque effect, forming a girdle that looped at her hip. Except for the lace frill at the gently rounded neck, the gown depended on the richness of the color for drama. She smoothed the silk charmeuse across her flat belly, amused as she recalled the sidelong glances she'd been subjected to when she and Hillary wed after so short a courtship. There had been even more talk because of Elliot Maveen, but she tuned it out totally. Hillary's conscience bore more guilt than her own, but he assured her he and Elliot had talked endlessly about the turn of events, and that their marriage had Elliot's blessing. Rachel insisted on sending the Maveens a wedding invitation. They had sent a gift of luxurious table linens along with their regrets. It had been more than a year since Elliot's return from France. He was still a recluse in the Maveen house on Darien Hill.

She closed the door on the past and turned away from the glass. Outside the apartment she stood a moment feeling the hotel around her. It had been difficult to accustom herself to living here. She felt like a caged lioness looking through bars at freedom out of reach. The hotel was larger than an ordinary house, but she was confined to one corner. Now Hillary wanted to build on it. She glanced along the wall that adjoined Mrs. Johnson's property, trying to imagine the expansion. She shook her head; she couldn't visualize anything beyond the patterned wallpaper. No, she would have her house first. Then it would be time enough to push out walls.

In the dining room she inspected the table the girl had set in one of the small alcoves with bay windows overlooking the sea. The alcoves afforded magnificent views beyond the bluff, with ship lights bobbing on black waves in the distance and the luminescence of the amusement pier near the heart of the city. It never failed to impress visitors seeing it for the first time.

Because it was the first time they were entertaining any of Hillary's friends, Rachel had instructed Elvira, the most reliable waitress, to use the Limoges china and sterling silverware from Rachel's sideboard in the apartment. The wedding gifts sat untouched except for occasional dinners when her parents visited. But this was a celebration—at last! Satisfied that the table met expectations, Rachel worried if she should have arranged for dinner in their apartment. Hillary and Teddy Reno would have a great deal to talk about and might prefer privacy, but then she would have no place to escape to if she became bored with their reminiscing. No, the dining room was better.

Dark-haired Teddy Reno was taller than Hillary, with a taut figure enhanced by a handsome double-breasted alpaca suit. His looks didn't match Hillary's, but his movements were agile and he talked animatedly as they entered the lobby. In the sitting room Rachel waited, the book she had been reading open on her lap. Teddy Reno's heavy-bearded, rough features crinkled in a smile. He strode across the room and clasped her hand without waiting for introductions.

"Rachel! You're prettier than all Hillary's bragging!" He planted a friendly kiss on her cheek, still holding her hand. "I can't tell you how much I've looked forward to meeting the little gal who finally got old Hillary to the altar!" He nodded approvingly. "I can see why. You're as pretty as a picture." He picked up her book and studied the open page.

"Shakespeare! 'Beauty, wit, high birth, vigour of bone, desert in service, love, friendship, charity, are subjects all to envious and calumniating time. . . .'"

She smiled. "You are familiar with *Troilus and Cressida.*"

"Only because I knew you would be reading it when I met you. I am determined to make a marvelous impression on you so I shall always be welcome here."

She laughed softly at his nonsense, suspecting he was a gifted charmer. Hillary gave instructions to the boy carrying Reno's bags, then came to join them.

Hillary eased into one of the comfortable morris chairs as Teddy walked to the mantel to inspect the silver candelabra. The other guests had gone to the dining room, and they were alone in the sitting room. Reno moved slowly, his glance picking out the Sevres vase, a cut-glass bowl, and the silver Augsburg charger. Clasping the Shakespeare volume like a scholar, he paused at the bookcase to scan the titles of the other leather-bound volumes. Finally he came back and laid aside the volume Rachel had been reading.

"You are a fortunate man, Hillary. A beautiful wife, a hotel that is more comfortable than most homes I've been in, and Emerson, Dickens, and Shakespeare to read! Yessir, you're a lucky devil." He grinned at Rachel. "Your husband was always the one with big plans. Now here he is carrying them out just like he said he would. California's been good for him." He laughed ruefully. "I never believed the stories about this being such a wondrous place of golden opportunity and sunshine, but I have to eat those words. Judging by Hillary's success, I'd say they weren't exaggerated a bit!"

She knew his geniality was exaggerated for her benefit, but she found herself liking him in spite of her reservations. "Are you planning to stay in California long, Mr. Reno?" she asked.

"I may leave before dinner if you keep calling me 'Mr. Reno.' Nobody does that except creditors when I owe them money! It's Teddy, just Teddy, Rachel."

Elvira came in with a silver tray holding a wine decanter and glasses. Hillary said, "Bring the whiskey bottle from the apartment, Elvira. I think Teddy would find this a bit mild for his taste." The girl glanced at Rachel, who nodded.

Reno settled into an easy chair and crossed his long legs. "Thank God you haven't succumbed to the insanity of Prohibition."

Hillary laughed. "Would you believe this city has been dry since the turn of the century? It's written into the city charter."

Reno made a face of mock horror.

"It's easy enough to get liquor," Hillary said. "This town can give bootlegging lessons to the rest of the nation."

"Hillary! Teddy will think us immoral," Rachel admonished.

"On the contrary—enterprising, I'd say. A city without spirits is a city without spirit." He waited while Elvira set down the liquor bottle, then lifted the glass Hillary poured for him. "To Rachel and Hillary, and their lovely hotel, which is an oasis in the dry desert of southern California!"

Sipping her sherry, Rachel listened to Reno's fanciful de-

scription of his trip to California. He was an excellent story-
teller, and he made the most trivial incidents amusing. She
was surprised that he had not come from New York but from
Oklahoma, where he'd been scouting oil leases. If Hillary had
mentioned this, she'd forgotten. She asked Reno if he worked
for one of the big oil companies.

He shook his head. "I'm with Independence Oil. It's just
getting started. I've been with the big ones—Union, Standard
—the biggest. But I don't like to see them cutting the throats
of the little guys who made oil what it is today in this country.
They have Texas and Oklahoma tied up tighter than a dry
well. The independent wildcatter is vanishing like the American buffalo. It costs too damn much to finance a well these
days. Small companies are having a hard time competing unless they get an edge by getting in there first, so they hire
crackerjack scouts like me to explore for them." He broke off
suddenly. "I didn't mean to make a speech. I'm boring you."

"Not at all," she insisted. "Are you scouting oil fields in
California?"

He dropped his voice to a whisper as he glanced toward the
dining room. "Right here in Ocean Beach, though I'd be
obliged if you weren't to mention that around."

Rachel smiled indulgently. "There is no oil here. Several
years ago one of the companies drilled a test hole and came up
with nothing."

"Union," Teddy admitted. "They punched down to thirty-
four hundred feet, but one dry well doesn't change the favor-
able reports on the geology. There's oil, all right, and we aim
to bring it up."

It seemed impossible that he believed the old tales, but
Rachel listened politely, then with growing interest as he told
how some geologists were betting on a strike in the area soon.
Copies of surveys and a lot of hearsay had prompted his company to send him on a mission to buy on the potential oil-
bearing anticline. He was taking a chance telling them all this,
but he'd trust Hillary with his life, and now that he'd met
Rachel, he felt the same way about her. If word of the proposed test well got out, Union and Standard would buy up
everything available for miles around.

After second drinks for the men, they adjourned to the
dining room, where they ate a magnificent meal of roast beef,
fresh-caught red snapper, garden peas, onions and peppers,

and a salad of crisp greens topped with tender early avocados.
Teddy delighted in each dish, praising the chef lavishly.
Rachel was beginning to realize that everything Reno said was
exaggerated, but his exaggerations were part of his charm. He
entertained them with stories of his exploits in the oil fields.
He skipped over the part of his life that covered the war years,
but Rachel was sure he had not seen service.

When they adjourned to the apartment for coffee and
brandy, she coaxed him for more details of the well his company wanted to drill.

"At the moment we have an advantage," he confided. "We
know for a fact that Standard's had a damned good geological
report on Darien Hill. But they're hesitant about drilling
within city limits. It leads to a lot of politicking they'd just as
soon avoid. But the government's got an open door policy on
oil now. Foreigners are coming in. There's a rumor that a
Dutch company wants to lease acreage on the Hill. If I could
beat them to it—!" He snorted. "There I go—talking like a
rich man. I'm afraid I get carried away because I *know* what's
going to come. The truth is I haven't got the money or the
credit to buy a corner of your front yard."

Rachel noticed the slip from *we* to *I*, and she studied their
guest in the soft glow of the lamp. "You're so certain of this
that you'd risk your own money—if you had it?" She couldn't
make up her mind if it was just talk or if he really meant it.
There'd been desultory gossip about oil on Darien Hill for
years, and nothing had come of it. Still . . .

"Every penny I could put my hands on," he declared. "I've
had luck come and go. It pains me to have wealth within
grabbing distance and have to stand by and see someone else
get it. I've done some wildcatting. Nothing beats the exalta-
tion of having a well come in a gusher."

She wondered what happened to that wealth when he had
it, but she refrained from asking. Hillary leaned back in his
chair and swirled the brandy in the snifter. He'd been silent
until now, but his eyes burned bright.

He said, "If you feel that strongly, why don't you find
someone to back a well?"

"Easier said than done," Teddy answered. "Unless I can
persuade you and Rachel to back me." He smiled as if to say
he was joking, but his eyes glittered.

Rachel sipped her coffee and watched him over the rim of

the delicate Limoges cup. It made a tinkling clatter as she replaced it in the saucer. There was a long silence as Teddy and Rachel faced each other. In the corner of Rachel's vision, Hillary did not move.

Reno's voice was as soft as the wind rustling through the palms outside the window. "Would you back a well for me, Rachel?"

The silence lengthened again as she considered her answer. Finally she said, "Everything Hillary and I have is tied up in this hotel. I don't know the first thing about geology and drilling oil wells."

He leaned forward. "You don't have to, that's the beauty of it!" he said. "The drilling companies do the worrying about men and equipment and test holes. The easy money's to be made in leases. Let the oil companies take the risk along with their profit. You sit back and just let them drill on your land."

"My land?" She glanced sidelong at Hillary, annoyed that he had confided so readily and completely in Reno. "Those paltry few acres?" The bell chimed, signaling Hillary he was needed at the front desk. He looked relieved to escape.

"They only need enough space to put up a derrick, and access rights, of course. They could sink a hundred wells on your land." Reno's eyes glinted like the sea under a gray sky. "You'd be rich when the strike comes in."

She studied his face. "Why are you telling me this? If what you say is true, the oil companies will contact me sooner or later with lease offers."

He slapped his knee and grinned. "I like your style, Rachel. You're a businesswoman." His face sobered. "You're absolutely right. I'm not one to put charity before my own needs. I want to get in on the boom that's going to come. Trouble is, I have no ready cash. What I propose is a fair trade, sort of a partnership. You put up the money and I put up the knowledge of which land to buy. I've got maps that pinpoint it, Rachel. We can't miss. Now, I know what you're thinking, but hear me out. You've been connected with that real estate office quite a while now, and you know your way around. And your daddy's been picking up lots here and there long enough so no one's going to blink if you and he buy property. And your daddy's credit at the bank is A-one." He held up his hand, his white teeth flashing in a quick smile. "Now, don't get riled about me being so nosy. I had to be sure before I spoke my piece. I admit, when I decided to come to Ocean Beach, I was hoping to get Hillary to throw in with me, but it didn't take long to find out he's all tied up here. Nothing to be ashamed of, but he can't take a step without you and your daddy." He sighed. "Yessir, this town can be proud of people like you and your daddy. You're farsighted citizens who believe in the future of Ocean Beach. No one's going to have anything but praise for the two of you if you buy more property. This city's going to grow."

Despite her anger, she felt a reluctant admiration. Reno was a careful man who knew what he wanted. He'd galvanized her imagination. Without knowing it, Rachel's intensity charged the air—as it usually did.

Trying to ignore her allure, Reno pointed past the darkened park behind the hotel toward the twinkling lights on Darien Hill. "It won't be long before there's a forest of oil derricks up there, as far as the eye can see. Don't let this be another Huntington Beach, Rachel. The city got there first in that land grab. It *could* happen here." He sat back with the air of a lawyer resting his case, looking squarely at her. "Now, can you give me one good reason why the city should gobble up all those lovely oil royalties when nice folk like you and me can have our slice of the pie?"

She studied him evenly. "What of your loyalty to Independence Oil?"

He chuckled. "I think you already know the answer, Rachel."

"You are Independence Oil."

He nodded. "The way I see it, there's enough to go around. Help me get mine, Rachel, so Union and Standard don't guess I'm behind it. When we've sewed up what we want, let them pick up the leftovers."

It speared her to imagine the serenity of the Hill destroyed by noisy oil wells. She'd seen—and smelled—the ungainly rigs at Santa Fe Springs. But if Reno was right, the wells would spring up with or without her participation. And if he were wrong? What harm could come of owning land on Darien Hill? More, she'd been feeling a yearning, an odd dissatisfaction that she couldn't explain. A new irritation involving Hillary, and the hotel's slow, glacial evolution. If this was the opportunity they needed to surge ahead, so be it. She'd shirk no responsibility, let no bold risk pass.

❧ *Three* ❧

MILLS GRANT LISTENED when Rachel confided Teddy Reno's plan. They occupied a rich, luxurious corner of the apartment parlor, his daughter, looking unself-consciously sensuous as usual, draped in a blue wingback chair. She waved a soft, silky hand for emphasis, and while he listened, he stroked his beard and looked on.

"I figured it would come sooner or later," he said, sighing. "I've been hearing oil rumbles ever since the war. The world's going to automobiles and machines that need oil to run. Any likely spot is worth trying."

"But do you believe that they will find anything here on the Hill?" Rachel's violet eyes widened in anticipation.

"Striking oil is like finding water—it's there if you drill in the right place. That well Union sank in '16 or '17 could have been a pace off center or two feet short of the pool." He looked at his daughter, surveying her for a reaction. She seemed to be musing.

"Teddy is vague about his past. It may not be above reproach. He's the one who'll bend the truth to suit his needs."

"Do you think he has enough background to give credence to his story?"

She frowned. "I'd say Reno is an opportunist who, when he gets on the trail of something that may make him money, is not apt to abandon it. I can't vouch for his working for any of

42

the companies he named, but I'd say he's been around enough to pick up the scent of money."

"Let me make a few inquiries. If there's anything out of line in Reno's background, I'll find it. Tell him he'll have his answer day after tomorrow." Mills Grant looked at his daughter with frank admiration. "You're a good businesswoman, Rachel. Most men feel cheated if they don't have a son to carry on their business, but I've never had reason to entertain that notion for a minute. I'm proud of you, Rachel, mighty proud."

Her answer to Teddy Reno was yes. Her father's inquiries revealed that a law firm, which could very well be fronting for an oil company, had been investigating lease rights on the southeast flank of Darien Hill. No negotiations were underway, nor had a precise site been selected. The law firm was making a marked effort to mask its activities. They were, as far as Mills could determine, the only ones showing interest, which seemed to indicate Reno's information was valid. There was also a distinct possibility he had come by it illegally.

Teddy Reno wasn't bothered by the fact that Rachel confided in her father. His own investigation had shown Rachel's personal funds were tied up in the hotel and in her property. She'd have to go to her father for any large sums, and Mills would give them to her. He was surprised when Mills Grant did not insist on being cut into the deal but was content to let Rachel frame it independently. She offered Teddy three percent. He was astonished, then wounded.

"That doesn't make me much of a partner," he said. "I was thinking in terms of thirty-five percent."

Rachel snorted. "You're not putting up a dime."

Reno tapped his temple. "This is worth as much as cash."

"Not from a practical viewpoint," she declared. "We already own property on the Hill. We can go out and buy up anything else we can put our hands on and run less than ten percent chance of failure. Your maps may pinpoint the best locations, but they don't exclude lesser plots of land. We've already learned the interest is primarily in the southeast flank."

That surprised him, but before he could answer, she said, "If the strike is as rich as you predict, three percent can mean a tidy sum."

Reno stopped short and weighed a response. "Five percent."

Rachel tilted her chin, her lustrous brown curls framing her beautiful but defiant face. For a moment Teddy Reno was mesmerized. "Three and a half. I'll sweeten the pot by letting you stay at the hotel without charge."

Reno laughed and pounded the chair's arm with his balled fist. "You drive a hard bargain, Rachel. That's an admirable quality for a woman. I accept."

Rachel was aglow. Once the agreement had been signed, Teddy unfolded a map. Comparing a city map with the geological survey, he blocked out the prime areas on Darien Hill. Rachel saw that there were other pools indicated along the harbor and the dry riverbed, but Teddy discounted these quickly.

"It'll be years before they're worth drilling. Darien Hill is the place to concentrate on now. It's sitting right on top of the biggest goddam—excuse me, Rachel—pool you ever saw."

Almost anything on the Hill was drillable, especially on the southeast slope. The parcel Teddy claimed Standard Oil sought flanked Rachel's dowry land. It was owned by a family named Farwell, who had never built on it. Rachel located them in Los Angeles. Drawing on skills she'd sharpened at McCutcheon's, and her natural persuasive talents, three days later she owned the land.

Teddy soared and wanted to go out immediately to survey the acquisition, but Rachel ordered him to stay away from the Hill. If his face was known to oil people, his presence might spark suspicion and complicate future acquisitions.

When Rachel tried to persuade her father to team up with her, he declined. "I'm not a young man, Rachel," he said adamantly. "My greatest pleasure is watching you develop a business sense that's going to serve you in good stead the rest of your life. Everything I have will be yours someday. No harm in your getting an early start."

"But I would be more comfortable if you were a partner—"

"No. The rest of your life you'd wonder if you got where you did because I gave you a boost, or if you'd done it on your own steam and natural giftedness. This way, no matter what happens, the decisions and the risks are yours, not only the rewards. I like the way you handled Reno. You're off to a great start, girl. I know I'll always be proud of you." His one caution was that she keep the acquisitions in her name alone to sidestep Hillary's penchant for extravagance and high living. They both had to acknowledge the truth that Hillary did not have the business sense they had first thought he possessed. It was Rachel's good sense that balanced the books and made over the hotel.

Much of Darien Hill lay undeveloped and an easy mark to buy. In addition to the Farwell property, Rachel acquired two large vacant lots and two with houses, totaling almost eight hundred acres that crisscrossed to the Hill, which according to Teddy's maps encompassed the lion's share of the oil pool.

Rachel was bitten. Feverishly she conducted business on her own. As a precaution, she left Her job at McCutcheon's so there could be no question of a conflict of interest. When she had acquired all fallow, promising land on the Hill, she tried to recall where the pools had laced the harbor and river on Reno's map. Teddy had dismissed them too quickly. If they were on the geological map, the pools existed. That was good enough for her. She moved more cautiously on these parcels, and since more time would lapse before any profit could be realized, she did not ask her father for financing. Instead she confided in Hillary, and with his cooperation, mortgaged the hotel, then used the money to buy a block of lots close to the beach downtown and make a bid for a city-owned river strip. By December, Hillary had drawn up plans for the expansion of the hotel. They decided to give a New Year's Eve party to celebrate their glittering future.

The lobby and dining room were festooned with boughs of greenery and holly, trimmed with ribbons and streamers. Across the front entrance, a large banner welcomed the New Year of 1921. Hillary hired musicians, and the tables in the dining room were cleared away to make room for a dance floor. In addition to the hotel guests, townspeople came in response to the advertisements emblazoned in the *Tribune*. At five dollars a couple, the hotel was packed, the party a smash success.

Slightly light-headed, Rachel crossed the lobby with purpose. Hillary was dancing with all the women guests, as enchanted as he. Teddy Reno was also enjoying himself, dancing and making frequent trips to the bar for champagne, which Hillary's bootlegger had specially stocked. Judging by the suspicious bulge under Teddy's coat, Rachel suspected a flask was upended every time he stepped out onto the porch for a breath of air. But it was New Year's Eve, a time to celebrate. The police in Ocean Beach were accustomed to looking the other way.

She walked to the far side of the lobby where a window was open to stir the air. She inhaled damp fog that drifted in from the shore. The clock behind the front desk showed it was past eleven. She wondered if they had started too early. Some of the merrymakers would not last until midnight. She was aware of the front door opening and wondered which guest found it necessary to clear his head or have another swig.

"Hello, Rachel."

She turned to find Josh Fantazia smiling at her. He was wearing a tuxedo with a white scarf thrown carelessly around his neck. One end clung to the lapel of the velvet Chesterfield coat. He looked as handsome as ever, with chiseled features and those sparking eyes. He seemed elated to see her. "Hello, Josh. I—we weren't expecting you." She was angry to find herself stammering. She was even angrier to realize that the emotions she thought laid to rest surged as though she were still the child who'd kissed him good-bye at the station. She managed a smile. "I must have missed your name on the guest list."

He laughed softly. "I didn't make a reservation."

She knew the Fantazias were having a ball at the Rancho and he couldn't even consider attending the Oceanside party.

"I was driving by and stopped impulsively. This is the first time I've been here since you opened." He glanced around. "You've done wonders." The lush golden curtains and Edwardian-print chairs were softly backlighted by two colonial replica lamps. The floor to ceiling windows would look out over ocean in a magnificent view which they would see if it weren't pitch black outside. But even sounds of the waves crashing to shore drifted to their ears, and their eyes locked a moment in shared memory.

Rachel broke the silence, pleased Josh had noticed her changes. She smiled. "Can I get you a drink?"

He shook his dark curly head. "I have to get back. One of our guests had a bit too much and I drove him home." He regarded her with a curious smile. "You look marvelous, Rachel. Marriage agrees with you."

A blush rose to her cheeks. "Thank you," she said. "Is your wife well?" She felt foolish uttering platitudes, but she couldn't bring herself to let him leave.

He seemed to shrug but he had not moved. "She's fine."

Rachel recalled gossip that Collette was with child.

"I don't have to ask about Hillary." A smile played at his lips. "He's become quite a figure around town. The genial innkeeper."

Her jaw tightened. "He works hard."

"And you are working hard as well."

"I do what I can to help," she said coolly. She glanced toward the dining room, where the music had ended momentarily and the sound of laughter and voices surged.

"I should know better than to engage in word games with you, Rachel. I was referring to your sudden interest in real estate." He'd suddenly turned stern.

Rachel was stunned. Of course. He was on the city council, and the council channeled her bids for the river lots. She kept her expression hooded and did not lower her gaze.

"Would you mind telling me why you are so interested in property along the river? That land has been on the city rolls since Ocean Beach incorporated. No one's so much as asked about it until now."

She allowed herself a small smile and shrugged. "My father is getting on in years, and since truck farming is not an occupation for women, he thinks I should get into something more suitable."

"Don't tell me you're considering putting up another hotel?"

She was amused. "I believe in diversifying my interests."

He arched an eyebrow and studied her skeptically. "In the past few months you've bought seven hundred and sixty acres on Darien Hill and twelve parcels along the beach. Now you're after a hundred and fifteen acres of useless land along the river channel. Are you planning to take over the city?"

He'd made it his business to know exactly where she stood, and he was going to drill her for all it was worth. Anger surged in her, and her stomach knotted. "Hardly. My purchases don't begin to compare with what your family already owns."

"My family's holdings span several generations. Your interest is sudden."

"I don't see that it concerns you," she said evenly.

"Anything that concerns the City of Ocean Beach concerns me."

She laughed. "An honest, concerned politician? Such pretense of devotion may have influenced your appointment to the council, but it doesn't impress me. It would be more believable for you to encourage my purchase of useless land that is a drain on the city coffers."

He straightened his long elegant form, as if offended, but a glint in his eyes indicated he accepted her challenge and admired her for it. "Is it useless?"

"The description was yours. I believe my land has value in and of itself. I'm willing to gamble."

He stared, taking her in. "I'm in a position to help you get what you want, Rachel." His tone was so intimate she was taken aback.

"That's very generous of you," she said, still astonished by his manner.

"I am also in a position to prevent your getting it." His soft voice and arched brow—not to mention his very presence in her home—made her listen closely. But he offered no further explanation, forcing her to poke and prod. Fantazias apparently played close to the chest, and a dangerous game at that.

"That sounds like a threat of some kind, though I can't imagine in what way," she finally said. "I have nothing to hide."

"Who is Teddy Reno?" he demanded in a low whisper.

She had to answer instantly. "An old friend of Hillary's from the East." With effort, she kept her gaze from sweeping the crowd in the dining room. She smiled stiffly as three guests waved, then came in from the veranda. Had Josh heard rumors of Teddy's connection with the oil industry? It wouldn't be hard to unearth if someone smart looked into the records. Josh was smart, and if he sensed a gold mine beneath Ocean Beach, he'd make it his business to dig further. "If you'll excuse me, I must get back to my guests." She turned but he grabbed her arm. For a moment his touch sent a wave of paralyzing warmth through her, then she pulled away angrily.

He was smiling his charming grin again. "I have something to show you. I think you'll find it very interesting."

Curious, she waited for him to go on.

"Will you meet me tomorrow?"

"I don't see—"

"You will tomorrow. I'll be here at nine in the morning." Smiling, he lifted her hand to his lips and bowed over it. He straightened, turned his broad back, and strode out the door before she recovered from the shock. She could feel the warm, moist imprint of his lips still hugging the back of her hand as the door slammed shut against the winter chill.

She glanced out the lobby window the next morning, sure he would not come and even surer she would not get into his car if he did. The hotel was strangely quiet after a festive, raucous party that had rolled into the early morning hours. Hillary had returned to bed in the hope of easing his hangover. There was no sign of Teddy.

A new model Studebaker touring car turned at the corner and slowed to a halt at the curb that fronted the hotel. She had only a glimpse of the driver, but she knew it was Josh.

"I won't be gone long, Jeremy," she said to the bellman behind the desk. Quickly she drew on her coat, pulling the fur collar high across her face, and opened the heavy carved door.

"Sure, Mrs. Upfield. Take your time," he said with a wave.

She let herself out and was stunned by the biting wind that whipped across the bluff. She held her hat with one hand as she hurried down the stairs. Josh leaned across the front seat to open the door. Puffing, she settled onto the leather seat. She glanced at him as he put the car in motion, made a wide turn on the boulevard, and headed north on Cherry Street. He looked handsome in his tweed pants, argyle vest, and cap.

"Where are we going?" she asked.

"You'll see in a bit. It's not far," he said, his eyes riveted on the road.

"Why the mystery?" She was amused by his solemn face. "Am I being kidnapped?"

He laughed as he looked at her, his dark eyes widening as he took her in for a moment. The car bumped over a bit of rough pavement and he returned his attention to his driving. "Would you have gotten in the car so readily if you thought that?"

"Maybe." He glanced at her again but only for a moment; his solemn expression fled completely. She pulled off her gloves with slow deliberation. "I have not seen you for sixteen months. Suddenly you can't resist the impulse to stop at the hotel when you are supposed to be at a Rancho ball. And you must see me—take me somewhere—on a morning when everyone in town is sleeping off the effects of last night's party. I find that intriguing, to say the least. Very mysterious."

"Ah, you cannot resist a mystery, eh? From now on I'll know how to get your attention."

Smiling, she studied the deserted street. They were still driving north on Cherry, and she wondered if he was headed for Darien Hill. Certainly he wasn't going to take her to his house? It would spark more gossip in his world than in hers if they were seen together on the Hill.

She'd already eliminated the river lots as their destination when they turned north. His insistent invitation had come on the heels of the discussion of her purchase offer, but that's not where they were headed now.

They drove past Darien Hill and several miles farther before turning eastward. He'd fallen silent since the exchange of banter, and she was determined not to ask any more questions. The road was poorly paved here, and she knew they were close to the city limits. Finally he turned again, and she saw the sign: Rancho del Cielo. Was this his idea of a joke? She looked at him, her eyes narrowing.

"We're not going there," he said, reading her thoughts.

She let out a breath as he turned a moment later onto a trail almost hidden beneath low-hanging willows. The branches dripped wetly across the windshield, leaving spatters of moisture on the glass. The car pitched in deep ruts. Once it skidded slightly in a low spot where fog and dew had collected in a mud pool. Rachel tried to picture the precise outlines of the Fantazia rancho on local maps, but the boundaries were indistinct in her mind. Were they still on the grounds? Probably, at least as far as the river.

Finally Josh slowed to a crawl and pointed the car onto an almost invisible path under a thick canopy of leaves. Branches scraped as the car jounced into a clearing. Josh stopped and set the handbrake. The damp, chill silence was broken by the sound of a crow cawing overhead.

A stone cottage stood on the bluff overlooking the river-bed. When the winter rains came in full force, the river would become a torrent, sweeping mud and debris in its current and churning over rocks and brush. But it wouldn't jump the banks and destroy the cottage, only menace it with new drama. Josh held back a wet willow branch as he helped her out. He took her hand and walked toward the well-tended cottage.

Satiny geranium plants hedged the door stoop and a variety of jade and other succulents bordered the facade. It had been carefully planned to require minimum attention.

"Like it?" Josh asked, his chiseled features squaring around to face her.

"Yes, though I can't imagine why you've brought me here. Are you interested in selling it?"

He laughed. "Always practical Rachel." He unlocked the door with a key on a silver chain. He stood a moment on the threshold, gazing across the river to the opposite bank, which was covered with pampas grass and twisted oaks. Rachel caught the faint scent of citrus but couldn't see the grove.

Josh made a sweeping gesture. "As far as you can see, the land belongs to my family. Both sides of the river. My great-grandfather rode two days without coming to the end of his land."

"Is this what you wanted me to see?" Rachel didn't try to hide her annoyance. Despite the warm coat, the dampness made her shiver.

"Don't you understand?" Josh said. "All this is mine—or so close to being mine that it doesn't make a difference. My father has put control of it in my hands. Like you, I believe in the land itself, but I believe in the profit to be made from it. I've had an offer to buy. It's tempting, considering nothing's been done with this area since my grandfather stopped running cattle. Eventually the city will grow this far out, I suppose, but in the meantime, I'm trying to make up my mind if I should hold or sell it."

"Are you asking my advice?"

He gripped her shoulders, for a moment massaging them, then stared at her. "I'm asking you if there's oil here. Your friend Reno is scouting oil sites. He's been flagging you about prime property."

She challenged his flickering gaze.

"And you brought me here to plead with me? You want me to cut you in on a good thing?" She laughed derisively. "Why should I?"

"Because I'm in a position to see that no questions are asked about your activities. Did you think no one would notice that you're casting a net for land? Did you think no one would ask why so many abandoned lots that have always been so much dead weight are suddenly in hot demand?"

Rachel tilted her oval face, lifting her perfect chin. "Let them ask! It's too late."

His grip tightened until she could feel his fingers digging into her flesh. He loomed over her, his eyes smoldering with sex. He raised one hand, and for a moment she thought he meant to strike her, but his fingers came down gently to her face and stroked it as if such beauty deserved worship, not marring. "It's never too late," he said so softly she wasn't sure it had not been the wind. His face came closer, lips parted so that his hot breath whispered across her mouth. She tried to push him away, but he would not release her. He drew her into his arms, gazing at her as though seeing her as never before. She shook her head, denying the hot rush that flooded through her. Her lips parted, admitting him as he searched and demanded, rekindling the desire he stirred in her. Desire long dormant but not forgotten.

"Rachel . . . Rachel . . ." he murmured against her flesh as he trailed his lips across her face.

She clung to him, all thoughts of oil and real estate erased as passion engulfed her. She gave herself hungrily to him. And when his hands slid under her coat to her gowned flesh, she shuddered uncontrollably.

"Do you have any idea how much I've wanted you ever since that day at Union Station?"

She drew back to look at his face. "I don't believe you," she whispered hoarsely.

"It's true. I thought about you often while I was in France. Possessing you . . ."

How could he speak so tenderly when he'd married another woman? She tried to pull away, but he would not release her.

"I married Collette in a moment of weakness. I've had months to regret it." He lowered his gaze as though he were ashamed of the admission. "Her family was driven from their home by the Germans. They had no food except what I managed to steal for them. Then, when her parents were both killed, she was alone. I—" He shook away the memory. "Forgive me, Rachel, forgive me."

He kissed her again, driving away the questions that crowded her mind. Weak with desire and his promise of fulfillment, she let him lead her inside. She barely noticed the lush but casually furnished room with large casements facing the river and narrower cathedral windows gracing the other walls. Josh set a match to the fire laid in the stone fireplace, and flames leaped quickly, driving the chill from the room. Rachel moved in a hazy dream, aware only of Josh's warm hands on her waist as he escorted her to the wide bed in a corner. Her heart throbbing, she stood very quietly as he removed her bonnet and worked at the fastening of her dress, then slipped it down over her pale shoulders. She had to be dreaming; she willed the dream not to evaporate. And when at last he drew her to him under the eiderdown coverlet, and she gripped him to her as he plunged deep into her, and began the journey that made them soar, she knew the dream was real.

Much later they sat at the sunny table with mugs of cool water from a stone crock. They were silent, uncomfortable now with the whispered words of love they'd cried in passion. Rachel glanced at the patterned shadows outside. The sun had climbed almost straight above in the blue sky. The morning was gone.

"I have to go," she said.

He watched her finger trace a wet circle on the wood. "Tell me what you're thinking."

She didn't look up. Her dark curls, in disarray, haloed her beautiful chin. "That we've been foolish giving in to a moment's passion."

"I'll never believe that."

She met his gaze, her violet eyes setting his heart to throb faster. "Will you divorce Collette?"

He averted his gaze.

"You can't, you've already told me that by admitting your reason for marrying her," she said for him. "She has no one here, just as she had no one in France. And she's done nothing to deserve being cast aside any more than Hillary deserves to learn that his wife has been unfaithful. They're innocent. The guilt is ours."

"Is that what you feel—guilt?" He tried to take her sensuous hand, but she drew away.

"Some." She smiled ruefully. "Not enough to erase the pleasure."

He smiled, and kissed her. "I want to see you again. Whenever we can manage."

"No, it's not wise."

"The hell with wisdom," he said.

"A scandal won't help either of us."

He shook his head. "I won't promise never to see you again. No one has to know."

She didn't answer immediately. She was torn between the desire to see him again—as often as possible—and practicality. Their being together was no accident. She couldn't ignore the real reason he'd brought her there, no matter how much she enjoyed the consequences. Had he seduced her to put her in the mood to cooperate? She couldn't discard the possibility. Regardless of how she would abhor a sordid affair, she knew she could not stay away from him. He looked so handsome in the silk robe that exposed the matted fur on his broad chest, and his dark eyes glowed in the way she remembered. Yes, it had been desire, though in her youthful innocence, she hadn't understood that.

"What about the oil lands?" she asked point-blank.

His bushy brows knit together. "Are you admitting my hunch is right?"

"Yes."

He scrutinized her expression as though evaluating his best approach. Finally he said, "You can't afford to buy the whole town."

She laughed, a seductive chime to his ears. "Perhaps not, but that's a poor excuse for giving it away." He nodded, and she knew he was considering her with new respect. "I had in mind something practical for both of us."

"Such as?"

"A partnership. My information is as valuable as your cash, under the circumstances."

"That's ridiculous—"

"Is it?" She got up and hugged herself inside her coat, as he buttoned on his shirt and vest, never removing his eyes from her. "Oil pools are peculiar formations. A dry well can miss by a few yards or hundreds of feet. Of course, you could buy up the entire city of Ocean Beach. *You* would be able to do that." She moved toward the door. "Take me home, Josh."

"No—wait."

She turned, knowing she had won.

"Not a partnership. A corporation. It's easier to manage and harder to trace. And not fifty-fifty. The risk is all mine."

"Sixty-forty."

"Seventy-thirty."

"Done."

"I know a lawyer in Los Angeles who can handle the details. He can also be the resident agent, if that's all right with you."

"If you're sure he can be trusted, I have no objection." It would be far safer than having the corporation's third party someone in Ocean Beach.

Josh smiled as he came around the table and his muscled arms took her into his warm embrace. The kiss was an exchange of power, the seal on their bargain, their step into the future. When he released her, Rachel's eyes shone. Josh looked at her for a long time.

Then softly he said, "What about *this* land, Rachel? Should I sell it?"

She closed her eyes in order to recall an image of Teddy Reno's geological map. Smiling, she opened her eyes to gaze sensually into his.

"Keep it, Josh. It would be a shame to let it go."

Laughing softly, he escorted her out of the cabin and locked the door behind them.

❧ *Four* ❧

SHE'D BEEN UNABLE to stay away, despite her resolve. From the window of her bedroom in her parents' house, she stared at the winking lanterns that cast grotesque shadows up the Hill. The creak of the grinding bullwheel and the hiss of the boilers and engines filled the night, rattling the window-panes. As though tuned to the excitement, the night was brilliantly clear, with a carpet of stars around a pale gibbous moon. A sea breeze fluttered the curtains at the open window, spreading the odor of salt air into the room. Rachel lifted the soft hair from her neck and held her face to the cool night. The temperature had dropped since sunset, but she was warmer now than she had been in the broiling sun.

Teddy was sure the well would come in before morning. Oil men read signs, just as sea captains read the weather or businessmen read the statistics to forecast market trends. Oil was less predictable than barometers and wind gauges. More like the market. But even that could match men's expectations.

She paced, bypassing the pressed bed her mother had turned down. Would some warning signal be broadcast when the strike was near? She went back to the window and peered up the Hill. There'd be little sleep on the Hill tonight, even for those accustomed to the noise of the drill. Lights blazed in every house, creating a toy village below the derrick that resembled a wooden Christmas tree. Only the Fantazia house was dark. Collette had refused to live in the shadow and clamor of the well, and Josh had moved the household to Rancho del Cielo.

There was a tap at the door. Her father appeared, butlering a wine decanter and glasses on a tray. She noticed he'd grown heavy over the years, his hair thinned to a bare patch on his head.

"I thought you might be able to use a little company." He grinned and poured.

She smiled. "Do you really think it will come in?"

He set the glasses on the marble-topped table near the window and poured the wine. Handing her a glass, he said, "If not tonight, soon. I've talked with several people who know a bit about drilling. They say every sign points to it. They've drilled more than three thousand feet down. There were unmistakable indications of oil and gas at twenty-seven hundred. Do you think all those leeches would be hanging around to grab up leases as fast as they jot names on the dotted line if they didn't believe there was oil?" He raised his glass. "To your new adventure in oil—and prosperity."

Rachel smiled. Her dark hair had grown out, and framed her oval face in waves to her shoulders. There were fatigue lines around her mouth and eyes, but otherwise she looked like a woman in her early twenties whose beauty still hadn't peaked. She had developed a calm at her core, a sort of confidence over the last few months that others would recall later as the beginning of a chill, a will of steel, that no matter how strong, would never overshadow her femininity. She sipped the dry sherry. "If I've been wrong, we'll lose everything." She glanced sidelong at him. "I worry about the loan against the hotel."

"It will be paid back long before the note comes due. This is no time to lose faith, girl." He put his hand on the shuddering window sash as the drill spiraled deeper into the earth. "Feel that? Let it sink into your bones, Rachel. It's destiny calling. And your name is at the top of the roll!" he said proudly.

She linked her arm through his as they turned to gaze out the window. "It will all change," she said softly.

"Everything changes, Rachel. Places and people and—"

She glanced at him questioningly.

"And situations. I wasn't going to mention this for a while, but maybe the time is as right as it will ever be."

A small pain pierced her chest as she regarded his serious expression. He looked old all at once. Tired lines bracketed his eyes and mouth, and his skin had a grayish cast. He'd been working too hard.

"I read the profit-and-loss statement Dawson did on the hotel. It isn't good. Hillary's expenses are running fifty percent higher than they should be. He's got more going out in overhead than he takes in. With only four or five summer months when he can be sure of a full house, it doesn't balance the rest of the year. All that rain last winter took a heavy toll."

She felt enormous relief. Her father's health was not at question. Frowning, she gave thought to what he was saying about the Oceanside. "Is there any danger of bankruptcy?"

He met her gaze, then looked away. "Hillary asked me not to mention it, but you have a right to know. I'm surprised you didn't come across it on your own. You would have if these leases hadn't tied up so much of your time." He sighed as though reluctant to go on. "I made the bank loan payments most of the winter. Hillary should be able to handle them now through the summer, but he's going to have to face a few facts. He can't go on spending the way he's doing. You'll have to talk to him."

She waited for emotion to fill her, but there was a void. No anger, no disappointment. Perhaps a faint guilt that had she not been so involved with Josh, her emotions and reactions to Hillary might have been more finely attuned. He might have shared his problems—their problems. She could not make excuses for him to her father, or for herself.

After a bit she said, "All right, father. I'm sorry you had to go through it. I'll repay the money."

"Nonsense. You know that's not why I raised the issue."

"I'd feel better doing it that way. You've done so much already. I won't let Hillary take advantage. We'll pay it back."

"If it makes you happier."

"It does." She smiled. "Thank you for telling me. I'll talk to Hillary, but first I'd like to see Dawson's statement. I prefer going into the discussion armed with practical suggestions, not just complaints."

Mills wagged his head. "You're remarkable, Rachel.

There's not many who can have the cool head for business you do and still be totally a woman." He kissed her cheek affectionately. "You deserve to be very happy. The subject is closed." He glanced out across the darkened hillside. "Girl, do you realize the changes that are going to come when that well comes in? This area is going to explode." He emptied his wine glass and set it down. "So will our lives, Rachel. I hope to God we're ready for it."

"We are," she said. "We are."

The low murmur sounded on the edge of her awareness for some time, like a persistent insect buzzing around her head. When at last she realized it was the sound of voices, she sat up. Glancing at the ogee clock on the dresser, she saw several hours had passed. She had drifted along the perimeter of consciousness while her body relaxed. Now she was fully awake. She sprang to the window. The crowd near the derrick had swelled to an enormous size. People milled across the darkened Fantazia yard; figures dimly outlined by lantern light stood or sat on the stone walls surrounding the property. The road was clogged with people and cars. Where had they all come from? She estimated thousands!

Quickly she searched out the contours of the derrick against the sky. It was ghostly in the wavering lamps the drillers had hung to light their efforts. She made out the tower's faint sway as the drill plunged on.

She ran from the room and down the stairs. The parlor was empty, though a lamp had been left on the bentwood console table. She went quickly down the hall to see if her father might be in the kitchen, but it, too, was empty. The aroma of coffee lingered in the air. A freshly brewed pot stood on the stove. A half-filled cup was on the table as though someone had put it down hastily.

Out the back door she picked her way through the yard and crossed over to Darien Road. The moon hung low in the sky but cast enough light to let her see clearly. The murmur that had wakened her grew as she neared the fork. She halted in astonishment as she saw that the crowd had spilled forward this far. The porch lights had been switched on at the Maveen house. Elliot's father and two brothers patroled the yard warning people not to trample on the flowerbeds or lawn. Neighbors who had not had such foresight were trying helplessly to clear trespassers from invaded yards.

In spite of the mob an air of joviality surged in the pre-dawn darkness. A celebration. A mood of anticipation. Rachel looked for familiar faces as she worked her way to the Maveen fence.

"Thomas! Thomas!" She waved when the towheaded lad craned his head to see who summoned him. For a moment she thought he was going to ignore her, but finally he approached at a slow pace. He was a gangly lad of eighteen with a serious expression that mirrored Elliot's.

"Thomas, what is happening? What's drawn so many people?"

His green eyes regarded her as though weighing his response.

"You should know, Rachel. I hear it's your land they're drilling on," he said, a look of repugnance distorting his features.

She cast a quick glance at the wooden struts towering above the oaks. "But they haven't brought the well in. They're still drilling." She had to raise her voice to be heard above the din.

"They've been hauling up oil in the mud since midnight. The men say it's a sign they're close to the pool. It can't be long now. Hey, there—" He waved at two men who were pushing the gate open. "We'd appreciate it if you'd stay outside the fence. We've got an invalid inside needs sleep. Thank you kindly." He shepherded them out and relatched the gate.

Rachel pushed back into the crowd. Several voices called out as she forced her way up the Hill, but she was unaware of them.

She revised her estimate of the number of people who packed the Hill. The news had spread quickly. Half the populace of Ocean Beach had come to stand vigil. Surprised, she realized she was hearing as many expressions of anger as of glee. She smiled in the darkness. Let them scoff. Let them laugh or ridicule or whatever vented their shortsighted minds the most. Coming to a standstill against a knot of men exchanging money and bets, she closed her eyes and drank in the excitement. She felt the intoxication of power and success, knowing she had done the impossible, the impractical, the unbelievable. She inhaled, and the stench of grease and pitch and dirt and gas filled her nostrils like the sweetest perfume.

She threw her head back and laughed aloud.

"Is she crazy?"

"More likely drunk."

"I wish *I* were! That's Rachel Upfield."

"It's her lease—"

"Wouldn't you laugh, too? She'll be worth millions before the sun comes up!"

Rachel opened her eyes and smiled at the staring men. "Thank you, gentlemen." They nodded at her, somewhat in awe. It wasn't often that such a beautiful woman became a millionairess overnight. She moved ahead as they opened a pathway for her. She felt their eyes on her long after the crowd closed its ranks.

"Rachel!"

Her father pushed toward her. She craned her head and, seeing him, beamed a full-lipped smile. Grabbing her arm, he elbowed a path for them until they reached a clear spot under a misshapen oak that towered over a small knoll.

He leaned close to be heard above the clamor of the drill and crew. "I talked with Happy Yowell." He grinned. "It's coming in, Rachel. Any minute now. Any minute!"

She gulped in air to steady her nerves and stared at the framework of the derrick. The sky had turned from black to gray, foretelling dawn.

She felt it first. A trembling beneath her feet. An upward thrust of power that seemed to surge through her before it radiated outward. Then she heard it. A low growl, like a dog chained in a hollow barn that echoed. A rumble like a train hurtling forward past its station.

"It's here, Father, it's here!" she cried.

The ground shook. A piercing, whistling scream filled the night. The stunned crowd gasped as the derrick shuddered like a child's pile of sticks, then sent a dark spume skyward. Pandemonium erupted. Shouts drowned out the sound of the hissing and oil. Men slapped each other's backs and shouted, waved, and pointed at the gusher as though they'd found land after a long tempestuous sea voyage.

Rachel couldn't pull her gaze from the black monolith of the derrick. She was aware of the jubilant crew trying to regain footholds on the platform, and begin the work of capping. She wanted to shout at them to let the oil soak the crowd and saturate the soil. Oil! Her father hugged her exuberantly and shouted in her ear, but she couldn't hear his words in the uproar. She laughed and returned the hug without taking her eyes off the wondrous sight. Black mist clung to her face and arms. Her dress was damp, and her shoes soaked. Some of the crowd fell back to escape the worst of the spray. When her father moved away, Rachel stood her ground. Oil! Laughing, she glanced around and shouted the word aloud: "Oil!"

Near a workshack a man stood alone staring up at the gusher. Like hers, his clothing had been showered with the black gold, his face a sticky mask. Rachel's breath caught as she recognized the familiar stance. Quickly she made her way to him. He didn't notice her until she walked up to him.

"Josh!" she cried.

He broke into a grin. "A gusher, Rachel! They've brought in a goddam gusher!"

She reveled in the pride she saw in his eyes. Any vestige of doubt he might have had about their partnership was gone. She'd proved herself. She took his arm and yanked him down the path toward the dark carriage house of the Fantazia estate. They had been circumspect about being seen together. It would be a mistake to become careless now. At the carriage house she pulled him inside and shut the door.

Wordlessly he swept her into his arms and their lips met hungrily. As he crushed her against his sodden coat, the dampness of oil was more erotic than the feel of silk against her bare flesh.

"Josh—"

"God, Rachel—I can't believe it! Do you know what this means?!" His voice was hoarse, his black hair in disarray. She could feel his muscled body against her, sending another charge through her.

She smiled. "Believe it, darling."

His excitement could not be contained. He pulled away distractedly and began to pace in the musty darkness. Shafts of moonlight through the long, high windows gave the cavernous room an eerie, pale glow so Josh's figure was a shadow among darker shadows. Occasionally his handsome features, tanned face, were illuminated when the light from one of the wells broke through the oil shower. Finally he came back to grip her arms.

"I never doubted you for a minute, Rachel," he whispered.

"We've done it—we *own* this city!"

She swayed against him. She felt as though she owned the world! In the past months the Fielding Corporation had quietly purchased hundreds of acres that would yield oil as surely as this one. What would Teddy Reno say when he learned she hadn't confined her purchases to the Hill? He had no part of the Fielding acquisitions; he'd been too shortsighted to realize he had to see farther than the end of his nose. It was hers and Josh's—all of it!

She circled Josh's neck and drew him back to her lips. The kiss was powerful and unhesitating.

"I couldn't stay away," he said, as though reading her concern at his appearance.

"The crowd is so excited, they wouldn't notice if Jesus Christ were walking among them," she said with a smile. "It's a day for celebration."

He laughed, then devoured her mouth in a kiss that left her breathless. Before she recovered, he lifted her and whirled her in a mad dance until she begged him to stop, terrified he would lose his footing and send them both sprawling. He set her down, still holding her.

"This is only the beginning, Rachel, the first gusher. Money! Power! We'll have it all." He hugged her until she struggled for breath.

Didn't she feel the same? Wasn't she as charged by power and limitless horizons as he? So much all at once . . .

When he pulled away from her lips, he laughed. "Your kisses are oil-flavored, but they are the sweetest I have ever tasted!" He reclaimed her mouth, his tongue searching and demanding. She felt their breath mingle. She felt, too, the hard pressure of his arousal. She devoured his kiss as her hands explored the broad strength of his back under the fine silk shirt. His hands lifted her dress as he pressed her against the wall. He pulled aside her chemise as she tugged at the buttons of his trousers, fumbling with his drawers until she found his swollen member. She clasped the hot, hard flesh and directed it into her ready body. Gasping, they coupled with urgency. Rachel's body sang with a thundering pulse. When she closed her eyes, the room spun in its own orbit.

He drove into her with a steady rhythm, his need spiraling to meet hers. Rachel welcomed the sting where oil had

smeared their flesh. Heat surged through her. She was at the
top of the world, arms outstretched, body welcoming,
receiving. . . . She took in his power, claiming him fully.

Dawn had crept over the horizon when she let herself out
of the carriage house, Josh still asleep. The gusher sprayed a
steady, sullen roar of rocks and sand and oil and the terrible
stench of gas. The crowd had swollen as the news spread. As
far as she could see, the road was clogged with cars, trucks,
and people pushing up the hill. The trespassing throng poured
over the Maveens' yard. Everyone wanted to see and feel the
oil, to be anointed by the flux.

Rachel looked for her father, but she couldn't spot him in
the mob. A phantasmagoria of activity unfolded on the drilling
platform, but in the thick, slimy brown fog she couldn't
screen out the confusion. She made an effort to push her way
through the throng but abandoned it when two burly figures in
workshirts blocked her path. She had no choice but to move
with the riptide of jostling, exuberant humanity until she was
at the far end of the Fantazia yard. Then, taking advantage of
a momentary lull, she plunged through, close to the house,
and ran across the slippery grass toward the road.

The Maveen fence had been trampled into the lawn that
was now a sea of mud. The entire house was stained brown in
the glow of the rising sun. In places tiny rivulets of slime ran
down the walls like tears. The flowerbeds that Thomas and his
brother had guarded so fiercely only a few hours ago were
bogs. She started to turn away when suddenly someone
grabbed her arm and yanked her back. Expecting to see a
jovial celebrant, the indulgent smile froze on her lips as she
faced a furious Thomas Maveen. His mouth moved in indistinguishable rage. She tried to free herself, but his grip tightened as he pulled her toward the porch. She stumbled in his
wake as he dragged her up the steps, then inside. The door
slammed, shutting out the cacophony.

Handcuffing her in an iron grip, Thomas towed her down
the hall to the back parlor and shoved her inside. She was only
vaguely aware of the door closing behind her. The furor outside seemed remote from the darkened, hushed room.

Elliot was sitting in a chair near the window. His face was
gaunt, framed in a gray stubbled beard. He wore a collarless
shirt that showed slack folds of skin at his throat. His lap was

covered by a crocheted afghan. She realized she was staring at the single shoe that showed beneath it, and her face flushed. Aware of her bedraggled, filthy appearance, she tugged at her skirt to straighten it.

"It doesn't matter," he said. His voice had lost its timbre. He'd lost his beautiful voice; no audiences would he enthrall again.

"Hello, Elliot." She struggled to regain her poise, impatient with herself for being tongue-tied and awkward when she should be angry. But she was still too surprised to react with anything but confusion.

He glanced at the opaque, oily window. "Armageddon."

She had the fleeting thought that the stories of his mental derangement might have substance. "Despite the ugliness of this morning, most people see the beauty of the well, Elliot."

He turned as though it took concentration to command his muscles. His eyes were as opaque as pools of oil. When Rachel tried to smile, her face was stiff and unyielding.

"Beauty?" he demanded with the first spark he'd shown since she entered. He thrust his hand toward the window and wagged his arm. "You have brought destruction!"

"I'm sorry you feel that way, Elliot." There was no point in the conversation, and she wondered why he'd summoned her. She turned to leave.

"Stay!" The command was so strong, she leaned against the door and gaped. Even in confusion, her hair and clothes in disarray, she had a sensuous, exquisite beauty.

"You're young and beautiful, Rachel. But have you given thought to what will become of the people on the Hill?" His voice was suddenly calm, almost matching its former elegance.

"The poor will become wealthy, and the rich richer," she answered.

He laughed mirthlessly. "Ah, yes. Money is your god, I'd forgotten."

She bolted straight. "It is not my god," she retorted, "but neither do I pretend it has no place in the order of life." A resurgence of reason overcame her fear. Elliot couldn't hurt her; he couldn't hurt her physically, and she could battle him with words. They were on equal turf.

"And your order of things includes wiping out everything people on the Hill have worked for for generations? Destroying homes and families, raping the land?" he demanded.

"That's a narrow viewpoint," she said, her shield impenetrable.

"What other can a man have while he watches his world vanish? Like me, it will be awhile dying, but it will surely die."

"Nothing is being destroyed," she said angrily. "Change is part of life. Perhaps this change is more dramatic than ones we've seen before, but it is only change. Progress, if you will. No one will be forced to move or to lease oil rights if they don't wish to."

"Yes, they can choose to live in the shadow of the derricks." He glanced toward the window as though visualizing the future. "Every day will be as dark as this morning. We'll be in the middle of a forest. A dark forest." The breath seemed to go out of him. "You've sold your soul, Rachel. You've opened the doors of hell."

Impatience entered her voice. "There's no point in discussing it, Elliot. I'm sorry. I had hoped we could be"—she hesitated only a moment—"friends."

His thin, gaunt, almost transparent face twisted into a fierce mask of hate, making her breath catch. "You've become ruthless, Rachel. When did that happen? You were beautiful, gifted, and now you're hard. You say, 'Poor, crippled Elliot, dangle him from a chain like I do Hillary'? No, Rachel. I am not much of a man, but I can be proud of the fragment that I am. I won't let you take that."

She stared, mouth open, words swallowed. She felt as if she had received a horrible blow to her midsection. Her breath escaped with a pained sound. What was he saying? Was it his own jealousy and loneliness that made him accuse her of spitefulness and malevolence? Trembling, she opened the door and turned to leave.

"Whore!" he cried. The epithet hurtled after her as she ran down the hall. Outside a fresh spray of oil greeted her and mingled with her tears. As she ran down toward the boulevard that lead to the hotel, she couldn't shake the image of Elliot's long face, looking so gaunt and sickened, twisted in revulsion.

❧ *Five* ❧

RACHEL GAZED AT the the wind-chopped ocean below the bluff. Soon after the oil strike, she'd tired of the dark little apartment behind the hotel lobby and had converted four front rooms on the third floor to their new living quarters. She rarely fixed meals, since the hotel chef always supplied extra food for the Upfields. There'd been no need for more than a kitchenette where she could brew a pot of tea or morning coffee. The apartment was a practical suite that could some-day be put to use for guests.

She had shelved her plans for a large house on Darien Hill for the time being. The Hill was a forest of derricks with all their accompanying noise and dirt. The lot on which her house would someday stand was crisscrossed with the wooden struts of prosperity. The Hill had become an oil town and its rural life had dried up. Gushers still spewed black gold over the hillside. Only a few houses remained; most families had in-vested their oil-lease riches in extravagant households else-where. Her own parents had abandoned their house when her mother's health began to fail. They lived now on a quiet, tree-lined street in Belmont Shores.

For several months after the strike, Teddy joined the cele-brators who roamed the Hill, passing hip flasks among one another. Teddy no longer had to stay in the background, where

it was safest to speculate on oil. Among the more knowledgeable drillers and roustabouts, he was tolerated with amusement. Among drinkers and gamblers, he was a prince whose
money flowed freely.

Rachel soon realized how fortunes slipped through his
fingers as quickly as they fell within his grasp. For days on
end he absented himself from the hotel, only to return in a
sorry state with empty pockets. It was obvious that if he remained in the highly charged atmosphere of Ocean Beach he
would never have a penny left. In one of his more sober
hours, Rachel cornered him for a discussion of their financial
arrangement. She insisted they set up a bank account into
which she would deposit his royalty monies to free her from
having to contact him. She was relieved to find his room
empty one morning a few weeks later, a clean sweep of clothing and personal items testifying to his hasty departure during
the night. In his wake, rumors of worthless oil stock sold to
unsuspecting buyers made the rounds.

Despite the blight, the new era was a source of pride and
excitement for the city. Ocean Beach basked in worldwide
publicity. Five years later, locals and tourists clogged the Hill
on Sunday afternoons, eager to view the wells and inhale the
smell of oil and sea air.

The atmosphere of the city had changed, too. Men from
the rigs came off their shifts keyed up from constant danger
and exhaustion to seek diversion in dance halls, saloons, and
pool rooms. They played hard and spent lavishly. The economy of the city boomed. Merchants extended credit and padded their own pockets. An abundance of restless hopefuls for
whom there was no housing trailed into the town. Tent cities
sprang up in the harbor area as ugly pustules overflowing with
energetic children and weary adults. The men took whatever
jobs they could get as roustabouts on the rigs or unskilled
laborers on construction crews. Women hired out in canneries
and laundries, and they cooked in community kitchens over
common gas burners and ovens. The children crowded the
schools, streets, and Salvation Army gym. Some of the most
primitive accommodations were gradually phased out, but the
tent cities acted as a constant reminder that instant riches did
not come to all.

Rachel recalled in anger that Hillary had taken to playing
poker in Seaside Camp, and worse, that he had taken cash

from the hotel drawer to finance his gambling. When he returned reeking of whiskey, his pockets empty, they had quarreled violently for the first time in their marriage. She warned him that if he ever tapped the cash drawer again, she would see to it that it was the last time.

Hillary had not taken well to prosperity. His extravagance had boomed out of control. They had refurbished rooms, added a dining room wing, and doubled the staff. To Rachel, the Oceanside already stood leagues ahead of other establishments. It was gaining a regional reputation as a lush, elegant hotel with beautiful views, excellent food, and recreation. The hotel had installed an indoor pool, and shuffleboards on one patio. But the bills continued to exceed the accounts receivable. She hired an accountant to keep Hillary on a tight leash. Hillary spent more and more time away from the hotel, and his gambling debts quickly squandered the salary he took from the business. He was still filled with plans and dreams, but none came to fruition. Perhaps some of the fault lay with her. He had fewer responsibilities, but she'd been forced to step in when she realized he had no head for business. He was a glad-hander, the genial innkeeper, who preferred drinking and chatting with guests to spending time with the ledgers. He was well liked, she couldn't deny it, but he would have bankrupted the hotel if she hadn't intervened.

She sighed, thinking how much their marriage had changed. And how much more it would change. She pressed a hand to her belly and felt the new life there. She hadn't told Hillary yet, but soon the pregnancy would begin to show, the child due in June. June, it seemed, marked a time of changes in her life. She had no doubt it was Hillary's, no matter how much her heart longed for it to be Josh's. Long ago she'd banished the specter of guilt that shadowed their trysts at the Rancho cottage. For all their infrequency, they were fraught with danger. Each interlude was separate from the rest of her life, an island of pleasure to be savored sweetly long after they had taken place. Yet each was so completely a part of her, she wondered if she could live without them. She was sure Josh shared her feelings, but they never spoke of their most intimate emotions. They both knew that their lives did not allow acknowledgment of their love. Josh's wife, Collette, had borne him a son and was expecting another child before Christmas. Josh doted on young Judson, who was a winsome, dark-eyed child, strongly favoring the Fantazia bloodlines. Collette's health was fragile, and Josh catered to her whims. They spent winter months in Palm Springs or on extended trips to warmer climates. Collette had never overcome her dislike of the ocean. When they were in town, they lived at Rancho del Cielo, far from the sound of the pounding surf and city life. She rarely accompanied Josh into town except for gala functions where the promise of glamour overrode her distaste for the city. Rachel had last seen her at the opening of the posh new Pacific Club, with its marbled archways, paneling, stained-glass windows, and carved wood mantels. The new construction division of Fantazia Enterprises had built it.

Was she foolish not to consider the construction business? The real estate and land management company she'd opened soon after the oil strike was soaring. At times she was restless for new ventures. Her father encouraged her to expand into allied fields. He'd become interested in the development of Belmont Shores, which he predicted was destined to become one of the community's most exclusive residential districts. Southern California was undergoing a tremendous building boom, he said. Construction was the wave of the future, as oil had been in the past.

It would be a challenge. Why did she hesitate? Was it because she would have to compete with Josh in yet another area? Was she afraid to be too competitive in his eyes? She knew he admired her ambition and success. After all, she'd made him huge profits by sharing her knowledge of oil lands. And there was more to come. Their investments in city properties hadn't been plundered yet. When the bonanza of Darien Hill eventually cooled, oil companies would expand their horizons. She knew that Teddy Reno's old maps would prove as right for beach and river properties as they had for the Hill. And she and Josh monopolized the high cards.

She turned her attention to the architectural blueprints on her gilded desk. They, too, had been drafted without Hillary's knowledge. Plans for the new hotel. If she formed a construction company, she could build it herself. The idea galvanized her senses. She studied the drawing of the building with tall, columned facade and arched windows. It would be the show-place of Hillary's dreams. The Virginia would pale in comparison. The new Oceanside would sprawl over four additional lots flanking them now, three of them already acquired. Hillary knew she'd bought the adjacent lot where Mrs. Johnson's rooming house stood. At first she hadn't told him about the others because she wanted to surprise him with the *fait accompli,* but now she was no longer sure. If he knew they had the land, purchased in her name, he'd want to enlarge right away. His dreams and plans would soar. Was it that she didn't want to face that burst of enthusiasm he always showed only to see it eventually wither? Was she losing faith in Hillary's follow-through?

She locked the drawings away, then began to sort the bills for the month. She worked quickly and efficiently as she readied the books for the accountant.

She hesitated now over a produce bill and reread the figures in the spend column. Frowning, she opened the ledger and glanced at the previous month's entry, then for several months before then. The bill for October was four times that for July.

Carbello Wholesale Produce.... When had they stopped dealing with Pitman Brothers? She leafed back several pages, running her fingertip down the neat columns. The first Carbello entry was in May. Six months. About the time she had issued the ultimatum to Hillary about the cash drawer.

She felt sick. Her suspicions were unfounded. They had to be. She wanted them to be. *Hillary, Hillary . . .*

It took her a week to uncover, but Hillary was harvesting kickbacks from Carbello Wholesale Produce. The hotel chef verified that orders rarely fluctuated. She obtained a price list from Carbello; their prices had held steady since early spring. She made discreet inquiries and learned that Carbello Produce, new to Ocean Beach, worked separately from the daily Farmers' Market in Lincoln Park. They dealt directly with hotels and restaurants on a thirty-day net basis. Their prices were higher than competitors', but they did not lack for steady customers.

She located the driver who delivered to the hotel. He was a swarthy, curly-haired man who scowled when Rachel compared the bill with the company's price list.

"Your husband made the arrangements, lady. You got any complaints, talk to him."

At the hotel, Hillary was at the wet bar in the corner of their apartment sitting room. He gave her a rakish salute. The dark circles below his bloodshot eyes gave his handsome face a drawn look.

"Fix you something?"

"I want to talk to you, Hillary."

From the pocket of a superbly tailored gray suit Rachel was sure she hadn't seen before, he drew out the fourteen-karat-gold Illinois Springfield pocket watch she'd given him for Christmas. "Will it take long, darling? I have an appointment."

"It won't take long if you give me some direct answers."

His eyebrow lifted inquisitively.

"Why did you switch the produce account from Pitman to Carbello?"

"Their produce is fresher. The chef was complaining about wilted lettuce and bruised strawberries."

"We've dealt with Pitman for years and never had problems."

He shrugged. "They had trouble with late plantings. The season was getting off to a bad start, so I had to find someone who could fill orders promptly."

She set the most recent Carbello invoice in front of him. "Eight hundred dollars a month is a high premium to pay for promptness."

His gaze flashed to the bill, then away. He sipped at his whiskey and water, absorbed in the ice.

"Comparable merchandise from Pitman would have cost two hundred and forty dollars. I checked."

His eyes flashed. Anger? Fear? He took another swallow of whiskey.

"I'm trying to understand, Hillary, but you're not helping. *Why?* Surely you can see it isn't practical." She had difficulty controlling her impatience.

"Even a dolt like me should see that?" he said with heavy sarcasm.

"It's a matter of numbers—"

"Ah, yes, numbers. I'm sorry, darling. You should know by now that I don't have the fantastic Grant knack for numbers. I'm only a poor hotel operator who knows how to make guests happy."

She hid her annoyance. "Making a profit is part of being a good hotel operator."

He gulped the rest of his drink and fixed himself another.

His stance was tense and a faint flush showed above his collar. She was handling this badly, but there seemed no way to make him understand. She had no choice but to plunge ahead.

"I think we should switch back to Pitman."

Without turning he said, "Is that an order?"

She flinched. "Can't we discuss this rationally? We're talking about the hotel—it's a business venture. *Our* business."

He turned. The blue eyes that had always been so alive and twinkling looked cold and hard. *"Ours?* As long as I dance to your tune, it's ours. You and your father think I don't have the brains of an ant. One or the other of you is always looking over my shoulder, ready to tell me how to do so something better. Maybe it's time to stop the pretense, Rachel. Maybe you should take away the last vestiges of my psuedo-power here. Tell the staff you're giving the orders from now on. Perhaps you can place me as an assistant bartender or something."

Pain radiated from her heart toward the child in her womb. "Is that what you think of me?"

"Do you deny it? You've got Clarkson doing the books and watching me like a hawk. Your father stops in several times a week to offer 'suggestions.' You make every final decision about staff, linens, decorating. Had I known how many strings would be attached to your father's magnificent wedding gift, I would have refused both it and his daughter's hand."

She recoiled from him. He hunched protectively over his drink, his blond hair curling above his collar, long overdue for a haircut.

"Why do you keep me around, Rachel? My judgments are questioned. My duties have been taken over by you or your guard dogs."

"Hillary, please—" She trembled with hurt and anger.

"Please? Believe me, Rachel, I try, but there's no pleasing you."

"That's not true." It was a hoarse whisper.

He looked at her, then gulped down his whiskey. The air was suffocating with tension. Rachel closed her mind against the nausea that engulfed her. Her own doubts and misgivings were horrible condemnations from his lips. She could see them in the bar mirror—her flashing eyes, his downcast ones —a beautiful couple, whose relationship had soured.

"I'm sorry you feel that way, Hillary. We don't seem able

to discuss things anymore." Was she guilty of what he accused? Her mind struggled in a fog.

"I have a great deal of time to think with so little to do," he said helplessly.

She forced herself to hold his gaze in the mirror. "I spoke with the driver from Carbello."

His mouth twitched, but he was silent.

"I know you're taking kickbacks."

His face was carved of stone.

"Why, Hillary? Why didn't you ask—" She broke off as his rage erupted, and he whirled to face her.

"Why didn't I *ask* you? Would you have given me more money? Would you have given me back my self-respect? I think not."

Pain engulfed her; she realized her hand covered herself as if to shield the child from the ugliness of the scene. She drew it away. He made no excuses for his deceit. He saw no harm in cheating . . . stealing . . . She realized that he did consider the hotel hers, despite his name on the deed. Guilt swept away her anger.

"Oh, Hillary, I'm sorry. I'm sorry!" She threw herself at him and pressed against his chest, encircling her arms around him. She wanted everything to be right, to go back to what they'd had at the start of their marriage, to share the love and closeness they'd known. His body was stiff and unyielding. Finally he put aside the glass and took her in his arms.

"I'm a fool, Rachel. Forgive me. I don't want to hurt you."

He stroked her silky long hair. She trembled as tears welled. They *could* go back. They *could* start over. They would.

"I'll do whatever you say," he whispered, kissing her.

She shook her head. "I don't want that. We'll make decisions together."

He rocked her gently. "Darling, I want so much to please you in every way. Believe that. I love you."

She savored the words and let her guilt wash away. She would not see Josh again. She would devote herself to Hillary and rebuild their precious marriage. They would be partners in every way. Softly she told him about the baby.

He held her at arm's length, astonished. "A child? Are you sure?"

She nodded. "I saw Dr. Haverman two weeks ago."

"And you've kept it from me until now?" He laughed and hugged her tightly, then quickly released his grip as though terrified of crushing the tiny life in her womb. He squeezed more gently and grazed her forehead with his lips. "You are a cruel and wicked woman, but I love you. You must promise to do everything the doctor says." He looked solemn until she nodded. "That's a good girl. And you must slow down. You do too much, Rachel. I think it's time you had a regular office and staff to handle as much of your real estate business as possible. I'm sure your father would agree. It's one thing to be a good businesswoman but quite another to run yourself ragged. Promise you'll think about it?"

When she promised, he smiled happily. His eyes were no longer glacial but tenderly warm and inviting.

"Your appointment?" she whispered.

"I'd rather be with you."

She embraced him in a wave of stirred passion and lifted her face to his. His tongue tasted faintly of fine whiskey, but his breath was warm. Arms encircling each other, they walked to the bedroom.

The winter passed in cycles of bright sunshine and gloomy rain and fog. Hillary spent more time with Rachel that he ever had, asking for her opinion in every phase of the hotel operation. He also showed interest in her real estate ventures. When he occasionally took a night off to play a friendly game of poker with friends or guests, it was with her blessing. Business prospered, despite the off-season, and the hotel was filled to capacity. Rachel avoided criticizing his work as she recognized the effort he put forth to handle his responsibilities. They continued to buy produce from Carbello after Hillary explained that he had signed a year's contract with them. The kickbacks ceased, however, and the bills were no longer outrageously high.

True to her promise, Rachel looked into opening a real estate office. She found a hot location on Ocean Boulevard across from the chamber of commerce, and hired staff. As much as possible, she let them handle property showings, listings, and appraisals. Though she still took care of every closing personally, her work load considerably lightened as her pregnancy became apparent.

It was an easy pregnancy and she enjoyed the bloom. Her

body felt awkward and heavy, but Hillary assured her she was more beautiful than ever. She believed him as she basked in their renewed relationship.

Spring burst on the coast in warm weather and colorful new life. Tourists swarmed over the beaches. Rooms at the Oceanside were booked weeks in advance, and Rachel almost told Hillary about her plans for a dazzling new building, one that would draw clientele from around the country. Instead she decided to surprise him after the baby was born. With her confinement only weeks away, she linked up with her new office by telephone only. Her father took over most of her duties and brought papers for her signature to the apartment several evenings a week.

She was expecting him one Wednesday night, and when a knock sounded, she called a cheerful "Come in." She was sitting near the window with a glass of sherry, enjoying the cool evening breeze that fluttered the lace curtains, when she spotted the lithe, tall figure of Teddy Reno.

"Hello, Rachel. It's been a long time," he said from the doorway.

He was still tanned and fit and his stride was agile, but lines creased his eyes, and dark circles underscored them.

"Hello, Teddy," she said flatly.

His gaze drifted to the swollen front of the lightweight crepe Pasha skirt and loose shirtwaist. She wore her hair up, and she had lightly applied her cosmetics. She hadn't aged a day, and if anything, looked more beautiful than he remembered. "You're looking well. Always beautiful, eh, Rachel?" he said, looking around uneasily. "I trust Hillary is well?"

She nodded. "He's out for the evening. He'll be sorry he missed you—unless you're staying in town for a while?"

He laughed. "Same Rachel, eh? Curious and cautious. I'm staying in town. Actually, I came to see you."

He'd undoubtedly asked at the desk and knew she was alone. She indicated a chair and the wet bar. He crossed to fix himself a whiskey before he sat.

"I've read interesing things about Darien Hill," he said. "You've done very well."

"It's an easy matter to calculate your percentage against my profit," she said.

"I have done it many times," he said solemnly. "Many times. And it always comes out wrong, the way I see it." He glanced around appreciatively, noting the fine antiques and extravagant decorating. "You and Hillary have done wonders with the hotel. I am surprised you still live here. I thought you'd have a mansion by now."

She ignored his comment. "Why have you come back?"

"Yes, a fine job," he said, glancing about again as though he hadn't heard her. He studied a Renoir nude and a Pissarro watercolor on the wall. "It must have cost a pretty penny." He gave her a wide grin. "I never could have done it on my share of the oil money. I couldn't have come close." He sighed heavily. "Matter of fact, Rachel, I'm broke. I came back to see if we couldn't renegotiate our little deal. Where would you be if I hadn't put you on to those leases and convinced you they were worth a fortune?"

She looked at him without surprise. "The income from the oil was not what made me wealthy. It was how we invested it that mattered."

His smile was derisive. "No matter how you look at it, Rachel, it comes back to the information I gave you."

"Sold me."

"Much too cheaply. I could have gotten a lot more elsewhere. A dozen men right here in Ocean Beach would have paid more than a measly three and a half percent. You took advantage of me, Rachel."

The baby kicked. The fluttering movement disrupted her thoughts momentarily. "We both signed the agreement quite willingly, as I recall."

"Sometimes a man has no choice, even though he knows he's being cheated."

A suspicion lurking in a corner of her memory surfaced. "Or a man has no choice because he has gotten his information illegally."

The quick wariness in his eyes told her she'd struck a nerve. He had stolen the geological maps from Union, something she always suspected. He had had to be very careful whom he approached with them, lest his ploy explode in his face.

He finished his drink. "That makes you an accessory, Rachel, though I doubt Union's going to kick up a fuss at this late date. Still . . . they might find some legal angle that would cut your royalties. They've got a battery of lawyers."

She tilted her chin. "Then your share would suffer as

well," she said. "You're cutting off your nose to spite your face if you're threatening me, Teddy."

His eyes changed colors like a chameleon. "I was hoping you'd see reason." He set aside the whiskey glass and unfolded some papers from his pocket. He rose slowly, as though he hated to make the journey to the chesterfield sofa. He held out the slips, but when she put her hand out for them, he recoiled. "Just look, don't touch. Not that I don't trust you, Rachel, but a man can't be too careful."

She studied the top paper. *IOU $2000. Hillary Upfield.* Teddy shuffled the slips slowly. They totaled more than twenty thousand dollars. There was no question the signatures were Hillary's. Each slip carried the embossed gold crest: The *Lucky Lady.*

"How did you get these?" she said coldly. The breeze that had been delightful a short time ago felt like a winter wind over a grave.

"At the moment I am working for Mickey Carbello. He owns the ship."

The *Press-Telegram* had carried numerous stories about the gambling ship anchored beyond the three-mile limit. An eastern corporation supposedly owned it. Carbello's name had not been mentioned, she was sure. Carbello Wholesale Produce. Nausea rose up her throat. She pressed a hand to her mouth and closed her eyes. She heard Teddy move away, then the clink of ice as he fixed himself another drink.

"There are more, Rachel. Carbello only gave me a few. Hillary's in to him for close to a hundred thousand dollars."

She reached to draw down the window, unaware of her tears until they coursed over her lids in the cold sting of the wind. She wiped them hurriedly. Hillary's promises had been lies. Their new start was a sham. She'd been a fool. She turned back to Teddy as he seated himself in the cretonne-covered chair.

"Why did Carbello give you these?"

He grinned. "I told you, I'm working for him."

She eyed him speculatively, knowing he had found a way to work off his own gambling debts. Had it ever occurred to Hillary to find a way to solve his problem?

"What makes Mr. Carbello think he can threaten me?" An icy calm pierced her as she recovered from her shock.

"Threaten? I haven't made any threats, Rachel. Our business, yours and mine, is quite apart from this." He rustled the IOUs, then jammed them back into his pocket. She didn't believe him, but she said nothing. "Mr. Carbello is getting impatient about Hillary's failure to meet his obligations. He's been generous to let them ride this long, but Hillary's a mighty convincing talker. I'm sure after six years you've discovered that for yourself. Talk's one thing but eventually comes a time when it isn't enough. Mr. Carbello wants his money."

"I will not pay Hillary's gambling debts!" Her anger exploded like dynamite.

"Mr. Carbello wants you to remind Hillary that he has ways of collecting."

"He'll have to discuss that with Hillary. If Carbello is fool enough to advance credit, it's his problem, not mine! Hillary gave me his word——" With sickening clarity, she realized Hillary had never promised to stop gambling, only to end the kickbacks from the produce company.

Reno sipped his whiskey. "I don't think you should be hasty, Rachel. I told Mr. Carbello you're a businesswoman who knows the value of thinking over a deal before accepting or turning it down. He's agreed to wait twenty-four hours for your answer."

"The answer is *no*. Twenty-four hours from now it will still be *no*," she said emphatically.

Teddy emptied the whiskey glass and set it on the marble-topped Queen Anne table. He got to his feet with a casual air and tossed a card into Rachel's lap. "Call me at this number before six tomorrow." With a mock salute, he retrieved his Panama hat from the brass tree and let himself out.

Rachel hurled her sherry glass after him. It shattered, spraying glass over the floor. She picked up Teddy's card and tore it into a dozen pieces. Gradually the hot, suffocating anger began to ease. She breathed deeply, then stared miserably at her swollen figure in the hall mirror. She felt her stomach flutter as the baby kicked.

She'd been susceptible to Hillary's lies because of her altered physical and emotional condition. And Hillary had taken advantage of it. Of her. . . .

She pushed herself out of the chair ponderously, resenting her bloated body. In the kitchenette, she found a whisk broom and dustpan, then returned to sweep up the shards of crystal.

Straightening, she felt a sharp twinge of pain in her back.
She'd be glad when the child was born so she could emerge
from this restrictive life.

In the morning she was gone before Hillary woke. She'd
heard him come in late but pretended to be asleep. There was
nothing to say, and she didn't want to hear any more of his
lies.

She drove to Darien Hill and parked the Buick below the
Fantazia house and sat watching the pumping and drilling
equipment. She'd heard a count of nearly a thousand wells.
She thought it not exaggerated as she viewed the skyline. The
Hill had changed drastically. The few homes and carriage
houses that remained were overshadowed by the towering derricks and had taken on a dirty brown hue as though to blend
with the ugly landscape. Most had been torn down or moved
out of the path of progress. With wells every few feet, the
land's value soared higher than if studded with the grandest of
homes. There were sixty-nine wells on her Hill land—sixty
thousand barrels of crude oil a day.

She listened to the steady *whump-whump* of the pumps.
She knew the output of each well, their income, and their
projected lifetime. What she didn't know was her husband.
Were there facts and figures she could compute that would
give her a clear picture of him? Could she have foreseen his
deceit and penchant for gambling if she'd been more obser-
vant?

She glanced down the road toward the Maveen house. She
hadn't seen Elliot since the morning the first well came in.
The Maveens had moved the previous year, and word was that
Elliot's health had declined precipitously. He refused to see
anyone—not even Hillary could gain access into Elliot's
sanctum in San Pedro.

Elliot had accused her of destroying the Hill and of robbing
Hillary of his pride. Had he know what kind of man his friend
was? Had the loss of his beautiful tenor voice and promising
future destroyed his judgment?

She drove to Belmont Shores. Her parents were surprised
and delighted to see her. Rachel let her mother fuss over her
and fix tea. Rachel noted the frequent glances her father gave
his wife, knowing she was taxing her strength, but knowing,
too, that her pleasure at seeing Rachel overrode all. Althea

had failed badly the past years. The doctors were unable to diagnose anything more specific than a stomach ailment and anemia. Mills talked of taking her east to one of the large clinics that specialized in diagnoses, but Althea put him off. *She's dying,* Rachel realized. *One day she'll just be gone, and none of us will be able to prevent it. Thank heaven she'll live to see her first grandchild.*

Mills persuaded Althea to rest after they finished tea. Then he and Rachel closed themselves in his study while she recounted Teddy Reno's visit. Mills Grant listened somberly. He was far more knowledgeable about the owner of the *Lucky Lady* than she.

"I'm not sure it's smart to dismiss Carbello so lightly, Rachel," he said. "I don't like his reputation. He seems able to convince the police to look the other way when he doesn't want his business subjected to scrutiny. It's rumored—just rumored, mind you—that he ordered Perry Kranzle killed."

Three months before, Perry Kranzle, son of a wealthy San Diego family, had been shot after a night of partying and gambling. His body had been found in a Naples marsh, far from the water taxi that had brought him and friends back from the gambling ships. Kranzle insisted on driving his own car while his friends cabbed to a speakeasy on the west side of town. Kranzle never arrived.

"Why?"

"According to the rumors, a scuffle on the *Lucky Lady* erupted because they wouldn't give him any more credit. His father had paid off earlier IOUs but put Carbello on notice there'd be no more. That night the kid rang up a twenty-thousand-dollar tab. He didn't have the money. The next day he was dead."

"And you think Carbello did it?" She was alarmed by the similarity between the Kranzle story and her own ultimatum to Teddy.

Her father drummed his fingers. "I wouldn't want to owe Carbello anything."

"Did the police have any evidence?"

"No evidence, no suspects, no clues. Case closed." Mills took a Havana from his pocket. He snipped the end, then lit and puffed it silently for a few moments. "I don't like the idea of your being involved with Carbello in any way, Rachel. He's dangerous. I think you should pay him off. Kranzle was an object lesson." He looked at her through a blue-gray wreath of smoke.

Her chest tightened. "Do you think he'd harm Hillary?" Despite her anger, the thought of Hillary being hurt or killed horrified her.

Her father pointed a finger. "I'm more concerned about you. Carbello sent Reno to talk to *you*. I don't like that." He puffed a cloud of smoke. "I'd feel much better if you stay here instead of going back to the hotel."

She shifted her weight and gave her father a rueful smile. "I'm perfectly safe at the hotel. Besides, it won't be long before your grandchild makes his appearance. Then I'll be tucked away safely in the hospital, with Dr. Haverman's staff to watch over me. Please don't worry. You know mother would overdo if I were here."

Mills sighed. "All right, I won't try to persuade you. But you will be careful?" She nodded. "Good. And we have your promise to call us the moment you're off to the hospital? Your mother wants to keep track of you every minute."

She promised. She felt better even though she had come to no decision about Hillary. Her father was a good listener, and it helped sort her thoughts to use him as a sounding board. She felt a tremendous surge of love and admiration for him. He did not condemn Hillary or censure her, though she knew he was keenly disappointed that her marriage had turned out so badly. Would he be shocked if she decided to divorce Hillary? Perhaps not, but it would kill her mother. Especially now that there was a child. A child needed parents, a family.

It would be a relief to welcome her final labor, no matter how painful it might be. She'd avoided women who reveled in the tales of their childbearing ordeals. Not so her mother, who translated every twice-told tale of misery to concern for Rachel. She was certain Rachel's labor would be difficult and wanted Dr. Haverman to use nitrous oxide to cushion her pain.

She stood, easing her back which seemed to ache constantly of late. Dr. Haverman warned her that first babies rarely followed schedule. According to his calculation, the child would be born in about two weeks. She prayed it would be no longer.

"Let's stroll in the garden," she said. "I'll stay until mother wakes, then I must get back."

❧ Six ❧

HILLARY WAS GONE when she returned to the hotel, and she wondered if he was aware of Teddy's visit. It would be like Hillary to avoid a direct confrontation, hoping the problem would solve itself or vanish miraculously. He'd been growing more detached over the years, until he now seemed to relinquish all responsibility to her. The change had been glacial, but steady.

She spent the rest of the day going over the books. To her relief, she found no discrepancies to indicate Hillary had tampered with the accounts.

She dined alone with a tray filled with garnished lobster, creamed asparagus, and sautéed potatoes ordered from the kitchen. She felt vaguely out of sorts and uncomfortable and not up to putting on a cheerful face for the dining room. When Hillary didn't return, a nagging worry began to form in her mind that she had put him in danger by rebuffing Teddy last night. When the telephone rang on the Edwardian foyer table, she rushed to answer it.

The night clerk informed her that Mr. Reno requested her to join him downstairs.

"Ask him to come up," she said in annoyance.

"He says he has something to show you, Mrs. Upfield. He's already gone back to his car."

Stunned a moment, she hung up and grabbed her shawl. An object lesson . . . Her tongue was metallic and her mouth sour. If something had happened to Hillary because of her stubbornness . . .

She reached the lobby out of breath and hurried to the door. A sea breeze acted as a cooling balm on her flushed body. Darkness had enveloped the bluff. Beyond the light pooled around the hotel's entrance, she could make out a dark sedan at the curb. Nervously she walked down the steps.

Teddy Reno leaned to unlatch the passenger door. "Good evening, Rachel. Please get in." She noticed white peppered his wavy hair, and his skin sagged with an unhealthy pasty look. He was alone. "What do you want?"

"Get in," his voice commanded, his eyes refusing to meet hers. She hesitated, then started to turn away, but a figure emerged from the shadows and loomed over her. He was large and powerful, with broad shoulders under an unbuttoned suit coat. When he spread his arms to block her path, she saw the heavy gun in a shoulder holster. He jabbed a thumb toward the car.

Frightened, she backed away. There was no one on the street, no curious eyes at the hotel windows. No help. . . .

"Get in, Rachel," Teddy said wearily.

She stumbled in her haste to avoid the hand the big man put out. He slammed the door after her, then climbed into the backseat. His presence hung like a threatening cloud.

"What's the meaning of this?" she demanded.

Teddy started the car. "Mr. Carbello wants to talk to you."

"He has an unusual way of calling!" She was furious with herself for walking blindly into Teddy's trap.

Reno laughed. "He usually gets what he wants. It will be interesting to see the two of you meet head on."

"This is kidnapping. I'll have the police on you."

He glanced at her sidelong, his gray eyes unreadable. "You came down to meet me of your own free will. We're just going for a friendly ride."

She snorted. "And I suppose your friend back there will testify to that."

His teeth flashed a smile. "You should have called, Rachel."

She pressed her lips in a tight line. Her father was right. Carbello was dangerous. It was only a few hours past the deadline he'd set. She'd been a fool to put herself in jeopardy.

When they turned off Ocean Boulevard, she knew they were headed for the Seventh Street landing where the water taxis left for the *Lucky Lady*. Fear began to creep up her spine. Aboard the ship, Carbello would be surrounded by his people. She would be alone. Nervously she glanced at the busy streets. No one paid any attention to the car as Teddy maneuvered it through the throng at the landing. As soon as he stopped, the bodyguard jumped out and opened Rachel's door. He reached to help her, but she jerked away. She climbed out without assistance. Laughing merrymakers clustered on the pier waiting for Kip's Water Taxi, but Teddy steered her farther down the pier to a dimly lit flight of steps. He started down, motioning Rachel to follow. She had no choice with the heavyset man at her heels. She clutched the railing as the cold wet breeze clung to her, the shawl slapping around her, creating the impression of either an angry seductress or a bewitching angel.

A small boat was moored to the quay, its running lights on. As Teddy climbed aboard, a light switched on in the cabin, illuminating the deck. Teddy took her hand as she stepped onto the bobbing boat. He steadied her, then helped her into the cabin. His weakened condition—probably the result of late-night hours and too much booze—made her wary, her senses alert.

"Mind your head."

She ducked, holding the side of the doorway, then sat down quickly in a chair just inside. Teddy sat beside her. Almost immediately the engine sprang to life and she heard the heavy thump of the mooring ropes as they were cast off. From the landing a cry went up as the waiting group roared its disapproval at being left behind. Rachel wished they could have accompanied her.

As the boat plunged on, she looked around her surroundings. The cabin was pleasantly decorated, unlike the stark water taxis. Club chairs and tables were bolted to the deck. There was a fully equipped bar, with special racks to prevent glasses and bottles from sliding. Teddy made no attempt at conversation. She listened to the low rumble of the powerful engine and the slapping of the waves against the hull. As the lights of the landing receded, darkness enveloped the boat slicing through the water. She refused to let herself think about what was waiting at the end of the journey. Before long, tiny specks of light appeared in the distance and grew to a garish splash of color. The gambling ship was branded with a huge, bulb-flashing marquee hung above the deck. Across the center a banner of lights spelled out LUCKY LADY. Music slashed through the darkness in undulating jazz rhythms. A flotilla of sex, jazz, and gambling bobbed in the seas before her.

The boat slowed and bumped against a landing platform, where several deckhands scrambled to grab the lines. The big man was halfway up the stairs when Rachel stepped from the cabin behind Teddy. He waited for them on the deck, then led them aft.

Rachel pulled the shawl about her ungainly body. Through the long windows of the main cabin, she saw the huge gambling room and heard the clatter of chips and dice and the droning calls of the croupiers. The music came, she now saw, from a forward lounge, where couples in formal attire crowded the dance floor and bar. There was no attempt to conceal the sale and consumption of liquor. Rachel wondered if Carbello had the same kind of influence with federal agents as he had with the local police.

Teddy marshaled her into a passageway, again warning her to watch the low heading. She found his odd mixture of force and concern almost humorous. He knocked at a cabin door, then ushered her in.

A sumptuous cabin opened to her. Thick carpeting deadened sound; heavy drapes adorned the windows. The walls were paneled in rich dark wood and wall sconces held electric bulbs that resembled candles. A dark-haired man in a tuxedo, his hair oiled down and brushed back, sat behind a large desk in the center of the room. He dismissed Teddy with a flick of his gaze. When the door closed, he turned the full force of his brown, specked eyes on Rachel, his thick brows knit together. He motioned her to a chair, but she ignored him. She felt a quick surge of satisfaction as his scowl deepened. He wasn't accustomed to being defied. He was also at a disadvantage by having to look up at her.

His lips twitched, then he said, "Please sit down, Mrs. Upfield." Not an order. A pleasant request.

As Rachel lowered herself into the chair, she felt him scrutinize her cumbersome movements. She kept her hands on the chair arms so she wouldn't look like a frightened Buddha. She had to separate fear from her physical being in order to keep her wits about her.

"I don't like dames who don't do what they're told." Carbello's voice was rough, as though the sea air made him hoarse.

"I am not a dame," Rachel said evenly. "And I do not like being given orders, especially by people I do not know." She met his dark gaze without flinching. She saw a flicker of astonishment in his eyes.

"I tell you to call, you call," he said. He hunched forward, anger creasing his broad forehead.

Rachel didn't answer. That seemed to satisfy him for a moment. He leaned back, clasping his hands across his thin waist. She was not sure what she had expected, but she was surprised by Carbello's age—not beyond thirty, she was sure —and his ordinary appearance. He was not handsome, but flashed a Hollywood attractiveness: well-defined features, softened angles, high cheekbones, and a shock of unruly hair controlled with macassar oil. His fingers, though interlocked, looked as delicate as a musician's or artist's.

"Why was I brought here?" she asked when the silence lengthened.

"Your husband owes me a hundred grand. I want it," he rasped.

"I am not responsible for my husband's gambling debts."

He kneaded a lip between even white teeth as though considering her opinion seriously. Then, abruptly, he swiveled his chair in a gesture of disdain. Staring at the wall, he said, "A man comes to gamble on the *Lady,* he needs one of two things. Either he shows the color of his money or he proves he is worth it so we give him credit." The chair swiveled back like a lighthouse beacon. Carbello's eyes were hidden under the heavy brows. He stabbed a finger toward her, his eyes raking her. "You're a great-looking girl, even now," he said, referring to her pregnancy. "But aside from that, I know you're worth a hundred grand ten times over." His lips curled in a smile. "You and your old man and your property and oil wells. A wife's got a duty by her husband, the way I see it."

"If I ran my business on the blind faith you seem to run yours on, I would undoubtedly find myself with as many bad debts," Rachel retorted.

"I collect, one way or another," he said, licking his lips as his gaze wandered over her again.

She lifted her chin to hide her inner trembling. "Don't you dare suggest—" she began.

He straightened in his seat and squirmed. "Okay, lady. Then let's talk real estate. I hear the Oceanside is a pretty nice place," he said.

Emboldened by his backing down after a sexual advance, Rachel firmed in her resolve. She suspected he knew about her Fantazia connection and would tred very carefully. "It isn't worth a hundred thousand dollars!" she snapped. "If Hillary told you it was, you're a fool for believing him!"

Carbello's face darkened. Nobody called him a fool. Who the hell did she think she was?

"We had a gross income last year of fifty-six thousand dollars. Operating expenses run almost eighty percent, which leaves a net of around eleven thousand dollars. That's a far cry from a hundred thousand dollars."

"The property's worth plenty."

Fear stabbed in her stomach. "Granted, Ocean Beach isn't suffering the current depression as badly as the rest of the country, but I doubt we could find a buyer willing to pay one hundred thousand dollars."

His smile was frightening. "I got one. All I need is the deed, lady."

Anger engulfed her, cold unreasoning, blind rage. "I won't let him throw away everything I have worked for! He has no right—" She gasped as pain seared around her body, taking her breath away. The baby seemed to lurch in her body.

Carbello was startled, then watched her warily. He knew she was having a kid, but he hadn't suspected that she was this far along. Christ, he had to get her out of here as fast as possible. Some of the color came back to her face, easing his panic.

"He's got no more credit here, take my word for it," he told her. All idea of forcing an affair on her had flown in these circumstances. "But he ain't gonna walk owing me that kind of dough. Either I get the money or the hotel. If not—"

"Otherwise what? You'll have him killed like you did Perry Kranzle?!" Her rage exploded. Words dredged from a deep black spring of frustration and anger at Hillary these past months—years—erupted like seething lava. "He gambled here because you let him, Mr. Carbello! I can't stop him, that's obvious. If he's taken you, that's too bad. He's taken me, too! He's a dreamer. His big chance is always coming next week or next month or next year! Or on the next flip of the cards. You seem to have looked closely into my affairs. You must know that I am not without influence. It's possible I may be able to cause you more trouble than killing Hillary would be worth!"

He stared and shook his head like an enraged bull. She was threatening him. Nobody had ever done that, especially a dame. He didn't care how beautiful or *angelica* she was. Furiously he sprang from the chair. She jerked back as if he'd struck her. He took a step, but she began to shake all over. She wasn't even looking at him. She was—jeez!

"Hey, you okay?" He moved closer, warily. A thin sheen of perspiration covered her face as she bit her lip. "Jesus—" He bounded to the door and yanked it open. "Phil!" The big man ran in, gun drawn. "Put that damned thing away!" Carbello ordered. He jerked a thumb toward Rachel, who was having trouble sitting upright. Phil holstered the gun under his arm, looking bewildered. "I think she's having the kid. Get her out of here!" Carbello's voice cracked.

Phil stepped toward Rachel, but stopped abruptly when she moaned and her body folded over in pain. "What'll I do?" he whispered, looking helplessly at Carbello.

Carbello wiped the back of his hand across his mouth. Did it take long to pop a kid once it got this far? Maybe Sheila—hell, no, she'd start screaming like it was her. He stepped in front of Rachel.

"Can you get up?"

She shook her head and closed her eyes against another wave of agony. His voice came from a far place as though she were underwater. She was consumed with pain, eclipsing room for anything else.

"Get a doctor," Carbello ordered. Phil looked blank. "For crissake, there's gotta be one in the casino! Ask Johnny who's on board tonight. Maybe Hudson—the old geezer with the muttonchops. Or that bird from San Diego—what the hell's his name?" When Rachel moaned again, he shoved Phil toward the door. "Find someone, dammit!"

Carbello paced, terrified to be alone with Rachel, but not daring to leave. She was as white as a starched shirt. Did women die having kids? Why the hell did she have to have it now—here? Jesus! He looked at her nervously. Shit, she had guts. She hardly made a sound and she had to be hurting badly. Why the hell wasn't she in a hospital? Why the hell hadn't that deadbeat husband of hers seen to arrangements?

But she was certainly a fighter. A beautiful woman caught in this kind of trap? He muttered to himself, his Italian blood boiling. In awe, he knelt beside her. In almost no time her body began to tense again. He took her hand. Her fingers gripped his like a vise.

"Phil's getting a doc. It's gonna be okay. Yeah, don't worry. . . ." He kept talking in a low tone until her grip relaxed and her head fell forward; she panted instinctively. "It's gonna be okay," he said. "You're okay. . . ."

Phil ran in dragging a gray-haired man in a tuxedo behind him. The doctor bent over Rachel, touching her abdomen and gauging her pulse. He turned to Carbello.

"Get my wife and the other woman in our party. Hurry, there isn't much time!" he ordered.

Carbello jerked his head, but Phil was already moving. "Send Jake in!" he screamed after him. Jake slipped inside the cabin almost instantly. Carbello ordered him what to do and to get whatever the doc needed, then he escaped from the office.

In the casino, he wandered aimlessly, hardly noticing the players who occasionally spoke to him. Some of the women gave him hesitant smiles or outright invitations, but he ignored them until Jake finally appeared in the doorway. Carbello went to him.

"She okay?"

Jake's face paled as he nodded. "She had a girl. The doc says they're both okay."

Carbello expelled his breath, letting the news sink in. A girl. Damn, but that beauty was a fighter.

"The doc wants her to stay put, but she's squawking to go ashore. Whatta I tell him?"

"She wants to go ashore, that's what she does. Tell the doc he goes with her and the kid. And he stays with them until they're all set in the hospital, you hear?"

Jake nodded and started to leave, but Carbello grabbed his

arm. "Send some of the boys along to find that bastard Upfield. He's the kid's old man. He should be at the hospital with
them."

"Sure, boss."

When Rachel woke, Hillary was sitting beside the bed in
the predawn gray. A low night-light kept the room in eerie
shadows. The doctor had given her something which left her
euphoric, as though she were swinging in a hammock of
clouds.

Hillary came to the bed. "Rachel?"

Great gaps yawned in her memory, but she knew the baby
had been born and Carbello had allowed her to be taken off
the ship. When had Hillary come?

"How do you feel? Can I get you anything? Shall I call a
nurse?" Hillary's whisper charged the stillness with his fear.

When she shook her head, he squeezed her hand. She remembered Carbello holding it to soothe . . . Carbello . . .
Hillary was unhurt. She looked at him as something tugged in
her fogged mind. Hillary spoke, but she couldn't concentrate.

The next time she opened her eyes, the room was light.
Hillary dozed in the soft chair, his chin on his chest and his
legs stretched out. A nurse bustled in, smiling at Rachel.
Bending over Hillary, she nudged him.

"Time to go, Mr. Upfield. We have to get our little mother
ready for the day."

Hillary kissed Rachel's cheek awkwardly. "I'll come back
as soon as they let me."

"Visiting hours begin at two," the nurse said cheerily as
she shook a thermometer.

Hillary nodded obediently and left. Was it Rachel's imagination that he was glad to escape? The nurse put the thermometer under Rachel's tongue. Rachel took it away.

"Get me a telephone."

"Mrs. Upfield! Please—" The woman tried to rescue the
thermometer, but Rachel held it out of reach.

"First the telephone," she insisted.

"That's impossible."

Rachel threw back the covers and started to swing her feet
over the side of the bed. The nurse gasped and grabbed her.

"All right. Let me see what I can do. This is highly irregular, you know that. I'll have to speak to Mrs. Dunbar—"

"Speak to anyone you like, but either bring me a telephone or I'll walk to one!"

The woman scurried out. Rachel fell back onto the pillows. She could not believe she could be so weakened, but she would walk to a phone if she had to.

Josh entered the hospital room with a sure stride and a warm smile. The Fantazia name was sufficient to open doors despite the non-visiting hour.

"Congratulations," he murmured, and kissed her fully on the lips.

When she started to speak, he cautioned her to silence. The door opened and a nurse came in with a huge bouquet of yellow roses. "Mr. Fantazia brought them. Aren't they lovely?" She fussed with the vase on the dresser until she was satisfied the arrangement was perfect, then left with an envious glance at Rachel, who had the privilege of entertaining the distinguished visitor. Josh was instantly recognizable, since his picture often appeared in the social and business sections of the *Press-Telegram* and the *Los Angeles Times*.

"Thank you for coming," Rachel said. "I didn't know where to turn." A single phone call had reached him at his office, to her relief. Even though they had not seen each other for months, he agreed to her urgent plea immediately and without question. She knew he was the only person who could help her at this juncture, and though it pained her to see him again, and when she looked like such a recuperating patient, she knew there was no other course of action.

He searched her face with a concerned expression, noting the sensuous lips, the high cheekbones, slightly gaunt now. "What is it, Rachel? Has something happened?"

As succinctly as possible, she told him about Hillary's gambling debt, and Teddy Reno's resulting visit, and muscling her to the *Lucky Lady*. She marveled at her dispassion. She had no tears left to shed.

"I won't lose the hotel, Josh. I've fought too long and worked too hard. It's mine, not Hillary's." She decided Carbello's sexual advance did not merit discussion with Josh, who'd be enraged. There were other ways to skin the cat.

He pursed his lips. "Carbello has a reputation."

"He's not a god. He can be beaten. If the city ignores his

activities, I have no quarrel, but I won't let him take what's mine."

He studied her composed face, the glint of steely willpower in her dazzling violet eyes. "What do you propose?"

She answered instantly, no longer doubting her decision in the slightest. "Put the hotel in my name. Hillary can't throw away what isn't his."

A frown creased his handsome face. "Have you talked to him about this?" he prompted.

Rachel shook her head, a curl released from the tight way she had wrapped it up, the sheen slightly lackluster. "No, nor do I intend to. There's no time. God only knows how Carbello will force him, but you can be sure he'll move quickly. He may already be putting the pen in Hillary's hand. We've got to beat him to it!"

"How?"

She felt a wave of relief. He was not questioning her need for his help. She glanced at the door, which remained firmly closed. Could someone be listening? She lowered her voice, just in case. "A new grant deed. Your office has everything necessary to draw one up. With your notary seal affixed, no one will ever question it."

"You want me to sign his name?" Josh immediately responded, talking in lowered tones as well, as he noted her caution.

"Do it for me, Josh. Draw it up and file it this morning before Carbello can act."

He was silent. Her request would be an easy undertaking. He'd done the same and worse to obtain lots. Names from unpaid tax rolls traced to deceased persons or families that had moved away. Property that would have reverted to the city if he had not "purchased" it. Property that would tap untold millions in oil revenues when the Harbor District opened for drilling. And not all of which had been channeled through the Fielding Corporation.

He also loved Rachel. For the last eight years that she'd been his mistress and business partner, she'd never disappointed him. In bed she'd been an ingenious, sensuous lover who compensated for Collette's fragile-flower nature. He loved both women, but whereas Collette appealed to his protective instincts, giving him the children he wanted, Rachel appealed to the lusty male in him. Even when his bonds to

Collette were strongest, he admitted he could never deny himself the charged atmosphere Rachel created around her. He was savvy enough to know that her skillfulness in bed was not her only appeal. Her business acumen, her sensuous physical gifts, switched him into overdrive. Yes, he truly loved her.

"I'll take care of it." He clasped her hand and leaned over to draw a long, exploratory, loving kiss. Then he scanned her features, as if memorizing them. "Rest and regain your strength. You've been through an ordeal."

She clung to him, drawing his strength into her depleted body. "Thank you, Josh," she murmured in her unconsciously sensuous way. "I knew I could count on you. You're the one person I can trust—always." She drew him down and offered her lips again to seal the renewed alliance, and after exploring each other again, even more fiercely, he smiled and pulled back. Massaging her tender breasts carefully, he admonished her again to rest, and said that they would see each other soon, then he departed. For a long time she lay wrapped in the contented cocoon left by Josh's presence. Much later, she wondered how long it would be until Hillary discovered what she had done.

Teddy relaxed with his feet on Rachel's redwood and gilt coffee table and blew a gray cloud of cigar smoke. Hillary looked as if he'd been dragged across the desert by a mule team. He'd had too little sleep and a lot of worry about Mickey Carbello. The previous night Carbello's heavies had tracked Hillary down to a poker game on the west side. They dumped him at the hospital with orders to stay at his wife's side until she let him go. Too bad he hadn't returned home and hit the sack instead of calming his nerves with an uncountable number of stiff brandies.

"Can't we take care of it later, Teddy? I'm beat."

"It's Carbello's time schedule, not mine." It wasn't exactly true—Carbello had put *Teddy* on notice: deliver the deed to the Oceanside before the evening crowd forms, or else. Or else Teddy Reno's ass was in a sling right along with Hillary's. Carbello was giving him one last chance. Either he made this deal or he was back on the books for the six thousand he'd lost at the tables. And then Carbello would send one of his boys to settle the whole mess. With a gun.

"Rachel will kill me," Hillary whispered.

Jesus, he had become such a whining kid. Teddy swallowed some of the imported whiskey he'd liberated from Hillary's dry bar. "Take your choice. She kills you or Carbello does. Personally I'd take my chances with Rachel. She'd do it a lot less painfully."

Hillary blanched. He tangled his fingers, then ran them again through the locks of his blond hair. "If only I had a little more time! I could get the money somewhere."

Teddy grunted and reached for the bottle. He refilled his glass. He gulped the liquor in one swig, then wiped his stubbled chin with the back of his hand. "The county recorder's office closes at four. We haven't got much time."

Hillary staggered up like a condemned man, brushing back his tousled hair in a helpless gesture. How would he tell Rachel? Maybe he should wait until she was out of the hospital at least. But suppose Carbello's buyer wanted to take over immediately? He wouldn't have a place to bring Rachel and the baby home to. God, how had he gotten into this mess!

Teddy pocketed the document Carbello had given him for Hillary's signature. A nice clean deal. Hillary signed the place over to Teddy, Teddy signed it over to Carbello's buyer. Everybody's debts were canceled and Carbello wasn't on record for anything. That's the way he wanted it, and that's the way it was going to be.

The girl behind the counter shook her head. "I'm sorry, Mr. Upfield. The other deed was recorded this morning. You can't sign a second one." She turned the ledger and tapped an entry with a well-shaped, red-polished fingernail. "See for yourself. Rachel Upfield is owner of record now. Only she can change the deed."

Hillary stared at the entry. Dazed, he looked at Teddy, whose face mirrored his own shock. Hillary's lips moved soundlessly. Teddy snatched up Carbello's prepared document and grabbed Hillary's arm.

"Thank you very much, miss. There's been a mistake." He propelled Hillary out into the hall. The broad corridor of the spare, institutional-looking building was empty. Teddy slammed Hillary against the wall. "What the hell are you trying to pull?!" He grabbed Hillary's shirt and coiled it savagely around his fist.

Hillary gasped for air, his blue eyes darting around desperately for escape. "Nothing, I swear." For a moment he thought Teddy was going to slam his head against the marble. He was taller and more muscular, and while Hillary over the years had grown more delicate, Teddy, with his black hair and rough-bearded face, had grown more hoodlike. Why he hadn't terrified Rachel so she'd aborted the child was a miracle. Teddy had become dangerous. The sound of tapping heels saved Hillary. Teddy let go abruptly. He waited until a middle-aged woman disappeared into the office, then he turned viciously.

"You know what you've done? You've just killed the two of us!" Teddy cried.

Hillary stepped away, his face pale. "I swear, I don't know what happened! The old man gave it to *me*. She couldn't have—"

Teddy turned away in disgust. Rachel was two steps ahead of them. She'd outfoxed Carbello, and the two of them. Jeez! Carbello would knock the pins down one at a time, beginning with Teddy Reno. Rachel needed to be put in her place, but it wouldn't be by him. He wheeled and headed for the exit.

"Teddy—wait—"

Teddy didn't break his stride. His life depended on being far gone by the time Carbello realized he wasn't bringing the deed. *Let Hillary face him, not me.* He pushed open the heavy outside door and walked rapidly down the street.

IRENA

❧ Seven ❧

Ocean Beach, March 1933

IRENA RACED UP the steps, too excited to remember her mother's constant admonitions to walk like a lady. Miss Rogers had made her stand outside the classroom door after recess because she was fidgeting so much.

The doorman smiled as he pushed open the heavy wrought-iron door. "Good afternoon, Miss Upfield," he said, just as he did to grown-up guests.

Irena tried not to giggle. "Good afternoon, Horton." Then, too exuberant to pretend, she exclaimed, "Mama's taking me to Los Angeles! We're going to ride the Big Red car, and we'll see the whole city! The Bradbury Building and the Farmers' Market and Hollywood, and Angel's flight!"

"My goodness!" Horton looked appropriately impressed.

Irena tossed her blond curls imperially. She was a gorgeous little girl, a real princess. She had that angelic, high-cheekboned beauty of her mother, only she was fairer, like her father, and softer around the chin. Her mother possessed a perfect oval face, and Irena had a rounder, fleshier look—but she was still a real beauty.

She wore her hair in short curls around her tiny ears, and a silk, polka-dot pinafore hemmed around her knees.

"We shall have tea with Theda Bara. Mama is selling her a house, you know," she enthused.

"My goodness," Horton said again with a broad smile.

"Have a wonderful day, little one." He watched as she ran through the lobby and danced up the wide stairs.

Irena slowed as she reached the third floor. It wouldn't do to have Mama see her all flushed and out of breath. She forced herself to a ladylike walk as she entered the apartment.

It was empty. Her steps quickened as she scampered through the rooms, but Mama wasn't anywhere. Maybe she was waiting downstairs, impatient to get underway. Then Irena was at fault. Irena remembered to latch the door as she went out, then flew down the steps, her patent-leather mary-janes barely touching the carpet.

She glanced into the sitting room. Several guests were sitting on the sofas chatting or reading magazines, but Mama wasn't there. Irena went to the front desk and slipped under the partition. Leon glanced up from his work.

"Hello, Irena, you're home early today."

"I ran all the way." She pressed a hand to her mouth. "Don't tell Mama." Ladies did not run.

Leon winked. "Mum's the word."

"Where is Mama? Have you seen her? She's taking me to Los Angeles today!"

Leon's face sobered. "I haven't seen her. Best you ask your daddy, eh? He's in back."

She slipped out quickly and hurried down the back hall. The rear apartment had been made into offices; one was her father's, others for the bookkeeper and secretary who typed so fast her fingers blurred over the keys. The woman never glanced up as Irena raced past.

Her father's startled frown gave way to a wide grin. "Hello, princess!"

She flung herself into his arms and kissed his cheek. "Mmmm, I love you, Daddy!" He hugged her. She relished the smell of the bay rum he used. He was so handsome, with her soft hair color, but so different with such rugged cheeks and a big hard body. She wriggled to look up at him. "Have you seen Mama? She's taking me to Los Angeles today!" She squirmed as his arm tightened. He was for a moment so quiet, she squirmed herself free. When she looked at him, she saw that his smile had vanished and his eyes had clouded over. "Daddy?"

He started. "Today? Are you sure, princess? I thought it was next week."

She shook her head, and the honey-gold curls splashed over the shoulders of her dress. "Today! I marked it on every calendar!"

"Did you talk with Mama about it last night? I mean, just to make sure nothing had come up?"

"I waited up as long as Louise would let me," she said, pouting slightly. Louise came evenings, as Mama had to work, and made sure Irena stayed close to the hotel, took her bath, and was in bed by eight. "Mama was late. She was gone this morning when I got up."

He nodded, his blue eyes cast away. "Tell you what, princess. Give me ten minutes to make some phone calls, then we'll see what we can do about finding her. A deal?" He kissed the top of her head and she slid off his lap. "Go have some lunch in the dining room. Tell Judy I said you could sit by the window."

"Mama and I are going to have tea at Theda Bara's." Lunch at a window table overlooking the cliffs and the sea, with the scents and color and clamor of the famed restaurant around her, was very tempting. Maybe she'd be hungry again by the time they got to Los Angeles.

"Axel has cucumber sandwiches and strawberry tarts. He'd feel awful if you didn't try them."

"Well, maybe one of each."

"That's my girl. Run along. I'll see you in the dining room."

She ran out, her disappointment momentarily held at bay. As soon as the door closed, Hillary lifted the telephone. He had only half listened when Rachel dressed to leave. Maybe he'd heard wrong. Maybe she was going to the office first and later to Los Angeles. Maybe—

"Upfield-Grant," the cool efficient receptionist answered.

He no longer bothered making small talk with Rachel's employees. "This is Mr. Upfield. Is Mrs. Upfield there?"

"No, sir, she's out for the day."

"Where?"

The woman hesitated as she considered answering his faux pas in kind. Hillary could have sworn she lowered her voice before telling him, "She's gone to Los Angeles, Mr. Upfield."

"She's already left? You're sure of that?"

"Yes, sir. She left at nine-thirty. I believe she had a luncheon engagement at noon. I'll be glad to take a message, but she didn't expect to return to the office today. She may call in."

"No—wait, one other thing. Did she drive or go by train?"

"She drove, Mr. Upfield. She had several engagements and needed the car."

"Thanks." He hung up. She'd done it again, damn her. He didn't give a damn if she treated him like garbage, but Irena —poor kid. And now it was up to him to try to mend the injury. Damn Rachel!

Around them swarmed the midmorning brunch and lunch crowd who came to the Oceanside Hotel for its legendary atmosphere, magnificent views, and gourmet food. The hotel's reputation had spread wide and far the last five years, drawing not only a local crowd, but also—after Rachel hired the German chef, with a Parisian background, from a major restaurant in Los Angeles—a regional clientele. In fact, people from all over the country were beginning to lodge here for vacations, or to drop in for a delicious meal. Most learned of the hotel by word-of-mouth, as Rachel had intended. She only occasionally ran ads, and then she was highly select. She picked a specific month in a season, knowing instinctively when people would be thinking of travel and food. And she picked only certain newspapers. The L.A. *Times, The New York Times, The Sacramento Bee,* The *Press-Telegram.*

Irena was licking traces of strawberry tart from her fork as he sat down. Her golden hair and blue eyes and delicate features favored his mother's, considered a beauty for her time. That she resembled his family rather than the Grants gave him secret satisfaction.

"Well, princess, do you think I should fire Axel or is his cooking improving?" he asked seriously.

She suppressed a giggle and played the game. "Let's keep him a bit longer."

He nodded as though she had given him much needed advice and put his mind at ease. Irena was the darling of the staff and had the run of the hotel. Rachel imposed limits, but these were quietly ignored when she wasn't there to enforce them. Even the most loyal of Rachel's hand-picked employees had a blind spot when it came to the angelic child with the enchanting smile. What she lacked in attention from her mother, the staff supplied ten-fold.

"Did you find Mama? Is she ready now?" Irena laid her

fork carefully across the plate and wiped her fingers on the white linen napkin.

"Well, princess, there's been a little problem." He saw the glow in her eyes fade. "Something came up and Mama had to leave early. It just couldn't be helped. She felt awful about it, but you know how it is sometimes in business. This was a really big deal, and if she didn't get there—" He shrugged, watching the small face look pinched. He put on his most dazzling smile. "She left a message, though. The trip is only postponed, not canceled. And when you go, how would you like to see a movie studio?"

"A real one?" Irena asked hesitantly, her lower lip quivering.

"Absolutely, positively! You can watch them making a picture."

"With Jackie Cooper?"

"It's possible." He grinned, watching her intently and willing away her hurt.

"Okay," she said finally. "I'd rather see Jackie Cooper than have tea with Theda Bara." She regarded him with a solemn expression. "You promise, Daddy?"

"I promise. And if Mama can't make it, I'll take you myself! Now, what would you like to do this afternoon? We can't just sit around feeling gloomy, can we!"

She smiled, but shadows lingered in her eyes. Hillary felt a stab of pain for her innocence. He furrowed his brow in mock concentration. "We could bake a cake . . . but Chef Axel might not like us messing up his kitchen. We might go for a swim . . . no, it's a bit chilly for that. Besides, you've grown so much since last summer I'm sure you'll need a new swimsuit. Ah, we can play a game of gin . . ." He shook his head in exasperation. "No, that won't do. You're getting so good at your numbers, you beat me all the time. Hmmm . . ." He looked astonished, then elated. "I have it."

She gazed expectantly, her eagerness overtaking her disappointment. "The Pike!" he declared. "It's a perfect afternoon for the merry-go-round and saltwater taffy and hot buttered popcorn!"

She bounced delightedly. "Oh, yes, Daddy! The Pike! The Pike!"

"Run up and get a coat, the wind's chilly. I'll meet you at the desk in five minutes."

* * *

It was late when they finally started for home. The afternoon breeze turned biting and a hint of rain clung to the air. Hillary bundled Irena in her coat and turned the little fur collar up around her flushed face. He had indulged her shamelessly, letting her ride the carousel a dozen times until she caught the brass ring; swaying at the top of the Ferris wheel and claiming the entire city as their prize; even plunging on the terrifying Cyclone Racer, which left them both pale and giggling. They feasted on hot dogs and cream sodas at Marfleet's, watched the machine pull taffy at Magruder's, then bagged a supply to eat while they played the arcade games. Hillary won Irena a fuzzy, floppy-eared dog that she insisted on carrying although it dwarfed her. He looked dashing in his breeches and argyle sweater, which he'd towed along in case of a chill.

Rachel hadn't returned when they got back to the hotel. Hillary was just as glad not to face her when he was angry. He shooed Irena upstairs to wash her face and hands while he made perfunctory rounds. It had become such a habit, he rarely thought about it anymore. Six years ago Rachel had given him an ultimatum: Stay if he wanted, but he'd have to follow her orders.

The dining room was equipped for the dinner hour; silver pitchers of ice water studded the service carts, ready for pouring. Another cart encased desserts and exotic pastries in glass. The new pretty dark-haired waitress cast him a shy smile as she set tables, with the others. When he winked, she blushed. He glanced into the kitchen bustling with cooks and waiters, but didn't invade Axel's sacrosanct territory. He smiled as some guests enjoyed aperitifs in the sunken lounge not far away while they waited for the call to dinner. As he turned toward the lobby, the front doors opened and a tall man dressed in a dark topcoat and fedora strolled in. It took a moment for Hillary to recognize him. Teddy Reno extended a hand.

"It's been a long time, Hillary."

"Yeah," he said, studying the man. Teddy was as tall and solid as before, though gray peppered his black hair and beard. Lines creased his eyes—not from laughing.

"Not a very warm greeting for an old friend," he said.

"It's more than you'll get from Rachel." ·

Teddy laughed, a sound like a snicker. "I took the precaution of telephoning to determine if the little lady was on the premises. I admit a touch of surprise that I find you still in a state of grace."

Hillary shot a glance at the sitting room. "Keep your voice down, you fool!"

Teddy's smile only widened, his self-assurance grating. "I suggest we retire to your office and celebrate our reunion with some of that good booze you keep in the dry bar."

Hillary steered him out of the lobby, eager to get him out of sight. No one seemed to notice as activity began to get frantic with the approaching dinner hour. A group of loud patrons had entered the lobby, and two waiters ignored Hillary as they brushed past in search of the maître d'.

Settled in his library, Hillary poured two glasses of whiskey. Hillary settled in a wingback chair. "Why'd you come back? If Rachel finds you here—"

Teddy arrogantly took the sofa. "I'll be gone before she returns."

"She's due any minute."

Teddy shrugged. "She'll be awhile yet." He sipped the whiskey. "You haven't changed, buddy. A little paunchy, but still the good-looking lad I remember. Life treated you well?"

Hillary shot him a curious look. Crazy or foolhardy? Better not waste time. *He* wanted Teddy out as soon as possible.

"So? Why are you here?" he said shortly.

Teddy snorted, an iciness taking over.

"I need money."

Hillary laughed. "You came to the wrong party. They don't come any broker than me. Rachel gives me a niggling allowance that gets me as far as the Spit and Argue Club."

Teddy laughed, then suddenly stopped. "There haven't been any deposits to my account for several years. She owes me that money."

Hillary shook his head. "Good luck. Rachel has a long memory. She hasn't forgotten the part you played in Carbello's scheme. When you ran out, he came after her. You didn't know that, huh? She paid a hundred thousand dollars to buy my life, but believe me, she'd sell yours for the first buck someone put on the line."

"She paid Carbello?" Teddy was stunned. "Why the hell didn't she do it in the first place and avoid the whole damned mess!" He slapped his hand on the desk, then beamed those shifting brown eyes on Hillary. "You say she knows about me?"

Hillary did not like this man, who didn't intimidate him the least. "You'd better believe I didn't cover for you. She got the whole story."

Teddy's eyes narrowed. "Damn it, the oil royalties have nothing to do with that business. She has no right cutting me off."

Hillary laughed derisively. "Maybe she's taking the hundred grand out of your hide as well as mine. Be thankful you're not in penal servitude like me."

Teddy sipped the whiskey moodily and shrugged. "You never did know how to handle her."

"And *you* do?" he snorted. "Don't be an ass. Get out of here before she remembers how much she hates you. I wouldn't put it past her to swim out to the *Lucky Lady* and tell Carbello you're here."

Teddy clambered to his feet. "Now, there's a gentleman I don't plan on paying my respects to. Rachel may have gotten you off his list, but I'd lay odds my name is still right up at the top." He put out a hand. "So long, Hillary. When I find a way to work this out, you'll be hearing from me again." They shook hands, Hillary out of pity, then Reno retrieved his hat from the desk and dejectedly walked to the door.

Hillary watched him leave. If Teddy knew what was good for him, he'd keep right on walking and never look back. Did he really think there was any way to beat Rachel? What she couldn't do herself, she could hire someone to do. She was Mrs. Bucks, right up there with the Fantazias in wealth and power. Her real estate company flourished, in spite of the depression that gripped the rest of the country. Hell, Rachel could make a buck off her own funeral. The company had grown from two assistants to fourteen salesmen and a full office staff. And now Rachel was thinking about expanding into construction. He admired her guts. It wouldn't be easy. There were plenty of builders who wouldn't like the idea of a woman moving into their territory. The hell of it was that Rachel would do well, as in everything else she did. Except raise Irena.

He wandered out to the lobby and started for the stairs, glancing at the banjo clock behind the registration desk. Ten minutes since the dining room had opened. Time enough to

check on Irena. She couldn't possibly be hungry after all she'd
eaten during the afternoon, but if she didn't collapse from
exhaustion, they'd have a light dinner later, the two of them,
with candlelight and wineglasses (ginger ale in hers) and
music. As he started up someone hailed him.

"Mr. Upfield—"

He suppressed a sigh and smiled as Mrs. Sheffield Porter
ran toward him, her corseted figure shimmering like a silver
lamé tank.

"Have you been able to confirm our reservations for the
Fourth of July weekend? Sheffield and I do *so* want to enjoy
the festivities here."

The Porters had telephoned only three days in advance for
their first stay at the Oceanside. Now they were regular patrons, who appeared like clockwork every spring.

"I'm working on it, Mrs. Porter, but I'm afraid I have no
good news yet. We're completely booked, but I've put you on
the waiting list." They had as much chance of getting in as she
did of floating off on the breeze. Maybe he should suggest she
reserve now for next year.

"I'll be crushed if we don't get to come. I *love* it here. I
can't believe I never *heard* of the Oceanside before the Crom-
wells told us about it." She simpered. "You shouldn't adver-
tise in the Los Angeles papers so often, Mr. Upfield."

He gave her a disarming smile. "But then we couldn't remain open year-round and accommodate perennial guests like
yourself."

"Oh, dear, I suppose you're right—" The words froze and
the woman looked startled. Her surprise turned quickly to fear
as she looked about wildly.

Hillary felt the first rumble, a small tremor as though he'd
stepped on loose rock. Instinctively he grabbed the banister,
which shivered unmistakably under his hand. Then the floor
heaved with a heavy rolling motion. Above them, the
wrought-iron chandelier swayed like a child's swing gaining
momentum, making shadows leap back and forth across the
lobby. Without warning, the whole building began to shake.
Chimneys around the lights crackled and sprayed glass like
fireworks. Mrs. Porter shrieked.

Earthquake! Hillary clutched the banister as the stairs
pitched with a cracking sound. The walls swayed so badly, the
room seemed to dissolve. Mrs. Porter tried to run, but she fell

headlong onto the undulating carpet and gripped it for dear life, screaming.

Hillary wheeled to scramble up the stairs. Irena! When the railing snapped away, he flung himself prone to keep from falling sideways down to the first floor. Crawling, he ignored the shuddering, groaning wood beneath his body. A cloud of plaster dust billowed down the stairwell, choking him. He pushed on blindly, groping for steps he prayed were still there.

Irena! He had to reach his baby.

Steps had split away completely and he had to time his maneuvering carefully to cross the gaping holes upward. All around him the sound of crashing mortar and bricks and splintering wood chorused in his ears.

By the time he reached the third floor, he could hardly breathe. The main tremor seemed to be over, but in its aftermath the hotel shuddered ominously. He groped for the apartment door. When it stuck, he slammed his weight against it. Ceiling plaster showered over him as the door finally flung open.

"Irena!" The cry was a strangled cough as dust filled his lungs. "Irena . . . Irena . . ." He tried to brush his eyes clear of the stinging debris, but it blinded him. Tears streamed down his face. "Irena!"

"Daddy! Daddy!!"

He plunged forward, lifting his head to hear his daughter's voice more clearly.

"Daddy! Daddy!!"

He ran, pinpointing the location of her plaintive cry. Suddenly the floor under him cracked, split, and yawned open in front of him. He never reached his little girl's bedroom. Miraculously the air cleared in time for him to watch the front wall of the hotel collapse into a pile of rubble. Then he was skidding down the steep chute the floor had become, into an eddy of dusty debris and splintered wood beams three floors below.

"Will you be in Los Angeles again soon?" Rachel asked, basking in the warmth of his naked body. Her hand smoothed his bare thigh and his muscles responded, until he leaned his silky flesh into her suggestively.

"I can arrange it." Josh lay against her arm while his fingers played erotically with her nipples. When he smiled, her breath quickened. "Can *you* invent a reason to come again soon?"

Her lips trembled. She needed only one reason—her desire of him. When he had phoned this morning at her suite of rooms, she'd left them immediately. He was already waiting in the hotel lobby of the sumptuous Alexandria Hotel when she arrived. She carried a briefcase as a decoy. But alone upstairs, all pretence vanished as they savored each other's bodies with abandon, as if they'd been starved for weeks. And they'd gone through this scene only five days ago.

"There's always something that needs checking," she murmured. She would invent excuses, she knew, but when his call came, she would come anyway. His lips blazed a trail over her throat and breasts. She closed her eyes as his exploring hands and tongue stirred whirlpools of passion in her.

Their clandestine meetings had been far too infrequent. The Rancho cottage, their old secluded hideaway, was now encircled by new development, and the risks of rendezvousing there had soared. Since Fantazia Enterprises maintained a suite at the Alexandria Hotel in Los Angeles for visiting clients and consultants, they swallowed their irritation at the inconvenience and met there.

"Actually, we have business to take care of," he said, then continued to explore her softest places with his tongue, which whirled in excruciatingly sweet circles.

It was difficult to concentrate. "What business?" she asked as warm waves lapped over her.

"Perkins wants to see us."

She snapped out of her reverie. Garson Perkins was the resident agent for the Fielding Corporation, which she and Josh had formed to purchase oil lands. Over the past ten years she'd seen the owlish young man only at the annual meetings that were more ritual than anything else. The Fielding Corporation owned considerable land throughout Ocean Beach, mainly in the Harbor District and the flood control channel; many of the parcels were leased for industrial purposes, netting the company a respectable income while reserving all mineral rights.

"About what?" she asked.

"He wants figures so that he's armored when the first question of oil leasing comes up."

"You've heard something?" There had been no new activity

since residents of Belmont Shores, alarmed by the advancing derricks, had pressured the city council to vote down residential drilling. Fortunately, and not accidentally, the controls did not extend to the tidelands.

Josh focused his attentions on her breasts, but Rachel was not distracted. "What is it, Josh? Tell me."

Laughing, he fell back onto the pillow. "All right, business first, then pleasure. New rumors, but they persist. As far as I've determined, they may be valid."

"What?"

"Geologists at General Petroleum are working on a technique to locate oil and gas reserves with sound waves."

Incredible! she thought. But quite feasible. Oil technology had skyrocketed since the roughly sketched maps of Teddy Reno's days. The day of the wildcatter was gone.

"They can go as deep as eight miles, Rachel. Eight miles." His eyes gleamed, mirroring her reaction. He was more pleased with her spark of intrigue than anything else. He knew that she had instantly grasped the import of the news. Eight miles did not have to be straight down. Wells could be drilled and whipstocked horizontally, under the river channel. Not only would the tideland leases tap a bounty of new income, but the restricted city lots east of the channel could be exploited, too. They were perched on a gold mine.

"How soon?"

"Within two years at most. The city council isn't eager for word to get out. They know that every company with a truckload of pipe will be up here bidding. There's talk of several big companies forming development groups. The council is going to hold out for eighty-five percent. They'll get it if they deal with a bloc."

"And our land?"

"Perkins thinks we should channel some leases through outside corporations. When it comes down to city versus individual holdings, there's going to be a lot of close scrutiny. If we diversify now, there'll be fewer questions later."

She didn't like Perkins's intervention, but maybe Josh was right. It worried her that she knew so little about the attorney, but she couldn't fault his handling of their corporate affairs. The Fielding Corporation grew continually, and markedly when they followed his counsel. But what Josh was saying

now was that Perkins wanted to set up a dummy corporation
to feed money back to Fielding. Untraceably.

"Fielding is legitimate," she said with a frown. "I don't
think we should risk juggling assets."

He steadily met her gaze. "It's too late, we already have.
Perkins needs us to come in and sign the papers."

"You went ahead without telling me?" She studied his
always-striking features, the sensuous lips, the velvety eyes
she had always found so appealing. They were set in the way
she knew signaled his determination to get what he wanted.
Now when he didn't answer, she sighed. "We seem to have let
the afternoon slip away. I guess we'll just have to come back
very soon."

Her hand moved across to his manhood, where she coaxed
him with firm, stroking motions until he responded and
melded his body over hers. They soared in perfect harmony to
the inner beat of a music only they could compose. Their
lovemaking grew to a frenzy, each driving the other to ever
higher peaks so magnificent it took their breath away.

They lay side by side a long time until their breathing grew
steadier. The room had grown dim, the twilight entering
through the open silken drapes which they'd kept apart because they knew they could not be spied upon in their lofty
aerie. The champagne bottle in the silver ice bucket lay empty
after their afternoon of pleasure. Finally Rachel glanced at the
lavaliere watch she'd put on the nightstand. It read 6:00 p.m.

"It's late!"

He laughed. "Is that so terrible?" He drew her back into the
circle of his arms.

She dug more deeply into him. "Of course not."

"You don't turn into a pumpkin if you're not home by dark,
do you?" he teased.

"I would not be surprised," she said solemnly. "When one
lives in a fairy tale, one must expect all sorts of supernatural
events."

"What would you say if I asked you to stay the night?"

She raised her head and looked at him. His velvet dark
eyes gleamed sensually, lighting the elegant features of his
handsome face. "Are you asking me?" Her mind whirled. To
spend the night in his arms . . .

He nodded. "I'm not expected back. You could invent an

excuse about being delayed. With this fog, no one could blame you for staying over. We could see Perkins in the morning."

She licked her lips. To wake up beside him . . .

"Will you, Cinderella?" he prodded.

"Yes." She answered without hesitation. "I'll have to call home, though." She hadn't booked the babysitter, Louise, for the evening. She'd expected to drive home before dark. Good Lord. Irena! She'd completely forgotten her promise to bring the child to Los Angeles today! How could she have forgotten? Her smile vanished.

"Something wrong?" he asked, his brow furrowing with creases.

She inhaled deeply. "Just something I remembered a bit late."

"Important?" His hand stroked her bare shoulder.

The guilt was already beginning to recede. "I can take care of it another time." She'd tell Louise to give Irena a special treat before bedtime. Tomorrow she'd stop at Bullock's Wilshire and buy Irena something extravagant.

"I have a marvelous idea," Josh said with a grin, biting her shoulder. "Let's have dinner at Bernard's and go dancing at the Ambassador."

She looked dismayed. "I'm not dressed for those places!"

He laughed as he massaged her silky buttocks and then reached for her soft breasts. "My dear, you are dressed for only one thing!" he said with a suggestive leer, and rolled on top of her. "We could call room service."

"Let me call home first," she said, and squirmed to the phone. Josh pulled away and watched on a crooked arm. A smile lingered on his full, soft lips that she found appealing. When the operator answered, Rachel enunciated the number in Ocean Beach, and waited.

The girl sounded breathless. "I'm sorry, ma'am, all the lines to Ocean Beach are down."

Rachel swung her legs over the bed as she sat up. "Whatever do you mean?" Josh, alerted by her abrupt manner, sat up and leaned back against the carved wooden bedpost, watching.

"The earthquake—didn't you feel it? My goodness—of course it was much worse there. . . . we had a fair jolt, though, not ten minutes ago. . . ." the receptionist stammered in agitation.

Rachel's hand shook so badly, she could hardly rehook the telephone receiver. Josh reached out to her, but she pushed his hands aside and got up. She didn't realize she was pacing until Josh scuttled across the entangled sheets and grabbed her.

"What is it?" he asked, worry in his voice as he stood.

"An earthquake. The operator said all the lines are down. In Ocean Beach. It was worse there."

"My God!" Josh cried, then released her to snatch up the phone and cry out a number to the operator. When he hung up, his face was ashen. Rachel was already dressing. Josh strode to a cabinet and snapped on the radio. Static blended with excited voices. Rachel sat on the edge of the bed to slip on her stockings.

Ten minutes ago, and they'd felt nothing. They'd been so engrossed in passion, in each other's bodies, they had missed the tremors.

Josh adjusted the dial until a newscaster's voice enunciated clearly.

"—just minutes ago. The temblor seems to have been centered in the harbor just off Ocean Beach. Reports of damage are beginning to flood in. The city of Ocean Beach lies in ruins. Entire buildings have collapsed. Telephone, electricity, and waterpower are out. Workers are shutting off main gas lines to prevent further fires or explosions. We've had a call from a man in Artesia who says he can see flames shooting up from the oil wells on Darien Hill. There is no estimate of the number of wells burning." He paused a moment, and they could hear paper rustling. "We have a report that a naval emergency field radio unit has been erected at the Ocean Beach police station. We hope we will get some official reports soon. We've been asked to tell our listeners that roads into Ocean Beach are closed to anything but emergency traffic. Do not try to drive into the disaster area. We repeat, ladies and gentlemen, *do not* drive to the Ocean Beach area."

Rachel fastened the leather belt around her wool challis dress. With only a glance in the mirror at her hair, she pulled on her cloche and picked up her coat. Josh was still standing in front of the radio, dazed and naked. He looked startled when she raced to the door. By the time she closed it behind

her, he was already pulling on his clothes, worried about her
and her family; worried, too, about his own.

It was almost midnight when she finally reached Ocean
Beach. She had been stopped a dozen times but had ignored
the warnings not to proceed. Several times she had made de-
tours to avoid the roadblocks, but she found circuitous routes
on side streets. At the city line, slowed to a crawl, she blun-
dered into streets filled with rubble, broken pavement, or
yawning pits and crevices. A pall of smoke hung over the city,
but the fires on Darien Hill had apparently been successfully
contained. From time to time flames erupted in the darkness,
but they flickered out as waiting firemen scurried to snuff
them out with blankets or to hose them down.

At Pacific and Tenth in downtown Ocean Beach, she abandoned the car. She could move faster on foot; too many streets
were completely blocked. People strayed about like lost
sheep, unsure of where to begin the awesome task of cleaning
up, or searching the rubble for loved ones or cherished items.
The reports of devastation were exaggerated, she realized with
relief. Many buildings stood untouched, but there was no
denying the damage was considerable and widespread. To her
dismay she saw, too, that brick structures had fared the worst.
Huge piles of debris pooled around steel girdings.

An ambulance siren screamed in the distance. At the end of
the next block a bonfire flared in the darkness, encircled by
people trying to ward off the night chill. Rachel's hands were
numb. She'd lost her gloves somewhere. At Seventh and
American, farther downtown toward the hotel, four men shoveled broken bricks and glass in front of Ward Drugs. A ring of
lanterns lit their horrible task. In the next block half of an
apartment house had collapsed, the other half stood unscathed. Houses sat askew on their foundations. She followed
the Pacific Electric tracks toward Ocean Boulevard, then east,
seeing destruction and rubble everywhere. By the time she
arrived at the Oceanside, she felt both fatigue and horror.

For a moment her mind refused to comprehend what her
brain registered. The entire front of the building was gone.
The rooms were exposed like a giant dollhouse without a wall.
Brick, mortar, and glass littered the street; close to the building, rubble was strewn several feet high. Numb, she crossed
to what had been the entrance.

"Here, miss, you can't go in there!" A policeman with a lantern blocked her path.

"I must—"

"'Sorry, no one's allowed any closer." He spread his arms to show he meant business.

Rachel forced her mind to frame an explanation. "I am Mrs. Upfield. I own the hotel."

The policeman peered at her. She was dressed less spectacularly than usual, but he noted the high cheekbones, curvacious body, and dark curls hanging loose from a designer hat—still quite a specimen for a woman past thirty. "Ah . . ." He shook his head. "I'm sorry, Mrs. Upfield. I didn't recognize you in this light. But you can't go in there. The whole thing could come down."

She gulped down tears. "My husband and child—"

His gaze faltered.

"Are they all right?" She didn't recognize the hoarse whisper of her own voice.

He looked relieved as a man stepped from the shadows and came toward them. Rachel recognized her father. He walked like a very tired old man, and she knew . . .

He opened his arms and she went to him. For a moment they embraced wordlessly in the flickering light, then Mills put his arm around her and led her away. His car was parked in the next block. After helping her in, he squeezed in behind the wheel.

"Irena is safe," he said. "Badly frightened, but no physical injuries beyond a few scratches." He looked at her across the gloomy darkness. "Hillary is dead. Leon saw him race up the stairs after the first tremor to find Irena." His tired breath was a long sigh. "He was buried when the front wall collapsed. Irena was safe in a corner bedroom."

The facts . . . laid out simply . . . for acceptance or rejection. No . . . they could not be rejected this time. Hillary was dead. The Oceanside lay in partial ruin. All the expansion, all the restoration and decorating . . . gone.

Minutes dragged by. Mills waited to let the situation sink in to his daughter's mind. He wished he could shoulder her pain, but he knew she had to deal with it her own way. Everyone had to. Sitting in the dark silence, he thought about Althea's death four years before. It had been a long time coming. Even though expected, the pain had been no less to bear.

Rachel stared through the misted windshield. She could barely see the remains of the hotel a block away. The fog distorted everything. Just as well. Hillary's dream had crumbled. Crumbled with him. She remembered when they'd first met on Darien Hill and he'd shared his dream . . . both had been so young and full of fantasy.

She looked at her father's drawn face. "Where's Irena?"

"Seaside Hospital. It's damaged, but they're providing emergency services. It would be best if we took her home with us tonight." He thought about the crowded corridors and harried doctors and nurses. St. Mary's had been so badly damaged, patients had been evacuated to the Adventist church across the street.

Rachel gazed at the hotel sadly. Home?

"My house withstood the quake," Mills said quietly.

"Yes," she muttered.

In the aftermath the city bustled with activity. Even though the early reports by some news media had been exaggerated, the damage was extensive. Emergency services had been set up; ham radio operators linked Ocean Beach to the outside world, while the Boy Scouts ran messages; Pacific Telephone operators returned to work the following morning and resumed service at makeshift counters set up in the streets; fire stations kept equipment in readiness while they cleaned up building debris. Water was trucked in so people could fill buckets, pans, and jugs for the encampments sprouting everywhere, from yards to city parks. Clean-up crews shoveled, hauled, and swept in order to salvage what remained of their homes, shops, and public buildings.

Official reports indicated the quake registered a 6.3 on the Richter scale. The heavy damage in Ocean Beach was attributed as much to the shifting oil sands under the city as to the faultline. Ironically, the oil that had financed Ocean Beach's blossoming had also helped magnify the shockwaves to destroy it.

Rachel moved through her days mechanically. Irena was still too frightened to talk about her ordeal. She huddled in tears or silence, rebuffing Rachel's attempts to comfort her. Louise stayed with her while Rachel and her father attended a private funeral for Hillary. The service was spare and kept short. Ocean Beach had too many dead to mourn. Hillary was laid to rest at Sunnyside beside Althea in the Grant plot.

Worse, Rachel heard that Elliot Maveen had died, not the day of the quake or in it, but miles away, at an institution in San Diego, where he'd been shifted. He'd apparently been wasting away for years, withdrawing emotionally until he died a shell of his former self. He succumbed to starvation the day following the quake, apparently never aware it had taken place. The town mourned his death as well; the tragedy of his life, and the loss of his tremendous promise as a singer. He'd be buried in his family plot at Sunnyside, along with his father, who'd died about the time Rachel's mother passed away. Bleak had turned to bleaker.

Rachel, trying to grapple with the losses, was fortunately spared the ordeal of going through her dead husband's things; they had been destroyed along with the hotel. The entire facade of the building was rubble; the rest was in danger of collapsing. Rachel, to keep busy and avoid brooding about the past, hired a wrecking crew to pull it down. She salvaged a few items left miraculously untouched: A Sevres vase, the cherrywood table, some silver. The office safe was recovered from the debris, intact. She had it taken to the Belmont Shores house. The night after the funeral she sifted through its contents. She was surprised to find a bundle of Hillary's papers. Among them was his will, which left everything to his heir, or split equally between heirs, including the hotel. She stared at the document a long time. It was a useless piece of paper. She didn't recognize the law firm that had drawn it. Hillary never mentioned the will, nor had he bothered to repair it after the Carbello incident.

How long ago that seemed. She would store it in the safe in case Harper & Filman Law Offices contacted her for a reading. Then she would produce other documents, disproving its validity.

The schools would take years to repair and rebuild. Classes resumed in makeshift quarters, but Rachel kept Irena at home and hired a tutor to spend the day with her. The real estate office had escaped miraculously unscathed. A shattered window, a few chips in the masonry. That was all. She hired a structural engineer to inspect it for hidden damage. When it was pronounced safe, she reopened for business three days after the quake. Some families and merchants decided to relocate rather than rebuild. Rachel bought a quarter of a commercial block on East First Street and twelve homes within a half-mile radius. She also bought the Zorbel Construction Company, whose offices and yard had been demolished but whose equipment had survived intact. Rachel knew their work, and after investigating Zorbel thoroughly, enlisted him to head the new construction division of Upfield Land Management. He began by surveying the old blueprints for a new Oceanside Hotel, locked away until now. If Rachel had been hesitant about starting the project before, she was no longer.

She also began to look for a suitable house for her and Irena. She resisted her father's plea to stay at his Belmont Shores house, which was too big and lonely since her mother's death. Rachel knew she belonged in Ocean Beach. She would have chosen Darien Hill, but it was still jammed with oil equipment. Few of the old mansions remained amid the forest of wooden struts; Rachel's own land was covered with wells. She chose a lot near the base of the Hill that afforded a good view of the sea, but was far enough away from the noise and smell to nourish peace of mind. In July, Zorbel's crew went to work building the house.

It would hug the hill in four stepped-back floors, ceiling-high windows facing the sea on two of them, terraces and patios, a very modern, Frank Lloyd Wright design stressing horizontal planes. Outside, the house and patio would be hedged by bushes and flower beds, filled with azaleas, crocuses, honeysuckle, and an assortment of blooms. Inside, Rachel would again aim for sumptuous Old World luxury, with rich cherrywood period pieces, silver, and gilt-edged ornaments of British and French design. There would be a wing for servants and rooms for weekend guests. It would be a manor house, of modern design and conveniences.

In the hectic weeks that followed, Rachel didn't see Josh. She'd received a brief formal note of sympathy penned by Collette after the funeral. Rachel went to Los Angeles several times. Once she called the Alexandria, but Josh had not been in, and the concierge didn't know when he would book the suite. She didn't leave a message.

❧ Eight ❧

IRENA PEELED OFF her dirndl skirt and silk blouse, then threw them casually to the bright beach blanket. She was showing off her latest purchase—a two-piece bathing suit. Ruth Fantazia's mouth formed a startled O.

"Your mother will kill you!"

Irena thrust out her well-formed breasts, the contours displayed clearly in the tight suit, then lifted her beautiful face to the early afternoon sun in mock imitation of a model. She ran long, manicured fingers through her blond poodle-cut hair. "What she doesn't know won't hurt her," she quipped. She'd bought the suit, considered brazen and suggestive for 1942, just two days before in Los Angeles. The salesclerk had sniffed disapprovingly until Irena handed her twenty-one dollars in cash.

"Do you like it?" she asked, and pivoted. The bottom half clung to her curvacious figure so closely, she might rival a Hollywood starlet. The bright blue color enhanced her complexion and eyes. She was certainly a well-endowed girl, advanced beyond her teenage years.

"It's too divine!" Ruth said, ecstatic and envious, and a little nervous. A year older than Irena, her figure was more gamine. No breasts or behind to showcase in such a brazen way. She was her mother's daughter—delicate and slim, and she had a weak heart from a childhood bout of rubella. Her

119

father called her his "petite sweet," but figures like Irena's
were the ones that magnetized the admiring glances of the
boys.

Irena lowered herself onto the blanket with considerable
undulation of her hips. "Good. Maybe it will attract us some
interesting specimens," she said. The girls giggled. Irena
glanced along the waterfront with studied nonchalance. It was
an unusually hot summer, and the beach was jammed with
bodies. This past week two ships from the Pacific Fleet had
anchored in the harbor, and sailors swarmed all over town.
Irena tried to decide which of the muscular young male bodies
belonged to the Navy. Those who'd been in Ocean Beach long
enough to visit the tattoo parlors on the Pike were easy to
spot. The blue and red dragons, hearts, flags, and garlanded
names promised exotic adventure. Maybe she'd get some guy
to have her name tattooed on his arm.

Her gaze lingered on two well-muscled youths sitting a few
yards away. Their white towels were Navy issue. "How about
those two?" She made a subtle motion as though she were
brushing away an insect. Ruth blushed as she glanced hurriedly. The two youths were sandy-haired, with deeply tanned
arms and torsos, signaling service in the South Pacific; body
tan meant they worked above decks. That was good. Irena
remembered an oiler she'd picked up on the Pike one Saturday
night. Things had gotten pretty rough. He had brushed off half
her suit when she was scared enough to blurt her true age.
Actually officers were best, but they weren't as free spending
as the enlisted men who never knew when they'd shove off.

"Well, what do you think?" she asked Ruth. "Will they
do?"

Ruth threw another fleeting glance toward the two males
and nodded, still blushing. Irena saw the excitement in her
eyes. Poor Ruth. She had the Fantazia delicate beauty—dark
wavy hair, large obsidian eyes, a trim figure without the lush
curves that Irena seemed blessed with. The two had journeyed
through the same private, elite schools in the area, and had
gravitated to each other almost instinctively. Neither knew
why, but they enjoyed each other's company. Irena suspected
that the reason they had succumbed to each other's almost
opposite charms was that they came from the two most respected families in Ocean Beach, and among the great families of California—the Fantazias and the Upfields. Both their

parents wielded power and commanded extensive empires of oil and real estate and construction. Rachel ran a hotel and inn, too, that had developed a national reputation. The whole community knew about the two girls and focused on their progress, their promise, from grade school on. It came as no surprise to anyone that both girls were precocious for their ages. And so it was natural that an Upfield and a Fantazia would find each other on the playground and in the school corridors, and later in the after-school snack shops everyone frequented, even when their parents were business rivals and refused to socialize. They had their cliques of friends, separate ones, but some of their friends were also mutual. The two girls shared a rare, symbiotic relationship that others couldn't intrude on. It had journeyed through dolls, playground games, to discussions of Saint Augustine, George Eliot, and H.G. Wells, until now they tittered over the dozens of romances they'd lately consumed.

Each shared fascination reflected a new stage they entered —together. Like sisters, both ranked at the top of their classes, but Irena's body had bloomed early, and Ruth suspected that problems at home exacerbated Irena's increasing brazenness. She sailed through school, even though she neglected her studies, and she would no doubt finish well. But Irena's physical precociousness was becoming difficult to keep up with.

Irena now laughed loudly as though Ruth had told her a funny story. Her gaze swept toward the target and caught the two sailors staring. Her smile was an open invitation. They smiled back. She fluffed her hair so they got a complete view of her stunning suit.

"Here they come!" Ruth whispered.

"Which one do you want?" Irena talked through her teeth without relaxing the smile.

"Oh, dear—"

"Okay, yours is the one on the left." He was a little shorter and lighter. Big guys dwarfed Ruth.

"Hello, girls." The two squatted near the blanket. "Can you tell us where the Pike is?"

Irena laughed, flashing pretty teeth. "I'll bet you say that to all the girls!"

They looked at each other and laughed. "Maybe we need a new line?"

"You need something."

"You're absolutely right," the tall one said, easing himself onto the blanket beside Irena. He was light and resembled the actor Clark Gable. Just her type: macho. "My name's Phil. I've been off fighting the Japs to make Ocean Beach safe for pretty girls like you. This is my first shore leave in eleven months. I haven't seen a woman in almost that long, so you are a magnificent sight for sore eyes. You're gorgeous." He grinned.

The other boy's name was Joe. He was darker than his friend, looking half-Hispanic. He was quite handsome. They were both from Illinois, and they were friendly as puppies. Before long, even Ruth was relaxed with the banter and laughter. They swam, walked along the beach and stretched out on their blankets to soak in the sun. When Phil went to one of the concession stands and came back with hot dogs and beer, Ruth refused the beer. Irena explained Ruth didn't like the taste, lest either of the sailors guess they were underage. She gulped hers and welcomed a second when Joe insisted it was his turn to buy.

As the afternoon faded, Ruth began to collect her things, saying she had to leave. It was her brother's birthday and the family was planning a party. Reluctantly Irena began to pack her tanning lotion and towel. Phil drew her aside.

"Are you going to the birthday party?"

"No." Both girls knew Ruth's parents didn't like Irena's growing reputation. They couldn't forbid their daughter from seeing her, but they could discourage her at every opportunity. What Irena didn't know was that the Fantazias considered her to be on a downhill track, and believed that nothing would reverse her direction.

"How about meeting me later? We could go dancing. You know any good places?"

Irena felt a surge of excitement. Why not? Her mother would be working at the hotel or the office. Irena would have only Mrs. Madison for company, guaranteeing another dull evening.

"I know a lot of good places," she told him. She could wear the blue sweater that was like Lana Turner's in *Honky Tonk*. But she couldn't let him come to the house. "I'll have to meet you. I told my boss I'd come back to work for a couple

of hours this evening. He has some letters for me to finish."
Did he believe her?

"Whatever you say, honey. How about meeting me by the
lifeguard station at eight?"

"It's a date!" she exclaimed.

She felt strangely elated as they strolled arm in arm along
the Pike, stopping at a shooting gallery, where Phil won her a
teddy bear, or at a vendor's, where they washed down ham-
burgers with cold frothy beer. They were boisterous and giddy
on the Dodg'em and Cyclone Racer. On the Laff-in-the-Dark,
Phil's hand secretly explored her breasts encased in the tight
sweater. She shivered with new excitement, and when he
passed her a flask from under his middy, she pretended to
enjoy the sharp biting liquor.

While they were dancing at the Majestic, some of Phil's
shipmates made remarks Irena didn't understand but which
made them all laugh. She laughed, too, knowing they thought
she was pretty and older than her actual fifteen years. Between
dances, everyone drank from the bottles they'd smuggled in.

Irena had trouble focusing her eyes, and she lay her head
sleepily on Phil's shoulder while they danced. When he suggested a walk along the beach, she welcomed the fresh air.
Her head ached. She wondered what time it was, but if she
asked, Phil might think she had a curfew, like some dumb kid.
They stumbled along, clinging to each other for balance, and
laughing when they failed to retain it. Once when they wandered too close to the water, Irena let out a yelp as a wave
curled over her shoes. Hanging on to Phil, she bent to yank
off the soggy sandals. With a wavering heave, she tossed
them into the dark water.

"Hey—"

"I don' need 'em." She giggled as the white straps sank
from sight.

He pressed the nearly empty bottle to her lips. She made a
loud gurgling sound as she drank, then hiccuped loudly. He
grinned. "Don't need 'em . . . don't need nothin' but you,
baby." He flung the empty bottle to where her shoes had sunk
from sight and grabbed her hand. He ran, dragging her along
and singing at the top of his voice. *"I got plenty of nothin' and
nothin's plenty for me. . . ."* Giggling, she struggled to keep

up with him. When he finally slowed, she was out of breath and dizzy. He grabbed her and pinned her against his body. She felt his hard muscles ripple against her breasts through her thin sweater. Her breasts seemed to pop out of the bra. She gasped as his hand touched bare flesh. Scared, she looked along the beach; they'd come far from the pier and no one was about. She took a deep breath as he got the hook on her bra undone and snapped it open.

He made a sucking sound as his hand cupped the naked orb and squeezed. Then he bent over and explored the nipple with his warm, moist tongue. Irena let her head fall back, pressing herself harder against his sucking mouth, reveling in the tingling wonder that filled her. She moved like a sleepwalker as he led her away from the water's edge, to the dark shadows below the seawall. Then they were on the sand, and he pulled her skirt down, then pooled her blue sweater around her shoulders so he could tongue and suck her. She squirmed as heat began to spread through her like warm oil. She felt the skirt at her ankles and kicked it away. She realized her panties had gone with it when she felt the sudden heat of his naked flesh against her. She breathed desperately as he straddled her, pushing a knee between her thighs.

"Come on, baby, open up for papa."

Heat engulfed her. She spread her legs and he plunged his swollen member into the dark cavern between her thighs. She felt the rough scrape of pubic hair against her flesh, then a hot driving stab as he entered her. The initial flash of pain vanished in a surge of moisture that quickly became a new kind of heat. Unbearably good. She moaned. He was pounding into her now, driving hard and pulling out to tease her. She cried out for him. He hadn't said anything since entering her, but she knew instinctively that he'd be finished soon. She concentrated on the prickling, tingling, tension where their flesh rubbed. *Yes . . . yes . . . do it . . . let me come. . . .* He exploded, grunting and heaving like a rutting animal. She gasped, then clasped her legs around him and rode with the motion of his pounding hips. She wouldn't let him stop now. . . .

She was on fire all over. Her flesh was crawling with hot needles. Her mind reeled and her stomach lurched as if she were back on the Cyclone Racer. Huge waves pounded through her in relentless succession until at last she lay limp on the cool sand.

He climbed off, pulling up his pants and straightening his jumper and neckerchief. She watched him, unable to stir. He found her skirt and underpants and shook out the sand, then held them out to her. "Hey, come on, get dressed."

"I like it here," she murmured. She never wanted to move again.

"Someone may come along. Come on, baby, get dressed." He squatted beside her. "Pretty good for you, huh?"

She made a gurgling sound. He laughed and slapped her bare butt. "Okay, party's over. Time to dress."

"Let's do it again." She tried to nuzzle his crotch.

"Hey, cut it out. Come on, get dressed. Up you go." He lifted her to her feet and tried to pull the sweater down over her bobbing breasts. She giggled and fell against him. He propped her against the seawall as he struggled with the bra. He couldn't find the hooks. "Shit." He tugged the sweater down, abandoning the attempt. She fell across him as he bent over to force her foot into the leg of her panties. Finally he got them started in the right direction and yanked them over her hips, supporting her weight as he stood her up. He braced her with one hand while he worked on her skirt. It hung lopsided. He brushed sand from it. "Upsadaisy. Come on, baby, help me."

"Mmmm, let's do it again."

"Not now, I'm beat."

"Do it again." She sagged and he had to hold her up again. "Mmm, do it again."

He grinned. "You liked it, huh, baby? Old Phil gave you a treat?"

She snuggled against him. The afterglow of pleasure left her limp. She didn't want to move, but he was determined to keep her on her feet. She squinted, trying to focus on his face, which kept blurring and fading. He grinned again, and her knees buckled.

"Hey, you be a good girl and zip your skirt. Time to go. Whatta you say you meet me tomorrow night, huh?"

She nodded eagerly.

"That's a good girl. You okay now?"

She straightened up, holding on to his arm. "Sure. Fine."

"Okay, let's go. I'll take you home."

She tried to remember why he shouldn't do that. Her mother. Yep, that was it. She started to giggle. "Dragon lives in the castle."

He scowled, then shrugged. "Okay, I'll put you in a cab."

"Walk." She peered at him. "Tomorrow. Eight—don' forget?"

"Sure, baby, come on now." He led her across the sand to the boardwalk. The Pike was crowded, though, so he steered her in the opposite direction. He checked her appearance when they came to the first street light. Jeez, she was a mess. He straightened the skirt the best he could. Her tits were jiggling like jelly under the sweater, but he wasn't going to wrestle with that damned bra again. He spotted a bench and pushed her onto it. Cabs in this town had phone numbers on the doors. You probably had to call to get one. Fishing in the tight pocket where he kept his bills, he unfolded a five and tucked it into her sweater. She wriggled as though he was making a pass. She was a hot one, but when they were shy about telling you where they lived, it usually spelled complications.

"Sit right there, baby. I'll look for a cab." He'd find a phone booth and call for one. But that would be it for the evening.

She nodded as though it was the most reasonable statement she'd ever heard and watched as he walked away into the darkness.

A hot pain pressed behind her eyes. She wanted to sleep but knew she shouldn't even though she couldn't remember why. There were big gaps in her memory that mystified her. She closed her eyes, but opened them quickly. Both maneuvers left her dizzy. Finally she staggered to her feet and began walking. The beach was dark; blackout curtains shrouded buildings so they looked like dark cubes against the subdued, wartime glow of the city. Occasional cars, with only parking lights on, roared past Ocean Boulevard.

Irena's feet were cold. But Phil was hot. And she was hot. She wasn't a virgin anymore! She clapped her hands and tried to do a quick pirouette, but she pitched forward onto the sand like a rag doll. It took a long time to get up.

What was she supposed to remember? Something she had to do? She shook her head but that produced a wave of nausea that engulfed her. God, she was tired. Gotta go home. Gotta sleep.

In a lucid flash she remembered. She couldn't walk home, it was too far. And her feet were bare. She creased her brow and tried to concentrate. She'd need a cab. That was it! She had to find a cab. She sighed with tremendous relief that she had solved the puzzle at last.

She looked down the beach. No cabs. Setting out doggedly toward one of the dark monoliths a few blocks away, she knew the best place to call a cab from was a hotel. She gauged her location to be a few blocks from the Oceanside. She smirked. That was one of the benefits of being the daughter of a celebrated businesswoman—you knew the location of every hotel in town, where there'd always be help.

When she finally reached it, she was incredibly weary. Her head felt like Gene Krupa was holding band practice. She tried to close her eyes, but she felt dizzier than before. A sudden splash of light made her blink. A uniformed doorman emerged from the imposing, ornate building.

"A taxi, my good man," she said, forming the words carefully.

He gaped. "Miss Irena?!"

She burped as he steered her away from the entrance. He shielded her from sight as he picked up a phone from the small niche.

"Gerry? This is Horton at the Oceanside. Send a cab. I need a driver who can keep his mouth shut. There's a fiver in it for him."

He hung up, praying no one would come out of the hotel before the cab arrived. He looked at her. What had she been up to? God, he didn't like to think. Mrs. Upfield would kill her. He shook his head. Irena was a good kid, but too good-looking for her own good, and always into crazy things. Why? Sometimes he figured it was to bug her ma. It was a crying shame.

A cab motored into the circular drive. Horton opened the door and helped Irena in. She crumbled on the seat like an empty sack.

"It's the Upfield kid," he said to the driver. "Take her home and make sure she gets inside. And none of this is happening, you understand? *None of it!*" He handed the driver two fives.

The man gave him a thumb's up sign. When the cab purred down the drive, Horton went inside to use the telephone at the bell captain's desk. Mrs. Upfield listened to his recital without comment until he finished.

"Thank you, Horton. You did the right thing."

Irena came to groggily as the driver lifted her out of the cab and helped her up the steps of the striking, angular home. The door opened immediately, and who should be straddling the threshold, but the dragon!

"Want me to help you get her upstairs?" the driver asked.

"That won't be necessary. Thank you." Rachel took Irena's arm and closed the door. Irena grabbed onto the bannister of the sunken foyer stair. She could hear the tick of the hall clock. Funny she'd never noticed it before. The house began to spin. Irena sat down on a step.

"Where have you been? Look at you!" Rachel yanked at the filthy blue sweater. One end of Irena's bra hung out like a flag. Patches of drying sand clung to her bare feet and skirt. Rachel stared at the scaly stains near the hem. "What have you done!?" she demanded.

When Irena giggled, Rachel slapped her. Irena blinked. "Don't you dare hit me!"

Rachel's hand struck again. "Don't tell me what to do, young lady! How dare you come home looking like a—a slut! Whom were you with? Who did this? Who—" Words failed her and she shook with impotent rage.

Irena smirked. "I was with a man. That's right. A beautiful specimen who screwed the hell out of me!" she spit in a fury built over a lifetime. To her, Rachel had found it easier to hire a succession of well-paid housekeepers and tutors than to spend time with her daughter. Rachel had squirreled away a fortune, yet didn't give two cents for her own kid. Rachel had been canonized for sainthood by the city, the state, the *whole* world, yet her own daughter hated her.

Rachel grabbed her, but Irena jerked away violently. "Don't touch me—I don't want you to touch me!"

Rachel's face blazed. Not trusting herself to speak, she clutched Irena's flailing arm and yanked her to her feet, then pushed her up toward the stairs. Irena stumbled and staggered, but Rachel prodded her forward.

Her drunkenness was offensive enough, but it paled in the

face of the indisputable evidence that she'd slept with a man.

Dear God, not one of her high school classmates! The story would be all over town by morning. Thank God, Horton had the presence to secret her into a cab to be ferried home. Had anyone recognized her before she got to the hotel? Shuddering, Rachel propelled Irena through the bedroom. Irena would have fallen across the bed, but Rachel forced her into the pink and gold bathroom.

"Leave me alone!" Some of the fight was gone as nausea engulfed her. Rachel reached inside the shower and turned the water on full blast. She shoved Irena in, then slammed the door and leaned against it.

Irena yelped, then beat against the glass. "Let me out. Let me out!" She pounded but Rachel held the door shut with the weight of her body. "Bitch! Let me out! I'll kill you! I'll kill you like you killed my father! Let me out!"

Rachel's pale face stared back at her from the mirror.

"Bitch," Irena sobbed. "I hate you!"

Then there was the dreadful sound of dry heaves set against the backdrop of splashing water. Rachel walked silently from the room.

September 1945

The ballroom shone in the dazzling light cast by the crystal chandeliers. Contractors had taken down the heavy blackout curtains covering the windows and boxed them up for storage as soon as the first bulletin came over the radio. V-J Day. The war was over. The kitchen staff in a celebratory mood polished silver and washed crystal and china while singing; chefs began roasting beef, lamb, pork, and chicken that had been stored in huge coolers. Rachel enlisted the town's most popular radio station to air an all-day invitation to the Oceanside's Victory Ball. Another call guaranteed that Jo Stafford would appear as a special festivity treat. The Oceanside's twelve-piece band and their jazz quartet would play nonstop throughout the night.

Rachel glanced at the long buffet tables and found them faultless. A huge ice sculpture, a map of the United States, and victory flags ornamented the cold-cuts table. Nearby a table brandished dishes of paté and caviar, salads, cold meats, fresh vegetables, and fruits. Axel managed the production on short notice, and Rachel questioned neither his ability nor his methods. Throughout the war he had kept delicacies on the Oceanside menu that other hotels had to forgo. Tonight's repast would crown his achievements. Smiling, she recalled the day he'd come to her suite and offered to resign. Anti-German sentiment had swollen in many quarters; if she felt it was in the best interest of the hotel, he would step down. She'd refused. Axel was the best chef in California and she would not sacrifice him to others' pettiness. She had taken the same stand about the Japanese gardeners, but that decision had been squelched when the government rounded up the Niseis and shipped them to internment camps.

She weaved among her guests, pausing here and there to chat and drink victory toasts with them. The mayor and his wife, president of the chamber of commerce, the police chief —out of uniform, thank heaven—were all there. The response to the broadcasts was gratifying. Celebrations were going on all over the city, but the guest list at the Oceanside read like the Four Hundred. The Red Book.

"Magnificent party, Rachel. A miracle on such short notice, or did Truman tip you off ahead of time?"

Rachel laughed. "A good hotelier doesn't tell her secrets, Senator. I'm delighted you are in town to join us."

"An invitation to the Oceanside would bring me running at any time."

Smiling, she moved on. Joe Pasternak introduced her to one of MGM's newest leading ladies, a pretty blond girl named Kathryn Grayson. Rachel promised to screen one of her pictures in the hotel's theater salon if Pasternak sent her a print.

She paused at the edge of the dance floor to watch the couples swirl in rhythm to "I'll Get By." She would dance later, when she was sure the party was running smoothly. She enjoyed dancing more now than she had when she was young, even though she did not have a regular partner. There were guests who always asked, lusty, attractive men who streamed through her life. She never lacked for escorts, dinner companions, or lovers when she wanted them. But since Hillary's death she had shied away from any deeper commitments. She liked being free and accountable only to herself.

There was Irena, of course, but even the scantest scrutiny showed the flaws in that relationship. It was one of the few things she could not control. Irena seemed bent on self-destruction, committed to a course that shamed and embarrassed the Upfield name. Irena had gone from minor naughty escapades to full-fledged rebellion. She wondered if that ugly scene three years ago was as branded on her daughter's memory as it was in hers. She sighed inwardly. She half expected Irena to show up tonight. Not because Rachel had requested it, but because so much fanfare had accompanied the Oceanside's festivities. She glanced around.

"Hello, Rachel."

Her heart warmed when she whirled to face Josh Fantazia's beaming face. "Hello, Josh. I'm delighted you could come." Her gaze met his without betraying their intimacy, then flashed to the dark-haired beauty at his side. "Hello, Ruth. You look lovely tonight."

"Thank you, Mrs. Upfield. Everything's so marvelous," Ruth said, glancing around the ballroom.

She had Josh's lustrous dark hair and a milky, pale complexion. She was much too thin, beyond ethereal-looking, to the point of frailty. Rachel knew that Josh worried about her constantly even though he permitted her to have the independence she desired in a small apartment of her own.

"People seem to be enjoying themselves," Rachel said. She considered asking Ruth if she knew Irena's whereabouts, but she refrained from quizzing her. She knew Josh didn't approve of Ruth's alliance to Irena's fading star. Irena's reputation often tarnished those closest to her, no matter how hard Rachel tried to keep Irena's name out of the gossip columns. "I'm really delighted you both could come. Is Collette with you?"

Josh shook his head. "She didn't feel up to it, but Ruth and I couldn't resist the excitement. A day like this calls for celebration. The entire country is hell-raising."

Rachel laughed. "We're planning special entertainment later. I think you'll enjoy it," Rachel said.

"I can't stay," Ruth demurred. "I've invited some friends to the apartment." She looked apologetic.

"We understand, dear," Josh said. "The young people want to celebrate on their own. Can't say I blame them, can you, Rachel?"

"Not at all. I'm pleased you stopped by."

Ruth looked relieved. They stood chatting about the changes that would come now that the war was over. After a few minutes Ruth excused herself and Josh and Rachel were alone.

"You look beautiful, so vibrant and..." He let the words trail off, but his glance completed his thought. "I couldn't stay away, Rachel. I associate you with all the happiest days I've ever known. I wanted to see you."

She smiled her understanding. The affair ignited twenty-five years ago had survived and sustained her. She loved Josh with a remarkable, all-encompassing love. They still enjoyed a passion that transcended their rivalry in business; indeed, their rivalry added piquancy to their occasional trysts. Josh alone understood her lack of sorrow after Hillary's death. And when it was followed two years later by her father's death, he was her strength and solace. He became more important to her than ever before. She no longer felt any resentment toward Collette, whom he would never leave.

Josh loved them both, but with Collette he had family responsibilities he would never abandon. Rachel was satisfied with the arrangement. She had freedom, yet she had Josh when she needed him.

She rarely thought about the chaotic past. After the earthquake, Josh never again mentioned the holding corporation they'd discussed while entwined in each other's arms. Almost superstitiously. He was still a member of the city council, which proved very advantageous when the Wilmington Oil Field opened. Their leased city lots netted large profits. Urban drilling restrictions allowed derricks to line only the west levee of the river channel, beyond Rancho del Cielo. The whipstocked wells went as far east as Pine. The Fielding Corporation had come under only the most casual scrutiny when Ocean Beach Oil Development won the bid to drill in the Harbor District. Garson Perkins had done his job well.

She had done well with the construction boom of the war years, too. Upfield Land Management, located in the center of the rebuilt downtown, rivaled Fantazia Enterprises, only a few blocks away on Ocean Boulevard. Despite her fears about competing with Josh on so many levels, he'd grudgingly admired her success. Upfield won the contract for the new Oceanside School when the old one was abandoned because of encroaching industry. Rachel's friendship with members of the school board enabled her to offer a substitute site and an acceptable construction bid. When Rachel and Josh met at the

Alexandria a few weeks later, their lovemaking had been explosive.

She smiled as a recently promoted Douglas Aircraft executive and his wife passed, then turned her attention back to Josh. He was in his late forties, his black hair streaked with gray and his face more creased, but his striking, elegant good looks still turned the heads of women half his age. "I didn't dare hope to see you, but I prayed I would. I remember the end of another war."

The handsome features clouded only a moment. "When I didn't tell you I was coming, and you weren't at the train to meet me."

Would their lives have been different? Nostalgia filled her. "The past is gone, Josh, we can't change it. We have only the memories, good and bad."

He winked at her lasciviously. "Not everything of the past is bad." He grew more serious. "I had a phone call from someone we'd both prefer to forget." When she gave him a puzzled look, he said, "Teddy Reno, our peripatetic troublemaker."

She was astonished. "He called *you?* Why?"

Josh snorted. "Maybe he's afraid to tangle with you again after the Carbello thing. As usual, Teddy wants money. The aroma of tidelands oil has lured him back. He smells a chance to reopen negotiations."

Rachel forced down her anger as several guests paused to comment on the party. When they moved on, she said, "He's already been well paid for his paltry contribution." He had almost cost her the Oceanside. She would never forgive him for that. Nor would she make any deal with him now.

"If he put half the energy he's spent cheating others into honest work, he'd be a rich man," she said bitterly. "I trust you told him to go whistling down a lane. He had a lot of nerve to approach you."

Josh glanced around casually, and she saw wariness in his eyes. When he was satisfied no one could overhear, he said, "He's resorting to the nastiest kind of blackmail. He knows about the Alexandria Hotel."

She tried to hide her astonishment. *"How?"*

"I don't know. He says he can produce dates and times and witnesses to swear we were there together. He wants a cut of the channel leases or he'll take his information to the council, the real estate board, the newspaper, and Collette, not necessarily in that order."

"My God—I'm sorry, Josh." His concern was for Collette and Ruth, she knew. Like her mother, Ruth's health was not robust and a constant source of worry. Neither of them could endure the nasty kind of scandal Teddy threatened.

Their eyes locked in compassion. She wanted to take him in her arms, but she had to settle for an innocent gesture of camaraderie as she touched his hand. "We'll find a way to handle it," she said gently. "When can we talk?" He'd come to the party because he needed to share his burden, but they couldn't discuss it here, not tonight. "Tomorrow? Any time you choose."

He nodded. "Not Los Angeles. The Rancho?" When she agreed, he said, "Noon?"

"I'll be there."

❧ Nine ❧

IRENA LAUGHED AS a sailor grabbed her. The Pike was jammed. She gave up fighting and let herself be swept along, crushed and exhilarated in the throng. The war was over. V-J Day! She raised two fingers in the victory salute as a passing sailor shouted something she couldn't decipher. He made a sudden change of direction and swept her into his arms, lifting her from her feet as he claimed a victory kiss. Irena matched the eager stabs of his tongue and felt the hard pressure of his crotch. Every swab on the Pike was horny tonight. When he released her, the throng pulled him on, but he glanced back, yelling. Irena blew him a kiss.

Thousands had swarmed to the Pike, gripped by the fever that infected the city. Music blared, shouts and laughter rang out, barkers cried, and air rifles cracked steadily.

She hadn't spotted Ruth yet, but it wasn't surprising in this mob. Besides, the evening was still young. The party at Ruth's apartment had been Irena's idea. A day like this called for some special fun. And Ruth had that super little place all her own, with no one to keep an eye on her. Irena envied her. She could just see Rachel letting *her* have an apartment. Ruth's old man was realistic. He cared enough for Ruth that he didn't try to imprison her. He gave her a super allowance and a long leash. Rachel still screamed bloody murder if Irena came home late.

I'm sick of listening to her, Irena thought. Now that she had graduated from high school, she sure as hell wasn't going to stick around much longer. She'd even graduated with honors, but her mother had refused to relax her rules. And no college, no matter how much her mother threatened. She couldn't tolerate the idea of more years under her mother's thumb.

Sounding off at her mother had become one of Irena's few sources of pleasure. Rachel was more devoted to that damned real estate business and hotel than to her daughter. Why did she bother having a kid? *I was probably one of those "unplanned" babies who entangled her life. A surprise result of a night's screwing.* The thought made her smile. She couldn't imagine her mother screwing. Steely, demanding Rachel. Men stared at her beauty, but she was as warm as a block of ice. A brief haunting memory of her father surfaced and made her shiver, but she shook it off quickly. She rarely thought about him anymore; sometimes she was convinced the memories were illusion, as if he'd never existed at all.

She shook off the somberness and stretched on tiptoes to look around. Laughing, she grabbed a freckle-faced sailor with carrot hair poking out from under his white hat. He gave her a shy smile, and she gave him a kiss he could write home about. He looked dazed as she was carried off with the crowd.

"Irena!" Ruth's head popped up and a hand waved frantically. Irena waved back, and wedged her way between a woman in a flowered dress and a soldier. The GI grabbed a feel as Irena went by, and she laughed.

"Irena!" Ruth bobbed up and down like a yo-yo. Irena elbowed past some boys huddled around a bottle. They held it out to her, and she took a quick swig before handing it back; they broke into gales of laughter that turned sour when they saw her get pulled away by the crowd. She shrugged helplessly at them.

Finally she reached her friend, and after they kissed each other's cheeks, Irena led Ruth to a clear spot near the wall of a building where they could hear each other.

"I've never seen such a crowd!" Ruth's face flushed, her velvet light eyes ablaze. She wore a Lilli Ann tailored skirt and plaid top and a light sackbacked coat. "Isn't it wonderful?"

Irena looked sexy in a curve-clinging silk skirt and pat-

terned blouse. "Fantastic! It sure beats those awful blackouts!"
They linked arms to keep from being separated. Irena pulled
Ruth close to make herself heard. "Have you seen anyone we
know?"

Ruth nodded. "Those four guys we met last weekend. They
said they'd come to the party."

Irena squeezed her arm. "What about Glen?" Ruth shook
her head, and Irena flashed her a quick smile. "Don't worry,
he'll show up. He wouldn't miss seeing you today." Ruth had
fallen so hard for the striking radio operator from a destroyer,
she was blind to the truth that she was just another girl in a
port. Glen had tumbled half a dozen girls on the beach or in
the backseat of a rented car. He'd made passes at *her*, for
heaven's sake. But Glen was the first guy who'd brought Ruth
out of her shy shell. If she thought it was love, so what? As
long as she didn't get hurt too badly, she'd be smarter the next
time around.

"Maybe we should stop at the Majestic," Ruth shouted.

"Are you kidding?" Irena pointed toward the winking lights
of the dance hall a block away. It might as well have been on
the other side of the ocean, the walk was so jam-packed. Besides, bouncers had linked themselves into a human chain
across the doorway, barring their chances of getting in anytime
soon. She steered Ruth in the opposite direction. It was like
weaving through a mine field. Any moment they were in
danger of being dragged into Skooter or Crazie Mazie or Marfleet's. Her eyes darted wildly around, absorbing the scene.
The war was over, and everyone had cast off their inhibitions.
This was what they'd been waiting for. Irena felt alive. The
end of an era. A new beginning.

It took them an hour to reach Ruth's car. En route they
acquired two GIs who had a quart of Scotch and loved the idea
of a party. They piled into the convertible and sang lustily as
Ruth drove the few blocks to Plaza Apartments. It was an
elegant, five-floor brick prewar building in a developing
quarter of the city. The rooms, with cathedral ceilings, were
spacious and graced with latticed windows and carved woodwork. One of the soldiers had a tobacco sack full of marijuana
and as soon as they were inside, he sat cross-legged on the
carpet and rolled joints. Ruth fetched glasses and ice from the
kitchen. They were half stoned when the doorbell rang and
four sailors joined the party. Irena squeezed into an armchair

with the Italian Fireman, who had brought a two-fifths bottle of booze.

The doorbell kept ringing and the apartment filled with people and sweet-smelling smoke. Someone stacked random records on the phonograph so the music was a mixture of Sinatra, Mills Brothers, and plaintive Gershwin. No one noticed. No one cared. The war was over. It was partytime.

Irena smiled at the tall, bearded older man who'd just come in. He looked out of place. For a moment she wondered if he was a spy sent by Ruth's father. He caught her staring and held out a brown bag.

"Reinforcements," he said, grinning as he handed over the bag. Whiskey bottles clinked inside.

Irena peeked in the bag. Three fifths! "Welcome, friend!" She leaned against him and offered her mouth. He thrust his tongue into her, and after a moment she pulled back, smiling. He was aroused, but a friend was behind Irena flagging his attention away. Someone behind Irena caressed her buttocks. She turned.

"Hi, baby. Some party." Glen Orlando took the brown bag. He was tall, his black hair short-cropped, but his pleasing features indicated he was quite handsome when his hair grew out. He wore a patched leather jacket over an unbuttoned cotton shirt. "Ruth's over there. . . ." She pointed vaguely. The small apartment was so crowded it was impossible to find anyone.

"I know where old Ruthie is." His hand massaged her rump playfully. "Old Ruthie doesn't like to play touchie-feelie when there's people around."

"She's my friend." Irena tried to slap his hand away but wound up falling against him. The caress moved up insinuatingly. "It's not nice to fool around with your girlfriend's best friend. . . ." She was bombed. Glen's face swam in and out of focus like the weird reflections in a house of mirrors. "Not nice," she said.

"So who's fooling? I mean business." He thought that was funny and laughed, hugging her in the crook of one arm. "Come on, let's get another drink." He pushed through the crowd, using the heavy bag as a wedge and dragging her behind. In the kitchen he pulled out one of the bottles. He whistled at the quality label. "You got some nice friends," he told her as he poured two glasses straight. He gave her one and moved so she was trapped in a corner near the refrigerator. "Victory kiss," he demanded.

His kiss was wet and nonstop. She tried to push him away, then surrendered. What the hell, the war was over. Everybody loved everyone. He came up for air and grabbed her hand.

"Come on, I want to show you something."

"What?"

"A surprise. You'll see." He dragged her toward the bedroom. She held back at the door, suspicious and afraid to be alone with him. But the bedroom wasn't empty. A sailor and a girl were sprawled on the bed necking. Another couple were entwined on the chaise longue. Glen dragged her toward the walk-in closet where the delicate scent of Ruth's perfume clung to the rows of dresses and suits.

"What's the s'prise?" Irena whispered conspiratorially.

He nuzzled her neck. She squirmed, and a silk dress slipped from a hanger and covered her head. He lifted an end to peek at her. "Hello, haven't we met somewhere?"

She giggled. "Where's the s'prise?"

"Toll gate. One kiss, one little smacker." He grabbed for her. She stumbled back, swatting at the tangled clothes. Her drink splashed down the front of her blouse as she hit the wall. In slow motion, she slid down to the floor. It was very funny. She giggled uncontrollably. Glen sat beside her. Then his arms were around her, and he was kissing her.

Deep inside her fogged head, a warning bell tolled, but Irena couldn't figure out what to do.

"Want the surprise?" he whispered hoarsely. "You like surprises, doncha?"

She nodded, but that made her so dizzy she had to close her eyes. His hand was under her skirt. Ruth's boyfriend. She tried to crawl away but he pulled her back. She was too drunk to resist. When he kissed her, it was all she could do to breathe. Gotta stop him . . . Ruth's boyfriend . . . She felt his rigid penis push past her panties.

"No—" But it was too late. He was in her, pumping urgently and making her wet and hot. "Oh, God—no—no—" But he wouldn't stop and she couldn't. She met his thrusts with wild abandon.

"You like it, doncha, you like it!" he cried.

"Yes . . . yes . . ."

It was over. They lay panting in the stuffy, tangled mess of

Ruth's clothes. He pulled away and fell in a crumpled heap, half on top of her. Irena roused herself enough to pull away the silky garment covering her face.

Ruth was standing in the doorway, her face ashen. Irena gasped and tried to sit up, but before she managed to push Glen off, Ruth fled. Irena buried her face in her hands. God, what had she done?! Her best friend . . . She sat up abruptly and pounded Glen's head.

"You bastard. You `stupid rotten bastard!" She pummeled him furiously.

"Hey—" He raised his arms to shield himself. When she didn't stop, he clipped her with a half punch. She fell back crying. "What the hell do you think you're doing?" he demanded. He got up, trying to arrange his pants.

"Get out of here," she snarled. Her lips pulled back in a grimace of hatred.

"Who the hell do you think you're talking to?"

"Get out or I'll kill you!" She threw a spikey stiletto shoe.

He scuttled out of range, stumbling in the doorway, still fumbling with his pants. She lunged, fingers clawing, and he scurried out the bedroom. Irena sank back sobbing uncontrollably. She covered her face and rocked back and forth.

"Please, Ruth, let me explain. God, I'm so sorry. He said he wanted to show me something. I thought he'd bought you a surprise."

Ruth sat in the chair by the window, her face averted, eyes closed, as though she couldn't force herself to look at Irena. Irena had found her like that when she finally emerged from the closet where she'd passed out. The party was over. Irena had no idea what time it was. The apartment was quiet. Empty glasses, overflowing ashtrays, and scraps of chips and peanuts littered the floor and tables. Irena wondered if she should clean up the mess. Her head was pounding and she was sick to her stomach. She wanted to go to bed, but she couldn't leave until Ruth forgave her. She crossed to the chair and knelt.

"Ruth, say something, please?" She laid her head in Ruth's lap. "He's a bastard. You're much too good for him. He's nothing but a rat. I know you love him, but he's no good. He's really rotten. He's been seeing other girls and letting you think you're the only one. He doesn't deserve you. You're much too good for him, honest." Irena's tears stained Ruth's dress. Her chest heaved as she sobbed. "Say you forgive me, Ruth. I was drunk. He said he had a surprise. I thought he bought you a ring. I didn't know. I didn't want—I tried to fight him off, honest. Say you forgive me."

The room was silent except for Irena's sobs. When she could stand it no longer, she raised her head and looked at Ruth's delicate, angelic features. They were beautiful, but strangely expressionless. Still sobbing, Irena crawled away, then stumbled to her feet and ran to the bathroom. She barely made it to the toilet bowl before she heaved. In misery she pressed a cold washcloth to her eyes, but nothing dulled the terrible ache in her head. A monstrous black agony engulfed her.

Back in the living room, Ruth had not moved. There was an empty glass beside her on the table. She'd been drinking and smoking, too. She must have gotten bombed. That was it. That had to be it. When she woke up, they'd talk. And Ruth would forgive her. She had to. She had to.

Irena sat on the sofa. From time to time, she jerked up as she dozed off. God, her head hurt. When she looked at her watch, she was astounded to see it was past three. She got up and smoothed her wrinkled torn skirt. She'd have to borrow a coat from Ruth's closet. Closet. Oh, God, she felt like a fool.

She crossed to the chair. Maybe she should wake Ruth and help her into bed. Irena had never seen her so smashed.

"Ruth?" Her voice was hesitant and pleading. Irena raised it. "Ruth, please, we've got to talk. I can't leave like this. You're my best friend, no matter what. Ruth?"

She shook her arm gently. Her arm slid from the chair into her lap. "Ruth?" She shook her again. Ruth's head flopped like a loose puppet's. "Ruth—" She picked up the hand. It was cold. "Ruth!" She shook her by the shoulders, violently, demanding a response. Ruth's body fell sideways in the chair, her dark hair flowing in a shimmering cascade around the deathly white face.

"Ruth!!!!!"

Irena fell sobbing across the body. "Ruth . . . Ruth . . . Ruth!!!!"

She sat up as hope filled her. Maybe she was still alive. Sometimes people seemed dead when they weren't. Get help. She had to get help. When she tried to stand, her knees buckled. Irena crawled to the davenport and reached for the phone on the end table. She lifted the receiver. Who? The dial tone was an insistant buzz. Who? Her hand shook. Trembling, she dialed the one number she could remember.

Rachel answered sleepily on the third ring. It was her private number and phone, and the servants were forbidden to answer—in case Josh called. "Yes?"

"Mother?" It was barely a whisper.

"Who is this? Speak up, I can't hear you."

Irena responded to the command automatically. "Mother, I need help."

"Irena?" An astonished pause. Her daughter rarely called this number. "Where are you? What have you done this time?"

"I need help... please... it's—" She glanced at the chair where she could see Ruth's serene body lying as if in sleep. "Oh, God, Mama, please come. You've got to come—"

"Where are you?!" Rachel sounded angry.

"Ruth's apartment. Oh, God, she's dead, she's—"

Rachel swung her legs, wrapped in a floor-length nightgown, over the bed. She barked into the phone. "Irena, listen to me! Stay right where you are, do you hear me? Stay there. I'll be there as soon as I can. Don't call anyone, don't do anything, do you understand?"

"Yes."

The line clicked dead. Irena huddled against the davenport with the phone in her lap.

Rachel quickly checked the girl's pulse for signs of life. There were none. Ruth's skin had already developed a waxy pallor. Rachel pressed a hand to her own temple where a throb threatened to obliterate her vision. She glanced at Irena cowering like a frightened child.

"Get up."

Irena pulled herself onto the davenport. She clasped her hands and wet her lips nervously.

"What happened?" Rachel's gaze flashed around the room. The sizable apartment looked as if a hurricane had struck. She glared at Irena.

"I—I—"

"Pull yourself together, you fool!"

Irena took a deep breath. Haltingly, she tried to tell her mother about the party.

"And?" Rachel demanded. "What happened? Did Ruth say

anything, do anything? Did she take any drugs?"

Irena chewed her lip. "We had marijuana. I don't know how much she smoked."

Rachel recalled everything she'd heard about the narcotic. Its intoxicating effect produced high spirits, much like alcohol, but could it kill?

"Anything else?" When Irena shook her head, Rachel studied her daughter. She was lying. She looked scared and guilty. "Something happened," Rachel accused. "Don't lie to me!"

Irena shook her head too quickly.

"Damn it, tell me what happened! Don't you realize that girl is dead? Ruth was your *friend*." *And Josh's daughter*, she agonized. *God help me.*

Irena cowered. When Rachel took a step toward her, she began to babble. "It wasn't my fault. He pulled me into the closet—"

"Who?"

"Glen . . . her boyfriend." Irena burst into tears and buried her face in her lap.

My God, did the girl have no shame? Was her body so worthless that she surrendered to every aggressive male? And to betray her best friend. Rachel felt sick. She went back to the chair where Ruth's cold body was an obscene accusation. Rachel ran her hands along the cushions and found what she suspected would be there. She held the vial closer to the lamp to read the label. "One tablet at bedtime for sleep. Do not exceed dosage." The vial was empty.

Irena sobbed, "I couldn't help it—"

"Shut up!" Rachel cried. She had to think. It would kill Josh to know Ruth had taken her own life. He would kill Irena if he knew she'd played any part in the events leading up to his daughter's death. Oh, God—what was she going to do? *Josh, Josh . . .* She looked around the room, then walked through the kitchen, bathroom, bedroom. Evidence of the wild party was everywhere. The smell of tobacco and—marijuana?—clung to the air along with the stale odor of liquor. Stains spotted the carpet where drinks had been spilled. The bathroom stank of nausea. Rachel rounded to the living room. It would take hours to clean the place up. There wasn't time. She'd have to *use* the party. Yes, it would work.

She went through the rooms again, looking carefully for anything that could be identified as Irena's. Only her purse under a chair. Nothing else. Then she went back to Irena.

"Stop crying," she ordered.

Irena hiccuped and sniffed as she raised her head. Rachel thrust a handkerchief at her. "Blow your nose and wipe your eyes." When Irena obeyed, Rachel threw the purse in her lap. "I presume you have makeup in there. Do what you can with your face." She stood over her while Irena powdered her nose and touched scarlet lipstick to her pale mouth. She looked at her mother for approval. "It will have to do. Now, listen carefully. We are going to leave. We'll walk to the end of the hall and go down the stairs, do you understand?" No one had seen her come in. Anyone awake at this hour would probably be too drunk to notice, but they still had to be careful. She knew the building; she'd sold it to the present owner. The stairs led to the alley. Her car was across the street.

She motioned Irena to her feet. The girl was still a mess, but they had no time for miraculous remedies. "Take your pocketbook, and not a word. Not a sound, do you understand?"

Irena nodded mutely. Rachel retrieved her own purse, then listened at the front door before opening it. She looked in both directions along the hall, then drew Irena out and closed the door behind them softly. They walked down the hall quietly. In the corner of her vision Rachel watched Irena for signs of panic. She seemed hesitant but eager to get out of the building.

In the alley they listened again. But the sounds of merriment took place too far away for concern. She gripped Irena's arm as they walked to the car. She breathed a sigh of relief when they turned off the boulevard and headed for the highway. Irena was slumped beside her. Rachel concentrated on driving. Without traffic, she could make Palm Springs in three hours. She would have Irena admitted to a private health spa that catered to an elite clientele. She'd been a guest several times and had handled real estate deals for the owner. Irena would be kept active and out of trouble. More important, she'd be off the scene so she couldn't blurt something stupid to create problems.

Ruth. Poor child. No amount of pity would bring her back. Nothing could do that. Rachel ached with the pain she knew Josh would suffer, but she knew it would pierce less for what he didn't know. How long would it be before he or Collette worried about not hearing from Ruth? Was she in the habit of phoning home daily? Did Josh call her? Perhaps with all the celebrations last night, he would refrain from calling Ruth right away. The longer the body went undiscovered, the more apt Josh would be to not question the cause of death. He'd be blinded by remorse and guilt. She felt like a traitor, but her calculating behavior was preferable to the alternative.

Belatedly she remembered her appointment with Josh. All thought of Teddy Reno had fled these last few hours. She couldn't read her watch in the dim light from the dashboard, but it couldn't be much past four. She'd be in Palm Springs by seven, then back again in plenty of time to meet Josh at the Rancho.

Or to hear that Ruth's body had been discovered.

❧ Ten ❧

SHE WAS AT the Rancho cottage ten minutes early. Long ago Josh had given her a key so she could let herself in any time. It was a wonder that the house had been allowed to survive. Across the riverbed, a canyon of oil wells pumped steadily. The cottage was the classy vestige of a bygone era.

She'd gotten back from Palm Springs an hour before. She'd had time to stop at the house to bathe and change. She'd called the office and the hotel, but there was no message from Josh canceling their meeting. If Ruth's body had been discovered, would he be too upset to think of calling? She'd listened to the radio all morning, but no station mentioned Ruth Fantazia's name.

She paced nervously until she heard a car engine rev then sputter dead, followed by Josh's footsteps on the path. Her heart caught at the sight of his handsome figure in a light summer-weight suit. He'd gotten better-looking over the years as a weight and gravity settled in his features and gray streaked his hair.

He closed the door before embracing her and kissing her affectionately. He was preoccupied, but no more than he'd been the previous night. It was obvious he had not found out about Ruth. He'd have been too distraught to even show. She felt an immense weight lift from her shoulders.

The thick adobe walls shielded the cottage from the midday heat, so inside it was cool and pleasant. They sat at the table in front of the window. Outside, the arroyo shimmered in the sun's rays, and cicadas chorused a high-pitched song.

He glanced at her, taking in the light rayon dress colored with red geometric lines. She was still a shapely woman, still had the power to enthrall him. Her hair was pinned up, her high cheekbones glowing with health, though he noticed her brow more furrowed than usual. He caught her scent—not flowery or sweet, but assertive, if not suggestive of her feminine allure. He braced himself for this meeting, sorry this was how they'd have to spend their time.

"He wants a hundred thousand dollars," Josh finally said.

"He's insane! Worse, he's getting greedy."

"He's also getting smarter," Josh said bitterly. "He's been snooping around the county recorder's office in L.A. He knows which lots we own and when they were purchased. He also mentioned the Fielding Corporation."

"He can't possibly know—" Scowling, she studied Josh.

He shrugged. "It's hard to believe he could have pulled the name out of the blue. He may be fishing. I let it pass as if it meant absolutely nothing to me, but I don't mind telling you, Rachel, I'm worried."

"Damn Teddy Reno!" She fumed silently, staring out at the wells beyond the riverbed. Would they never be rid of him? Ironic, since it had begun with him. He would haunt them whenever he needed money—forever. She sighed. "I wouldn't consider a penny if he weren't threatening you. Are you sure he's not bluffing?"

"I can't risk calling him," Josh said. "Do you realize what it would do to Collette and Ruth? Judson, too. No, Rachel, I intend to pay him."

She studied the creases in Josh's face. What did Teddy Reno have and how had he uncovered it? After all this time . . . She and Josh had never been chauffeured together to Los Angeles. Nor had they ever entered the hotel together. Like the cottage, Rachel had a key to the suite and let herself in without stopping at the desk downstairs. If they planned to stay the night, she always booked a room at another hotel, checked in, and hung out the Do Not Disturb sign on the doorknob before leaving for the Alexandria. Reno could not have known when they would be there, since they often didn't

know themselves until the last minute. Had they somehow
become too nonchalant?

"Half the debt is mine," she said. "I'll pay, too, but the
time has come to guarantee that this is the last time. And that
he keeps his mouth shut."

"A tall order." He stared out the window, his velvet eyes
pained. He was worried about Collette and Ruth.

"The only thing Teddy understands is power," she said.
"We have to hold something over him that's more dangerous
than anything he can hold over us."

He looked interested. "What?"

Her thoughts raced. The idea had been hovering at the back
of her mind ever since Josh had told her about Reno's return.
But Irena's call had crowded everything else from her mind.
"Suppose we could link him to murder?"

Josh's mouth fell open. "Whose?"

"Perry Kranzle. Teddy was in Ocean Beach at the time,
and he was working for Mickey Carbello. The murder was
never solved."

He frowned. "It's pretty well accepted that Carbello was
behind it."

"Exactly. But Carbello didn't do his own dirty work. He
sent Reno to threaten me. If we can come up with something,
anything, to link him to the murder, we'd have some bargain-
ing chips."

Josh blew a breath. "How could we do it?"

Rachel paused to think, sipping the Colombian coffee
she'd brewed for them. "The police reports. You can look at
them without arousing questions. All we need is a fact or two
that hasn't been made public. We invent the rest."

"He'd know we were lying."

"But he couldn't take the chance of having the investigation reopened. There's enough evidence to connect Kranzle to
Carbello and Carbello to Teddy. We can invent details to
match the facts. It will work, I know it will."

He was silent, staring out the window as he considered the
idea. He gulped down his cup of coffee. After a few minutes
he said, "All right. It's worth a try."

Rachel sighed and entwined her long sensual fingers as she
sat back. "We'll have to work fast. Can you get to those reports today?"

"I'll do it right away. There'll be no problem wandering

around the city hall basement. Everyone's still in a holiday mood." He sighed. "You're a genius, Rachel."

"No, desperate," she said modestly, though others had described her that way. "Do you have a meeting scheduled with him?"

"He said he'd call today. He gave me time to contact you."

"We'll see him together. Call me as soon as you find what we need. I'll wait at the office." She clasped his hand. He caressed the soft skin on top of her hand, admiring its texture and tone. "I wish I could do it all, Josh. You don't deserve any of this."

He shook his head. "I'm in it as much as you. What if I set up a meeting for tonight? I want it finished. Collette's planning a party for Ruth's birthday the day after tomorrow, then we'll be leaving for Tahoe."

The mention of Ruth made Rachel cringe, but Josh was too distracted to notice. "I'm sure we can."

"Good." He took both her hands in his, and kissed them. He looked at her tenderly. "I don't know what I'd do without you, Rachel. You always have an answer to problems." He came around the table and pulled her into his arms. "Sometimes I wonder what our lives would be if you *had* met my train when I returned from that other war." They kissed again, and in that timeless moment Rachel mused, If only we could change the past.

A package of photostatic copies was messengered to Rachel's office by four o'clock. She locked herself in her office after telling her secretary to rebuff any visitors. On her cherrywood, gilt-edged desk, she fanned out the package's contents, studying every sheet. There were copies of the investigation report, coroner's report, and autopsy findings, plus transcripts of a dozen interrogations of witnesses and suspects. Mickey Carbello had been questioned; there were pages of testimony to prove he had not left the *Lucky Lady* the night of the murder. An employee roster did not include Teddy Reno's name. One item caught her eye. In the coroner's report a catalog of Perry Kranzle's belongings noted two IOUs to the *Lucky Lady* signed by a Collin Wilcox.

She sifted through the interviews again until she found Wilcox's. He'd known Kranzle for years, and the two often were in the same party aboard the gambling ship. Wilcox stated that he'd lost heavily the night of the murder and had to write the IOUs. He had no idea how Kranzle had obtained them. She leafed through the stack of papers to the interrogation of Carbello. She could almost envision his hard face as he gave curt replies to police questions. A man accustomed to dealing with matters in his way.

Lt. Jeremy:	Why would Kranzle have someone else's IOUs in his pocket?
Carbello:	He bought 'em.
Lt. Jeremy:	How could he do that when he didn't have enough money to pay his own off?
Carbello:	Kranzle came aboard with cash. He had no credit with us anymore, he knew that. He was winning early in the evening. Wilcox was losing. When he ran out of dough, Kranzle bought his markers so he could keep playing.
Lt. Jeremy:	Then Collin Wilcox owed the money to Kranzle, not to you?
Carbello:	That's right.

Rachel studied the excerpt. The more she read, the more apparent it was that Teddy had lied. He may have been working for Carbello, but not the way he'd led her to believe. Carbello was a businessman, who never would have given Hillary's IOUs to anyone. Teddy had bought them, just as Perry Kranzle bought Collin Wilcox's. When Hillary couldn't pay, Teddy tried to collect from her. He'd probably bargained for time on his own markers by claiming Rachel would pay Hillary's larger debt.

Lies beget lies, she thought. All I have to do is be as extravagant.

Josh phoned her at six while she listened to the evening news in her living room. The newscasters had not reported Ruth's death, and in spite of her inner impatience, Rachel felt relieved. If Josh learned of his daughter's death before they settled with Teddy Reno, he would be distracted. She needed his strength, his charismatic presence.

"We're to meet him at ten," Josh said into the phone.

"Where?"

He gave a mirthless laugh. "Darien Hill. It meets the requirements for seclusion and accessibility, as well as what Reno calls 'returning to the scene of the crime.'"

She ignored Reno's gibe. They would see who laughed last.

"I need to see you first. I have what we need."

"What is it?" His voice was full of hope.

"It's better not to discuss it until we meet. Say nine? At my house."

He hesitated. "All right. I was going to have dinner with Ruth, but she doesn't answer her phone. She's probably forgotten and gone out with friends."

Rachel flinched, then framed a fiction he might accept. "If she's spending her birthday with the family, she probably wanted to celebrate now with her friends." She was amazed how readily the lie fell from her lips. But she had to keep Josh occupied until the meeting with Teddy was over.

He seemed to accept her story.

"All right, nine."

Rachel's hand shook as she replaced the receiver on the phone cradle. She looked around the sunken living room furnished with Edwardian chairs, Chinese Chippendale tables, and collector paintings. The room looked ironically serene. Remembering her task, she rose and set to work frantically.

At eight she fixed a cup of tea and forced herself to eat a lobster salad prepared by the cook, who'd left for the day. She needed her strength, not only her wits. She had to be alert to Reno's every move, his expressions. Surprise was an important element that would work in their favor. She was counting on it.

When Josh arrived, she showed him the papers she'd readied and told him her plan. He was dubious but hopeful as he listened, looking handsome in his flannel shirt and khaki slacks. He'd brought the money, now all he wanted was to be rid of Teddy once and for all. They drove to the top of the Hill and parked off the road in the darkness. Above them, derrick lights winked like stars as they sat listening to the steady clamor of the pumps. When a set of headlights parked behind them, they got out and walked to the rear.

Rachel was dressed in riding pants, a dark jacket, and leather shoes with broad, flat heels. Her silky hair was pinned up to frame lightly blushed cheeks, and her full, sensuous lips colored red. Only her creased forehead showed determination as she undulated over the rough terrain. The earth was pitted and mounded. Rainy seasons made it a quagmire; summer baked it to rock hardness. Scraps of drilling pipe and litter were strewn about like forgotten toys, making the footing treacherous. There were no wells being drilled at present, but the rumbling pumps of old ones were silhouetted in the darkness. Rachel studied the shadowy figure approaching on foot. His step had lost some of its bounce and he seemed older. She could discern a paunch under his raincoat. His hair and beard were peppered white except for his black bushy eyebrows. His complexion looked creased and sick, as if he drank heavily. He gave her a mock salute.

"It's been a long time, Rachel. You look comfortable here amid your castles."

Rachel laughed derisively. "And you are reverting to character by resorting to blackmail. I had hoped never to see you again."

He clucked. "Those are harsh words from one with so much to lose. Or should I say two?" He glanced at Josh wryly. "But don't worry. I'll be on my way as soon as we settle this little matter of money."

"I told you once before that I wouldn't be blackmailed," Rachel said.

"That was your late husband's debt," he said. "This one is yours. Yours and his." He glanced at Josh with a cruel smile. He'd never met him, though he'd enjoy humiliating this kind of privileged scion of California nobility. Brown eyes, trim build, poised demeanor—a real prince. "Unless the two of you want your sordid little affair to be made public. You have a lot less to lose by paying me off. You have too many secrets, Rachel, too many."

She suppressed her loathing. "You can prove nothing."

"Maybe not, since your meetings take place behind sumptuous locked doors, but what I have will certainly stir up a lot of interest. A corporation that's picking the city's coffers? The prince and princess of Ocean Beach, pillars of the community, conducting love trysts in Los Angeles? The gossip columnists would love it. I have enough dates and times to lock up the front pages for weeks. Colorful real trash. I don't have to prove one damned thing to make a hell of a stink. Don't tempt me, Rachel. I'd give them what I have just for the pleasure of seeing you squirm."

"How do we know you won't do it even if we pay?" Rachel demanded.

Reno laughed and bowed. "My word as a gentleman," he mocked.

She snorted, aware of Josh's rising fear. "That's not enough," she said. "I'm taking steps to guarantee you won't be back."

He seemed amused, but there was a wariness in his voice. "What kind of steps?"

Rachel pulled the papers from her briefcase and gave them to him. He squinted at them in the pale glow of the rig lights. "They're copies," she told him. "The originals are in a safe place."

"What the hell are they?"

"Your IOUs to Mickey Carbello and a signed document in which he swears you killed Perry Kranzle."

His black eyebrows lifted in fear. "That's a lie! Where did you get these?"

"From Carbello. You took me to him yourself, have you forgotten?"

He trembled like an enraged bull. Rachel blessed the darkness that kept him from seeing her triumph.

"They're faked. There never were any such papers," he said.

"The originals are in an envelope in my lawyer's safe," she told him. "He has complete instructions for what to do with them in the event it becomes necessary. The police haven't closed the file on the Kranzle murder. I'm sure these would lead them to reopen the case. Do you have an alibi for the night of the murder after all this time?"

He glared at her, shaken to the core.

Her violet eyes blazed. "I thought not. When you read Carbello's statement, you'll see he swears you were gambling aboard the *Lucky Lady* that night. After Kranzle bought some of your markers, you went ashore with him. Later you came back with the markers. The police are going to wonder how you got them."

"You're crazy! I never had them! You're lying! You—" He sputtered out of control.

Rachel flashed him an icy smile. "Do you deny Carbello traded markers as a way of minimizing his own debts?"

"Carbello pulled out of here years ago. . . ."

"The police would undoubtedly be able to find him. I daresay he could hardly refuse to testify in a murder trial." She smelled his fear, and knew she would win. It didn't matter if Carbello had written these documents or she. Reno couldn't afford the gamble.

Breath hissing, Teddy said, "You're bluffing."

"Am I? How can you be sure? You took me aboard the *Lucky Lady* yourself. You were foolish enough to give your name to the hotel clerk when you came for me. I have the clerk's deposition. And the doctors who brought me back from the ship. I'm not a fool, Teddy. When I was forced to pay off Hillary's debt, I made sure I was rid of you once and for all. Actually, I found Carbello easy to deal with. His opinion of you was not any higher than mine."

Teddy's glance darted from one to the other. Events had turned unexpectedly, and he was frightened. Rachel felt no pity. She nodded to Josh, who reached for the money they'd brought despite her objection. Reno was scared enough to flee without it, but Josh insisted on a fair settlement before Reno departed.

Josh's sudden movement took Reno by surprise. He panicked like a startled jackrabbit. Before Josh could pull out the packet, Teddy lunged, grabbing him with a tackle that sent them both sprawling into the rutted road. Josh's breath *wooshed* as he hit the ground. Reno was on him like a tiger, pummeling as he tried to pin his arms.

"Bastard—!" Reno jammed a knee in Josh's groin. Josh moaned.

Rachel grabbed Teddy's coat and tried to wrench him off, but he swung backhand and sent her sprawling into a swishing heap. She was stunned by the impact. Her briefcase had been flung away, and dirt encrusted her clothing. Lights danced before her eyes as she tried to sit up. A pain stabbed her shoulder, and she winced. Teddy was straddling Josh, hands around his throat, pounding his head against the ground. Rachel crawled toward them, every breath searing her lungs. She tried to call out, but her voice only eeked a croak. Inching forward, her hand encountered a length of pipe. She lifted it, then swung with all her might. It struck Teddy's head with a sickening thud. He came up as though it had flagged his attention. When he tried to turn around, Rachel raised the pipe again and brought it down more sharply. Teddy crumpled. Josh pushed free quickly, his face mottled as he gasped for breath. Blood trickled down his split lip, and his face was already swelling from the pummeling he'd received.

Panting, Rachel crawled past Teddy to smooth Josh's ruffled black hair, now embedded with dirt. Her hand came away bloody. "Are you all right?"

He nodded painfully, extracting a handkerchief that he held to his head after wiping his lip. His dilated eyes went to Reno's sprawled form. He looked at Rachel fearfully. She stood and walked to Teddy. Was he unconscious or—? Trembling, she crouched down and, fighting nausea, forced herself to lean close to listen for his breathing. Only the steady *whump* of the pumps echoed in the darkness. Even in the gloom she saw the bloody gouge on Reno's skull. Blood trickled along his face in grotesque patterns. She started to back away, then remembered the papers. She searched until she found them, stuffing them in the pocket of her jacket before she went back to Josh.

He looked at her. "Is he—?"

"I think so. I had to stop him, Josh. . . ." She glanced back at the still, dark form. "What'll we do?"

Josh touched his head gingerly. "Give me a minute." He squeezed his eyes shut as he pressed the handkerchief to his temple. The pumps droned a steady low throb that seemed to say, "Mur—der . . . mur—der . . . mur—der . . ." Rachel clenched her fists so tightly the fingers went numb.

When Josh looked up, he whispered, "We'll leave him where he is."

"We can't—"

"We must. He'll be found in the morning, there's nothing we can do about it. It's less risky than trying to move him. We need time." He glanced at the sprawled body again. "Check his pockets."

Rachel shuddered as she methodically fished through

Teddy's coat and trousers, collecting his wallet, car keys, and a hotel key which she handed to Josh. "That's all," she murmured, feeling repulsion pulse through her.

Josh examined the hotel key. "The Waterside," he said. It was an old, cheap hotel in a section of town due for renewal. "I'll have to check it out." When he tried to get up, Rachel took his arm, helping him and holding on until she was sure he was steady on his feet. They walked slowly to the car. Instead of getting in, Josh put Rachel behind the wheel. "I'll have to get rid of his car. I'll park it down by the beach. Follow and retrieve me."

At Rachel's house Josh bathed in the sunken tub of her upstairs suite of rooms. A dark bruise colored one cheek, and his lip was puffy. Rachel cleaned the gash on the back of his head, but he refused to let her bandage it. It would be less noticeable the way it was. She brushed and sponged his suit so it would pass casual inspection.

When he left, she bathed and wrapped herself in a silken Japanese robe, then sat by the phone waiting for his call. When it came, she almost leaped from the chair.

"Yes?"

"It's okay," Josh said.

"You found—"

"He had a list, nothing more."

She thought about her own pretense about papers in safe-keeping with a lawyer. Had Teddy—?

"I think he was bluffing," Josh said. "It was all suspicion, nothing more."

"Can we be sure?"

He sighed. "We have no other choice. Rest well, Rachel, I'll talk to you soon."

"Yes, soon. . . ." She was frightened to be alone and longed for the comfort of his arms. They had taken so many risks. They needed to be together.

In bed she lay staring in the dark. She had killed a man. No matter how much she hated Teddy Reno, she had not meant to kill him. It was an accident because she was trying to help Josh. Teddy was a madman. His deranged mind imagined Josh reaching for a weapon. The irony of it . . . they were going to pay him! The faked papers were meant to ensure his silence, no more. The ruse had worked too well . . . and now she was a murderer.

Worse . . . she remembered Ruth's undiscovered body. With huge wracking sobs, Rachel for the first time in years began to cry.

The phone shrilled. She reached for it groggily. Her head ached and her eyes were swollen. "Yes?"

"Good morning, Mrs. Upfield. This is Bernadette at the office. Mr. Caffrey is here and wonders if you've forgotten your appointment with him."

Rachel looked at the clock and was astonished to see it was almost ten. She swung her feet out of bed. "Give him my apologies. Something unexpected has come up. If he can't wait, I'll meet him any time that's convenient. I'll hold."

How could she have overslept? It was essential now of all times that everything seem normal. Had Teddy's body been found? At least there were no police waiting at the office to question her.

Bernadette returned to say Caffrey would wait. Rachel promised less than half an hour. She was on her way to the shower the moment she hung up. She was never late for appointments, especially clients like Caffrey. Should she invent an excuse or let the matter drop? She was as nervous as a cat. She snapped on the bedroom radio while she dressed, but there was no newscast. She listened to the car radio as she drove. Still nothing.

She went through the day mechanically, talking to people, seeing to correspondence, stopping at the hotel as she always did. Every time she could she listened to the news stations. When it came finally, it was not how she expected.

The night clerk, a heavyset man with a mustache, came to her suite at six o'clock to tell her he'd seen an ambulance and police cars at the Plaza Apartments on his way to work. Knowing the Fantazias had been at the victory party two days before, he'd stopped to ask what the commotion was about. People milled all over the lawns and in the courtyard, and a passing resident had leaned into his car to explain. Josh Fantazia had found his daughter dead in her apartment.

Rachel thanked him numbly. The man, grim at having to convey the news, bowed and left.

Rachel sat unable to move. No tears came. It was too late for that. She'd committed herself to a silence that could not be broken. Josh . . . Josh . . . Her pain matched what he was suffering now. And she could offer no comfort.

There was still no news of the discovery of Teddy Reno's body. She dared not make inquiries. Did it matter? Did anything matter now? Josh . . . Josh . . . her mind wailed.

Ruth's funeral was private. The family requested donations to the Heart Fund in lieu of flowers. Rachel sent fifteen thousand dollars in her and Irena's name. She did not see or hear from Josh, which was understandable, though hard to bear. Josh and Collette left the day after the funeral for an undisclosed destination. They told the newspapers they needed a place to mourn privately.

Every day Rachel scrutinized the *Press-Telegram* for mention of Teddy's body or Josh's destination. After a week she gave up. With the constant activity on the Hill, Reno could not have gone undiscovered. The only possible explanation was that his corpse had been written off as an unexplained death. A transient, killed in one of the brawls that frequently took place among the hard-drinking roustabouts on the rigs. Teddy had no identification. If he'd been traced to the Waterside, the squalid room would confirm his itinerant existence. Ocean Beach police had more important matters to fill their time, and the *Press-Telegram* had more important news to cover.

Three days after Ruth's funeral, Rachel received a call from the spa in Palm Springs. Irena had walked out and not returned. Rachel asked that the final bill be sent to her. She did not try to trace Irena's whereabouts.

She threw herself into work until gradually the aching pain receded. Even the horrible memories began to blur, and she was left with only the memory of the pain. Upfield Land Management was engrossed in a number of major projects. The war's end pushed construction into high gear. Housing boomed. Commercial enterprises had prospered during the war years due to an economy bolstered by servicemen and war contracts.

Fantazia Enterprises was in the hands of Judson Fantazia, Josh's son. Judson, who had his father's dark hair and complexion, though he was slighter in build, was well trained but lacked his father's fire. He viewed projects unemotionally and logically. Rachel quickly discovered this gave her an edge in winning contracts that would have gone to Josh before.

Though she was forced to accept his absence, she thought of him often and worried she might never see him again. Periodically, tidbits emblazoned the paper; the Fantazias were cruising the Caribbean; they had sailed for Europe; they were in residence in Palm Desert, the newest California enclave of the wealthy.

She accepted the separation from Irena far more easily. It was a relief not to have her stirring up dissent and scandal. Irena called or wrote occasionally; the purpose was always the same: to ask for money. Rachel wired funds to Denver, Chicago, New York, and the Bahamas.

❧ *Eleven* ❧

BY 1949 THE City of Ocean Beach had netted millions of
dollars from drilling in the Harbor District. Money from tidelands oil had also swollen city coffers; the harbor bustled with
activity. Channels were dredged, docks and wharves built; the
never-ceasing sound of construction beat to the rhythms of a
city on the move.

Litigations by the state on tideland claims were a small
cloud on the horizon. Tideland millions were impounded until
a U.S. Supreme Court decision giving the Navy paramount
rights along the shore could be cleared. Congress had passed a
bill quitclaiming the tidelands, but it had been vetoed by President Truman. When a second bill was also vetoed, Rachel
followed the news with interest. She was positive the quit-
claim would indeed come before too long. The drilling sites in
question were city-owned, but the entire waterfront came
under scrutiny and made her uneasy. She had lots bordering
municipal land, and she set about selling them off quietly and
discreetly. Those she and Josh owned through the Fielding
Corporation were, according to Garson Perkins's assurances,
untraceable.

Without Josh to keep her informed, Rachel took an active
interest in politics and the urban climate. She cultivated politi-
cians whose platforms included using tidelands money, when

it was freed, for general and worthy purposes. The prosperity of the Oceanside Hotel was linked closely with that of the downtown area, and she encouraged redevelopment. The City of Ocean Beach had made her a wealthy woman; it was time to repay the community in some measure. Another factor spurring her on was boredom. She was restless and eager for new challenges. The real estate and construction divisions of Upfield ran smoothly. The hotel no longer required anything more than general supervision. Its excellent staff maintained the high caliber of service she demanded. She paid for, and got, the very best. The hotel's reputation continued to soar, becoming a West Coast shrine for the wealthy who wanted ocean scenery, excellent sumptuous surroundings, food, and closeness to Los Angeles, without being directly on top of it.

So Rachel decided it was time to become active in the cultural growth of the city. She'd always been a member of various groups and had financed worthy projects. Now she decided to expand the construction end of Upfield Land Management into an arena controlled for years by the Fantazias: civic and cultural buildings.

She hired young, forward-looking architects who would depart from the Victorian buildings of the past and the boxlike efficiency of the war era. The only guideline she set was that their designs fuse Ocean Beach's elegant past with its sparkling future. Within months, Upfield won contracts for a small art museum and an addition to the state college. Even though the jobs were not large, she considered them a major triumph. Upfield had a foot in the door; it was only a matter of time before its reputation surpassed Fantazia's. She wondered if word would reach Josh, if he cared any longer.

She thought about him often, but the painful memories had begun to fade. It was as though she'd always known they would be apart someday and was prepared for it. From time to time she heard mention of him and Collette or read an item in the *Press-Telegram* or the *Los Angeles Times,* but they never returned to Ocean Beach or to the Rancho. It was as though they had divorced themselves completely from the specter of Ruth.

Rachel found the ultramodern manor house on Ladera Street lonely. She no longer took pleasure in clinging close to the Hill, and she spent more and more time in her lush penthouse suite at the hotel. The hotel rose fifteen stories and was one of the highest buildings in post-war Ocean Beach, though even taller ones were rising here and there farther downtown. It was closer to the office, which was the pulse of her life. She went to the house several times a week, checking in on the full-time housekeeper, as well as the gardener and a staff of daily servants who kept the house clean.

The opening of the art museum created a newsworthy stir. The Women's City Club, Junior League, chamber of commerce, Art League, Ebel Temple, and countless private individuals supported the effort fully. The grand opening was a spectacle composed of the elite, wealthy, artistic, and curious, as well as the press, who covered the event thoroughly. Present were the wire services, radio, television, and two national magazines. The building looked dramatic, as it curved around sea and shore and gave a feeling of freedom. Art critics called it magnificent. Architectural critics dubbed it "a stunning new concept in dimension." Ocean Beach officials declared it the dawn of a new era in modern city planning.

Rachel was interviewed and her picture appeared on printed pages and television screens throughout the country. One of the networks covered the Art Ball which followed the opening. Rachel had donated the facilities of the Oceanside for the event so that all the proceeds could go to an art acquisition fund. Midway through the evening the mayor mounted the dais and the band struck up a chord. When the room quieted, he expressed the city's appreciation to the woman who had made it all possible. He called Rachel to stand beside him and presented her with a plaque naming her Ocean Beach's first Woman of the Year.

Rachel made a very brief speech of thanks, then retired to the sidelines, looking stunning in her scarlet Schiaparelli gown. A bevy of well-wishers crowded around her. Rachel accepted congratulations graciously but commanded the band to resume playing. Gradually people drifted back onto the dance floor and toward the buffet tables. Rachel escaped to the terrace.

"Hello, mother."

Rachel saw a figure in the shadows beneath the tall palms that had been potted into the terrazzo floor. Irena was dressed in soft green chiffon that flowed in loose lines from the shoulders to her knees, with a wispy scarf tied at the neck. Dressy, but not formal. More appropriate for an afternoon garden party than a ball, but she would not jar anyone's aesthetic sensibilities if she went inside. She looked like a young beauty—but without her mother's ravishing sophistication. Her light hair was different, longer and with soft bangs across her forehead. The effect was striking but did little to mature her.

"Hello, Irena."

"You don't seem terribly pleased to see me," she said bluntly.

Rachel shrugged, her long hands clasped. "Surprised, perhaps. You have a way of turning up at odd times for your own convenience."

Irena's blue eyes flashed, her gaze shifting to the ballroom. "Are you afraid I'll embarrass you in front of your guests? Has the city of Ocean Beach forgotten that you have a wayward daughter?"

Rachel ignored the taunt. "What brings you back?"

"We were in L.A. and I heard about you on the radio," Irena said. "I thought it would be interesting to come down and say hello. I hoped you might be glad to see me."

"I'm always glad to see you. Will you be staying at the house?"

"Is that an invitation?"

Rachel couldn't quite put her finger on what bothered her about Irena's attitude. It was neither friendly nor hostile, but something in between. It wasn't like Irena to concern herself with amenities. Perhaps she was growing up after all.

Rachel smiled. "You don't need an invitation in your own home. I'll call Mrs. Dryer and ask her to expect you."

"There are two of us." Irena's gaze flickered momentarily in defiance.

Rachel waited silently for her daughter's explanation. She's nervous, Rachel thought. *I wonder who's with her. A man, that's for certain.*

"I'm married, mother."

"Married?" Rachel couldn't hide her astonishment. It was not what she expected. A boyfriend, perhaps, some hanger-on who dogged Irena's sexy heels. But a husband? "When did this happen?"

Irena lifted her chin. "Two months ago."

"And this is the first you thought to tell me?"

Irena laughed harshly. "Would you have sent twelve settings of sterling or a silver punch bowl?"

Rachel studied the bitter lines curving around Irena's mouth. Why couldn't they get along? She was tired of constant bickering and trouble.

"I'm not sure what I'd have done, but now that you're here, I offer my congratulations. I look forward to meeting your husband."

Irena's gaze roved behind her. "He'll be here any minute. He went to park the car."

Rachel wondered why he hadn't used the valet parking service. She prayed he was presentable. Judging from Irena's gown, she kept herself well dressed. The sound of footsteps relieved them of further small talk. Irena turned to watch the man coming toward them, fingering one end of the chiffon scarf nervously as she smiled.

He was medium height—not much taller than his wife—and strongly built. Brawny was the word that came to mind. He was tanned, and had chestnut hair and black eyes the color of oil. He was ruggedly handsome, like an unfinished sculpture. He was wearing a nondescript gray suit that was poorly tailored and had undoubtedly come from a store rack. If he was uncomfortable under Rachel's scrutiny, he didn't show it. He looked at her appraisingly, as if comparing her against an image he'd already formed.

"This is my mother, Drew."

He bowed his head. "Howdo." His voice was deep.

"Drew—?" Rachel pointedly indicated she required another name to go with it.

"Hamilton."

She stretched out a long sensuous hand, which the other grasped firmly. "Irena has surprised me. I offer my congratulations, late as they are. Are you from this area, Mr. Hamilton?" She would not call him Drew as though he were already an accepted member of the family. Where had Irena met him?

"I've been around six-seven years." He glanced at Irena, wanting her to take up the slack in conversation.

She said quickly, "Mother has invited us to stay at the house. Isn't that wonderful?"

Rachel couldn't read his expression, but she had the feeling he hadn't expected the invitation. Or perhaps not wanted it. He pocketed his hands and looked around uncomfortably as if searching for an escape route.

"If it suits your plans," she said, hiding her irritation. "Do you intend to stay in Ocean Beach long?"

"Depends."

"Drew's looking for a job," Irena said. "I told him this was the place to get one. This town's booming again."

"What do you do?" Rachel asked.

He stopped his perusal of the terrace and looked at her squarely, as if this part in the conversation intrigued him. "Oil. I work the rigs."

A thought flashed through Rachel. Oil-field trash . . . That's what she'd seen in him. Animal sexuality, the earthiness of a man who pitted himself against the land. He looked ill at ease in the gray suit because he probably had been forced into it. He was the type who had only one, and it was stored away in some attic for weddings and funerals. And for the grand introductory performance staged before his wife's mother.

Rachel nodded. "There are enough of them about if a man's willing to work. I'll have a word with Johnny Brinks on the Parker Number Four."

His mouth twitched. "Thanks, but I'll do my own talking."

"Drew," Irena said in an admonishing and pained voice. Irena cast down her glance when her husband shot her an angry look.

Rachel smiled in her feline cat way. "I admire a man who knows the value of making his own way. Or a woman." She didn't look at Irena, but she hoped the remark struck home. It was refreshing to think that Irena might have met her match and married him. Rachel began to feel a grudging respect for this stray that Irena had brought home. "Shall we join the party? Unless you're tired after your drive. . . ."

"We'd love to!" Irena locked arms with Drew so he couldn't bolt. He looked as if he were being led to his execution. Rachel wondered if he had ever been at a formal ball before. Irena was tactless and cruel to expose him to the stares of the high couture-fashioned crowd inside. There was no way the man wouldn't suffer by comparison. The women dripped with sequined gowns and jewels; the men wore glistening formal wear. Well, he'd married Irena. Sooner or later he'd learn for himself what she was like. Rachel led the way inside; at least she wouldn't embarrass herself or Drew by introducing the newlyweds publicly. She glanced at Drew. He was uncomfortable under the chandelier lights, the reporters' eyes, but

determined. She supposed he'd promised Irena this introductory overture to home and family and would see it through. At
least he wasn't a fawning gold digger looking to exploit the
Upfield millions.

Irena saw that the glittering perfection of the ballroom had
not changed. It was as dazzling as it had been on V-J Day.
The huge crystal chandelier glowed with hundreds of lights
that sent rainbows dancing on the walls and made the
women's gowns shimmer like precious metals. When Drew
hesitated, she tugged him insistently away from Rachel.
Thank God the first confrontation was over. Sparks but no
explosions. She was anxious to get away before Drew reacted
to Rachel's obvious snobbery. She led him toward the buffet
tables.

"Let's get out of here," Drew said in a harsh whisper.

"You promised—"

"I've met your mother. That's enough." He glanced at the
men in formal attire.

"A few minutes won't kill us," she said defiantly. "Besides, I'm starved." She wouldn't let go of his arm. A white-
jacketed waiter with a tray of champagne glasses stopped.
Taking a glass, Irena shot Drew a meaningful look. He took
one and bolted it down like a shot of whiskey.

At the buffet she filled a plate with cold shrimp, caviar,
and open-faced sandwiches. Drew put a few things on his
plate mechanically. When they found an uncrowded spot, he
ate without appetite.

"Pretend you're enjoying yourself," Irena said petulantly.

"Why?"

"You're impossible! Can't you get it through your head
we're broke and hungry? My God, at least we have a bed to
sleep in tonight and full bellies if you stop being so pig-
headed."

"I don't like sponging."

"We're not taking anything that doesn't belong to
me—us." She whisked off another glass of champagne from a
silver tray as a waiter came by.

Drew finished the food and set the plate aside. Coming
here had been Irena's idea, and he liked it less now than when
she had first suggested it. He'd heard and read enough about
Rachel Upfield to know he didn't want any part of her bejew-
eled and gilt-dazzling world. Except Irena. He wondered if he

would have fallen in love with her if he'd known she came
from this. They'd met in a Texas bar frequented by oil riggers.
Irena stood out from the women who were casually bought for
a few drinks. His buddies jokingly called her the Ice Princess,
bone-certain she'd freeze them out when she tired of slum-
ming. Irena thawed as she and Drew danced and later walked
under the Texas stars to unfog their blurry heads. She'd done
more than thaw when he took her back to the hotel. Before the
week was out, he knew he loved her. They were married on
the second-week anniversary of the day they met.

He never made the connection to *the* Upfields until she
began talking about her mother.

Anyone whoever smelled oil knew the name Upfield. Rachel Upfield was Mother Oil. And Mother Money. He put his
foot down when he found out Irena got checks from the old
lady. He had no idea she was such a stunner for her age. Even
so, his wife was going to live on his income, dammit. A few
months into their marriage they had their first big blowout,
and Irena walked out for two days. He'd been frantic, but
when she came back, he was so relieved and glad to see her,
he didn't mention the checks again. He fooled himself into
thinking they'd ceased until Irena showed up with a dozen
new dresses or shoes that sure as hell didn't come out of his
budget. When his contract at the well ended, she demanded a
honeymoon before he signed on again. Mexico City, Aca-
pulco, Los Angeles. Their cash ran out. It was time to get
back to work. Ocean Beach. He wouldn't have any trouble
getting work in a city whose lifeline was oil, so he'd agreed to
meet her mother. He hadn't counted on staying at the Upfield
house or barging into a party at the Oceanside. Thank God,
Irena hadn't arranged for them to stay here. He felt as if he'd
stumbled into the queen's chambers.

The way Irena talked, she never liked being a feature of her
mother's world; she'd run as far from it as possible. Now he
wasn't so sure. He glanced sidelong. There was a hungriness
in her eyes, as if she'd been longing for excitement and glamour. Had he read her wrong? Was this where she belonged?
She said she hated her mother and everything she represented.
That was easy to believe when she told him she hadn't seen
her mother for five years and didn't care if she ever did. But
now. . .

"Let's dance," Irena said, setting her empty plate on a table and wiping her hands on a cocktail napkin.

"Uh-uh."

"Come on . . ." She tried to pull him onto the floor, but he wouldn't budge.

"No way I'm going out there looking like a skid row bum among the uptowners."

"You look fine!"

He laughed. "Sure. The waiter didn't know whether to give me champagne or a broom to sweep up other people's crumbs. Let's get out of here. We'll find a bar that's got music."

Her eyes flashed, then she grinned. "Okay. But let's make it an early night. We'll go home and climb into the sack so I can give you an official welcome to Ocean Beach."

His black eyes glinted. "Now you're talking. Do we have to say good-bye to the duchess?"

"The hell with her. Let's go."

Rachel received a daily report from Mrs. Dryer, but she never got time to visit the house. She hadn't made up her mind about Drew Hamilton. He was coal among diamonds, but there was always the possibility that he could be polished. Not to a high gloss, but buffed enough so he'd be presentable. She also realized her growing admiration. Mrs. Dryer reported that he had gone out the first morning and been hired at the Padres Number One. The Padres was a new well tapped by Standard on land Rachel had leased them. She wondered if Drew would have taken the job had he known. She was amused by his refusing her recommendation of Johnny Brinks at the Parker well. Drew Hamilton was proving to be his own man.

According to Mrs. Dryer, Drew was off each morning before Irena stirred. When she got up, Irena lazed or drove Rachel's Buick into town. Drew walked up the Hill to the drilling site; his delapidated Ford stayed parked in the garage unless they went out in the evening. He refused to drive or ride in Rachel's car. He didn't like Irena doing it, but when he wasn't there, she did as she pleased.

Rachel didn't encourage Mrs. Dryer to spy on the young couple, but neither did she turn a deaf ear to the reports Mrs. Dryer gave. The arguments Irena and Drew had were usually loud enough to be heard by the servants, if not the neighbors. *He* wanted to take an apartment in town. *She* insisted there

was no need to waste money on some hovel when they had
Rachel's house and all its amenities at their disposal. It was
typically Irena, lazy and easily bored. Rachel pitied Drew,
who was probably in for a rude awakening when he found out
what Irena was really like. But if he didn't find a way to
handle her, the marriage was doomed.

One evening, when Irena and Drew had been there two
weeks, Rachel received a frantic call from Mrs. Dryer.

"Holy Mother of God, they're going to kill each other!
You've got to do something!"

The housekeeper babbled on. Rachel heard shouting and an
occasional ominous crash in the background.

"Saints preserve us—you've got to come, Mrs. Upfield!"
Mrs. Dryer broke off with a small yelp as a thunderous crash
was followed by the tinkling sound of glass breaking.

"I'll be there."

The house was ablaze with lights. Noise reached her ears
as she turned into the long curved driveway. Rachel stormed
up the steps. Mrs. Dryer hurried from the back hall, wringing
her hands.

"It's worse," she moaned. Her eyes rolled as another crash
and a high-pitched scream from Irena pierced the air. "I sent
Higgins up, but she threw a clock at him. The language, oh,
my..." The housekeeper wagged her head as though she'd
glimpsed perdition.

Rachel marched up the elegant, gleaming mahogany spiral
steps. Her footfalls were soundless on the thick hall carpet as
she approached the battle. Irena and Drew had taken Irena's
old suite of rooms, equipped with adjoining bath and sitting
room. The suite occupied a back corner of the house and faced
the foot of the Hill and city beyond.

The suite looked as though a major earthquake had hit. The
tabletops and mantel had been swept of ornaments by Irena's
anger. They lay shattered on the pink carpet: a Royal Copen-
hagen figurine, a Lenox vase, a teacup and saucer of ugly
pearlescent glass that Irena had treasured since winning it on
the Pike.

A badly dented and glass-cracked clock lay near the door
below a gouge in the wall. The bouquet of red roses which
Mrs. Dryer arranged each day was scattered amid the mess
like bloody footprints.

From the bedroom Irena's voice shrilled. "Jackass! Stubborn and stupid! You can't tell me what to do! I'm not your slave!"

There was a thud as another missile struck the wall. Drew cursed, and something whizzed past the open door. Irena yelped with pain.

"I wish I had never laid eyes on you! Damn screwing bastard! Just because you're hung like a horse you think you're so damned hot! Well, I've had better fucking from drunken sailors who couldn't find their—"

"Irena!" Rachel's voice rang above her daughter's hysterical screams. Irena spun about, one hand clutching a silver-backed mirror from the dresser set. Her hair was disheveled, her skirt twisted off center, and the buttons of her blouse ripped open, exposing her heaving breasts. "Put that down this instant!" Rachel's gaze impaled Irena until her hand finally lowered. The mother and daughter faced each other in a contest of wills. Irena's eyes blazed and she breathed like a spooked cat, ready to do battle with anyone who crossed her path. They were both beautiful specimens, though Irena's blondish beauty looked askew and deranged.

"You are making a spectacle of yourself," Rachel said angrily. "If you can't settle your domestic problems without wrecking the house, I'll have to ask you to leave."

Irena's tiny nostrils flared. "It's my house, too!"

"Only by my suffrance, young lady!" Rachel imagined she heard a chuckle from the direction of the bathroom, where Drew had taken refuge.

"Half of everything is mine! I was too young to fight you when my father died, but you can't cheat me out of my share!" She glanced toward the bathroom as Drew's chestnut-haired head poked out; without hesitation she heaved the mirror. It struck the doorjamb and glass showered on the tile and carpet. Drew's head vanished.

"You're being a fool, Irena. Stop it this instant!" Rachel cried. She grabbed Irena's wrist as she reached for another missile. "Stop it!"

Irena was no physical match for Rachel. In the past, Irena had used her rapier tongue to defend or attack, and relied on a sluggish indifference when these failed. Now she struggled with the desire to strike her mother. Rachel read the rage clearly. She let go of Irena's hand and locked gazes until Irena finally put down the hairbrush.

"Come out, Drew," Rachel ordered.

Drew came but didn't approach Irena. He was laughing silently. Rachel's fury mounted. "I do not find any of this amusing," she said.

His laughter became audible. "I suppose not," he admitted. "I wouldn't like it if a little spitfire hellion wrecked my house. Ain't she something?"

Was he out of his mind? Where was that bravado when he was hiding in the bathroom? "Your energy might have been put to better use preventing this—destruction!"

He grinned. "I learned a long time ago, ma'am, sometimes it's better to back away from a fight. Irena wasn't exactly listening to reason. I wouldn't want to clout her, even though she deserves it, God knows. I've never hit a woman. So it seems smarter just to get out of range. I knew she'd calm down eventually or run out of ammunition."

Rachel was too astonished to argue. She wondered what kind of man Drew Hamilton was. Her respect for him was in danger of eroding. But even more amazing was Irena's quiet acceptance of his little speech. The fight was drained from her, and she looked almost contrite. Was it possible that Drew had discovered the secret of handling her fits?

Rachel glanced around. "It will take a full day's cleaning to make this room habitable again. I'll have Mrs. Dryer make up one of the guest rooms for the night."

"That won't be necessary, Mrs. Upfield." When Rachel gave him a questioning glance, Drew grinned. "That's what we were . . . ah, discussing when you came in. I rented us an apartment today. I put down a month's rent so's we can move right in. Irena thought maybe we should stay on here a while, but I think she's gotten over that notion now."

"I see." Rachel watched Irena, who said nothing. She was submitting like a kitten. Astounding. "Very well. If you need any help packing, Mrs. Dryer will see to it. Of course, you're welcome to move your things out at your leisure."

"Thank you, ma'am," he said formally. "I think it's best we take it all now, and not put temptation in Irena's path, so to speak."

"I'm sure everything will work out for the best. Please leave an address in case—"

Irena shot her mother a glance filled with venom. Rachel didn't bother to finish the thought.

"I'll leave you to your packing." She went out, still marveling at the way Drew had handled Irena.

She was sipping a glass of sherry in the sitting room when Higgins brought down the bags. Irena went out without a word. Drew paused in the doorway.

"Thank you for your hospitality, Mrs. Upfield. Maybe when Irena's had a chance to think it over, she'll call."

Certainly when no allowance check was deposited in her account, Rachel thought. While she'd been sitting there, she'd decided to give this strange young man a chance to tame the shrew in his wife.

"Good luck," she said without malice.

He smiled and went out. A few minutes later she heard the sputtering cough of the Ford as it motored down the drive.

Drew left Irena to her own thoughts until they neared Fourth Street, where he'd rented the apartment. Then he tried to coax her back to good humor.

"It's not a bad place. The landlord says it was a nice address a few years back. And the apartment's freshly painted. In a month or two we can get rid of the furniture that's there and buy some stuff of our own."

She gave a noncommittal shrug and took out a compact to inspect her lipstick. She didn't look up until he slowed. They were on a block of older buildings. The apartment he had selected was plush enough—a two-bedroom completely refurbished and carpeted. The furniture was serviceable but not so comfortable that Irena couldn't replace them with some of the antiques she insisted were hers.

Irena studied the facades as Drew searched for the number. She felt a clutch of terror as he pulled to the curb in front of an arched entrance to an apartment court.

"This is it." Drew shut off the engine. "Come on." He jumped out of the car and strode to her side. Irena sat frozen as he took her arm. She shivered and her lips trembled. He started toward the court, but she hung back, her face pale.

"Hey, come on. Give it a chance. You'll see—"

"No!" She tried to free her arm.

He tightened his grip. "Damn it, let's not start again." He scowled as he saw the terrified look on her face. "What's the matter?"

She shook her head dumbly as tears filled her eyes.

"Jesus, do I have to pick you up and haul your ass in there? The rent's paid and this is where we're staying. I'm telling you, it's not bad. It's a hell of a lot nicer than that place I had in Texarkana. You didn't have any objections to sleeping in my bed there!" He was tired and angry. Why the hell did she have to act like a damned kid whenever she didn't get her own way? He headed for the entry, dragging her along. He'd get the bags later. Right now he needed a drink. He'd bought a bottle and some soda when the landlord gave him the key.

She was practically dead weight, though her feet kept moving. For a minute he thought she was going to balk again when they started down the second-floor corridor. She was whimpering when they reached the door of the apartment. Still holding her arm, he fished for the key. He pushed her inside as he flicked the light switch.

Irena's gaze darted around the room. Then she gave a pitiful moan and collapsed at Drew's feet.

He knelt beside her quickly. "Irena—" Her hands were cold as ice and there wasn't a drop of color in her face. He chafed her wrist and slapped her face gently. "Hey, baby—what happened? What's the matter?" Her eyelids fluttered. "Irena . . . Irena . . ." His voice was soft and tender, his anger gone. She opened her eyes. He gave a tentative smile. "You okay? Want some water?"

She shook her head. He put an arm around her and helped her sit up. "Come on, I'll help you into a chair."

"No!" Panic filled her eyes.

"Okay, okay, take it easy." He watched her with a worried frown. He'd never seen her like this. After a time her breathing became regular and there was a touch of pink in her face. It gave her even, delicate beauty a healthy glow. "Come on, beautiful, you feeling better?"

She nodded, but he wasn't convinced. "You should rest. A good night's sleep is what you need. Okay?"

Her head moved again like a slow-motion gypsy fortune-teller in an arcade machine. He scooped her into his arms and carried her to the bedroom. She gave another convulsive shiver and hid her face in his shirt. When he put her on the bed, she lay with her eyes closed.

"I'll get you a drink."

He came back with the bottle and a glass. He sat beside her and lifted her head. "Drink, baby."

She drank obediently, gulping the whiskey in two swallows. He poured again. When she finished the second shot, he set her head back, her blond curls spilling over the pillow. Her color was better. She was coming out of it. He was curious as hell, but this wasn't the time to ask questions that might throw her off balance again. He sat beside her until her breathing fell into a regular pattern of sleep. Then, as gently as he could, he pulled off her shoes and stockings and got her under the covers. When he was sure she wouldn't wake, he went down to the car and brought up the suitcases.

In the morning Irena's head ached and she stared at the gray ceiling in confusion. All too quickly she recalled where she was and bolted up in bed. In front of her the closet door gaped open, revealing a few wire hangers on the rod and a piece of torn shelf paper. She leaped out of bed, angry, and slammed the closet door, then ran out of the room. She stopped in her tracks in the living room.

"Oh, God!" She covered her face and tried to blot out the image of Ruth's body sprawled in the chair by the window. Of all the apartments in the whole goddam city, how could Drew pick this one?! She sobbed until her stomach began to heave, then gulped hard and fast so she wouldn't have to run to the bathroom. For five years she had blacked out the images that burned in her brain. Now they flooded through, drowning her in an inky black quagmire.

When she could finally move, she walked to the kitchen in a daze. Without interest she read the note Drew had propped on the table:

> *Take it easy today, baby. You scared the hell out of me last night. I bought coffee, eggs, and bread. Make sure you eat. I'll try to get off early. Love, Drew.*

She opened the fully stocked refrigerator, the cupboards filled with colorful porcelain dishes. In one next to the sink she found the bottle of whiskey. Drew had rinsed her glass and left it on the drainboard, along with his breakfast dishes. She picked it up and carried it with the bottle to the living room. She sat on the couch and poured the glass full. Drinking slowly, she fixed her gaze on the armchair near the window.

It's just a chair, she told herself. She wasn't even sure it was the same one. It couldn't be. Maybe she should tell Drew —tell him what? That she killed her best friend? That she let her mother hide her terrible secret so the world wouldn't know the truth about her?

The glass was empty. She filled it again. Drew wouldn't understand. Nobody would. She hadn't meant to kill Ruth any more than she'd meant to screw on that closet floor with— what the hell was his name? She didn't even remember any more. Screwing with Sailor No-name.

She wiped the tears rolling down her cheeks. Why did Rachel have to be the one who knew? Why had she called Rachel that night? She filled the glass again and tried to solve the conundrum. Rachel hated her. Rachel hated her because she knew about Ruth. No, Rachel hated her long before that. Daddy knew it. Daddy tried to make believe Rachel didn't do spiteful, cruel things. Like forgetting to take her to Los Angeles when she promised. Daddy pretended, but Irena knew.

Whiskey trickled down her chin as she raised the glass unsteadily. Daddy knew. Daddy loved her. Another trapdoor swung open, and Irena heard the roar of the earthquake inside her head, felt the terrible tremble of the building, saw the plaster clatter with a crash to the floor, the wood beams begin to splinter.

"Daddy—Daddy!"

It was a piteous sob as once again she heard the wall collapse, knew her father clutched for anything to halt his momentum as he cried out her name, knew he disappeared into a cloud of dust and bricks.

"Daddy." It was a whisper.

Crying, she refilled the glass.

❦ *Twelve* ❧

DREW SAT IN the parked car staring at the Upfield Building. In two months he'd heard enough about his mother-in-law to know she was highly respected even if she wasn't always liked. Some idolized her. To them she was strong, brilliant, a leader. Others found her ruthless in her dealings. He supposed your reaction depended on which end you were on. But any way you looked at it, she'd earned the right to carve her name in stone over a doorway.

He got out and entered the lobby, looking around like a country rube at the marble and gleaming brass. He studied the roster of tenants. Upfield Land Management had the top three floors. He stabbed the elevator button.

Maybe he should have gone by the apartment and changed into his suit, but Irena would have wanted to know where he was going. He brushed the front of his windbreaker as the elevator hummed to a stop.

He uttered his name to a pretty, rouged receptionist sitting behind a desk in a lushly carpeted room the size of their apartment. The girl fluttered her blue eyes at him as she spoke into a phone. A moment later she looked disappointed as a secretary shepherded him into Rachel's office.

Rachel did not rise. "Hello, Drew. Would you like coffee?"

He eased into a sumptuous Dakota leather chair, shaking his head. He hadn't seen Rachel since the night he and Irena had moved out. He hadn't even talked to her until today. She agreed to see him and made an appointment the same as she would for some client. If she was curious about his reason for calling, she wasn't letting it show.

She was sitting behind a huge lacquered redwood desk. It was strewn with papers, in rough piles. The room looked out over a terrace, with French glass doors leading to it. The room was furnished with a mix of classical styles, but what startled Drew was the astonishing variety of pieces—tables of different heights in the corners encircled by chairs; there was a black lacquered chaise longue of striking geometric design. Clay and metal sculptures, modern and nineteenth century, graced the tables, and the room was lined with ceiling-high bookshelves. He wondered where Rachel got the time to read, if she did. Was it just decor? She was smart. Very.

"I know you're busy, so I won't take much of your time, Mrs. Upfield. I wouldn't come except I don't know what to do. You're her mother. Maybe you can help."

Rachel frowned. "Is something wrong with Irena?"

"She's really down. I've never seen her like this."

"Down? In what way?"

"Sad, miserable, I dunno—lost." He shrugged his broad shoulders. "She isn't eating or sleeping right. She mopes around and doesn't go out unless I force her to. A couple of times I dragged her to a movie, but she didn't even know what unreeled before her." He looked at his calloused hands and rubbed at a grimy knuckle.

Rachel arched a slim black eyebrow. "Has she seen a doctor?"

He shook his head. "She won't go. She says she's fine." He looked at Rachel to study her reaction. "She should. See a doctor, I mean. She's pregnant."

Rachel was mildly surprised. "Is she sure?"

"I don't even know if she knows, but *I'm* sure. She hasn't had a period in three months. Do women get the blues like this when they're pregnant?"

"I'm hardly an expert, but I suppose it's possible. Do you think she realizes her condition and is unhappy about it? Have the two of you discussed having children?"

Drew again hunched his big shoulders. "No, but hell, what's to discuss? Everyone wants kids. We got married, didn't we?"

She was amazed at his naïveté. "The two don't necessarily follow, sad to say. A woman may feel that a child will bring about a change in lifestyle she's not quite ready to accept. I speak with honesty and without malice when I say that Irena is not emotionally mature for her age. Her father died under tragic circumstances when she was quite young. She's never gotten over it. They were quite close."

"She told me he died in an earthquake. I don't think that's what this is, though." He studied the carvings on her broad desk, as if they held the key to the mystery. "I dunno, I have the feeling it's something bigger, something worse. I could be all wet, but I'm worried. Especially now with the kid to think about. If she doesn't start taking care of herself and quit drinking so much—" He hadn't planned to mention the booze. He sighed. "She's putting down a fifth a day. That's not party drinking, Mrs. Upfield, that's solid two-fisted boozing. I don't buy any, but she's got a store that delivers. She's gonna kill herself."

Rachel was shocked. Irena had never drunk heavily. That was not one of her vices. Drew was right. She needed to see a doctor. What in heaven's name had brought this on?

"I'll call our family physician and persuade him to see her. He'll make a house call so she can't ignore an appointment. I'll be sure to be with him. I doubt that I can talk any sense into her, but I will try. Can you give me any background the doctor may find helpful? When did this begin?"

He looked pained. "The night we moved out of your place. Or more accurately, when we moved into the apartment. She acted funny right off. She fainted when we first got there. I should have called the doctor then."

"Irena fainted?" He estimated three months into a pregnancy. She would have been a few weeks along.

"She just crumpled in a heap without warning. No, come to think of it, she shivered like she was cold. I figured she took a chill, and what with that rip-snortin' argument we'd had . . ." He shrugged.

Rachel twitched the ends of the reading glasses her optometrist, Michael Barker, had demanded she get. "I've never known Irena to faint before, but it would seem a sign of some physical problem. I'll call Dr. Champs immediately." She glanced at her watch. "I'm sure he'll make time to see her today." She reached for the phone, then withdrew her hand

and picked up a gold mechanical pencil. "I'll have to have the address."

He gave it to her. She wrote quickly, then frowned. She looked at him, and for a moment he thought he glimpsed the same haunted fear mirrored in Irena's eyes. They were both beautiful—but in different ways. Except for this look, they rarely resembled each other. The puzzled crease stayed between her brows as though he'd suddenly started babbling in tongues.

"What's the matter?" he demanded.

She tapped the gold pencil at the paper. "You live in the Plaza Apartments?"

"Yeah."

"What number?"

He told her. She closed her eyes and her face paled. What the hell . . .

When Rachel opened her eyes, she took a deep breath. "We may have found the explanation you've been searching for, Drew. Lord, you had no way of knowing." She tried to soften the blow as much as possible. "Inadvertently, you've rented the apartment in which Irena's best friend died. It was unfortunate . . . the girl had a weakened heart since childhood. Her family indulged her desire to have an apartment of her own. Because she lived alone, the body wasn't found for two days. They found her on her birthday. Her family was grief-stricken. Irena was away at the time, but given the close friendship between the two, I suspect Ruth's death caused her a great deal of pain. Walking into that apartment must have awakened memories Irena doesn't want to face."

"Jesus!" Drew cried. He set his creased brow on his balled fists. He felt sick. He'd put Irena through hell. He had to get back and let her know it was all right. He'd find another apartment. He'd take her to a hotel—anything. Jesus. He got to his feet.

"I'm ten kinds of an ass, Mrs. Upfield. Me and my damned pigheadedness. I had to find us an apartment when I didn't even know the goddam town. What a jerk."

"You had no way of knowing."

"Well, I know now. Look, call your doctor and get him over there as fast as possible. I'm going home. I'm not going to leave her alone in that place again." In quick strides, Drew raced out the carved redwood doors.

For a moment Rachel sat motionless except for her churning mind. How much did Irena remember of that night? Would it be necessary to probe those dark memories in order to bring her out of her depression? The matter had long ago died along with Ruth's corpse. Let it be . . . let it stay buried. . . . Slowly she dialed Dr. Champs's number.

He moved her flung-aside silk blouse and dungarees from the foot of the bed and sat watching her. Her eyes were closed, the color washed out of her once glowing, now sunken cheeks. Her blondish hair was limp and lackluster. There wasn't any whiskey bottle in sight, but he smelled its stale odor and knew there'd be an empty in the garbage.

"Irena?"

She didn't open her eyes, though he sensed she had found no sleep and was awake.

"Honey, if you don't want to talk, it's all right. I understand. It's taken me long enough, but I understand, baby. Just listen, then if you want to say something, okay."

Her eyes moved nervously behind the closed lids, and she murmured. In a low voice he told her about his visit to Rachel. He asked her to forgive him and promised to start looking for a new place. It was going to be okay, he assured her. Everything was going to be okay.

Tears crept from under her lids. He took her in his arms, pressing her to his body and rocking her gently, murmuring against her tangled hair.

"I love you, baby. It's going to be all right. Try not to think about it anymore. We'll get out of here, and you don't have to think about it anymore. When the well is finished, we'll go someplace else. There's a new field down in McAlester. Some of the guys are heading down there. A couple of wildcats are coming in. I'll find a great job. What do you say?"

He rocked and showered her with warm, tingling words. Suddenly she began to cry. At first it was a little shiver, then a shudder, finally huge sobs that tore from her. He held her as she poured out her grief.

"I can still see her in the chair—she was so beautiful—I'd never touched a dead person before—I tried to wake her up—Oh, God, she was dead—dead—"

He stroked her hair and handed her his handkerchief, which she blew into, then wiped her long black-lashed eyes that looked fawn-like now. "It's okay, baby, it's okay. . . ."

Gradually her sobs subsided. She lay back, closed her eyes, and fell asleep. Her face was puffy, but a glow had returned to her normally silky complexion. Softly he tiptoed from the room and closed the door. He sat at the kitchen table until Rachel and the doctor came. Maybe now the ghost would rest in peace. Maybe now Irena could concentrate on building herself up and having a healthy kid. He'd meant what he said about Oklahoma. It would be good for her to get away from this whole damned town. He never should have let her talk him into coming here, into staying after he had met that witch, Rachel. Rachel had to control everything and everyone around her. If not with her millions, then by her witchy, mesmerizing beauty. He wondered if she'd ever given Irena a chance.

Well, this was her chance to come through for the kid. If she brought a good doctor and the two of them talked Irena into forgetting the booze and eating right . . .

There was a knock and he hurried to let in Rachel and a stocky iron-haired man carrying a professional black bag.

"I've told Dr. Champs the pertinent facts, unless you have something to add?" Rachel said.

"She was pretty well soused when I got home. I told her I was sorry about causing her such hell."

"Did she talk?" Rachel asked.

"She babbled a little but mostly she cried, then she fell asleep." He looked at the doctor. "Can you help her, Doc?"

"I'm not a psychiatrist, Mr. Hamilton, but I'll do what I can. I would say determining the basic cause of the current depression, which I understand is this apartment, may be a giant step forward. Only time will tell. I am more concerned with the immediate problem of the suspected pregnancy. Mrs. Upfield tells me there is no doubt whatsoever in your mind?"

"Hell, I can count. She missed her third period last week."

"Emotional trauma sometimes causes cessation of menstruation. I'll have to do laboratory tests to ascertain the pregnancy beyond question."

"Whatever. Just get her well."

The doctor picked up his bag and looked at Rachel. She said, "Irena will be less frightened if I'm there. Perhaps you should stay here, Drew, so she won't feel inhibited in what she wants to confide."

"Sure, sure." He waved them down the hall.

Rachel opened the bedroom door and saw that Irena was still asleep. She went to the bed while the doctor opened his bag and took out a stethoscope.

She touched Irena's shoulder. "Irena. Wake up, Irena. Someone's here to see you."

Irena's large eyes fluttered sluggishly. Her appearance was unflattering, and Rachel fought to keep the disgust from her face.

"Dr. Champs is going to examine you. You haven't been taking care of yourself. We don't want you to be ill."

Irena wet her lips slowly. "Drew?" It was barely a croak.

"He's in the other room. He'll come in as soon as the doctor is finished." Irena's gaze locked on her mother's clouded figure. Even ill, she could see her mother had dressed to the hilt, in a light tweed suit of fashionable herringbone gray. Her dark hair was pinned up; her cheeks lustrous, and lips slightly rouged. How like her mama to be worried about "appearances."

The doctor sat on the side of the bed smiling clinically as he listened to Irena's heart and lungs through his stethoscope, counted her pulse, palpated her chest cavity. When he pressed her abdomen, Irena winced and looked frightened. Dr. Champs asked her a few questions, which she answered thickly. She was still drunk. Rachel thanked heaven Champs could keep his mouth shut.

"Well, young lady, I would agree you have not been taking care of yourself. Your mother tells me you've always enjoyed excellent health. No reason why you shouldn't again."

Irena looked confused. Rachel covered her and went out with the doctor, shutting the door. Drew came toward them quickly. Rachel turned him back toward the living room.

"Is she okay? Is she pregnant?"

"She's run down, but I don't think there's any permanent damage if the self-abuse is stopped now. I'd like to give her liver shots and put her on a high-protein diet. She has some tenderness in the abdomen and I can't rule out the possibility of infection. As soon as we determine definitely that she's pregnant, we can do some other tests. I'd say the important thing is to keep her comfortable and rested—and away from alcohol. If she goes on this way much longer, her liver may be

damaged beyond hope. She should be in the hospital where
she can have constant care."

"She won't like that."

"I don't want to interfere, Drew," Rachel said, "but may I
suggest that you and Irena come back to the house? Irena
knows the servants and is comfortable with them. She'd feel
less as though she's being guarded, and your mind can be at
ease knowing she's well taken care of. There's no question she
must get out of this apartment."

He rubbed his temple where a dull ache throbbed. Maybe
Rachel was right. He had to think about Irena now.

"I told her we'd move to Oklahoma. The Padres Number
One will be capped in ten days or so."

Rachel's jaw set. When she armed herself for battle, her
beauty took on almost a supernatural air. That a woman near-
ing fifty should retain such physical appeal and personal magnetism was astonishing. Worse, it was intimidating. Drew's
muscular legs drew apart, his hands set on his hips as he
braced for a confrontation.

Dr. Champs cleared his throat. "Unless she gets the proper
care *now,* she'll be in no condition to travel."

"Could she go in two weeks?"

"If she builds herself up."

Drew sucked in his breath, looking at Rachel. "All right, if
it's okay with her. Let me talk to her."

"Do it now," Rachel said. "The sooner we get her out of
this place, the better."

MCALESTER OK 09–03–50 1054A CST

RACHEL UPFIELD
OCEANSIDE HOTEL
OCEAN BEACH CA

BABY GIRL BORN SEPT 2 10PM IRENA AND CHILD FINE

DREW

September 5, 1950

Dear Irena,

*I am delighted with the news of my first grandchild. I
hope the birth was uncomplicated and the baby is*

healthy. I'm sure you're happy to have the long wait over. The hot summer must have been unbearable.

I presume you have been busy these past months. It takes time to settle in a new place. I have only the first address you sent; I hope it's current. Not knowing what baby clothing, equipment, and furniture you already have, I am enclosing a check so you can buy what you need. I was tempted to purchase a complete layette—in actuality, I was so overwhelmed and charmed by the darling dresses, sacques, and buntings I wanted to purchase several layettes!—but since I'm not sure that the Oklahoma weather is as close to perfect as we enjoy here, I console myself with the certainty that your selections will be more suitable. I do hope, though, that they include a pretty pink, lacy dress from her loving grandmother.

What name have you decided on?

As to the matter of the christening, please consider the possibility of having it here in Ocean Beach. I took the liberty of speaking with the Reverend Mr. Daggett at Trinity. He would be delighted to officiate. Since both you and I were christened at Trinity, Irena, I feel this would be most fitting. You can stay at the house; I spend most of my time at the office and hotel, since I find the house empty of family a bit lonely. It would give me great pleasure to have you use it, though I shan't promise not to come often to admire and hold the baby!

If this is suitable, I'll have Mrs. Dryer bring the christening dress from the attic. It has been wrapped in tissue and sealed in airtight packing. It will be ready whenever you are.

I won't bore you with trivia. Life has a way of going on much the same year after year. We are expanding the construction end of the company and hope to win the bid on the new library.

Do write soon and answer the questions I've asked. I cannot wait to see a picture of the baby, and, of course, the child herself.

Affectionately,
Rachel

October 17, 1950

Dear Rachel,

   We're coming to Ocean Beach on the 26th, if the car holds together. The well's in and we're tired of this godforsaken place. We might as well have the christening there. The church here is a shack that stinks of oil, like everything else. Drew doesn't want to stay at the house, but unless you start sending my checks pronto, we have no choice. I've never looked into details of my father's estate, but there must be plenty left. Maybe I shoud make an appointment with that law firm.

   We named the baby Paris. She's taking the place of us having a trip there.

Irena

PRESS-TELEGRAM/OCTOBER 30

THE INFANT DAUGHTER OF MR. AND MRS. DREW HAMILTON WAS CHRISTENED SUNDAY MORNING AT TRINITY EPISCOPAL CHURCH OF OCEAN BEACH. THE REV. MR. USHER DAGGETT PERFORMED THE CEREMONY. THE CHILD, PARIS ELAINE, IS THE GRANDDAUGHTER OF RACHEL GRANT UPFIELD, PROMINENT REAL ESTATE DEVELOPER OF OCEAN BEACH AND OWNER OF THE OCEANSIDE HOTEL. THE INFANT WORE A WHITE SILK AND BELGIAN LACE HAND-SEWN DRESS THAT BOTH HER MOTHER, IRENA GRANT HAMILTON, NEE UPFIELD, AND THE GRANDMOTHER WORE AT THEIR CHRISTENINGS AT TRINITY CHURCH. MR. AND MRS. HAMILTON ARE SPENDING A FEW WEEKS AT MRS. UPFIELD'S HOME ON DARIEN HILL.

PRESS-TELEGRAM/NOVEMBER 15

COLLETTE MARTINE FANTAZIA

   PHOENIX, ARIZ.——COLLETTE MARTINE FANTAZIA, A LONGTIME RESIDENT OF OCEAN BEACH, DIED SATURDAY IN PHOENIX, WHERE SHE AND HER HUSBAND WERE WINTERING. MRS. FANTAZIA HAD BEEN IN POOR HEALTH FOR SEVERAL YEARS. A NATIVE OF ST. GERMAIN-EN-LAYE, FRANCE, MRS. FANTAZIA WAS BORN FEBRUARY 7, 1902. SHE CAME TO OCEAN BEACH IN 1919 AS A BRIDE. HER

HUSBAND'S FAMILY HAVE BEEN RESIDENTS OF THIS AREA
SINCE 1834, WHEN ALONZO RAPHAEL FANTAZIA, COUSIN
OF GOVERNOR FIGUEROA, PURCHASED 60,000 ACRES OF
THE ORIGINAL NIETO LAND GRANT. MRS. FANTAZIA'S
WIDOWER, JOSHUA SIMON FANTAZIA, STILL OWNS THE
ORIGINAL FAMILY RANCHO. AS WELL AS NUMEROUS
OTHER PROPERTIES, HE ALSO OWNS FANTAZIA ENTER-
PRISES. MRS. FANTAZIA WILL BE BURIED IN A PRIVATE
CEREMONY AT THE FAMILY CHAPEL AND CEMETERY AT
RANCHO DEL CIELO.

SURVIVING ARE HER HUSBAND, JOSHUA, A SON, JUD-
SON SIMON, OF OCEAN BEACH, AND ONE GRANDDAUGH-
TER, SHANNA MARGARET. MR. FANTAZIA PLANS TO TAKE
UP RESIDENCE IN OCEAN BEACH AFTER AN ABSENCE OF
SEVERAL YEARS.

PRESS-TELEGRAM/DECEMBER 3

DREW HAMILTON HAS ACCEPTED A YEAR-LONG CON-
TRACT WITH ARAMCO OIL COMPANY TO WORK AT THEIR
NEWLY DEVELOPED FIELDS IN SAUDI ARABIA. MR. HAM-
ILTON LEAVES OCEAN BEACH IMMEDIATELY FOR HIS AS-
SIGNMENT. HIS WIFE WILL REMAIN IN OCEAN BEACH WITH
THEIR INFANT DAUGHTER. MRS. HAMILTON IS THE
DAUGHTER OF RACHEL UPFIELD, WHO WAS VOTED OCEAN
BEACH WOMAN OF THE YEAR FOR 1949, AND WHO IS A
MEMBER OF THE CHAMBER OF COMMERCE, WOMEN'S
CITY CLUB, EBEL TEMPLE, CALIFORNIA BUSINESSWO-
MEN'S ASSOCIATION, ART LEAGUE, OCEAN BEACH SYM-
PHONY LEAGUE, MEMORIAL HOSPITAL ASSISTANCE
LEAGUE.

SAUDI ARABIA 09−02−51 0900 GT

PARIS HAMILTON
1510 LADERA STREET
DARIEN HILL CA USA

HAPPY BIRTHDAY BABY

LOVE DADDY

SAUDI ARABIA 09–12–51 1800 GT

IRENA HAMILTON
1510 LADERA STREET
DARIEN HILL CA USA

NO LETTER FOUR MONTHS WHAT IS GOING ON

DREW

OCEAN BEACH CA 09–27–51 1100A PST

DREW HAMILTON
ARAMCO OIL
SAUDI ARABIA

EVERYTHING FINE IRENA VISITING FRIENDS IN
HAWAII PARIS GROWING FAST AND MORE BEAU-
TIFUL THAN EVER WILL SEND SNAPSHOTS OF
FIRST BIRTHDAY PARTY SHE SENDS DADDY
KISSES.

RACHEL

SAUDI ARABIA 11–24–51 11200 GT

IRENA HAMILTON
1510 LADERA STREET
DARIEN HILL CA USA

OFFERED NEW CONTRACT DECISION BY DEC 15
CAN LEASE HOUSE WILL YOU AND PARIS COME
LOVE

DREW

OCEAN BEACH CA 11–30–51 1150P PST

DREW HAMILTON
ARAMCO OIL
SAUDI ARABIA

YES

IRENA

December 30, 1951

Dear Drew,

It is with a heavy heart that I write to tell you that Irena and Paris will not be joining you after all. They are both well—set your mind at ease on that score. Perhaps I should start at the beginning. After Christmas I insisted she have a complete physical. Dr. Champs assured me that it was nothing more than general post-partum malaise. Having a baby puts considerable strain on the constitution; meeting the demands of caring for an infant intensifies it. Since Irena has not for some years taken the best care of herself (which we both must recognize), all this had its toll. Dr. Champs suggested a rest and change. I suggested Irena take a brief trip to some pleasant clime where she could recover her strength. She arranged to visit friends in Amarillo and to spend a few weeks in Mexico, perhaps also stopping in New Orleans to enjoy Mardi Gras. She was to return to Ocean Beach in early April when the rainy season was over. She left the first week in January. I had frequent cards and notes assuring me she was improving and that the rest was performing wonders. And of course she inquired after Paris, who stayed here so Irena could truly be free from strain. I hired an excellent nursemaid, an old-fashioned nanny, to take care of the darling. She is in excellent hands. I am enclosing several snapshots from her birthday party. You may recognize the doll she is holding. It was your gift to her. She loves it.

I suppose I should have realized Irena's delay was a danger signal, but I admit I was so delighted to have Paris, the time passed quickly. When Irena had not returned by June, I began to worry. Her postcards became infrequent. Then stopped altogether. I was worried and hired an investigator to locate her. I won't go into details. You've been through as much pain as I, so you know the problems she gets into when she is partying more than is good for her. The investigator located her in Hawaii. That was in September. We could not persuade her to come back of her own free will. Short of going to Honolulu and bringing her back forci-

bly, I had no choice but to contact the medical people recommended by Dr. Champs and have her placed in a hospital where she could once again obtain the rest she needed to rebuild her strength. She remained a month, then was brought home by a man in my employ.

I wish I could say a happy new beginning followed, but Irena was depressed and uncooperative. Her moods were mercurial, but at least with constant vigilance, her physical health definitely improved. When your cablegram came in November, she was delighted with the chance to join you. She made eager plans, including talking to friends who might advise her on the climate, clothing, etc. The next thing I knew she was not returning home in the evenings, following one round of parties after another on the winter circuit. I have not seen her for three weeks. I am reluctant to send the investigator after her again, but if she doesn't return soon, I will, for her own good.

In the meantime, be assured that Paris is well taken care of. She's growing and learning fast. She walks without assistance, and her vocabulary is multiplying rapidly. She knows your picture and calls it "dada." Her version of "grandmother" sounds suspiciously like "gum," but it delights me nevertheless.

When Irena returns, I shall see that she writes and makes plans to join you. I presume you leased the house you mentioned. Is it fully equipped or should she plan to bring linens and other necessities? I can arrange to have them shipped separately. I hope you had a wonderful Christmas. Please do not worry about Paris. She is a delightful child and grows to look more like you every day. You can be very proud of her.

> *My very best,*
> *Rachel*

SAUDI ARABIA 05–22–52 1000 GT

RACHEL UPFIELD
1510 LADERA STREET
DARIEN HILL CA

IRENA NOT ON FLIGHT WHAT HAPPENED

DREW

OCEAN BEACH CA 05–25–52 1130A PST

DREW HAMILTON
ARAMCO OIL
SAUDI ARABIA

PLANS CHANGED SUDDENLY LETTER FOLLOWS

RACHEL

May 29, 1952

Dear Drew,

I am completely out of patience. Irena has once again run off. I despair of her ever changing. Her ticket was bought, her bags packed. The morning of the flight, I found a note saying that she could not bear the thought of living in a primitive, foreign place. She said she was going to visit friends and left no forwarding address. Thank God Paris is too young to understand. Her nanny is a gem and has smoothed over the disappointment of Paris not going on her "twip." I recognize your commitment there. It would be a shame to break your contract in the hope of changing Irena's ways, I fear. Let me assure you again, Paris is well cared for and loved. You need not worry on her account. She is a happy, very bright child—a delight to have around. I spend far more time at home now than I ever have in order to be with her. You can be sure we are both looking forward to your furlough in the fall. What fun you will have getting acquainted with the little lady your daughter has become. I know Irena looks forward to your furlough as well. This temporary flight is only panic at leaving the security of everything she knows. When she sees you, I'm sure she'll want to accompany you. In the event the two of you would like a second honeymoon while you are here, I will be delighted to keep Paris. I'm sure I will hear from Irena before long. I will write immediately when I do. I have not sent the investigator. There seems little point.

My best,
Rachel

SAUDI ARABIA 09—02—52 0900 GT
PARIS HAMILTON
1510 LADERA STREET
DARIEN HILL CA

HAPPY BIRTHDAY SWEETHEART FURLOUGH CANCELED
HOME FOR GOOD APRIL HUGS AND KISSES FOR MY GIRL

DADDY

February 20, 1953

The Superior Court of the County of Los Angeles, State
of California, hereby appoints Rachel Grant Upfield
temporary legal guardian of minor child, Paris Elaine
Hamilton, born September 2, 1950, to Irena Grant
Hamilton, née Upfield, and Drew Edward Hamilton,
removing the legal guardianship from said parents until
such time as they are able to prove responsibility in
providing adequately for said child. This case has been
heard before the Children's Court, Judge Rupert Col-
linger presiding.

MELTON & ROBERTS LAW OFFICES
Armstrong Trust Building
Ocean Beach, California

January 24, 1954

Mr. Drew Hamilton
American Hotel
Ocean Beach, California

Dear Mr. Hamilton:
    We regret to inform you that your appeal to
set aside the temporary guardianship of your
daughter has been turned down. I am enclosing
a copy of the decision, which in essence states
that you have failed to show you can provide a
suitable home and environment for the child.
Mrs. Upfield's documentation that your wife is
an unfit mother, which was submitted at the
time of the original hearing, weighed heavily in
the decision. Your wife did not appear for this
hearing.

Naturally, this decision does not preclude another appeal. We suggest you submit evidence of a permanent place of residence and gainful employment. Character references from Ocean Beach residents who have known you some length of time would also be advisable.

Please advise us if you wish this office to set in motion the divorce action we discussed. Though it is not impossible, it is rare for the court to award custody of a minor child to the father in divorce cases. We can, however, protect your rights of visitation.

> Very sincerely yours,
> Theodore Roberts

He needed a drink but he had to keep his wits about him. Rachel had already tried and convicted him. This was his court of last appeal. His mouth twisted wryly. What the hell could he appeal to? Sentiment? Rachel's sense of fairness? Shit.

He pulled the ancient, wheezing Studebaker into the driveway. The Ladera Street manor, originally ahead of its time with its strong horizontal planes, high narrow windows, stepped-back levels that hugged the Hill, was still stylish and timeless. A uniformed maid showed him into the front room and said Mrs. Upfield would be with him in a moment. He paced nervously, needing a cigarette but not daring to light one. He saw that the car was right in line with the window, and he cursed himself for not parking it on the street. It didn't add to an appearance of prosperity. Nothing he did would fool Rachel. He'd be willing to bet she had a complete dossier on him, down to his last buck and the cheap café where he ate last night. But he had come armed with a last resort of his own. Blackmail.

He felt her presence, like a vibrating platform before a gusher comes in, and turned.

She stood there, watching him. The creases on her oval exquisite face were set in determination, he saw. Gray streaked her hair, pinned up in a chignon, and she wore a red Chanel suit and blue pumps. Though the lines in her face deepened with age, she'd always remain a stunning woman. "Hello, Rachel," he said.

"Drew. Please sit down." She chose to reign from a high-backed Victorian chair in the sunken living room, and led him to the area, where she sank gracefully into the cushions. He perched on the edge of the Regency sofa, a flower pattern embedded in the chintz fabric. It doubled his sense of impotence to be led this way, and surrounded by her luxury—as the ruthless witch no doubt intended.

"The court has set weekends for visitations."

He swallowed an acid taste. "I came to see you, not Paris."

Her expression flickered. Anything he said was going to come out wrong. He wanted to banish rage and despair from his voice.

"You and I got off to a bad beginning. I'm sorry as hell about that, but I'd like to start over. If it's possible." He caught his hand as it moved toward the pack of cigarettes in his pocket. "I admit I'm probably not exactly what you would have picked for a son-in-law. Irena never told me much about you or her life here before we were married. I knew she was a mixed-up kid, but I loved her and that seemed to be all that counted. No matter what it looks like, I tried to make a go of the marriage. I'd have given her the moon if I could."

"What is it you came to discuss?" Rachel said flatly.

Just like he wasn't trying to be polite. His hands began to tremble and he locked them together. He had sworn he wouldn't lose his temper. He'd take whatever shit she shoveled.

"I came to ask if we couldn't set aside our personal differences and come to a better understanding about Paris. She's my kid. I love her. I may not be the right husband for Irena but I'm Paris's father. I have rights." His voice cracked despite his resolve.

"You have been given visitation rights."

"To see my own kid on weekends? What the hell kind of a deal is that?!" Oh, shit, he was blowing it. Why couldn't he play it cool? "Sorry, I didn't mean to yell."

Even that didn't get a rise from her. She sat giving him that arch witchy look as if he were some kind of peasant the ravishing queen was forced to hear. How could others worship her as a shrine? She was power, corrupt and unchecked.

"It's not easy for me to be in the same city knowing she's here and not being able to see her. If Irena doesn't want to see me, I can take that. She's an adult and can make up her own mind. Paris is a little girl. She doesn't understand why her daddy goes away after a few hours and why she can't stay with me."

"Do you think she wants to stay with you?"

The tone said it all: stay in his rat-trap room, stay with a sitter while he worked, give up everything she had here? A dull ache throbbed in his ears.

"A father has a right to know his own kid. I don't want her growing up not remembering me or thinking I'm some guy who brings her a new toy every Sunday. How can she know me if she never has the chance to be with me?"

"Precisely what did you have in mind?"

"Let me have her for two weeks. I'm rolling up my clothes on this job in a couple of days. I have a little put by so I don't have to sign on again right away. Let me take Paris on a little trip. Just the two of us."

"It's out of the question."

"Why? I'm not going to run off with her. I don't need to be knocked over the head to know you'd turn your dogs loose on me if I tried anything. I just want to be with my kid. Is that so much to ask?"

"Where do you propose going?"

He felt a glimmer of hope. "San Diego. They've got some great beaches there and the weather's nice. She'd get a kick out of the zoo."

"She's too young to appreciate animals in a zoo."

The hope began to dim. She wasn't giving an inch, no matter what he said. Her mind was made up before he walked in. He had no choice but to go for the jugular. His blackmail would have to have its day.

"I want those weeks," he said.

"It's not in Paris's best interests. I'm sorry, but if that's all—"

"That's not all, dammit! I've been trying to be nice. Now I'm telling you, I want two weeks with my kid, and I'll do whatever I have to to get them!" His hands unlocked and his fists clenched.

Rachel looked amused. Their gazes locked. "I read in the paper where Upfield Construction has bid on the new hospital

complex. The final decision's down to you or Fantazia." He
saw the flicker of interest in her brilliant violet eyes at the
mention of the Fantazia name. "According to scuttlebutt,
you've been beating Fantazia's ass because the old man lets
the son handle things. He hasn't had any interest in running
the company since his daughter died." The flicker became
wariness. "What would happen if the old man got back into
the act?"

"Josh is an excellent businessman. His presence would en-
ergize the organization."

Drew didn't lower his guard. "Maybe if Josh Fantazia
knew that Irena was at Ruth's apartment that night and that
you didn't let her call anyone, he might figure you were worth
fighting." Jesus, her eyes glinted like ice chips. "He might get
mad enough to put up a real fight if he found out you knew all
along his daughter was dead. I checked the newspaper stories.
It was two days until the body was discovered, but you knew
—you and Irena. You were there. What was it, some big deal
going you couldn't afford to jeopardize?"

Rachel's voice was as cold as an Oklahoma wind in winter.
"Sometimes the past is better left buried. It would not be
pleasant for Irena to have those memories revived. Her one
encounter with them was tragic enough. It could have been
worse if I had not intervened."

"The hell with Irena! And the hell with you! You covered
up the whole rotten mess because you were looking out for
yourself—not for her. You're always number one and anyone
else be damned. You *used* Irena's guilt to protect your selfish
interests. What kind of mother are you? You let her think her
best friend died because she didn't call for help. It took me a
long time, but I finally got the whole story out of my poor
confused, miserable wife. Even then I didn't want to believe
it. Like a jackass, I left Irena and Paris here and went off on
that Saudi job." His laugh was bitter. "I really believed she'd
come over. I win the blue ribbon for stupidity on that one.
When I think of all those letters and cables and how you
strung me along . . ." He sucked in air deeply as he tried to
control his swelling anger. But he'd hit home. Rachel's exquisite face was bloodless. Maybe some of the pain she dished
out to others would finally rebound.

His breathing and the ticking of a clock were the only
sounds in the room. Their gazes locked in a duel of wills.

After a long time she shifted slightly and seemed to shrink into the high-backed chair. Her voice was so low he had to strain to hear.

"Everything I did was in Irena's best interests. That may be difficult to believe, but it's true. I am not entirely ruthless, Drew. Irena believed she had killed Ruth Fantazia by negligence. You say she told you the entire story. I doubt it. Irena remembers only what suits her, and she was drunk and drugged that night. When the effects wore off, she held on to only fragments."

"She told me enough," he insisted.

"Did she tell you that she let Ruth's boyfriend have his way with her while the party was in full swing? While Ruth was in the next room? Or that Ruth discovered them together in a compromising position? Her best friend, Drew. Irena's had the morals of an alley cat since she was fifteen. I'm not proud of what she is, but I couldn't let her destroy a good family because of her lack of moral fiber. It was bad enough that Ruth was so hurt and shocked that she swallowed a bottle of sleeping pills. Ah, I see you didn't know that. It's true. Irena never cared enough to wonder how Ruth died at that particular time. I found the empty pharmacy bottle. I took it away in order to spare her family the added grief of knowing their daughter took her own life—because of Irena." She sighed. "So there's your truth. Are you willing to have it come out? Yes, it will hurt me, but it will hurt Irena more. And the one who will suffer most is Paris, the one true innocent. Make no mistake, the reverberations will be national, not just limited to Ocean Beach. Are you willing for Paris to grow up under the shadow of scandal?"

A cold wave washed over him. He'd lost . . . he'd gambled and lost. He would never hurt Paris, and she knew it. He tasted bile as he got up slowly. His body was heavy and hard to move.

"I know you love Paris," Rachel said in a surprisingly gentle tone. "I do, too. I never knew it was possible to love a child so much. I want what's best for her. I will never keep you from her, Drew, that I promise. But neither can I allow you to take her off someplace where the temptation to keep running might be too seductive. I won't lose her. She's become my world. I will give her everything she needs and see that she is educated so her life won't be wasted like her

mother's. Marymount, Radcliffe, Harvard graduate school.
Let me have her. Don't fight me. I give you my word I have
never, nor will I ever, say any unkind or untrue things about
you to her. She'll grow up loving you as she does now."

He looked at her sadly. She was giving him her word but
not his child. Her couture wardrobe, sumptuous house, national reputation as a preeminent businesswoman tycoon. How
could he fight her? She always won, always held the high
cards. The pain that had begun as a slow ache blazed into a
fire that spread to his chest now. He'd lost.

"Can I see Paris before I leave?" he asked.

"She isn't here. I wasn't sure what to expect, so I sent her
off with Nanny. If you'd like to wait . . ."

He shook his head. "I'll stop by before I leave town."

"Where will you go?"

"Texas, maybe back to Oklahoma." His broad shoulders
shrugged eloquently. He combed a hand through his lustrous
dark hair, the look of defeat etched on his handsomely rugged
features. "One rig's as good as another."

"If you stay in Ocean Beach, you'll be able to see Paris far
more often." The gentleness in her voice surprised him again.

He shook his head at the thought of that living hell. "I'll
come back." Right now he needed time for his wounds to
heal. "Maybe after a while you'll let me cash in all those
weekends for one nice vacation with her. When she's older,
you know . . ."

Rachel nodded. "I'm sure we can work something out.
Please keep in touch. I have no objection to your phoning
Paris, if you like."

"Sure. Well, that says it all. Good-bye, Rachel," he said,
rising from the chintz sofa, still stunned.

"Good-bye, Drew."

She leaned over the rosewood coffee table flanking her
chair and pushed a buzzer embedded in the underside.

A servant appeared, a plain woman masked behind a white
cap and black shirtwaist-dress uniform. She led the once-
jaunty man, with his animal magnetism now dimmed and his
head hung in defeat, across the spacious foyer to the oak-
carved front door that seemed to mock any pretension he
might have harbored.

PARIS

❧ *Thirteen* ❧

SEPTEMBER ENGULFED THE coast in a heat wave, stifling the normally stiff breezes and stranding the sailboats in the harbor so that they bobbed with slack sails like tired gulls. The afternoon sun made the parking lot shimmer like an impressionist painting as Paris motored into the area marked UP-FIELD PAVILION VISITORS ONLY and parked near the door. The heat was suffocating as she stepped through the hospital's side entrance. Her crisp pink linen suit was perfect wear for the air-conditioned corridors, while a tad too warm for the broiling outdoors.

A young intern slowed his pace as he watched a curvacious, exquisite woman with honey-blond hair and flashing green eyes walk briskly toward the elevator. Paris caught his glance as she whirled around inside, and smiled. He tripped just as the doors whispered shut. Laughing, she pushed the tenth-floor button beside the brass plaque engraved RACHEL UPFIELD PAVILION. It was good to laugh out loud again after the somberness of recent days. She'd be glad when Rachel was finally allowed to go home. It would spell relief, even though she had accustomed herself to the daily visits as the hour she relished most in her days. She missed having Rachel in the office flanking hers at Upfield Land Management's penthouse suite, or at home where she could easily phone her.

Rachel was the most admired woman in Ocean Beach, and one of the most east and west of the Mississippi. And she was a very important feature of Paris's world. Rachel was lucky this time. The stroke was not severe. A warning, Dr. Forest said. A warning to slow down. A warning Rachel would never heed. Paris sighed, thinking how much she loved that stubborn old woman who'd raised her. It hurt to see her—a woman so fierce in will and charisma—locked in a weak and helpless shell.

The Rachel Upfield Pavilion occupied the entire top floor of the east wing. It resembled more an elegant resort than a medical institution; patients were assured the utmost in comfort as well as the highest caliber, most technically advanced medical care. It had sheltered the city's leading citizens over the years: the wealthy, the famous, the infamous. The press had dubbed it "Ocean Beach Country Club," a title not undeserved. It wasn't particularly ironic that the woman who had endowed it fifteen years before, and who cast a long shadow over the community, roomed as a patient there today.

Paris stopped at the rosewood Duncan Phyfe desk in the carpeted foyer of the oval reception area, papered in a silver flower design and hung with reproductions of famous American painters, from Andrew Wyeth to Frederic Remington. The woman behind the desk looked up and smiled. "Good afternoon, Miss Hamilton." Dressed in blue silk, Elizabeth Aspenson looked like a charming guest who had paused to relax in the writing room of a posh private club. The desktop was piled neatly with work, and fronted by a gold pen and leatherbound notepad, opened with items checklisted in order of importance. Nothing about the woman indicated a nurse, except alert blue eyes that flashed concern and sympathy. A plain woman, but appealing in this atmosphere.

"Hello, Elizabeth. Did my grandmother have a good day?"

Paris took the paper Elizabeth held out to her. At Paris's request, the nurse prepared a daily report for her, a simplified version of Rachel's medical progress, physical therapy sessions, and behavior for the day.

"Excellent morning, but she's been a bear this afternoon," Elizabeth commented.

Paris scanned the report. Rachel's condition was stable, her vital signs in the safe range. The physical therapist reported slight improvement in Rachel's stroke-weakened left side, her vision, and her blood pressure. There was a notation that Rachel had asked again for a telephone in her room. *Denied.* Dr. Forest had known Rachel twenty years and recognized a phone would be her license to overdo. There was another notation that Rachel had read the *Press-Telegram* after her post-lunch nap, as was her custom. *That* accounted for the abrupt change in Rachel's mood, Paris knew. Rachel read the paper thoroughly, so she wouldn't have missed the story about the Oceanside, and she knew she had been furious when she read it.

On the surface an analysis of the proposed downtown redevelopment plan, the article read more like an appeal for the razing of the Oceanside Hotel. It quoted facts and figures that made it seem like the old hotel was a derelict in the way of progress. The hotel had been boarded up for three years. That in itself had been a hard decision for Rachel to make, but the Oceanside was no longer the money-maker it once had been. It had still offered elegance in accommodations, service, and cuisine, but upkeep dwarfed profits. And the character of the city around it had changed. Like most other metropolises, Ocean Beach had suffered urban blight. The fanciest hotel in southern California couldn't flourish in an area that had aged and been deserted except by big business.

But now, with a redevelopment project in the works, Upfield Land Management had submitted a plan to completely remodel and revitalize the hotel. Only the shell of the original 1933 structure would remain, with its lofty towers and elegant stone facade. The Oceanside, which had been Rachel's life for so long, would once again become a national watering hole. And it would be the core of the entire urban redevelopment plan.

Fantazia Enterprises had also submitted a plan. It proposed bulldozing the Oceanside and building luxury condominiums in its place. Or more accurately, Shanna Fantazia had. In addition to being Josh's granddaughter, Shanna Fantazia ran a very successful real estate office. She'd been part of the Fantazia organization for a few years, but her temper and tactics had put her in conflict with quite a few people. She'd even run awry with her grandfather and, in a fury, had quit her secure job, claiming she would open her own office. She had, and she had done very well. Long ago she and Josh had reconciled. Now she had a buyer for the Oceanside, who wanted to raze it and put up condominiums. Paris suspected Shanna was behind some of the "informed sources" quoted in the article. Swallowing her anger, Paris handed the report back to Elizabeth, who inclined her head toward the hall. "There goes Sumi." Sumi, a petite Japanese aide, turned and waved. "Follow me," she said, and Paris fell into line, waving thanks to Elizabeth, who turned back to her work. Sumi was carrying a tray with two wineglasses and a small carafe. Like Elizabeth, she was not dressed in institutional white, but in an emerald shirtwaist dress softly curving over her slim body. Only the medical duty nurses wore uniforms as a matter of practical expediency: they would be instantly recognizable and ready for emergencies.

Rachel sat in a blue velvet chair near the window. As soon as she'd been able to be out of bed, she insisted on dressing for the afternoon. Today she was wearing lavender crepe de chine dress with a diamond and pearl brooch pinned at the neckline. Her short curly silver hair softly framed the delicate oval of her face. She'd never been a big woman, and the stroke had shrunk her to appear all her seventy-nine years. One side of her face still slackened with the vestiges of paralysis, but her eyes flashed brilliantly as ever. Her lavender gaze followed her granddaughter as Paris came to kiss her, giving her a dazzling smile.

"Hello, darling. You look chipper today," Paris said cheerily. Except for inheriting Irena's fair hair and Drew's dark skin, she could be a younger version of her grandmother. She had the same high cheekbones, thin nose, and full sensuous lips. She did not have her mother's excessive curves. What Rachel approved of most was her spirit and intelligence.

"Chipper enough to have a phone," Rachel snapped, even though she was grateful to see Paris. There was only a slight slur to her words.

Paris sat in the chair across from her and waited for Sumi to leave. This half hour belonged to her and Rachel. Paris joined her grandmother every day at five for "cocktails," the single glass of sherry Rachel was permitted every day. As she coddled the drink—which she'd browbeaten out of her doctor —Paris related the day's business, or what she considered acceptable to convey to Rachel, who could get ruffled easily and, in her precarious medical situation, had to be treated with kid gloves.

"Dr. Forest doesn't think you're ready," Paris said. "He'd like to see your blood pressure down another ten points."

Rachel waved her good hand. "Spare me details."

Paris smiled, and sipped the excellent sherry. *Giving up* were words her grandmother didn't know the meaning of. The bony fingers of Rachel's hand, once sleek and sensuous, tapped impatiently on the chair arm until she suddenly became aware of it and forced them still.

"Drink your sherry and relax. There's nothing worth getting upset about," her granddaughter coaxed.

Rachel snorted. "Josh Fantazia would see me in my grave."

Again, Paris had to control her anger whenever the Fantazia name was mentioned. If it hadn't been for Fantazia Enterprises' opposition in the redevelopment plan, Rachel might never have had this stroke.

"Then don't give him the satisfaction," Paris admonished. "I presume you're referring to the story in today's paper? It's not unusual for the Fantazias to make sure a reporter gets a slanted view. They're taking advantage because you're unavailable for interviews."

Rachel sipped her sherry, calculating. "If Victor Sands recommends it, the city council will condemn the Oceanside. Josh was on the council for so many years, he might as well still have a vote!" Rachel's eyes flashed with fire reminiscent of her prestroke days. Normally Paris would welcome such spirit, but in Rachel's present condition, she held up a warning hand to calm her down. Rachel sighed heavily. In a more subdued voice she said, "Where did Sands get his information? I warned you he was dangerous."

Victor. His name in the article was enough to convince Rachel he was in league with the Fantazias. Victor Sands had been hired by the city to evaluate the redevelopment project and recommend the best way to accomplish its long-range goals. His opinion would be the deciding factor in which bid was accepted.

"There wasn't anything in the article that isn't a matter of record," Paris said. "Anyone with time and patience can cull it from newspaper files and annual reports." Or from talking to Shanna Fantazia, Paris thought angrily. And she knew Victor had been seeing Shanna . . . as she had. An image of Victor's taut, tanned body caught Paris with her defenses down. She was no longer able to separate personal feelings from business where he was concerned. In three months she had managed to complicate her life by falling in love with a man who was refereeing the power struggle between her and Shanna Fantazia.

She had to take the reins in Rachel's stead. And Josh never publicly supported his granddaughter's kamikaze schemes. His silence, however, was a type of support. So Paris considered the whole redevelopment project to weigh on her shoulders, and her opposition: Shanna Fantazia.

From the start Rachel had labeled Victor a parasite brought in to do Fantazia dirty work. She had encouraged Paris to woo Sands, even seduce him if necessary, to win him to their side. He was handsome enough, with wavy dark hair, a mustache, and gleaming blue eyes—a man Rachel would have looked at more than once in her younger days. She would not have slept with him for business, but then, times had changed, and the young had ploys in their arsenal less accessible to her. Paris had done it all—too successfully. Her grandmother didn't know, and never asked too many questions. There was just a knowing gleam in her violet eyes.

Her grandmother cocked her head, gazing intently. "Has Sands given any indication of his decision?" How much was Paris keeping from her?

"No," she said, quickly searching to detour the inflammatory topic. Paris opened her briefcase and drew out the papers she'd brought, leafing through them to make sure all were there.

Rachel ignored the proffered papers. "I want to talk to Josh."

"What?!" Paris cried. Astonishment lit up her face.

The older woman looked back at Paris, unruffled. "Tomorrow. Tell him to come at four."

Paris shook her head. "Are you trying to court another episode?"

"I will not get excited," she said finally.

"You're not temperamentally suited to being in the same room with a Fantazia. Your blood pressure will climb twenty points."

Rachel studied the gnarled hands in her lap. After an interval she said softly, "There was a time when Josh and I were friends."

She sounded so wistful, Paris looked at her keenly. As long as she could recall, the Fantazia name spurred a fighting stance from her grandmother. Rachel and Josh were both at the top, where there was supposed to be plenty of room, but they competed for contracts, prestige, and whatever personal satisfaction it gave them to beat out each other. If they had been friends, it had not been in Paris's lifetime.

Paris braced herself and sank into the chair. "Well, right now you're on opposite sides of an important issue. Josh would never let sentimentality temper his tongue. The two of you would be clawing at each other within minutes." Paris smiled gently. "Besides, darling, you know I'd have to get Dr. Forest's okay, and you know there isn't much chance of that."

Rachel's steady gaze didn't waver. Paris knew she was assessing her chances of persuading both of them. Rachel wasn't one to give in easily, nor was she one to waste breath on impossible causes. To her surprise, Paris saw no compromise in Rachel's amethyst eyes. She meant to have her way. Why did she want to see Josh? Did she think she could talk him into or out of anything?

"All right, I'll ask Dr. Forest, but don't start making any plans," Paris conceded. "I'll abide by his decision, and so will you."

Rachel sniffed, then glanced at the folder in Paris's lap. "What have you brought?"

Rachel had a knack for putting people off guard by abrupt changes in topics. Paris knew she'd have to keep an eye on her for a few days. She smiled inwardly. Anyone would think it foolish to suspect an old woman confined to a hospital room, but then, they didn't know Rachel as she did.

She handed her grandmother the first sheaf of papers from the folder. "Gunderson called. He hasn't been able to get clearance from the Harbor Commission. Frankly, I don't think he will. Sully-Ford has its eye on that piece of property for expansion." Gunderson Freight wanted to build a warehouse for electronic equipment imported from the Orient. The acreage on the waterfront was ideal for unloading, but the fast turnover of goods leaving the warehouse would increase pier traffic ten percent, which the Harbor Commission wanted to avoid. On the other hand, an expansion of the Sully-Ford Pipe Company would make only minor changes in traffic patterns.

It would also keep the pipe company from moving their plant elsewhere.

"They haven't made an offer," Rachel said. "Call Ashton and let him know we favor Gunderson's plan. We don't sell to companies that aren't an asset to the community."

Paris made a note to call the building commissioner, but she knew she wouldn't go out on a limb for the freight company. If Gunderson didn't get Harbor Commission approval, she'd sell to the pipe company. The land was better suited to their expansion than Gunderson's warehouse anyhow. Had the question cropped up before Rachel's stroke, Paris would have argued openly. Now she let Rachel enjoy the feeling of triumph.

Rachel awkwardly turned the pages in her lap. One of the nurses had suggested installing a mechanical page turner, but Rachel had stubbornly refused. Paris studied her movements and tried to detect improvement. She didn't see any obvious signs.

"What about the Mendahl job?" Rachel asked.

Paris briefly summed up what had been done to acquire the acreage for a shopping mall in nearby Lakewood. The project had originally been slated for Ocean Beach, but Shanna Fantazia had gotten to property owners before the city council voted, tipped off by Josh, no doubt. She got exclusive listings on three-fourths of the land Mendahl needed. Shanna wouldn't budge on the inflated asking prices, so Paris advised Mendahl to find another site. Shanna could sit on her listings until they expired. Lakewood was out of the jurisdiction of the Ocean Beach City Council. Paris had personally handled the real estate transactions for the land. She had a crew ready to start excavating next week.

Rachel nodded, her eyes full of admiration for the competent, beautiful woman Paris had become. And a fighter. It gave Rachel great satisfaction to know Paris had beaten Josh's granddaughter this time. Shanna was a dirty fighter, a woman who used people unscrupulously. Little wonder she hadn't been able to get along with her quiet, methodical father or her fiery-tempered, determined grandfather. Paris had run afoul of her numerous times and had not always come out victorious.

For the rest of the half hour, Paris and Rachel moved from one topic to another as they went over the day's work. At times Paris drew out a description or explanation as she sensed

Rachel was tiring. As a rule, she was pretty accurate about gauging her grandmother's strength, but it seemed diminished today. Reading that article hadn't helped her health. Paris felt a stab of pain as she returned the papers to her briefcase. She wondered if Rachel would ever regain the ground the stroke had deprived her of.

"I don't suppose your mother's been in touch?" Rachel asked abruptly.

"No," Paris said with surprise. It wasn't unusual for Irena to absent herself for months on end, but it was rare for Rachel to ask about her. "Is there something special you want to talk to her about?" If necessary, Paris could probably locate her mother, but it wasn't something she'd do on her own. The less she saw of Irena, the better.

Rachel snorted. "When did it ever do any good to talk to Irena?"

That didn't require an answer. Long ago Paris had accepted the fact her mother possessed a restless spirit, even a wanton one, and that no one would change her. That was fine with her, since she had so much more in common with Rachel, who had nurtured her as lovingly as a full-time mother would.

Reluctantly, Paris said, "Do you want me to get in touch with her?"

"No", Rachel said, but offered no explanation for why she had asked after Irena in the first place.

The door opened and the slim Japanese girl came to clear away the sherry glasses, a signal that the visit was over. Paris kissed Rachel's parched cheek.

"I'll see you tomorrow. Anything I can bring?"

"A telephone!"

Paris smiled and squeezed the frail hand gently. "Behave yourself. Have Elizabeth call if you need anything."

Rachel snorted, and waved her granddaughter away, though if she let anyone coddle her, it would be Paris.

Victor stood on the balcony watching the changing pinks and mauves as the sun neared the horizon. For a few minutes a dark cloud became a symphony of beauty as a golden halo embraced it, warding off the encroaching twilight. He turned and stepped inside the living room of his eleventh-floor apartment, assigned to him for as long as he needed to complete this job. Decorated in bold colors, furnished in traditional American, if it lacked personal touches, he was oblivious to their absence. He was not a collector of mementos . . . or people.

An image of Paris with the sun glinting in her hair crowded his mind. The way she'd tied her shoulder-length blond hair back the day they sailed to Catalina highlighted her high cheekbones and wide-spaced eyes. Her eyes were the color of the Pacific that day, deep sea-green with glinting yellow flecks that entrapped the sunlight. Her eyes changed color with her moods, and that day they'd been warm and loving. Would he be able to walk away from her when he finished here? He'd tried to analyze his feelings a hundred times this past month, but he still had no answer. He'd liked her right from the start, even though he knew it was bad policy to mix business and pleasure. There were so many things he admired about Paris. Paris was a fighter, a doer, and a hell of a good business-woman. He realized now that she commanded as much respect and admiration as the Old Lady. Rachel Upfield's stroke had coincided with his arrival, so he'd never met her, but he knew she was a worthy adversary, even tucked away in the privately endowed wing of the hospital. She was fighting her illness with the same determination she used to get to the top of West Coast business, society, and wealth. She fought to save the Oceanside Hotel just as hard . . . and Paris carried her banner.

The doorbell chimed, and Victor crossed with long strides to open the door.

Speaking of the devil. Or an angel. Paris, in a pink cotton sweater that followed her curves, and green dungarees, stood in the hallway, smiling. He put his arm around her as she came in. She looked tired. Was the strain of running the business and worrying about her grandmother wearing her out?

He kissed her. "Bad day?"

She sighed, then tossed her handbag onto a cinnamon tweed ottoman. "Not really. It just seemed longer than usual." In the room she felt protected in the warm circle of his arm. She leaned her head against his shoulder, and felt the tension ease from her neck. Being with Victor was the best relaxation she could ask for.

"I have a shakerful of martinis on the balcony," he whispered against her hair.

She turned to look into his velvety brown eyes and flashed him a grateful smile. In the fading light the planes of Victor's handsome face were strongly outlined: his broad forehead, deep-set eyes under heavy brows, his firm square chin. His dark hair was streaked by the California sun. Outside, a delightful breeze had sprung up to dissipate the heat. Victor took the chilled glasses from an ice bucket and poured from an insulated shaker.

"Cheers."

She raised her glass, then sipped. "Perfect." She smiled with affection, wanting to be in his arms again and to forget the hundred and one problems that clung to her mind. She relished the martini fully as she gazed across the expanse of Pacific which blended with the darkening sky. The purple streak of horizon grew hazy as she watched. Ships looked serene on the choppy ocean, and seagulls swooped lazily in the air. Unbidden, thoughts returned to her stoic grandmother. Victor put his arm around her.

"You're very solemn."

"Sorry, I don't mean to be. It's just that every time I see Rachel so helpless . . ." She sighed.

"She's better than she was two months ago, Paris. Give her time."

"Time? How much does she have left?"

"I don't think Rachel would trade any of her past for one day of the future. She's led a full life."

"I don't suppose she would," Paris agreed. "It's a shame that there has to be all this fuss about the hotel now. It's killing her to even consider the possibility of seeing it go."

"She'll have to let go eventually."

Paris looked at him quickly. "Does that mean you've made a decision?"

"No. I was speaking in generalities. Times change. People and places take new directions. Nobody lives forever, even Rachel."

"I've got to carry on her fight, Victor. I've been nurtured and shaped as much as the hotel and the company. From the time I was a child, we both knew I'd carry on where she leaves off."

"Whatever Rachel did for either the hotel or the company, she did before you even made an appearance in the world. She got what she wanted. Having you to take over for her is a bonus. Rachel knows you can't bank sentimentality."

Paris smiled ruefully. "I can't argue. Rachel would be the last to admit sentiment played any part of it, or does now. But it eats away at me to see her want something so much and not be able to fight her own battle. Business has never been a spectator sport to her." She turned back to the view that was rapidly losing the battle with darkness. In the harbor the well-lit offshore wells were enticing, cheery illusions. Rachel had been instrumental in persuading the oil companies to disguise platforms that would be seen from shore with mock towers to resemble resort hotels instead of letting ugly pumps and derricks destroy the view. There was hardly a place in Ocean Beach that Rachel hadn't played a part in forming one way or another. Paris looked back at Victor. Shadows played across the strong features of his face as darkness claimed the balcony. "She needs this final victory. I can't let her lose." She was sorry the moment the words were out. It sounded as if she were trying to influence his decision.

Victor took her arm. "Let's go inside. You can watch me put the final touches on dinner. We can't settle the problems of the world on empty stomachs."

She laughed softly, relieved that he had not made an awkward moment of her remark. "Are you always so practical?"

In answer he set her martini glass on the tray, then took her in his arms. "Try me," he whispered. He bent close, and his lips brushed hers invitingly. Paris melted against him. Her hands crept across the green sport shirt as she kneaded his muscular back. Responding to the shift in her mood, he murmured, "There isn't anything in the kitchen that can't wait."

Paris felt herself go pleasantly weak as desire stirred in her limbs. She succumbed willingly, molding her lips to his as they kissed again, searching each other's inner selves. Her hands slid to his firm shoulder, rode over the nape of his neck, and clasped behind him possessively. She wanted him. Everything else was insignificant to her flame. She drew away from the sweetness of his mouth long enough to glance toward the bedroom. Smiling, he led her there, releasing her only to pull back the deep green velvet spread and switch on the stereo.

As always, Paris was in awe of the ease with which they welcomed each other's bodies. Naked, they embraced as they stood beside the bed, pressing together with sensual awareness and complete pleasure. Victor's hands explored her flesh like a blind sculptor examining an exquisite statue. His power and gentleness hung in perfect balance, bringing her to heightened awareness that was nurtured by sharing. She touched his body, smiling, wanting, giving. They moved in accord as he lay beside her and once more soared toward the peak of desire. And when they coupled, it was eagerly, lingering to savor the wonder of flesh, male enfolded in female, bringing them to powerful fulfillment. When their hungers were appeased, they stayed locked in each other's embrace, communing in contented silence until they found the energy to stir.

They dined by candlelight. Victor had prepared Cornish game hens stuffed with wild rice and mushrooms, tomatoes Lutece, and broccoli and lemon butter sauce. Paris tried to keep her mind from returning to the subject of her grandmother and the newspaper article, but it was impossible. She brought it up over coffee.

"Rachel was upset today over the story in the *Press-Telegram*." She fingered the angular lines of the black Lenox cup. Victor's tablesetting was masculine, without pretense, yet richly warm and comfortable. Like him. She looked across the table and found him watching her curiously. "You hinted there were new factors that might affect the decision about the hotel. She wanted to know what they were."

For a time, Victor raised his cup and sipped the strong Costa Rican coffee, Paris's favorite brew. It bothered him that she was completely immersed in her grandmother's problems tonight. If he refused to discuss the article, she would conclude he had made his decision, no matter how much he denied it. Very carefully he framed his answer.

"The reporter hinted, Paris. I didn't write the article." He smiled.

"He got his insights from you."

Victor lifted a thick brow. "I'm not responsible for the conclusions he draws. The press release he got didn't contain anything I haven't already told you."

"And Shanna Fantazia!" It was out before she realized it, bitter words from the wellspring of pain deep inside her.

Victor felt their sting. The lingering euphoria from their lovemaking began to evaporate. He and Paris both knew Josh Fantazia had access to everything that crossed the city council desks. It was a fact of life in Ocean Beach he'd had to accept from the beginning. And if Josh shared his information with his granddaughter, that he had to accept, too. If Victor bore any guilt it was for discussing too much of his investigation with Paris. Victor had told Shanna far less. At first Paris had been a source of information, someone who could give him a history of the Oceanside Hotel and the city. But she'd been so accessible, so comfortable to be with, so damned attractive. . . .

Paris set down her cup with a clatter. "I'm sorry, darling. I'm being bitchy. I suppose I've been influenced strongly by Rachel's feelings, but I can't help it. She's been a lot more than a grandmother to me all my life. I think like she does. This whole business has become a crusade I've got to carry through."

Was the feud between Paris and Shanna Fantazia an outgrowth of rivalry between Upfield Land Management and Fantazia Enterprises, or was it more? he wondered. What was the explosive chemistry between those two families? "You can't be an extension of Rachel," he said. "She's her own woman and always has been. She built her empire by fusing her fortunes with the fortunes of this city. She was part of the city's growth, if not the cause of it. So was the hotel. Of course it means a lot to her, but if she has to give it up, she's going to have to accept the fact. She's done other things that have been just as difficult."

Paris narrowed her eyes, and impaled him. "What's that supposed to mean?"

He answered with a tinge of impatience. "It's not supposed to 'mean' anything. It was just an observation. You know as well as I do that Rachel came up the hard way. There had to be a lot of times she didn't like what had to be done but she did it anyhow."

Paris pushed her cup aside. "What specifically do you have in mind?" The sharp edge in her voice was like honed steel, but she couldn't suppress the anxiety and anger that clamored inside her. She'd known from the minute she walked in that Victor had found out something, and he wasn't going to share it.

Something about Rachel? she wondered.

Victor refilled his coffee cup from the pewter pot. When he held it toward Paris's cup, she shook her head. Damn. He didn't want to get into a discussion of Rachel. Was it possible Paris didn't know the things her grandmother had done? The full picture of Ocean Beach's and the West Coast's first lady had slowly emerged in his investigation, and it wasn't pretty.

"Let's talk about it tomorrow. You haven't forgotten we have an appointment in the morning?"

Paris refused to be sidetracked. "I want to know now."

"Darling—"

She shook her head, her honey-gold hair glinting on her pink sweater in the glow of the candles like burnished copper. "Don't patronize me!"

Exasperated, he said, "What the hell do you want me to do?! One minute we're lovers and the next you're carving up every word I say and spitting the pieces back at me! Is this a business discussion or a personal one?"

Paris pushed away from the table, too upset to control her temper. It was the Grant-Upfield temper, and would lend brilliance to anything she said. "Is there a difference?" she glared. "Don't you find me much easier to convince after you've taken me to bed? Isn't that why you set out to romance me?"

"Set out—?!" He drew in his breath angrily. What the devil had gotten into her? The delightful evening had suddenly become a street brawl.

Paris leaned on the table, bending toward Victor like a lawyer grilling a reluctant witness. "What about Shanna?" she demanded. "Does the famous Sands technique work equally well on her? Does it matter to you that Josh has sicced her on you like Mata Hari so he can beat Rachel?" She was out of control, shaking now with inner fury, knowing she was uttering horrible things but unable to stop. Her eyes swam with tears.

"Shanna's a real estate broker. You can't blame her for wanting a commission."

His calm logic infuriated Paris. "Do you deny you've been romancing her?" Shanna Fantazia could conveniently dig up a client for a deal when there was an attractive man involved. Paris trembled as tears spilled from her flashing eyes. She whirled and ran from the room in total frustration. Grabbing her purse, she headed for the door.

Victor stared at her retreating figure, reining in his anger. He'd never seen Paris so upset, but this wasn't the right time to tell her what he'd discovered. *Christ, would there ever be a right time?* The door slammed.

With the full force of a wave, the facts of his study came crashing down on him. Fraud, blackmail, possibly even murder . . . All of these composed the business life and times of one of the greatest businesses on the West Coast, Upfield Land Management, shepherded, piloted, *created* by Rachel Upfield, the grandmother of the woman he was very likely in love with. Paris might have the shrewdness of a Grant, but in her dealings with him, she'd shown she had limits that her grandmother likely never had. And her tears, even in a fiery blaze of anger, indicated she had a heart. Victor suspected that Rachel Grant never delivered her wrath with anything but steely composure. The woman had been, and probably still was, ruthless in all her actions.

But Paris—Paris was a kind of second chance for that family. Possessing all the strengths of her grandmother, and likely her mother, without the weaknesses. Except for that temper. It blazed into a conflagration at times.

Victor shook his head. It began to throb, and to radiate to his limbs in a hot flash. He sat in the quiet room, not hearing the soft music from the stereo, and instead, concentrated on counting backward from a hundred.

❦ *Fourteen* ❦

PARIS SLEPT RESTLESSLY, tormented by fragmented nightmares in which she fled from shadowy figures and ran into bleak walls or to the edge of a steep cliff overlooking the sea. In the morning she was tired and out of sorts. Her fight with Victor had left a miserable ache in her chest that she couldn't banish and which she hesitated to review carefully.

She declined breakfast in favor of black coffee, a pennance suited to her mood. Usually she enjoyed lingering in Rachel's sunny breakfast room at the Ladera Street manor house, but today the bright greens and yellow and the cheerful smile of the maid only added to her misery. She carried her coffee to the sun room.

Since Rachel's hospitalization, Paris had been spending several nights a week at the house in order to monitor Rachel's mail and the operation of the household. Long ago she had rented an apartment in a luxury highrise on Ocean Boulevard that Upfield had built and managed. Rachel wanted her to stay on in the big house where she'd grown up and which would be hers someday, but when Paris said she needed the freedom and independence of her own place, Rachel understood. Now, without Rachel, the house seemed strangely hollow.

A staff of eight servants ran the house, which was ridiculously large for one person. Darien Hill was in a state of flux.

Beyond the high arched windows looking toward the Hill, luxurious new condominiums sprouted like a crop of lettuce. Rachel's house, with its two wings, four full stories, and a huge attic under a slightly gabled roof, was magnificent but impractical in its changing environment. Long ago the mansions topping the Hill had given way to the oil fields that had fostered the city's astonishing wealth. This house had been built in the shadow of the unsightly but profitable oil derricks that had launched Rachel's prosperity, and the town's. Now underground pumps brought up the precious black gold, and the surface of the Hill was being reclaimed. Darien Hill was becoming fashionable once again. And when it reached full stride, would Rachel still want to live here? Yes. She was too old to move elsewhere, too much a part of the Hill, too tied to the past which was an integral part of her present. But Paris knew that without Rachel, she would find the house too full of memories.

She glanced through the archway to the spacious, sunken living room that was a page from Rachel's past. A high-backed, gracefully curved Regency sofa covered in Beauvais tapestry, an ornate gilt-framed mirror above the fireplace, rosewood tables with pink marble tops, crystal lamps, an exquisite Oriental rug on the gleaming hardwood floor. It was impossible to envision the room any other way. Paris had crawled on the deeply colored rug, taken her first halting steps between chairs and tables, sat savoring tea with Rachel on the sofa, or on the steps down into the living room where a fire on chilly nights blazed. The house was Rachel, she was everywhere.

Remembering her discussion with Victor the previous night, Paris wondered if she was a carefully groomed extension of Rachel rather than her own person. No, she could never accept that. Rachel had always given her the freedom to soar alone as well as to glide in the shadow of the eagle. Victor was one of those who couldn't imagine the sacrifices Rachel had made to take over the upbringing of a child whose parents had parted. If she had any memories of her father, they were long gone, thanks to his total disappearance from her life. And Irena? She always thought of her as Irena, not as her mother. Irena didn't know the meaning of motherhood. She'd been eager to discard her child and take off to her own pleasures. Beautiful, selfish Irena who flitted in and out of relationships—and trouble—without a thought for anyone but herself. And who had never shown the least interest in the businesses Rachel had built so staunchly, so brazenly. As long as Irena's allowance came regularly, it made no difference to her where the money came from.

Victor couldn't appreciate any of that. Victor was a machine that understood only business. Sentiment played no part in his life. She sipped her coffee, but it had grown cold. She set down the fragile Haviland cup with a sigh. She hadn't given Victor a chance the previous night to refute her accusations. Would he have? With a sick feeling, she realized that it wasn't Victor's innuendos about Rachel that had infuriated her as much as it was his not denying those about Shanna. *I'm jealous*, she thought with astonishment. She'd been aware for a long time that she cared a lot about Victor, but did she care enough to think in terms of exclusivity? Did she love him that much? Or was it that she hated Shanna Fantazia that much?

Victor had not denied seeing Shanna. Paris couldn't pull that barb from her heart. And Shanna wanted the Oceanside torn down, to be replaced by something vulgar, without the majesty and history of the inn and hotel. Paris would do whatever it took to make sure she didn't win. Picking up her briefcase and purse from the hall table where the maid had put them for her, Paris went out, slamming the big front door harder than necessary.

Her silver Mercedes was in the drive, the engine purring softly. She refused to have Rachel's chauffeur drive her, but he always brought the car around and had it ready no matter what time she came out. She got behind the wheel and drove down the long curving driveway.

Her mood lifted slightly by the time she turned the car over to the parking valet in the Upfield Building lot. She would phone the *Press-Telegram* and demand a rebuttal article on the Oceanside, since enough people recalled the glory of the old hotel and would rally to the cause of restoring it. Could she subtly instigate a petition to save the hotel? It would have no decisive value, but it might stir the city council enough to take notice. And Victor. It was worth considering.

As she pushed through the doors of Upfield Land Management, the receptionist held out an envelope. "This just came by messenger, Miss Hamilton."

Paris carried it to her office, her heart pounding erratically when she saw the Ocean Beach Memorial Hospital return address. If anything had happened to Rachel, Dr. Forest would have phoned. Dropping her briefcase and purse, she tore the envelope open. Inside was a sealed, postmarked letter in a heavy vellum envelope addressed to Rachel, and a note.

This came in the morning mail. No return address, but it's metered through the Fantazia offices. I thought you might want to see it. It was signed *Elizabeth Aspenson.*

Paris strode to the cushioned chair behind her curved walnut desk, staring at the envelope. The address was typed and offered no clue as to the identity of the sender. But Elizabeth was right, the meter number belonged to Fantazia Enterprises. Paris thought of Rachel's strange request to see Josh. It was inconceivable that she had managed to get a message to him. Paris slit the envelope with an ivory-brass opener that had been an offhanded gift from one of Irena's trips.

Rachel—I must see you. The hospital refuses to put through my calls or let me visit. It's imperative that we settle unfinished business. Find a way. You have my private number. Josh.

Paris reread the brief note, bristling with anger. Did Josh think he could demand—? That's exactly what he was doing. And only yesterday Rachel had demanded to see Josh. Puzzled, Paris tapped the sheet of paper absently on the desktop. Josh must realize his note might be intercepted. He'd been a patient in the Pavilion four years ago after a mild coronary. He knew the measures taken to protect patients when their physicians wanted to keep them quiet. *Unfinished business* . . . A threat?

Glancing at her grandfather's pocket watch suspended under a glass dome on the desk, she pushed the intercom.

"Yes, Miss Hamilton?"

"Fran, get me Josh Fantazia at Fantazia Enterprises."

"Josh—?" The secretary checked her surprise. She'd been with the company eight years and knew Fantazia Enterprises was their chief competitor in a rivalry that at times proved quite bitter. She had never before been requested to put through a call directly to Josh Fantazia.

"The old bear himself," Paris said firmly. She clicked off the intercom. The feud between Rachel and Josh was something she had accepted a long time ago. It went far beyond business rivalry, but it was a subject Rachel refused to discuss, and Paris had never pressed for an explanation. She'd been astonished by Rachel's remark yesterday that she and Josh had once been friends. She'd always believed them born enemies. The Fantazias were not easy people to like. She and Shanna had known each other since grade school, and even then she'd been a perfect little snob, haughty and condescending. Paris remembered the other girl's spiteful snubs, and the whispering to her classmates that Paris's father was nothing but a dirty roustabout in the oil fields. Cheeks flaming, Paris had punched Shanna with all the anger and frustration of a six-year-old. Nose bloodied, Shanna went screaming to the teacher. Paris had been forced to apologize and take a note home to Rachel describing the incident. Rachel cradled Paris on her lap and dried her tears. Yes, her father worked the oil rigs, but he was a good, honest, handsome man. Perhaps someday he would come to see her, but in the meantime, she was not to listen to crude remarks made by an ignorant little girl who thought she was better than anyone else because of her family name.

The phone buzzed softly. "Mr. Fantazia is on the line, Miss Hamilton." There was still a note of surprise in Fran's voice.

Paris lifted the receiver. "Josh?"

"Good morning, Paris. How is Rachel?" Fantazia's voice had the deep timbre of a man half his years.

"She's making progress. She's asked to see you."

There was only the briefest pause. "When?"

His directness irritated Paris and she had trouble keeping her tone even. "She *asked*. Dr. Forest hasn't given his permission yet. Rachel isn't strong and can't stand any excitement. Her health is our primary concern."

He cleared his throat. Paris sensed the effort the restraint cost him. "I'll make it brief."

"Like your note?"

There was another silence, longer and heavier than the first. "That was none of your concern."

"Anything that affects Rachel is my concern," she snapped. "Why not tell me what this is all about so I can decide if it's in her best interests to risk a visitor right now."

"It's personal," he shot back, unruffled and ready to close

the door on her completely. Paris had better listen, the threat in his voice seemed to say. "I'll limit myself to whatever time the doctor dictates, but I want to see Rachel alone. This is for her as much as it is me. Do what you have to, but arrange it." He hung up.

Paris slammed down the phone. She really hadn't expected Josh Fantazia to confide in her, but she couldn't countenance his peremptory manner, nor the secrecy with which this odd request was shrouded. But Rachel wouldn't let it go easily, and Rachel couldn't be ignored.

She glanced at the gold watch and began to ready her desk for the day's work. Victor's appointment was at nine-thirty. She had to set aside personal feelings and brace herself for a renewed fight. As he'd said last night, sentiment wasn't a bankable commodity. She couldn't let anything stand in the way of winning her battle with Shanna.

She unrolled the revised concept of the new Oceanside. Victor would be impressed, as Rachel had been when Paris came up with an idea for added wings that would blend the beach hotel with the new skyline of the proposed urban renewal plan. The architect had done a good job of depicting the subtle transition from new to old. If anything, the modern wings enhanced the beauty of the ornate older building.

She glanced at the clock again. Victor was late. It wasn't like him, but then, they'd never had a fight before. Was he going to skip the appointment without so much as a courtesy call to cancel it? That wasn't his style, but neither was that outburst last night hers. The acute pain of her jealousy and rage as she envisioned Victor in bed with Shanna made her insides churn. She buzzed Fran Markham again.

"Has Mr. Sands arrived?"

"Not yet."

At ten Paris admitted furiously that he wasn't coming. She picked up the phone. "Get me Ray Bart." When the head of the Upfield Construction Division came on the line, Paris told him to send a clean-up crew to the Oceanside Hotel as soon as possible.

"Is that a go on the project?" Ray Bart had been with the company twenty years. He was the best in his field, and he was as loyal to Paris as he'd always been to Rachel. At times he tended to be less formal than other employees, but his informality stemmed from personal affection for Rachel. Like her, he mourned the closing of the Oceanside three years before and was eager to see it restored and embellished to greater splendor.

"Not yet," Paris said, "but I want an accurate estimate of what has to be done structurally. Get B and S down to do an inspection next week."

"I can give you a pretty good idea by doing a walk-through on my own," Bart said. "Mrs. Upfield and I have gone over the original plans enough times that I know where every bearing wall is."

"How soon can you get it to me?"

"Tomorrow okay?"

"Fine. And the clean-up crew?"

"I've got one available Monday."

She felt better for having set the work in motion. She'd have the windows and doors unboarded, some of the interior clutter removed. It would only be a ghost of its former elegance, but when Victor saw its potential . . .

She glanced at the clock again, picked up the phone, and got an outside line. She dialed Victor's number, listening to it ring as she summoned cool detachment. *You can't bank sentimentality.* Impatiently she found herself counting the rings. Had he left? She was about to hang up when the receiver was finally lifted, but there was no familiar, brisk answer, "Victor Sands here."

"Victor?" Still no answer, only the open line. Scowling, she said, "This is Paris. Have you forgotten our appointment?" It was harsher than she had planned, but his silence irritated her. She couldn't squelch the Grant in her. He might at least have the decency to answer her.

She was aware of his breathing then, slow and heavy as if he'd wakened from a deep sleep. But that was impossible. He was an early riser, a dawn jogger who blazed a path on the beach every day. Could he be ill? She leaned on the desk.

"Victor? Are you all right? Is something wrong?" Her rage was forgotten as she counted his breaths. "Answer me!" Her voice caught.

Finally he spoke. "Yes . . . I think so."

He sounded strange. Confused. The noise of his breathing receded from the phone. Paris gripped the receiver and raised her voice. "Victor—don't hang up."

"I'm sorry . . . I don't . . . " He gave a tremendous sigh and the line clicked.

Paris was out of the chair instantly, grabbing her purse as she ran out. The astonished secretary looked up.

"See if you can catch Mr. Siddon before he leaves the bank. Make another appointment for him." In her gold shirt-waist and black tailored blazer, she crossed the reception room, heads turning to watch as she raced out. Her beauty, and consternation, made a jarring contrast.

She tried to regain her composure as the elevator descended. Something was wrong. She felt it on an intuitive level. Something was terribly wrong.

She concentrated on driving the few blocks to Victor's apartment as swiftly as possible. Once, when she changed lanes abruptly, she ignored the other driver's angry honking. When she pulled up in front of the awning-covered entrance to the swank building, she was out before the startled doorman, a bespectacled, light-haired young man, could open her door.

"Have you seen Mr. Sands this morning?" she demanded, handing him her keys.

"He hasn't been down, Miss Hamilton."

"Come with me. I may need your passkey." She was already striding across the blue and gold lobby. Donovan hurried after her.

"What's happened?" he asked, following her into the elevator as she selected a button, the fifteenth floor.

"Mr. Sands may be ill." Pain gripped her chest the way it had the night Rachel had collapsed. A few hours ago she had been angry at Victor. Now she was filled with worry.

At Victor's door Paris pushed the bell, holding her breath as she listened. She jiggled the doorknob, then knocked, at the same time motioning Donovan to use his key.

Victor was sitting in a tweed chair near the phone. His dark head was bowed, cradled in his hands, his eyes closed. He still had on the shirt and slacks he'd worn the night before, and his face was drawn. Paris knelt beside the chair.

"Victor?" He looked up, his blue eyes filled with confusion. Paris's heart wrenched. "Victor?" She touched her hand to his wrinkled brow and smoothed back his tangled hair. "Are you all right?"

He seemed to be studying her, but there was no spark of

recognition, no emotion in his gaze. She took one of his large, tanned hands in hers, tracing a path across the dark hairs on it without taking her eyes from him, as if she could soothe a response from him.

From the foyer the doorman whispered, "Should I call a doctor?"

Paris hesitated. She'd been terrified of finding Victor collapsed on the floor, or worse. But he seemed all right. Could he be in shock? Had he received bad news? His hand was inert, as if he weren't even aware of her presence. An accident? She raised her hand and stroked his head gently, feeling for evidence of an injury. Nothing. Her hand lingered on the thick dark hair as she glanced around the apartment. Nothing seemed out of place. Beyond the open bedroom door, she saw the bed as she had left it the night before, covers smoothed and tucked under the mattress, and the heavy green velvet spread still neatly folded over the brass bedpost. Had he slept? Her gaze shifted to the dining room. She could see only a corner of the table. Her cup and saucer still occupied the place she'd left them on the Lucite placemat engraved with Victor's initials. She looked back at Victor, whose head was bowed again. She touched his chin and forced him to look up.

"Victor, do you understand what I'm saying?" When he nodded, she asked, "Do you feel all right? Are you sick or in pain?"

He frowned. "No."

"Did you sleep last night?" She had the elaborate patience of someone speaking to a slow-witted child, but she didn't want to lose his attention. She indicated the bedroom. "Did you go to bed last night?"

He glanced toward the open door with a puzzled look. The creases between his dark, thick brows deepened. "I don't know." His eyes held a glint of sheer terror in them.

Paris swallowed against the dryness in her throat. "Who—" She tried again, struggling for a lighter tone. "Do you know who I am?" Her gaze riveted on him the way it had on Rachel when she finally regained consciousness after the stroke and Dr. Forest had tried to assess her brain damage.

The silence was unbearable until Victor finally shook his head slowly. Paris couldn't breathe. Behind her, Donovan gave an astonished cluck. Paris squeezed Victor's hand reassuringly.

"Can you tell me your name?" she asked, hiding her panic. *I sound like I'm doing introductions at tea,* she thought idiotically.

He moistened his lips as though buying time. "You called me Victor."

Her heart skipped a beat. "Do you know your last name?"

He let his breath out in a long, pained sigh, then dropped his head back into his hands. Paris put an arm around him but withdrew when she felt him stiffen. She spoke very softly as she would to a hurt child. "It's all right, Victor. It's all right." She got to her feet and motioned to Donovan. "Help me get him to the car."

"Maybe we should call a doctor." Donovan looked frightened.

"I'm taking him to the hospital." She and Donovan got Victor to his feet. He moved like an automaton, staring straight ahead, his expression blank. Paris wondered fleetingly if he could have had too much to drink last night. He'd been fine when she'd left, except for his anger. Drugs? She'd never seen him even smoke pot, but she supposed anything was possible.

When they bundled him into the car, Paris pressed a folded twenty into Donovan's hand. "If anyone asks, say he's out."

"Yes, Miss Hamilton." He touched the visor of his blue cap as Paris climbed behind the wheel.

As she drove, Victor stared ahead woodenly, as though cataloging what he saw for future reference. Or maybe searching for something he recognized.

Paris fought back her tears.

They made her wait outside the emergency room while they examined Victor. She paced the wide corridor, aware of the sounds and medical scents around her but her complete attention focused on the curtained green cubicle where Victor lay on an examining table. Knowing he was in good hands did little to relieve her anxiety. Why was it taking so long? Was that a good sign or bad? Rachel's stroke had been decisive and swift, felling her in midsentence and making her skin flush like a doll whose maker had applied too much color. But because there was no doubt what had happened, Paris had been able to summon the best physicians and medical treatment. What kind of help did Victor need?

She wiped her mind clean as a slate, telling herself he would be all right. Whatever had happened, he'd be himself shortly. He had to be.

The green curtains parted and a young doctor emerged in a white coat with a stethoscope dangling about his neck and curly red hair crowning his head like a surgical cap. Paris crossed the room with brisk strides before he could escape through a set of doors marked DOCTORS ONLY.

"Doctor, how is he?" She tried to read the clinically masked expression behind the horn-rimmed glasses.

"We're going to run some tests," the doctor said. He'd recognized Paris, one of the few true beauties in town, and an Upfield, the moment he saw her. He wondered what her relationship was to the man she'd brought in. "Can you tell us anything about his activities this morning?"

"I don't know. He was fine last night." *Furious but fine,* she thought. She glanced into the treatment room and saw Victor staring at the ceiling. She looked back to the doctor, trying to be helpful. "When I phoned this morning, he sounded strange, so I went over. I found him like this. He—he didn't know me or his own name."

"He's suffering some kind of amnesia. There's no sign of a head injury. Possibly it's traumatic. I've ordered some tests. He'll have to be admitted. They'll need his ID and insurance."

"I'll take care of it. Can I talk to him?"

The doctor nodded, glanced at the two of them speculatively again, then pushed through the double doors and picked up a phone, studying the chart on the clipboard.

Paris went to Victor. She touched his hand and smiled. "They're going to run some tests." A wounded look emanated from somewhere deep inside him. Paris kept her smile fixed. "There's nothing to worry about. They'll find the problem, and with a few days' rest . . ." She squeezed his hand, hoping for a response. Her eyes brimmed with tears, and she tried to blink them away. Victor moistened his lips. It was a gesture she'd never seen him use before today. A sign of hesitation? Victor, who was always so sure of himself, so definite, so forthright, now exhibiting caution as though one wrong word might shatter the fragile hold he had on reality.

Finally he said, "Thanks. I appreciate your help."

Tears trailed down her cheeks, and she wiped them away before he looked back at her. He was so vulnerable. "They need information at Admitting. Is your wallet in your pocket?"

Again his response was delayed a moment. Then he patted his pockets carefully and shook his head. "It doesn't seem to be."

"That's all right," she said quickly when the worry returned to his eyes. "Donovan has a key." At his puzzled look she said, "The doorman who was with me this morning."

His gaze held her for a long time, but it lacked the spark and tenderness she was accustomed to seeing. His face had lost its vitality. The doctor returned, penning notes, then tucked the clipboard to a peg on the gurney.

"He'll be on Medical Three." He wheeled the gurney past.

Paris watched Victor vanish down the corridor, her mind and heart torn with anguish. He had to be all right. She loved him.

❧ *Fifteen* ❧

SHANNA FANTAZIA SLAMMED down the phone. The jarring noise made the real estate agents in the outer office glance through the open office door, then quickly back to their own desks as they saw their employer's brown eyes glinting with fire. Working for Shanna Fantazia was like being caged with a jungle cat, sleek and purring one moment but capable of snarling and snapping the next. Out of earshot the staff dubbed her the Black Panther, but even when there was no chance of being overheard, the nickname was whispered. At thirty-two, Shanna Fantazia was tall, slim, raven-haired, possibly brilliant and ruthlessly successful; her temper was something most people avoided at all cost. She'd been known to read out agents for minor omissions on listing agreements or for failing to meet sales quotas she imposed. The opinion had been offered that her tongue should be registered as a lethal weapon, yet there was always a waiting list of hopeful real estate agents wanting to work in the prestigious Fantazia office. And those who were taken on and survived made high commissions, excellent bonuses, and the Million Dollar Club within their first year. But when Shanna was angry, as she was now, a hush fell over the office and everyone quickly found something important on his or her desk that required full concentration.

Where the hell was Victor? Shanna had been trying to

reach him since yesterday, and there was still no answer at his apartment. She'd even driven by his building and parked outside, hoping to catch him. Sands was a very attractive man but not the easy mark she'd expected. She still hadn't talked him into recommending the condo plan for the downtown redevelopment. Or seduced him.

Now the stupid doorman at the apartment building kept telling her Victor was out. Damn it, she knew he was out. *But where?*

She swiveled the red leather chair and focused her flashing eyes out the large window that overlooked Ocean Boulevard. The office's richly paneled walls, gleaming teak accented by luxurious, deep red draperies, and plush carpeting usually gave her a sense of power and pleasure, but in her foul mood, her eye was immediately drawn to the turreted monstrosity of the Oceanside Hotel looming in the distance. The damned thing should have been torn down years ago!

No, she thought, if it had been, she wouldn't have this sweet deal hanging fire now. The commission on a four million dollar sale ... And on top of it, knowing she beat Paris Hamilton. Shanna wasn't one to forget a rival who'd bested her more than once. Having Paris pull that Mendahl deal out from under her still rankled. A victory on the Oceanside would be sweet revenge. She hated Paris. She particularly hated Rachel Upfield. The crowned princess and queen of Ocean Beach! Watch her be topped!

More importantly, she wanted to show her grandfather he'd made a mistake in not backing her fully. He was forever telling her how to run her business and personal life. There were times when he flat out refused Fantazia Enterprises' full backing when she could have used it. Desperately. And in combat with Upfield Land Management, which had been a thorn in his side for years, she expected him to give his complete blessing. But he hadn't. For a while she thought he was going to cut her off completely, but he finally agreed to consider the builder she had in mind if he succeeded in buying the Oceanside site. Fantazia Enterprises would handle the rest of the redevelopment itself, but because they weren't in residential construction, that portion of the plan would have to be contracted out. To her.

Recalling the four years she'd worked in the family company, Shanna felt a glow of pride as she looked around her smart office. She'd come a long way, baby. Face it. Admittedly the Fantazia name had boosted her chances, but she'd done it on her own, her way, with no one to credit but herself. Maybe her father was willing to be a yes-man to Josh, but she wasn't. Her father had been president of the company for thirty years, but with Josh still chairman of the board, no one, including her father, could make a move without his approval. Josh had given her a job with the company despite his disappointment that she'd decided on a local business college instead of Harvard, as Paris Hamilton had done. She worked in a goddam secretarial pool until she got her real estate license and he finally moved her into Acquisition and Sales. Two years in that department had been enough to show her she wouldn't move ahead very fast if she stayed. Josh insisted she work her way up, then raged when her successful knack for combining business with pleasure usually brought excellent results. She smiled, thinking of the night Josh had returned to the Fantazia offices after hours once and found her with a minister whose tiny church was the only holdout in an acquisition of land on which Fantazia was going to build an office complex. She and the man of God had been past the main event in her spacious office, but there wasn't any doubt about the means Shanna was employing to close the sale. Josh didn't even relent when she brought him the signed contract the next day.

When she closed the Oceanside deal, Josh would have to admit she had what it took. She smiled in anticipation, then quickly warned herself not to trumpet victory until the deal was signed. When she knew Sands was going to recommend the Fantazia plan, it would be all she needed. She'd have Stanton Fields's signature within hours.

She wondered if she would have gone for the Oceanside deal if Stanton Fields hadn't been so so dynamic and convincing. When he'd shown her magazine articles about condo developments he'd sponsored in Arizona, Colorado, and Texas, and sketched his plan for the Oceanside site, his zeal fired Shanna's interest immediately, and his crusade for a luxurious condominium development in the heart of downtown Ocean Beach quickly became hers as well. Only hers was more pointedly motivated by greed and revenge than by any sense of duty.

Fields was an intriguing man in many ways. She judged

him to be a well-preserved sixty-five, but at times she caught glimpses of age that made her willing to add on a few years. She surreptitiously studied his white sideburns for facelift scars but couldn't find any. He was tall, a bit on the heavy side, though his slim hands gave evidence of a lighter bone structure than a first impression gave. His hair was snow-white, only slightly thinning, and he wore a neatly trimmed beard and mustache. When he walked into the office three months before, he wore a perfectly tailored cream-colored suit that minimized his bulk and reminded Shanna of Southern plantations and colonels. He gave her his card and explained he was a packager for real estate projects and specialized in bringing together outstanding developers and top real estate parcels for highly profitable results. At times he found it expedient to work with local realtors who were in tune with their communities. He wanted a broker in Ocean Beach. He'd made numerous inquiries before selecting her.

She was flattered but wary. Plums like Stanton Fields didn't fall in her lap very often. There had to be a catch. But after driving him around for two days, she decided he was the genuine article. She warned him the Oceanside wouldn't be easy to get. Developers had tried, but Rachel Upfield hung on with a vengeance. Now with her bid on the redevelopment plan, she'd fight harder than ever. Fields shrugged and said he might be able to pull a few strings.

The hell of it was, maybe he could. She'd been skeptical at first, but Stanton Fields had some kind of inside track. He told her about the city hiring Victor Sands before the news was public. And he seemed to anticipate Victor's moves and know what information he would dredge up. She wondered if Fields knew where Victor was now? It was only a few weeks until his report had to be presented to the city council. Everything Sands did now was vital.

Damn it, where was he? She hadn't see him for several days, and he'd been evasive the last time she talked to him on the phone. He was investigating both Upfield and Fantazia businesses, and something he'd found was making him nervous. Her suggestion that she stop by had been met with polite but firm refusal.

Did Paris Hamilton know where he was?

*   *   *

Steve Plisky geared lower as the pickup started down the steep grade. It wouldn't be easy to get heavy equipment down the narrow drive, and he wondered if there was enough turn-around space. The driveway had been built to accommodate car traffic which could easily be controlled for a hotel, but a full work crew needed a lot more space to maneuver in. He parked in the arc of the curve where a pile of cinderblocks and broken concrete barred his progress. Glancing over the canyon grass and weeds that had laid claim to the rubble, he saw that the rest of the drive past the barriers was clear. He turned off the engine and climbed out, stretching his squat muscular body as though the ride had confined him too long. He glanced toward the street as a yellow Camaro turned in and pulled up behind him. A tall, balding man in khaki work pants and shirt jumped out and put out a calloused hand.

"Morning, Steve."

Plisky shook hands. "The gate was open."

"I came by earlier and unlocked it," Ray Bart said. He pointed toward the entrance of the hotel. "That lock's been jimmied. So much for Palms Security."

" 'We're there when you're not,' " Steve quoted with a grin that crinkled his tanned, square face.

Ray Bart shook his head. "Maybe we should go to guard dogs."

"I heard about one over in Santa Ana," Plisky said. "Some clown tossed drugged meat, waited twenty minutes, then went in and cleaned out a whole warehouse."

"I guess it doesn't make much difference here now, but when we start work, I'll mention it to Miz Hamilton. We'd better get started."

Plisky pulled off his visored cap and wiped his brow as he followed the foreman around the rubble. Pushing aside the dangling padlock, the two men opened the heavy plywood door that had been erected over the space where the ornate hotel doors had once been hinged. Leaving the plywood open for light and to help air out the mustiness, they went inside. Bart snapped on a flashlight and swung the beam around the cavernous room.

Ray Bart remembered the Oceanside in its heyday. They were in what had been a lower level lobby that once served guests headed for the banquet rooms and ballroom. There'd been glittering lights, plush carpeting and furniture, and an elegant decor. Now the room was a dark cave with peeling wallpaper and gaping holes where mirrors and light fixtures had been torn out. The furniture and equipment had been sold off when the hotel had been closed three years before. There'd been a salvage auction for the fine woodwork, plumbing fixtures, mantels, and stained-glass windows. He'd been there, and he could still remember Rachel Upfield's expression as the lovely rooms were decimated and left bare. She'd been crestfallen and preoccupied. Now the building was only a shell.

He led the way across the lobby. They'd start at the top and work their way down. There'd be water damage upstairs, he supposed, but this place had been built to stand, and he didn't expect any major problems on the upper floors. He hoped the lower regions would fare as well. If there was any structural damage, it would be in the foundations or walls that faced the ocean. A couple of storms the past two winters had battered beachfront property pretty badly.

They climbed a flight of marble steps to the street-level lobby. Chinks of light filtered through the boarded-up windows; the room smelled of mold and dampness trapped too long in cramped quarters. Bart swept the light around. Plisky whistled softly.

"It must have been a beaut in its day." He was new with Upfield and to California, but he'd heard plenty about the Oceanside Hotel.

"There was a fortune in stained and beveled glass in those windows," Bart said nostalgically. "When the sun hit them in the afternoon, it was like being inside a rainbow."

"It must have been something to see. I'm surprised the old lady let it go into storage this way."

"It got too expensive with the old furnace, plumbing, and fixtures. Everything needed to be replaced constantly. And with the downtown area going to seed the way it did, it wasn't worth it anymore." He wondered about Rachel Upfield wanting to save it all now, rebuild. He supposed she sensed the new tide sweeping the country—a move back into the cities. One thing sure, if she did it, the hotel would be a showplace again. Rachel Upfield didn't do anything in a halfhearted way. And her granddaughter was just like her.

As they started across the room, a rodent scurried by them.

Bart played the light around again. Twenty feet above them a line of rose windows gaped like pale eyes. Elaborate carvings decorated the stone walls on either side of the boulevard entrance, meeting over it in an eternal garland. Shards of wood and bent spikes outlined where the front reception desk had been ripped out. A section of broken pigeon-hole mailboxes was still fastened to the wall behind it, splashed with purple paint by vandals. A thick, hardened pool had dried on the floor like blood. He swung the beam to the stairs.

Plisky whistled again. "Are those steps okay?" The magnificent double-curved stairway swept upward toward the mezzanine. The handrail and balusters were gone, and the steps were littered with dust and debris, but even so, the staircase retained the grandeur of a haughty dowager.

Bart started up. "This wood is as sound as the day it was put in. You'd have to chop it with an axe to make a dent in it. Mrs. Upfield insisted it stay. Good thing, too. The elevator went in the auction. Some guy bought it for a mansion down in Mexico City."

They climbed to the top floor and began working through the rooms, noting where walls or floors had buckled or sagged, where water had leaked through the damaged roof tiles. He tapped the walls and probed the plaster to determine how deep the flaws went. Bart called out figures into the warm, musty air while Plisky made notes. In the stripped, desolate rooms, doors had been removed for their rich paneling, mantels for the marble and exquisite workmanship. It was like picking over the bones of a skeleton.

When they finally reached the main level again, they found a badly damaged area where the foundation had sunk beneath the main lounge. Repair would be a major job. If Bart remembered right, the lounge was directly over the basement area where the hotel abutted the bluff. From where they were standing now, there was a drop of about fifty feet to the lower level, but the space hugging the cliff had been used for the boiler room. It would be a hell of a place to excavate if they had to replace footings.

"Let's have a look downstairs," Bart said. Plisky fell in step beside him, still gawking at the size and scope of the old building. As they came around a corner, Bart grabbed his arm.

"Watch it!"

"Jeez!" Plisky gaped at the yawning space caught in the

beam of the flashlight. The boards covering the opening had been torn away from the black hole of an elevator shaft. Plisky blew his breath. "Thanks, Ray. I'd hate to fall down that mother!" he said, glancing into the hole. "Hey—shine the light again." He pointed as the powerful beam swept the pit, exposing broken bottles, papers, beer cans, rags, and dirt. "There—"

The beam caught a fluttering, torn newspaper. In the draft sighing through the shaft, the paper rose and fell. When it lifted, a face stared up at them.

"What the—!" Bart centered the light as the newspaper settled back.

Plisky's voice sounded hoarse. "Some bum sleeping it off? How the hell did he get down there?"

At the bottom of the shaft the newspaper fluttered and rustled again, and drew back like a curtain. Ray stared down at the unblinking eyes and the waxy face of a corpse. "I think we'd better call the cops."

Dr. Marshall Forest steepled his fingers and looked at Paris. His white hair and trim mustache gave him a scholarly air. He had the coldest blue eyes Paris had ever seen, but he was without peer in his specialty. And he had taken over Victor Sands's case. They sat face to face across a teakwood table, in his plush, green-carpeted corner office at the Rachel Upfield Pavilion.

"Strokes can occur anywhere in the brain," he told her. "The size of the eruption and its precise location determine the damage. Rachel's was massive and showed up clearly on the CAT scan, and as you know, her entire left side was affected. She had hemiplegia." He put his hands down. "In Sands's case the damage is much lighter. However, there's enough evidence from the EKG and X rays to convince me that his amnesia is induced by a stroke rather than a traumatic incident such as a blow to the head."

"He's only thirty-eight—"

"Age isn't necessarily a factor in strokes. There are many causes. We suspect stress plays a vital role, or at least the way we handle stress. I understand Sands has no family here?"

Paris nodded, still numb from the news Dr. Forest had parceled out. She had requested this conference as soon as she knew he'd been consulted. "He's from the Midwest, but as far as I know, he has no family there either. At least I've never heard him talk about them."

"Then you don't know if he has a history of hypertension?"

"No. He seemed to be in top physical condition." Her chest ached as she thought of lying against Victor's muscular, lean body. "He jogged every day." *And made love often. . . .*

"The portion of the brain affected in his case controls personal memory," Forest said. "It's a more unusual occurrence than strokes damaging physical control. With physical impairment, another portion of the brain can often be patterned to take over the lost function. You've seen the progress Rachel has made." His glacial blue gaze studied her features for acknowledgement. She nodded.

She knew he was being totally honest with her, but she longed for a word of encouragement. "And with mental?"

He lifted his shoulders slightly. "It's difficult to say, but for all practical purposes, it's gone for good. Memory is like a slate. When it's washed clean, you can't bring the picture back."

The hard surface of the chair pressed against her spine. Forest's office was briskly efficient, absolutely correct, without frills. Grass paper on the walls, framed diplomas, an original Robert Thom oil of Hippocrates, expensive walnut furniture with uncushioned chairs to test the mettle of visitors and patients. Sit up and take it like a soldier. . . .

"Are you saying he'll never recover his memory?" She was haunted by a picture of Victor talking like a polite stranger. Forest nodded slowly. "He'll remember everything from this point on. He's suffering mild confusion about the first few hours after he was brought here, but the rest will stay in focus. His data memory is not affected. There's no impairment of learned knowledge, only his personal connection to it. He'll be able to swim, ride a bicycle, drive a car, if he did those things before. If he knew Mexico City in the past, he'll still know facts and be able to find his way around, but he won't have any personal memory of when he was there or with whom."

He would remember Catalina but not the joyful day they spent sailing there. "That doesn't make sense." It was a feeble attempt to reject the harsh truth, as if by doing so she might regain for Victor the precious gift he'd lost.

"It does medically. It's rare, but it happens. There have

been other cases. You'll just have to accept it. So will he."

"And he'll never know what his life was like before?" His work, their romance . . .

"Eventually he'll fashion a past of sorts for himself. People will tell him things. He'll read old letters or newspaper stories about himself. When there are enough of them, they'll blend with his post-stroke memories and begin to merge. He won't know where one leaves off and the other begins. The more he learns about his previous life, the less noticeable the gap will be."

A one in a million shot that only a handful of medical men understood. How could someone's complete past be wiped out in an instant? How could anyone live a new life without tying it to his past? Victor wouldn't know anyone, just as he hadn't recognized her. He was still uneasy with her, like a waking drunk trying to decide if he'd made a fool of himself the night before.

Dr. Forest leaned back. "The important thing is that the patient himself doesn't change. He'll have the same interests, the same skills. He'll probably like the same kind of people and activities he did before. Right now, he's suffering trauma. This is a lot for him to accept all at once. He may want to retreat, but others can prod him out of his shell—in fact, you can help him fight. You're his primary link to the world right now, the face and name he knows now. You can help him adjust." Forest tilted his head and studied her sleek nose and soft full lips for some reaction. The creases in her silky brow and her distracted green eyes indicated she was still stunned, but he was getting through to her. "We want to keep him here for a week or so, just to make sure we haven't missed anything. I'd also like to have Dr. Shaw talk to him."

"Neville Shaw?" Paris immediately lifted her chin. "Victor doesn't need a psychiatrist. You said only his memory was affected."

"I also said there's a lot of trauma. He needs someone to talk to, worry aloud to, if you will. Shaw will be able to pick up any danger signals if there are any. There is also a minor degree of motor interference on the left side. Physical therapy should bring it around. Face it, Paris, he's better off here than he would be trying to cope on his own right now. Call it a safeguard."

She sagged against the unyielding chair, still battling with her acceptance of the truth. "It's such a shock," she told Forest. "Someone you—" She almost said "love." "Know and care about suddenly stricken down this way. I want Victor to look up and say, 'Hey, the bad dream's over. It all comes back to me now.'" Her voice caught. "It isn't going to happen, is it?"

He looked at her solemnly. "No, it isn't."

His words were more cruel than he realized. The tenderness and intimacy she'd shared with Victor were forever lost in a dark chasm he couldn't cross. She was alone with their memories. Her eyes stung with tears. "It's so unfair."

"I suppose it is, but life doesn't come with money-back guarantees. It's a lot harder on him than it is on us." His voice was almost gentle.

Paris found a tissue and wiped her eyes. She'd cried when he told her about Rachel's stroke, too, then girded herself to help her grandmother in her long struggle to come back. She looked at Forest. "What can I do to help him?"

Forest was briskly efficient again, his voice as precise as his finely combed and trimmed mustache. "Visit. Talk. Tell him what he wants to know. Help him ease back to reality. Avoid any topics that would disturb him."

"What about his work?"

"He's capable of doing it if he wants to. It would help assure him he hasn't lost his skills."

She picked up her purse. "Thanks for giving me so much time, Marshall. I appreciate it. One other thing, Rachel is demanding either a telephone or that Josh Fantazia be allowed to visit her." His white brows peaked in astonishment. "I promised her I'd ask."

"It's out of the question."

Paris said, "I knew it would be, but you know how persistent she can be. I don't want to spend every evening being badgered about it."

"I'll talk to her later today."

Paris stood. "Do you think I should have Victor moved up to the Pavilion?" The homelike surroundings might help him adjust.

Forest considered it briefly then shook his head. "He's better where he is for now."

She was relieved. It was difficult to envision Rachel and Victor in the same hospital wing, even though Victor didn't know Rachel existed. She hadn't told Rachel about Victor's illness yet. She hadn't told anyone. She had no choice now.

Paris went to see Victor directly from Forest's office. Dr. Forest's diagnosis left her vaguely uneasy that the fragile relationship they'd established the past twenty-four hours might vanish unless she nurtured it carefully. She tried to imagine how Victor suffered knowing his past had fled forever.

She found him staring at his reflection in the mirror over the dresser. He was still dressed in the tan slacks and green sport shirt open at the throat that he wore when she found him. He looked so normal—so handsome . . . Paris paused in the doorway, watching him. When he realized she was there, he gave her a wry smile, his dimples showing in a lopsided way that made her smile in return.

"I haven't quite gotten used to that face looking back at me," he said, nodding toward the mirror. His gaze studied her as she sat in the blue vinyl armchair. He was in a private room, which Paris had insisted on. The last thing he needed was disturbing questions from a curious roommate.

He folded his arms. His eyes had a perplexed expression that wrenched Paris's heart. "I keep checking to see if it's changed, like the colors of a chameleon." His smile was sad. "Dr. Forest told me you were seeing him this morning. He says I'm going to have to start over and build from images and information I acquire." He leaned toward her and for a moment his muscular, athletic body looked boyish on the bed. "Who am I, Paris? Do you know me?"

The ache in her chest spread painfully. "I wish there was something I could say. 'I'm sorry' seems inadequate, but I'll do whatever I can to help."

"Inadequate? Inane? Insane? I'm not sure. Was I a person you'd be sorry to have vanish? Are there people who'll say, 'Good riddance. Victor Sands was a first-class louse.' Are there any who'll say, 'Poor old Victor, I wish he were here.'"

She tried to smile. "It will be 'poor old Victor' for the most part."

"I was a good guy, then?"

"A very good guy." She wanted to reach out and hold him, to kiss away the lines creasing his broad brow.

"Were we close, you and I?"

It caught her off guard and she felt her face flush. He

watched her with an intense curiosity she found unsettling because it stirred intimate memories. Despite the strange chasm of his memory loss, she felt irresistibly drawn to him as she had the first time they met. The electricity charged the air. Did he feel it?

"I see we were," he said, sitting back. He smiled, pleased. She was a very beautiful woman. Had that been what attracted him? No, it was more, he was sure. He felt an aura about her, in the way she moved, that told him their relationship had been more than casual. "All right, tell me about us. How did you happen to come to my apartment yesterday?" It sounded strange to his ears to claim an apartment he didn't even recall. He watched Paris with interest. She'd recovered her poise and answered without hedging.

"We've known each other three months. We met at a city council meeting. You were hired by the city of Ocean Beach as an independent consultant to evaluate the city's downtown redevelopment plans."

"Are you a councilwoman?"

She laughed and shook her head. She wore her hair swept in a side knot but for some reason, he envisioned it spread like molten gold across her shoulders. Her golden dress caught the overhead light, accentuating her curvacious body, and he felt a warmth engulf him.

"No. I leave politics to the jackals. My grandmother owns property that occupies prime real estate. She's an invalid, so I was representing her interests. My own, too, since our company is bidding on the contracts." She saw confusion cloud his blue eyes, as if he'd wandered somehow into a house of mirrors. She smiled reassuringly. "Maybe I should give you some background, if you think you want to get into it this soon."

"I don't promise I'll be able to make head or tail of it, but I've got to start somewhere."

She gave him a brief résumé of the competing plans submitted by Upfield and Fantazia. There was no flicker of recognition when she mentioned Shanna Fantazia's name, and Paris was relieved. She struggled to hide her antipathy to Shanna and made no mention of the personal conflicts that were as much a part of the rivalry as business. It would be unfair to present a prejudiced picture instead of facts. Victor listened intently, his gaze never wavering from her face, as if he were absorbing information with his eyes as well as his ears. Once he brushed a knuckle along the side of his jaw in a familiar gesture, and her breath caught. He noticed, and his brow furrowed. When she finished, he sat watching her until she looked away uncomfortably. It was impossible to be objective about him when she kept seeing the lover, not the businessman.

Finally Victor said, "I must have been ready to give an answer. What was it going to be?"

She said honestly, "I don't know."

"We didn't talk about it?"

"No. You kept your own counsel. After all, I was an interested party."

"I see. And what will happen now? Will the city council start over?"

"I don't know." Dr. Forest insisted none of Victor's mental functions or skills were impaired other than his memory. Would he really be able to complete the report?

"Well, I've got a lot to think about, haven't I?"

"We'd better leave it at that for now," Paris suggested. "I have to go," she said, glancing at her watch.

He stood up as she did, and once again his nearness sent a charge through her although he didn't touch her. "I appreciate everything," he said.

"I'll stop by later, if you want me to."

He wanted her to very much, but he remembered she had a company to run. "If it's not too much trouble."

"Don't be silly, darl—" She flushed. "Of course it isn't. I come every evening to see Rachel."

She was enchanting when her face colored. "Rachel?"

"My grandmother. She's been a patient here since her stroke three months ago."

"Do I know her?"

Paris shook her head. "She had the stroke just before you came to Ocean Beach." When Shanna began her fight for the Oceanside. When Rachel began gearing herself up to fight Shanna, Josh, Victor, the council, or anyone else who opposed her. "I see her every evening at five. She isn't allowed other visitors, so she looks forward to my standing appointment." *And your name comes up frequently,* Paris thought. "How would it be if I stop by after that? Can I bring you anything?"

He considered his answer carefully. "I guess we know each

other well enough for you to bring me some clothes. Would you mind?"

"Of course not. I'll pack a bag."

"I don't seem to have any keys."

"I can get in."

He gave her a curious glance, then said, "I have to start searching for good old Victor. I must have letters and papers. Can you bring them?"

"Are you sure you want to plunge in so quickly?"

He gave a wry smile, the dimples showing again, more evenly. "Nothing's going to change if I put it off. I've got all the time in the world right now. Two hours of physical therapy a day and occasional visits from doctors isn't exactly a demanding schedule."

"I'll bring what I can find."

"Thanks."

She managed to smile. "Until this evening, then."

In the hall she had to pause to regain her composure. Without memories for comparison, Victor didn't realize the polite strangers they had become. Did he have any idea how much she wanted to be in his arms and be kissed? *Were we close, you and I? Yes, Victor . . . we were close. . . .*

When Paris called the office, there was a message from Ray Bart.

"Did he say what it was about?" Paris asked Fran.

"There's some problem at the Oceanside. He wanted you to know his report will be late."

Leaving the hospital, Paris felt the hot slap of the noon sun. Trouble at the Oceanside? It had to be important to make Ray Bart late. It would be only a few blocks out of her way to drop by on the way back to the office. Whatever was wrong, she might as well handle it now.

There was a curious crowd of onlookers milling near the cyclone fence around the Oceanside. A uniformed policeman stood guard at the gate, and three police cars were parked in the driveway. Paris found a place to park near the bottom of the steep private street that led to the beach levels of the hotel. The policeman at the gate barred her way.

"You can't go in, miss."

Paris showed her identification. "Our company owns the hotel."

"Oh, sorry, Miss Hamilton. Go on in. Better ask for Lieutenant Chambers. He's in charge."

She went down the drive. Ray Bart's yellow Camaro and a company truck were parked in front of the police cars. Still wondering what had happened to bring the police, Paris entered the lower foyer. Electric lanterns that had been placed to give light cast huge shadows on the gray walls. Ghosts, she thought. Ghosts of a grand old hotel's past. She'd been inside only once since the auction, to let Victor see for himself a hint of the grandeur the hotel had once represented. Hand in hand they'd roamed the empty rooms as she shared her memories: visiting Rachel's suite on the top floor, where Paris had spent wonderful hours watching her grandmother go over ledgers or study reports; walking down the grand staircase beside Rachel as guests turned to watch the imposing old woman and the eager young child; eating in the huge dining room with its different settings and color schemes for each meal; dancing in the elegant ballroom under the shimmering rainbows cast by the crystal chandeliers.

Once again Paris realized how much she loved the hotel. She couldn't let it be torn down.

The trail of lights led down the back hall to an unboarded door to the basement. A crowbar lay on the floor. Another lantern stood on a landing halfway down, and there was a brighter glow emanating from the far end of the dark, gloomy basement. She made her way down, holding her pale gold linen dress close to her thighs so it wouldn't brush the begrimed walls.

Five men, two in police uniforms, stood in the harsh pool of light. She recognized Ray Bart and Steve Plisky. Ray started toward her, but the stocky man in a brown suit stopped him with a gesture.

"Lieutenant Chambers? I'm Paris Hamilton. I had a message there was a problem of some sort."

"We found a body," Bart said, ignoring the lieutenant's scowl. "Some bum fell down the elevator shaft."

A body. That meant the man was dead. Any compassion she would normally feel was overridden by the realization that any trouble connected to the Oceanside right now was illtimed. She looked at the detective. "I'm sorry to hear that, Lieutenant. I'm sure you'll do everything possible to find out who he was."

"As long as you're here, I'd like you to take a look at him. Maybe you can identify him."

She was taken aback at the suggestion she might know the dead man. She hesitated, frowning.

"It's your hotel, isn't it?" Chambers said.

"My grandmother's, but it's in the company holdings. Do you think this man may be someone local?"

"At this point we have nothing to go on but a hotel key, but we don't think he was alone here. We won't know the cause of death until the coroner sees him, but he's got a bad knife wound, and there's no knife lying around." He stepped back and swept his arm toward the elevator shaft. "If you don't mind, Miss Hamilton . . ."

Paris masked her surprise. Was he implying it was murder? She stepped forward as one of the uniformed policemen picked up a torch and extended it into the dark cubicle. The bottom of the shaft was a foot below floor level, and debris had collected in it. Atop filthy newspapers, crushed aluminum cans, and fast-food wrappers, the body lay on its back, one arm outstretched, the other folded across the chest. He was wearing dark slacks, a blue sports shirt buttoned to the neck, and a burgundy windbreaker. The clothes weren't new but neither were they as disreputable as the usual wardrobe worn by bums except for the large ugly stain that ran from the shirtfront down to the belt buckle.

She looked at his face. He was old. His sparse, yellow-gray hair was lusterless and long enough to reach to his coat collar. He had the ruddy complexion of someone who had spent a lot of time outdoors, but death had drained his face to a gray pallor. The lifeless eyes were filmed over. She turned away.

"I don't know him."

"You've never seen him before?"

"I can't swear to that, Lieutenant, but if I have, I don't recall it."

"Do you have any idea what he was doing here?"

"No, I don't. It would be a natural assumption that he may have been using the Oceanside as shelter." She glanced at Ray Bart, who gave her a quick nod.

"The padlock was jimmied," he said.

"I'm sure that's the answer," Paris said. "We'll replace it at once. I'm sorry this happened, Lieutenant. If you're unable to trace the man's family, Upfield Land Management will pay the funeral expenses. How soon will the body be removed?" She wondered if Ray had finished his inspection of the building.

"The coroner's on his way," Chambers said. "But we're going to have to seal the building until our investigation is finished."

"How long will that take?" she asked with a tinge of impatience.

"A week, maybe longer." He shrugged to show he wasn't going to rush to accommodate her.

Briefly she considered calling the police commissioner, but with Victor's report on hold, a few days wouldn't matter. She flashed Chambers a polite smile. "Is there anything else?"

"That does it, Miss Hamilton. Thanks for your cooperation." He tipped his hat, thinking how much warmer she was than her grandmother. But still shrewd.

"I'd like to talk to you a minute, Ray," she said as she turned away from the elevator shaft and its grim contents. Ray followed her upstairs and out into the bright sunshine.

"Sorry you had to go through that," he said. "I wouldn't have called if I'd known. When Steve and I first saw the body, we figured it was an accident. Then, when the patrol car got here, the cops saw the blood. They wouldn't let either of us out of sight."

"It's all right. I'll survive." It would be awhile before she forgot those sightless eyes. She suppressed a shudder. "Did you finish your walk-through?"

"Pretty much. I managed to have a look around the basement while the cops were waiting for Chambers. I can get the report to you late this afternoon."

"I guess there's no rush now." She glanced back through the ornate doorway, the gold still in place. "Have we had a lot of trouble with vagrants?"

"Not since we put up the fence. Once in a while a wino sleeps it off down on the beach. This is the first time we've come up with a corpse."

"I'm sure he'll turn out to be a vagrant with two percent alcohol in his blood who got into a scuffle over the last swallow of muscatel," she predicted.

Bart nodded. "Poor old duffer. It's a hell of a way to go."

There was a ripple of excitement as the coroner's van

stopped at the end of the driveway. Two men with a black body bag walked to the hotel.

Paris eyed the milling curious crowd beyond the fence. "If Chambers starts talking about murder, there are going to be reporters. Do what you can to play it down."

"Sure."

"And let me know as soon as you hear anything." When Bart nodded, Paris walked back to her car. She'd seen the bobbing flashlights and heard voices from the main lobby of the hotel, but she had no desire to see it now. She wanted to remember the Oceanside the way it had been, the way it would be again.

❧ Sixteen ❧

THE REST OF the day went so quickly, Paris barely made it
to the hospital by five. Elizabeth Aspenson warned her Rachel
was in a difficult mood and that Dr. Forest was with her.

Rachel occupied her circular velvet chair by the window.
She wore a deep rose-colored dress. A healthy glow colored
her cheeks and her eyes were diamond-hard and snapping.
Marshall Forest was standing over her, stiff-backed, his jaw
set. It looked as if they'd been battling for some time.
Rachel's gaze impaled Paris the moment she entered. Forest
sighed like a besieged general whose reinforcements had finally arrived.

Paris kissed her grandmother's papery cheek. "Who's winning, the lions or the Christians?"

"It's no joking matter!" Rachel cried.

"Since when did it hurt to smile?" Paris aped a scowl until
Rachel's frown softened. "Now, what's going on?"

Forest sighed with exhausted patience. "Rachel wants a
telephone or to be allowed a visitor. Neither is in her best
interests—"

"Rubbish!" Rachel snapped.

So Marshall Forest hadn't budged Rachel either. Paris
wondered what her grandmother would say if she knew about
the note penned by Josh. Was it possible both she and the

doctor were wrong? He for thinking Rachel could ever live any differently from the way she had always lived? And Paris for interfering in Rachel's personal affairs? They couldn't blame Rachel for being angry any more than she could blame them for wanting to do what was best for her.

Sitting across from Rachel, Paris said gently, "One of the first things you taught me, Rachel, was you should only pay for expert advice when you're willing to follow it." Rachel's gaze fell, and Paris felt a pang of regret for echoing Rachel's words from another time and place. But she had no choice.

The door opened and the pretty, slim Japanese girl came in with the cocktail tray. There was a third glass on it. "Thank you, Sumi," Paris said. Dr. Forest nodded politely, then poured. Handing the glasses around, he drew up a straight-backed chair and sat down, bracing himself for a continuation of the argument.

"This whole thing has really gotten out of hand," Paris said. She went on before Rachel could renew her arguments. "I don't see why the three of us shouldn't be able to come to some accord." Dr. Forest frowned. There was a spark of interest in Rachel's lavender eyes. "'First," Paris said, "how about telling us why it's so important to have a phone or to see Josh Fantazia right now?"

"No." Rachel's eyes glinted like wet steel. She looked at Forest, then at Paris. "I have not lived almost eighty years to be treated like a child now. I have been in this room for three months, and I have abided by your silly rules and restrictions. I have played the game *your* way, and I am sick of it. If this is what the rest of my life is to be like, allow me the dignity and freedom to shorten my sentence by doing as I please. Death is preferable to this"—she fluttered a tiny blue-veined hand—"nonliving. I take full responsibility for my actions. If they cause me another stroke, let me die with it." Her gaze swung back to Forest. "If it eases your conscience, put suicide on the death certificate."

Paris's fingers tightened on the stem of the wineglass. The anger behind Rachel's words frightened her, and she suddenly realized the terrible strain her grandmother had been feeling. Both Paris and the doctor had heightened her feeling of help-lessness by stealing her last freedom, the one of choice.

"Let's see if I have it right," Paris said gently. "You refuse to tell us why either of your requests is so important?"

"That's right!" Rachel's chin lifted in righteous indignation, but Paris saw the quick spark of curiosity.

"Okay. I accept that," Paris said. She turned to Dr. Forest. "She means business, so I guess it's up to us to find a compromise we can live with."

Forest was adamant. "It is not medically advisable."

"I accept that, too," Paris said. "But it isn't in Rachel's best interests to have her blood pressure zoom every time we refuse her. We both know she doesn't get over things like this readily, and that prolongs the inadvisable medical condition." She caught Rachel's look. It was surprised but also satisfied. Paris gave her a conspiratorial wink. "So it comes down to: How can we let her have the phone or her visitor? I presume, dear, that you are not going to hold out for both?"

Rachel sniffed slightly. "One will suffice." She lifted her sherry glass and sipped, watching Paris in wonder.

Paris said to Dr. Forest, "Rachel can set herself up for another stroke as easily by what she doesn't do as by what she does."

Marshall Forest thought how much alike these two women were. Paris's nature was softer, but neither of them gave up easily. He'd treated enough stroke victims to know that Paris was right. In Rachel's case, letting her get upset might be worse than giving in. Reluctantly he said, "All right, I'll agree only if it's under strictly controlled conditions."

"Such as?" There was an eagerness in Rachel's voice Paris hadn't heard in three months.

Forest said, "I don't suppose you'd consider a nurse or doctor in the room? No, I didn't think so. The next best thing, then, is to hook you back onto the monitoring system. The nursing station will be able to follow your vital signs. If they get out of line, that's it. A nurse comes in and out goes your phone or visitor. And from then on, we go back to my rules all the way." He looked squarely at Rachel, expecting her to challenge him.

"I accept," she said instantly.

Paris was astonished how simple it was when they all changed their perspective slightly. She smiled at her grandmother. Rachel's triumph was clear, and Paris prayed the victory would outweigh the potential danger.

Forest put down his empty glass. "I'll set it up for tomorrow afternoon when you're rested. Do you want the phone or the visitor?"

"The visitor."

"Very well," he said, getting to his feet. He lifted Rachel's wrist, his forefinger on her pulse, nodding, then patting the slender, fragile hand. "Thanks for the drink." Laughing, he walked out.

Paris wondered if she'd ever heard him laugh before. She smiled at Rachel. "Well, now that's settled, I have a confession to make." She reached into her purse and brought out Josh's note. It was a matter of conscience. She and Rachel had always dealt honestly with each other.

Rachel opened the letter and read it silently. Paris recognized her self-control in not fuming about yet another invasion of her privacy, but she knew she was being chastised silently. Rachel's hand trembled slightly as she held the paper, and Paris saw her mouth tighten to a thin, hard line. She didn't like what she was reading. Paris was consumed with curiosity, but she knew it would do no good to question Rachel. She prayed she'd been right in encouraging Dr. Forest to allow a meeting tomorrow between Rachel and Josh.

When Rachel finally looked up from Josh's note, she said, "What have you brought today?"

So there was to be no further discussion. Paris sighed. "It's been a day of surprises, none of them good."

Rachel's face was alert instantly. It seemed her life was crammed with the unexpected of late. How she hated not being able to handle her own affairs! Paris ran the office expertly and not a day went by that Rachel didn't thank the Lord for her, and that her genes had come from the Grant line, not the Upfield. But at times, Rachel chafed for action faster than Paris was willing to move. She missed the exhilaration of girding herself for battle before the enemy knew the war had started. Surprise could be a distinct advantage when it was on her side. She made an impatient gesture for Paris to go on.

Paris told her about the body that had been found in the Oceanside and that Lieutenant Chambers had roped off the hotel temporarily.

Rachel scowled. "The man is an idiot to think we're involved in any way. Every empty building attracts derelicts. Pressure him," she commanded, her violet eyes snapping.

"Better still, call the police commissioner. He owes us a favor for getting that zoning change for his brother's car rental agency."

"The delay may be insignificant," Paris said. "Something else has happened that can't be solved as readily. It concerns Victor Sands."

Rachel gave her a piercing glance. Had Sands made his decision? Something in Paris's tone warned her that there was more involved than she had revealed.

Paris told her about Victor's stroke as honestly as she could, including the details of how she had been involved and her consultation with Dr. Forest. She tried to play down her emotions but could not keep an occasional quaver from entering her voice. Rachel watched her with a curious expression.

When Paris had finished her litany, Rachel said, "You've become involved with him." It was a statement, not a question. She could see in her granddaughter's face an anguish that came only from being unable to help someone you love. She remembered seeing it in her own mirror when she longed to reach out to Josh but could not. Josh . . . She would not think about him now. Tomorrow was time enough to get ready to face him.

That Paris was in love with Victor Sands complicated matters, Rachel thought. How deep was the involvement? Paris had had lovers before, but none that made her consider permanent attachments. Perhaps Sands's memory loss would end the matter. It was a cruel thought, but life was often cruel. And with the city council deadline for the report only weeks away, they might be forced to start over.

"Does the council know?" she asked.

"I'm going to call Burt Douglas in the morning." When she had stopped at Victor's apartment to pack his clothes, the doorman told her Shanna Fantazia had come by. Paris knew she couldn't prevent the news from getting out.

"Find out if the council is going to replace him," Rachel ordered. "Time will be on our side if they have to postpone the vote. And tell Josh about it before he comes tomorrow. I don't want to waste any of the precious time God Marshall Forest is granting me discussing tangent factors with Josh." She sat back, her energy depleted.

Paris saw the exhaustion in her grandmother's face and quickly set aside the wineglasses. "That's enough for today."

She expected an automatic protest, but instead Rachel nodded. Paris said, "Shall I help you into bed?"

"No, Sumi can do it when she comes for the tray." Rachel smiled wearily. "Thank you for being in my corner today, dear."

Paris kissed her gently. "Have a good night, and try to behave yourself tomorrow, okay? I went out on a limb for you. Don't saw it off behind me."

Rachel squeezed her granddaughter's hand. Such compassion for one so young and ambitious. What would she do without Paris to carry on so capably?

Rachel examined the image in the mirror and patted her silvery hair. The pale, drawn face was a stranger; only her amethyst eyes hadn't lost their luster, though her left lid drooped slightly. Her skin showed a fine tracery of veins and was deeply creased with wrinkles. *I'm old,* she thought. *Much too old to feel excitement at seeing Josh.*

But she was excited despite the anger that was foremost in her feelings. When Josh returned to Ocean Beach a year after Collette's death, he had changed. He was remote and made no attempt to renew the closeness that had always bound them together. She saw him occasionally, but there was no intimacy; the terrible pain of losing Ruth and Collette had etched permanent scars on Josh, and Rachel's guilt prevented her from trying to heal them. Josh took an interest in the business again with some of his old fire, but it was not the same. Nothing was the same.

She put aside the mirror and relaxed against the pillows. Marshall had insisted she remain in bed, where she would expend less energy and could be more carefully monitored. She'd changed to a fresh gown and bed jacket, pale lavender, which she knew was a becoming color. Sumi had combed her hair and drawn it into a neat bun, dusted her face with powder and put a touch of rouge to brighten her cheeks. Pampering . . . but she wanted to look her best. She didn't want Josh to think he was dealing with a weakling who had no fight left. Now she had to stay calm. She was aware of the electrodes on her chest and the band that measured every breath, the blood pressure cuff on her arm. She fought off irritation as she pictured a nurse watching the screen that translated her life into squiggly lines like a seismograph.

No earthquakes . . . not even tremors, she warned herself.

The soft sound of the door drew her attention instantly. It opened to reveal Josh. He stood a moment as they studied each other. The thick, dark hair that had crowned his head when he was young had given way to a fringe of white around a bald pate. His eyebrows were still thick and also white, giving his dark brown eyes a more compelling intensity. But his square, elegant jaw had slackened. Loose folds of skin hung beneath his chin and deep lines creased his face. Yet he was still a handsome figure of a man in an expertly tailored tan suit, white shirt, and brown tie. For a moment Rachel was lost in memory.

Josh came toward her. The spring was gone from his step. Josh, who had always been so dynamic, had grown old with her, Rachel thought. And he hadn't mellowed. His angry expression reminded her that this was not a casual visit, and her fury returned in full measure.

"I'm sure Paris warned you they have me wired up, so let's not waste time on civilities," she said. His eyes glinted like coal, but before he could answer, Rachel brought her hand from beneath the covers with the greeting card she'd hidden. She dropped it on the spread in front of him. "What's the meaning of this?!"

Josh looked startled, then curious. He picked up the card, opened it, and read quickly. Beneath the saccharin verse was penned: *Has the city council ever looked closely at the deed to the Oceanside?*

Rachel's eyes smoldered. "How could you stoop so low?" she whispered fiercely.

"You think *I* sent this?" he demanded.

"You are the only one who knows! I would remind you that you have as much to lose as I if you think you can resort to blackmail at this late stage of the game! *Why,* Josh? Why after all this time?" Her face set into a mask of puzzled anger.

"Be quiet and listen to me!" he exploded. "I did not send this. Did you think I came here with the purpose of blackmail? Oh, Rachel . . ." He shook his head and sank into the chair that was pulled close to the bed. With a heavy sigh, he reached into the pocket of his coat and handed her an envelope. When he saw the awkward, uncertain movement of her left hand he remembered her afflicted arm. He drew out the greeting card and showed her the sad-faced cartoon witch standing by an empty mailbox. He opened the card and handed it to Rachel. Under the brief verse imploring the recipient to write was a handwritten note. *Has the city council ever looked closely at the ownership of the Fielding Corporation?*

Rachel felt a flutter in her chest. She closed her eyes, measuring her breaths until she was back in control. She felt Josh take her hand, and her heart fluttered again.

"Rachel?"

She opened her eyes. Josh was leaning over her, his face creased with concern.

"Are you all right?" he whispered.

She nodded.

He shook his head, still whispering as though the complex of wires leashing Rachel to the wall sockets might pick up his words. "I came here to accuse *you*. I thought you were prepared to use any tactics to keep the Oceanside." A ghost of a smile touched his mouth. "It would not be the first time." He sighed and squeezed her hand gently. "It looks as if we've both been fools."

Rachel felt a wave of sorrow and compassion. She was ashamed that she had believed Josh capable of such treachery and pained that he'd believed the same of her. How far apart they'd grown over the years. She tightened her fingers feebly on his. "Yes, old fools and two of a kind." She managed a wan smile. She was tiring fast and had to be careful Marshall's watchdogs didn't come rushing in before she and Josh had solved the puzzle. "Who, then, after all these years?"

Josh shook his head in bewilderment. "It's been buried for half a century. There's no way anyone could have found out."

"But someone has. What about Garson Perkins? He was in it from the start."

"He's been retired for years," Josh reminded her. "He's living in Mexico."

"You're sure he hasn't returned?"

"He's a senile old man who doesn't know his own name most of the time." Josh had not seen him for many years, but the monthly reports rarely varied: Garson Perkins saw no one but his household staff, and it was doubtful that he recognized even them.

"What about the lawyer who took over the practice?"

Josh mulled over the possibility. Perkins had turned over all the Fielding files to him before retiring. Josh kept them locked in a safe at home. Perkins had also arranged for the annual meetings of the Fielding Corporation to be waived when Josh and Collette didn't want to return to Ocean Beach. When Josh had finally come back alone, there seemed no point in changing the arrangement.

"Collingswood is completely in the dark. He's never seen the original papers. It would be impossible for him to trace ownership of the corporation without them."

Suggesting him had been grasping at a straw in the wind, but Rachel was stymied. Who then? And why? The deals channeled through the Fielding Corporation had been buried deep in the megabuck transactions of many oil companies. They never rated a second glance by any comptroller or auditor. The high risk that once existed because of the Fielding Corporation had diminished considerably. But if someone knew about the company and about the deed to the Oceanside, what other secrets had been uncovered?

She glanced at the two cards. "The handwriting is the same," she said.

"Double blackmail?"

"We both were involved with the Oceanside deed and the Fielding Corporation. We'd suffer equally if they were exposed," Rachel mused. "The redevelopment project must be the connecting link." There was no other answer to the timing of the threats.

Josh's brows creased into a frown and he rubbed his chin. She was right, if either of these things were made public, the city council would probably toss out both their bids. So much emphasis had been placed on a new, clean image for Ocean Beach, airing Upfield and Fantazia dirty linen would cause an outcry the council couldn't ignore. It wasn't like the old days when Josh had the power to control every decision.

Rachel's mind raced, skimming memories in search of clues. Two other companies had submitted bids, but neither she nor Paris had given them any consideration beyond a preliminary investigation. The final showdown would be between Upfield and Fantazia. Neither of the other two had enough influence or backing to launch the kind of investigation it would have taken to uncover these blackmail threats. If money wasn't the motive, what was? Power? Revenge? She felt the rapid beat of her pulse and drew a quiet breath, looking at Josh.

"Drew Hamilton," she said.

He looked astonished. "Paris's father? He's been gone for years."

"He didn't leave happily. He'd welcome the chance to see me squirm."

Josh said dubiously, "Why would he threaten me? I've never even met him."

"You represent power, and power has always frightened him." Drew had dug into the past once before, and his tar brush would have tainted Josh's life as badly as her own. Rachel closed the door on the bruising memory. "He has never forgiven me for taking Paris. When she was nine, he tried to instigate another lawsuit to regain custody. I obtained a writ to prevent him from seeing her. I never heard from him again." Until now. . . .

"You really think he's behind this?" It seemed farfetched, but Josh had nothing better to offer.

"We must find out. I can't do anything from this damned room. They won't even allow me a telephone. Help me, Josh. Find Drew Hamilton and stop him before he goes too far."

"Of course. I have a great deal at stake, too."

"I don't want Paris sucked into this, Josh. She's done nothing to deserve it."

"The sins of the fathers," Josh said sadly.

"Rubbish! We did what was necessary." Rachel would not wallow in regrets.

Josh took her hand and pressed it between his palms. "You love her very much, don't you? You must be very proud of her. She's done well." There was sadness behind his gaze.

Rachel felt a quick stab of guilt about Ruth, the daughter he had lost and whom he had loved so deeply. Judson was competent and successful, but his personality was at the opposite end of the spectrum from Josh's. The easy camaraderie they had shared during Judson's childhood had never developed into a close man-to-man relationship. His grandson, Phillip, had married and moved to New York. His granddaughter, Shanna, was a great disappointment to Josh with her unscrupulous tactics and sharp tongue.

"I am," she answered with pride and compassion. "That's why it's so important to nip this in the bud. Help me, Josh."

She had demanded his visit to berate him and counter his threats, and now she begged for his help. As she had once before from a hospital bed. Memories weighed heavily on her heart.

"I'll put someone on it today. Do you have any idea where he is?"

"Louisiana, the last I knew, but he rolls his clothes after every job. He'll be wherever they're paying the most."

"You're sure he's still working the rigs?"

She snorted. "The spots on a roughneck never change. Find him, Josh."

"I will."

For a moment they were awkwardly silent. Then Josh lifted her hand and pressed it to his lips. Rachel felt a faint shiver as she returned the pressure of his fingers when he held her hand against his cheek. She was overcome with longing for things that might have been. Tears filled her eyes.

"The years we have wasted," she whispered. "What would our lives be if we had not been such stubborn fools?"

He smiled with sadness filling his eyes. "I have always loved you. It was I who was the fool from the start."

"Josh . . . Josh . . ." Tears trailed down her cheeks. She closed her eyes as weariness engulfed her. She drifted to sleep with Josh still holding her hand.

By evening Rachel was resting comfortably. Josh Fantazia had been in the room twenty-two minutes. After the first erratic few minutes, Rachel's vital signs had leveled at a point only slightly above normal. Even though Marshall Forest was amazed at how well she'd done, he gave orders that she was to remain in bed for the rest of the day. He noted on her chart, however, that she was to be allowed more activity if she desired it, and if her remarkable progress continued, he would consider letting her go home.

Having read Elizabeth's summary of the medical report, Paris entered her grandmother's room with a cheerful smile on her face that evening. She found Rachel sitting up in bed, still wearing the lacy lavender bed jacket she'd worn for Josh's visit. The color in her cheeks now was natural. The wine tray was on the bedside table.

"Well, you did it, old girl," Paris said with an affectionate hug.

"Maybe now you'll listen to me. I've lived with this body

seventy-nine years. I should know it." Rachel spoke briskly, but there was pride in her tone. She motioned toward the sherry.

Paris handed her a glass. "Dr. Forest is impressed enough to mention the possibility of your going home."

"Humph. It's about time," Rachel sniffed.

Paris laughed softly. "You're a curmudgeon. I should know better than to get in your way when your mind is made up. I trust you solved the dilemma that brought all this on. Is there anything you want me to do?"

Rachel sipped her sherry, her eyes unnaturally bright. She seemed strangely excited, but her expression gave no clues to the cause.

"Nothing, thank you," she said at last.

Paris regarded her closely. "I have the feeling you're keeping secrets, darling."

"At my age I'm entitled to them." Rachel's chin lifted defiantly.

Paris laughed again. "I suppose you are." The change in Rachel was amazing. What in the world had she and Josh discussed? Had it something to do with the enigmatic remark Rachel had made the other day about her and Josh once having been friends? Surely after the bitter enmity of the past twenty years, there could be no reconciliation made so easily. And there could be no relenting in the fight against the Fantazias now, of all times. Paris was consumed with curiosity, but her grandmother made it clear she intended to disclose no more.

"What did you bring from the office?" Rachel asked abruptly.

"Nothing. Frankly, I expected to find you exhausted and trembling with rage. I didn't think you'd have the energy to deal with any business tonight."

Rachel sniffed again. "What about Victor Sands? Is the council going to replace him?"

Paris tried to ignore the quick stab of pain she felt at the mention of his name. "I don't know. Burt Douglas said he'd call me. If the council came to any decision, I haven't heard." She'd asked Burt to delay any vote until after Victor reviewed his work. If there was any chance he could finish the job, it was worth taking the risk.

Rachel was watching her closely. "You've seen him again?" When Paris nodded, Rachel asked, "Is there any improvement in his condition?"

Paris felt an ache tug at her heart. "He's still confused, but he wants to fit together the pieces of his past, including his work on the report. He asked me to bring the papers from his apartment."

"You'll read them first, of course." When Paris didn't answer, Rachel was silent a moment, then said, "Are you in love with the man?"

Paris hesitated.

"Don't bother to answer. It's written all over your face."

"Rachel—" Paris searched for a way to explain.

Rachel looked away. "I suppose it's been going on for some time? Well, I hope for your sake you don't let your emotions addle your judgment. Remember that the council chose Sands, and we can be sure Josh was influential in recommending him."

Paris rushed to Victor's defense. "Victor was hired because he is an expert. He doesn't take sides." Her cheeks colored as she thought of her own initial attempts to influence Victor, and her violent jealousy in believing Victor had succumbed to Shanna's charm.

"How can you be sure?" Rachel snapped. Then she regretted her sharpness as pain flashed in Paris's eyes. Rachel sighed. Her tone softened. "We're masters of our destinies, but we can't always master our hearts." Her love for Josh had been just as unpredictable and inescapable. Because of it, she understood Paris's suffering now. If the stroke had not felled her, Rachel would have seen the signs sooner, but she would not have been able to prevent it. Love was not something that could be diverted like a stream. She changed the subject.

"Has there been any unusual correspondence at the office or the house?"

Paris tried to catch up with the hopscotching conversation. "Unusual in what way?"

Rachel wagged her fingers impatiently. "Out of the ordinary. Indecipherable."

Paris frowned. "No. Why do you ask?" Her grandmother was indecipherable, if nothing else.

"No reason."

Paris set aside her sherry glass. "You are too mysterious

for me." She got to her feet and stood by the bed. "It's time for me to go. Mysterious or not, you still deserve applause for your magnificent performance today." Paris bent and kissed Rachel's cheek. "I'm proud of you. I'll see you tomorrow. Have Elizabeth call if there's anything you want."

"I would prefer a telephone to the applause you offer," Rachel said with a twinkle in her eyes.

Paris kissed her again. "You are a conniver."

"There's nothing wrong with conniving if it gets you what you want."

Paris smiled, her heart filled with admiration and love. "All right, I'll ask Marshall."

In her soft cotton top, and lushly pleated skirt, Paris hesitated outside Victor's hospital room as she heard voices. She'd made a brief stop at his apartment yesterday to pack some clothes, but hadn't had time to collect his papers. He hadn't questioned the delay, and she wondered if he suspected she was stalling deliberately. Rachel had gone right to the core of the matter: of course she'd sift through any papers she found before returning them to Victor. She'd been wrestling with her conscience, but she knew it was true.

She realized the voice coming from Victor's room was Shanna Fantazia's and felt a surge of anger as she waltzed in. Victor was dressed in gray slacks and a white knit shirt that gave his summer tan the deep glow of copper. He'd worn that shirt the previous month on their sail to Catalina. For a moment she saw him leaning against the boom, his face lifted to the spray left by their plunging boat, cutting a path through the choppy water. Her throat constricted as she forced a smile.

"Hello, Paris." Victor's smile was warm.

Shanna looked around sharply, annoyance on every feature of her pouty, beautiful face. Paris forced herself to say, "Hello, Shanna." Looking back to Victor, she said, "If I'm interrupting, I can come back another time." Being in the same room with Shanna made her bristle. If he wanted to see Shanna, she wouldn't stand in his way.

Victor felt tension vibrate the air. These two were more than business rivals. "Please stay," he said, offering Paris his chair as he sat on the edge of the tautly made bed. Shanna had arrived a half hour ago, sweeping into the room and hugging him like a lost lover. It had thrown him at first, but when she finally got around to believing he didn't know her, she gave him a rather glowing account of what they meant to each other. He was wary, wondering if he could ever have been as totally involved with a woman like her. She was a looker, but her sweater was too tight, worn for an effect, and there was something calculating and cruel in the way her full lips twisted.

When she had finally stopped her general banter, and had brought up her real estate client who wanted to buy the Oceanside, he was positive the love affair was as fictitious as her insistence that he had decided on the Fantazia development plan. He noticed that once again Paris hadn't brought his papers.

"You two know each other," he said, tossing the bait between them. Shanna grabbed it quickly.

"You might say we're competitors for your affections, darling." She gave a low, throaty laugh and looked at him seductively from under her mascara-thickened lashes.

Paris seethed at her lack of tact. What had Shanna already said to Victor? Had she regaled him with lies and fancifully embroidered truth? Paris wished she'd had the foresight to ask Dr. Forest to limit Victor's visitors as he had Rachel's. The thought brought her up short. A few minutes ago she had been championing Victor's fairness to Rachel, and here she wanted to deny him access to anything but what she had screened. She met Shanna's catlike stare, then smiled at Victor.

"I'm sure Shanna's told you that she and I are at different poles in the redevelopment project."

"Of course I did," Shanna said quickly.

Paris wondered suspiciously if Shanna was trying to keep Victor from divulging what she *had* said.

Shanna tossed her head, fanning her dark mane provocatively. In spite of the heat, she wore it loose across her shoulders, a style which gave her a sultry look. "I told him that my client is making a very respectable offer which no one in her right mind would refuse. Face it, Paris, the Oceanside is a dinosaur. Ocean Beach is a progressive city. The redevelopment project should enforce that, not preserve some monstrosity from a bygone era. That damned hotel should have been torn down years ago." She stopped abruptly, and turned a dazzling smile on Victor. "Victor knows that."

Paris looked sharply at him. Had he sided with Shanna

before the stroke? Was he convinced the Oceanside stood in the way of progress? Was that why he hadn't denied her accusation about Shanna that night? When Victor's gaze met hers, she saw confusion and uncertainty, like a trapped animal seeking a way out of a cage. He didn't know whether to believe Shanna either! Victor turned toward the window and the light caught his eyes. Without warning, Paris was overwhelmed by the memory of Victor across from her at a candlelight dinner. *He could not have been pretending then, any more than she had been.* . . .

She held his gaze when he turned back. "I didn't have time to collect the things you want, I'm sorry," she said.

He nodded as if it were of little importance. Shanna glanced from one to the other quickly, her feral eyes wary. "I'd be happy to get anything you need, Victor."

"I plan to take care of it as soon as I leave the hospital," Paris said, excluding Shanna from the conversation.

Sulking, Shanna tried a new tack. Indicating the newspaper on the table, she said, "I was telling Victor about the murder at the Oceanside. I suppose the police have questioned you." There was just enough insinuation in it to make Paris bristle again.

"I was asked to view the body before it was removed," Paris replied, as steely as possible. Shanna's face shriveled in disgust and Paris hid a smile of triumph. Why was it every confrontation with Shanna became a contest in which no holds were barred? *We fought like this in grade school and we're still doing it,* Paris thought. Getting up, she said to Victor, "I'm sure you aren't following this exchange as enthusiastically as we are. I'll go now."

He gave her a faint smile. "It's confusing but educational."

She laughed. "Well, school's out for the day. I'll see you tomorrow." Turning to Shanna, she said, "If you're going to visit again, I suggest you pick a time when you can have Victor's undivided attention. I visit Rachel every day from five to five-thirty and Victor right after that, so you can come earlier or later."

Shanna's mouth opened for an angry retort, then clamped into a frozen smile. "Of course. I'll be happy to," she said sweetly.

Grinning, Paris waved good-bye to Victor and hummed softly as she walked to the elevator.

✥ Seventeen ✥

PARIS STOOD AT the window watching the sunset, remembering how Victor had held her in his arms as they watched the sun vanish three days before. It seemed a lifetime ago, but the pain was a sharp, fresh wound. Seeing him with Shanna this evening had done that to her. She wondered if she had been foolish to leave the two alone. Realistically, she knew there was no way she could prevent Shanna from seeing Victor, but it didn't abate her jealous anger.

Beyond the harbor, the horizon of sea and sky blended as the sun disappeared behind a bank of red clouds. Victor was everywhere in the apartment. She hugged her arms across her breasts, remembering his smile as he touched her cheek . . . his deep voice telling her some bit of trivia or caressing her with words of love . . . his laughter as they shared the joy of experiencing each other.

Who am I?

Tears welled in Paris's eyes. She brushed them away furiously and sat down at the leather-topped walnut desk in the comfortable den. A man's room, rich in browns and blues, straight-lined furniture that spoke efficiency as well as beauty. American modern. She opened the top drawer and began going through the neatly arranged contents. She worked systematically, glancing at papers, arranging separate stacks for

personal and for business affairs. She laid out the folders from
the file drawer, reading the labels: Upfield Land Management,
Annual Reports; Oceanside Hotel, Financial Statements
1921–1933; Oceanside Hotel, Reconstruction 1933–35; Tax
Assessments, Ocean Boulevard properties . . .

Paris had a growing appreciation of how thoroughly Victor
had handled the work he was hired to do. He'd surveyed real
estate transactions within a ten-block radius of the Oceanside,
obtained current appraisals on locations along the boulevard,
and reviewed complete oil reports on city holdings. To Paris's
surprise, there was a folder on Rachel's oil leases and another
marked Darien Hill. Leafing through the contents, she saw
that Victor had compiled a complete dossier on Rachel. There
was also a considerable amount of background on her, including the names of men she had dated more than casually and
when her affairs had ended.

Paris felt violated, as if her personal belongings had been
exposed for public consumption. Victor had been able to distance himself from sentiment while he had methodically performed his job, no matter how unsavory. That there was a
similar file on Shanna Fantazia didn't appease her. She collected the papers and dropped them into the attaché case she'd
brought along. Would she be able to separate her heart from
business and hand over any ammunition he'd collected that
might defeat her and Rachel? Did she owe him any loyalty at
all? Slamming shut the file, she turned to the last drawer and
yanked it open, rummaging among the pens, stamps, and sta-
tionery. In the back she had found a packet of letters from
several midwestern cities. *Eventually he'll be able to fashion a
past for himself from what people tell him, old letters* . . . She
dropped them into the attaché case and locked it shut. With a
last look around the empty apartment, she turned off the lights
and left.

Her apartment was the penthouse floor of an excellent
building only four blocks from the Oceanside and five from
the Upfield Building. She had picture-postcard views in four
directions and an ocean breeze on even the hottest days.
Usually the white and gold decor with accents of apricot and
cinnabar lifted her spirits, but tonight any solace they provided
was gone. She left the attaché case on the hall bench and went
to the kitchen without checking the answering machine in her
office. She had a daily woman who, in addition to cleaning

and doing the laundry, always made something Paris could fix
for dinner easily. Tonight it was chicken and vegetables to be
popped in the microwave. It would be ready in ten minutes. A
drink first from the carved dry bar; she needed it. She fixed a
tall, cool vodka and tonic and carried it back to the living
room and settled on the white sofa that faced the floor-to-
ceiling sliding glass doors that formed a corner. She didn't
turn on a lamp. With only a glow from the hall and kitchen,
she sat in the semidarkness watching the lights of the city and
harbor.

Why had Victor probed her private life? Was it strictly to
acquaint himself with her part in the Upfield business? He
certainly had left no stone unturned as far as Rachel's life was
concerned. It hardly seemed necessary information for the
current project. Remembering Victor as he'd been the night
before the stroke, she knew something had been on his mind,
but his lovemaking had been as exciting and meaningful as
ever. He couldn't pretend that, could he?

The doorbell rang, startling her. She set down her glass on
the hammered brass coffee table and walked to the door. Only
a few people were able to get past the doorman without being
announced. When she opened the door, Irena swept inside,
eschewing the perfunctory kiss she usually bestowed in Paris's
direction. She glanced around the room like an appraiser evaluating antiques before an auction. Paris always had the feeling
she was checking carefully to make sure none of Rachel's
antiques had strayed to Paris's apartment, thus settling the
ownership question over which she constantly bickered. Paris
sometimes wondered what Irena would do with Rachel's
lovely things if she had them. Sell them, probably. There was
no sentiment in Irena's greed.

"Hello, Mother." Paris closed the door and followed her
mother into the living room, switching on a gold ceramic
lamp. At fifty-three, Irena's youthful figure testified to the
expensive spas she frequented. Her perfectly made-up face
showed less of the passing years than her lifestyle would dic-
tate. She was wearing a Dior silk suit of rich rose and kid
sandals that accented the slimness of her legs. Her hair was
drawn up in a loose knot with soft waves over her ears to hide
the face-lift scars. She sat in an apricot-colored chair and
opened her purse, digging for cigarettes.

"I've been phoning all day," she said with a quick glance at the slim gold Piaget watch on her wrist. "You might at least return my calls."

"I just got in," Paris said with annoyance. Irena was exaggerating as usual. There had been no messages at the office. Irena had probably called here and left an irritated message on the machine. Without guilt, Paris knew she wouldn't have returned the call if she'd checked the machine.

Irena extracted a thin, gold-tipped cigarette from a case and lit it with a diamond-studded Dunhill. The haze of smoke made her look like a vanishing Cheshire cat. "I've just come from the hospital," Irena said. "They refuse to let me see Rachel." She glanced around for an ashtray and, seeing none on the nearest table, settled for a Bavarian china candy dish.

Paris picked up a ceramic ashtray from the coffee table and shoved it in front of her mother, then emptied the flick of ashes from the candy dish into it. "Rachel is still in guarded condition. Dr. Forest—"

"Damn Dr. Forest and his stupid rules!" Irena said petulantly. "She's my mother. I have a right to see her."

Paris's jaw clenched. "Don't play the loving daughter, Irena. You didn't care enough to come back from Scottsdale when Rachel had the stroke three months ago. And what has it been since then? One phone call to ask about her? Or more precisely, one phone call to ask me to intercede and get more money for you. You'll pardon me if I question your devotion." Paris couldn't be with her mother five minutes without a flare-up of the bitter animosity that had always marked their relationship.

"Don't you dare talk to me like that!" Irena blew smoke like a straining locomotive.

Paris gave a cruel laugh. "Or what? You'll turn me over your knee? You won't bring me some little trinket from your next jaunt?" She sighed impatiently. "Please, mother, I don't want to argue. Why did you come?"

Irena's eyes glinted like ice floes in an Arctic sea. Her well-colored mouth formed a grim, determined line. As if suddenly aware of it, she rearranged her expression.

"I want to see Rachel. I have to talk to her."

First Josh, now Irena. What was going on? "About what?"

"It's personal."

"It's also impossible. She isn't strong enough to endure upsets."

Irena studied her daughter coldly. She had Rachel's icy calm and that same firm set of her jaw. She looked a lot like Rachel in snapshots as a girl except for the blond hair and green eyes. Even those were more like Drew than her, Irena thought. There was absolutely nothing of Irena in Paris, she thought. A sorry, but true, state of affairs. Her tone switched from indignant to wounded. "Is that what you think of me? An upset?"

Paris had heard the act too many times to be taken in. "Dr. Forest is doing what's best for Rachel. That's the way it has to be." Paris harbored no guilt in not telling her mother about Josh's visit.

Irena eyed her speculatively, sending eddies of smoke into the chasm between them. Finally she said, "How is she? Is there any improvement? I feel like a fool having to ask my daughter how my own mother is." She leaned to stub out the cigarette.

"Actually, she's making progress. She's been on a plateau for quite a while, but she seems to be doing better now."

"Will she get out of the hospital?"

There was something too eager and selfish in Irena's question. Paris shrugged instead of offering cautious optimism. Irena sighed. Paris regarded her mother's erratic displays of concern with suspicion. Irena never put anyone ahead of herself. When she seemed to, even briefly, Paris found herself taking a position of wary observer. Irena had never given cause for trust. As a result, Paris wasn't the least bit interested in her mother's problems. She let Irena stew in silence.

Finally Irena knew she had no choice but to try to have her message relayed through Paris. She suppressed her irritation and forced a smile as she crossed her slim ankles.

"I met a man in Scottsdale," she said, looking at a point beyond Paris's shoulder. "He's dreadfully attractive—but that's beside the point. He's in real estate, so naturally we have a lot in common. Believe what you will, Paris, but I have always been vitally interested in the family business, no matter what Rachel tells you. I make it a point to keep abreast of what's going on. With the hotel being mentioned in all the newspapers and magazines lately, it would be hard to ignore." She reached for another cigarette, then snapped her purse shut without taking one. She looked directly at Paris. "Is Rachel going to sell it?"

"She doesn't plan to," Paris said with forced patience. She wished her mother would finish whatever she came to say and leave. Only Paris's curiosity had let her endure the visit this long.

Irena felt swift, irrational anger. Rachel was a senile idiot! Irena chose her words carefully. "My gentleman friend tells me the property is worth close to four million." The sum still staggered Irena's mind.

"It's appraised at three point seven." Paris enjoyed the shock in her mother's eyes. Obviously she hadn't believed what her friend had told her.

"My God, Paris, do you realize—" She clamped her geranium-colored mouth shut as if the words had slipped out. She was thinking furiously, getting back her poise. "The real estate developer I told you about would like to make an offer." Irena masked her expression again.

"Have him submit it to the real estate division."

Irena's calm exploded. "Really, Paris, you're impossible!" Her nostrils flared and her hands clamped and unclamped in her lap. She struggled again for control. "My recommendation should carry some weight. I'm not an outsider!" She forced one corner of the geranium-tinted lips to a smile. "My friend would like to meet you. I've talked so much about you."

Anything Irena said about her wouldn't be good. Paris was getting impatient with her mother's silly pretenses. "Does this 'gentleman friend' have a name?"

"Stanton Fields. His office is in Phoenix, but he handles projects all over the country. He's been interested in Ocean Beach for some time."

Fields's name was familiar to Paris. He specialized in acquiring property for multimillion-dollar condominium projects. Boxes on boxes, spread across hillsides and beaches, or occasionally modern high-rise city towers. Was that what he envisioned for the Oceanside?

Irena watched Paris speculatively, waiting for comment or reaction. When neither was forthcoming, her jaw twitched. Her jowls sagged and faint bulges that had been double chins before the face-lift appeared momentarily before she tightened her neck muscles.

"Well?" she demanded.

"Well, what?"

"Damn it, Paris, don't aggravate me! Will you talk to Rachel about it?"

Paris spoke slowly and deliberately, as though to a naughty child. "No, Mother, I will not. Rachel has had a serious stroke. We are trying to protect her life. Her *life*, Mother, do you understand? It happens I care a great deal about Rachel, and I want her around as long as possible."

"Are you intimating that I don't care?" Irena shivered with indignation.

"I'm saying you're thoughtless and irresponsible if you expect me to plead Stanton Fields's cause on your behalf. You must have some idea what her reaction would be!"

Irena stiffened like a cat confronting sudden danger. Her eyes were chips of blue glass. "If she's that ill, she can't be handling any part of the business, which means it's been put in your hands completely! You're running things. You're in charge. You don't need Rachel's approval, do you?!" Glaring, she fell back in the chair. "Of course. I should have guessed. You've been currying Rachel's favor since the day you were born! *Grandma's little girl!* And now you've got it all, haven't you! Well, let me tell you something, young lady. That's not the final word. You can tell Rachel that this time I'm not walking away without a fight. I'm entitled to more than the pittance she doles out. I want what's mine. Tell her that, and tell her I want it now!" She picked up her purse and slid to the edge of the cushion, her sleek nyloned legs turned so her ladylike posture wasn't disturbed. There were high spots of color on her cheeks, and her breathing sounded harsh.

Paris's patience snapped. "Exactly what do you think is yours?" she demanded. "You've never worked a day in your life. You've never given a damn about me or Rachel so long as she picked up the tab for your high living. You've traveled, married, divorced, had whatever you wanted—and when that hasn't been enough, you've come back crying that Rachel owes you more! If you ask me, she's been too generous with you. You don't deserve or appreciate what she's done."

Irena sprang to her feet, her face livid, her mouth pressed in an ugly snarl. "What do you know about it, Miss High and Mighty? You're so much like her it makes me sick!" She jabbed a finger toward Paris. "That hotel is mine! My father left it to me and she stole it! Well, I'm not afraid of her anymore. She can't pack me off so I won't embarrass her. Not this time! Tell her—no, *you see to it* that Stanton Fields's offer is accepted. I'm staying at the Bonaventure in Los Angeles. You can reach me there." She jerked around as if controlled by invisible strings and stalked out, slamming the door hard enough to rattle the mirror above the hall table.

Paris sat back, stunned. What was that all about? The hotel *hers?* What gave Irena that ridiculous idea? And now, of all times? Was it that she thought Rachel was too weak to fight, easy prey? Fields couldn't be that important to Irena—nobody was. Had Fields planted the crazy idea in Irena's head that she had some claim on the Oceanside?

Rachel had explained to Paris that Hillary Upfield had died penniless, but she had set up a trust fund to provide for Irena's future. Rachel administered the trust until Irena was twenty-five, and it had grown tenfold. Put in Irena's hands after Paris was born, it had been squandered recklessly and self-indulgently through four marriages and countless affairs. Since then Irena had lived on Rachel's largess.

Now she was demanding more. Always more.

Paris vaguely remembered her father as a tanned giant, with dark good looks, rough hands, and a quick smile. He'd been a nebulous figure on the fringe of her early childhood, vanished completely by the time she was in school. Rachel had never spoken about him except the one time Paris had pummeled Shanna Fantazia for calling him a dirty roustabout. Paris had never heard Irena mention him. Paris wondered if Irena even remembered him. From what she could put together, Drew Hamilton had been nothing more than a brief episode in her mother's life, noteworthy only because he had fathered Paris. Even that hadn't been important to Irena, who flitted in and out of her daughter's life like a bright butterfly, rarely lighting for long. But what Paris lacked in parents, she found in abundance in Rachel.

Strange that the past she'd considered so neatly cataloged and put to rest could rattle so ominously after so many years. Victor's past had vanished. Hers and Rachel's were surfacing in murky pools that had to be cleared. Sighing, she picked up her empty glass and took it to the kitchen. She took the casserole dish from the refrigerator and put it in the microwave, then fixed herself a cup of tea while she waited for the food to heat. Then she arranged a tray and carried it into her study. The light on the answering machine was blinking, and she switched it on playback while she retrieved her attaché case. Irena's whining voice floated through the apartment. It was the only message. Paris reset the machine and opened the attaché case.

By 2:00 A.M., Paris was bleary-eyed and stiff. She rubbed the back of her neck where taut muscles protested the hours of bending over the desk. She couldn't absorb what she was reading anymore. Victor had compiled a complete account of Rachel's affairs, starting with her marriage to Hillary Upfield and the wedding gifts from her father which had laid the foundation for her financial empire. There were photostats of the marriage license, deeds for the original Oceanside Hotel, and a number of lots on Darien Hill, including the one on which oil was first discovered. There was a list of oil holdings, with dates of purchases and prices, many of them before the first strike. Paris had heard tales of the oil strike and the excitement it had generated, but Rachel had never attached undue importance to her holdings. The Oceanside Hotel and the Upfield Company had always played the more prominent role in her scheme of values.

Victor's file on the hotel was comprehensive. Yearly profit-and-loss statements showed the original Oceanside had not done well the first few years until Rachel took it over. Then it had made a sharp turnaround and showed an excellent profit. The first deed, dated 1919, was in Hillary's name. The second one, dated 1927, was in Rachel's name alone. Hillary had died in the earthquake of 1933. There was nothing to substantiate Irena's claim. The hotel had not been her father's to promise her. And certainly the new Oceanside, built after the earthquake and Hillary's death, was totally Rachel's. She had purchased the additional property, and Upfield Land Management's construction division had handled the work. Irena was making a futile, grandstand play.

Paris was disappointed at not finding any indication of Victor's conclusions. No notes, no draft of his final report. One surprising fact, though. In the file on Shanna Fantazia, he'd noted the name of her client interested in the Oceanside: Stanton Fields. He had also clipped a number of newspaper and magazine articles about the developer.

Both Shanna and Irena were involved with Fields. Paris didn't like it. It made her mother's appearance tonight and her demands more suspect than ever. Had Fields been interested in the Oceanside *before* he met Irena, or had Irena enlisted his cooperation for her own ends? It bore looking into. With Victor's investigation at a temporary standstill, Paris would have to take the matter into her own hands.

Wearily she piled Victor's papers and files back into the attaché case. She'd have Fran copy everything before she turned it over to Victor. The answer had to be there, but she needed time.

As soon as she arrived at the office the next morning, she used an outside line to phone a private detective agency in Los Angeles. She arranged to have both Irena and Stanton Fields followed, their various activities chronicled. Then she put aside the puzzle and devoted herself to company business.

Midafternoon, she was interrupted by a visitor who forced her back unwillingly to the problem. Lieutenant Chambers insisted he'd only take a few minutes of her time.

"Sorry to bother you, Miss Hamilton, but I wonder if you've recalled anything about the dead man found at the Oceanside?"

Paris answered the ridiculous question sharply. "No, I haven't. Has he been identified?"

"We traced the hotel key. His name was Theodore Reno. He came into town a week ago, as far as we can tell. We went through his things trying to locate his next of kin or a permanent address."

"And?" His deliberation irritated her, but she knew he hadn't come to keep her informed of his progress without a reason.

"He seems to be a drifter. We found a bus ticket stub from Amarillo. We ran him through R and I, but didn't come up with anything."

"I don't see how this concerns me, Lieutenant. I have a heavy schedule, so if you'll come to the point, I'd appreciate it."

"Sorry." He wasn't, but she waited for him to continue. "There were some papers in his duffel bag. One was a bill of sale and the other was a deed to the Oceanside Hotel."

Astonished, Paris said, "That's ridiculous. We haven't sold the property to anyone."

"These were dated 1927. Both are made out to Theodore

Reno and signed by Hillary Upfield. That was your grandfather, wasn't it?"

She nodded, her mind playing back Victor's dossier. The hotel had been deeded to Rachel in 1927. "That was long before I was born, Lieutenant, but I've never seen any record of the sale or heard the remotest hint that it could have taken place. The deed was obviously never recorded. My grandmother's was. You can check."

"I have," he said flatly.

"Then you know that whatever this man thought he had simply was not representative of the facts."

"It would seem so." Chambers gave her a courteous smile. "It sure makes me wonder how this Reno fellow got the bill of sale and what he planned to do with it. Seeing as he was killed in the Oceanside Hotel, there may be a connection."

What possible connection could there be? She wouldn't give Chambers the satisfaction of knowing he'd intrigued her, and said nothing.

"Policemen take a dim view of coincidence," Chambers said, "especially whoppers like this. I'd appreciate it if you'd check, maybe ask Mrs. Upfield? She may remember him. We'd like to get to the bottom of this."

"I'll do what I can, Lieutenant, but my grandmother can't be subjected to any lengthy interrogations. They might unsettle her."

His gaze sharpened. "Do you think this would upset her?"

"I didn't say that." She no longer hid her irritation. Maybe she should have called the police commissioner. "I'm just letting you know that if she shows the least sign of agitation, I won't push her. May I see this deed and bill of sale?"

Chambers drew two legal documents from his pocket and laid them on the desk. Paris scanned them quickly. They were legitimate forms, properly signed and dated, but without a notary seal. The amount on the bill of sale was $100,000. Her green eyes flashed toward Chambers.

"They seem genuine in intent, but I'm sure you've noticed that neither one is notarized, and as I pointed out before, the deed was never recorded. My grandmother was the sole owner of the property, so her husband couldn't sell it. I'll find out what I can, but whatever reason my grandfather had for making out these two documents may be buried with him." She didn't mention the coincidence of dates.

Chambers got to his feet, slipping the two documents back into his pocket. "It certainly makes a man wonder why Reno would hang on to these all this time, doesn't it?" He walked to the door. "I'll expect to hear from you."

As soon as he was gone, Paris called Ted Banyon of the legal department and told him to check the original deed, any liens that had ever been filed against the hotel, and every transaction that had ever taken place concerning the land on which the Oceanside stood before and after the earthquake. She demanded to know if a man by the name of Theodore Reno had ever had even a remote connection with the hotel, and if so, in what capacity.

Thoroughly puzzled, Banyon knew that when the edge entered Paris's voice, he'd better get on her request right away.

Victor watched Dr. Shaw leaf through a file. Dr. Forest had set up the appointment with the psychiatrist, and Victor had come reluctantly. Now, watching the bearded and bespectacled man's faint scowl as he read the report, Victor felt irritation without knowing why.

Laying the open file on his desk, Dr. Shaw looked up through the top portion of his bifocals. "How are you today, Mr. Sands?"

Victor shrugged. He'd spent two hours in physical therapy in the morning and some of his confidence had been restored by the therapist's enthusiastic praise at how well he did. The impairment had been minor to begin with, and now it was almost completely gone.

Dr. Shaw said, "Dr. Forest explained the reason for this interview?" When Victor nodded, the doctor said, "Good. Then you understand my purpose is to see if we can find a reason for your problem."

"Forest says the stroke is the reason."

"That's quite possibly the bottom-line truth. If so, there is probably no chance that the stricken portion of your brain will recover its normal functioning. How do you feel about that?"

"Pretty lousy," he said, thinking this man was an idiot.

"If there is a chance we can undo part of the problem, by whatever means, you'd be willing to go along, then?"

Victor's jaw tightened. "I'll go along as long as I feel it's doing some good."

"Excellent. Now, suppose you just talk. About anything

that comes to your mind. Your feelings since you've been here in the hospital, your impressions, whatever."

Victor sat back. He liked the interview less and less. He wasn't sure what he'd expected, but whatever was locked away inside his head signaled little patience for this oblique approach to a problem.

"My main feeling is confusion," he said. "I should recognize people and be able to find a slot for them. Whenever people talk to me, I wonder if I knew them. How and when? Did I like them, work with them, rap over a few drinks? I feel as if I'm walking around in a vacuum. And what do I say to the people who *did* know me and I don't remember?" He thought about the tears that had glistened in Paris Hamilton's green eyes when *she* remembered something he'd lost. Paris handled the whole thing well, but the other woman, Shanna, unnerved him. *But Victor, darling, surely you haven't forgotten the evening at the yacht club* . . . Innuendos, disbelief. . .

"Are you worried about leaving the hospital?" Shaw probed.

"Damned right I am. You can treat this as a fascinating case, but it's my life! Forest says only my personal memories are blanked out. How can I be sure? How do I know I haven't lost whatever I had going for me? How do I make a living if I'm a goddam vegetable?" His own vehemence surprised him, and he realized he was letting out all the frustration and fears he'd hidden so carefully the past few days.

Shaw jotted something on his pad. "How many people have you encountered who knew you before?"

Victor knew instinctively that Shaw forced him away from any one line of conjecture to make him examine his own feelings more closely. It was the way psychiatrists worked. Had he seen one before? Did he make a habit of blacking out when things got rough?

"Two," he told Shaw. "Both beautiful women."

"What's your reaction to them?"

Victor let his gaze drift to the green palms outside the third-floor hospital window. "Mixed. I like looking at beautiful women. I'm comfortable with the idea that they were probably part of my life, but I'm not exactly comfortable with the women themselves. I haven't the foggiest notion of what I've said or done with them in the past. The one who brought me to the hospital seems to have been on an intimate basis with me. She gets in and out of my apartment without difficulty, she knows a lot about the work I was doing. More than that— it's her eyes. They tell me she hurts for me. Maybe she loves me. Maybe I loved her. How the hell do I deal with that?"

Dr. Shaw was silent a moment, then said, "And the other woman?"

"She says we were intimate. She's good-looking enough that I might have taken her to bed, but I read her as a determined woman who's after something. Don't ask me how I've concocted that picture, it's just there." It was much easier to be objective about Shanna Fantazia than it was to be about Paris.

Shaw stroked his beard. "Perhaps that's an advantage right now. You can simply feel and think whatever you want."

"I don't have to put on a dog and pony show for anyone?"

Shaw's pale eyes were alert. "Why do you use that expression?"

"I don't know. Is it important?"

Shaw fingered his beard again. "I believe it comes from the development and construction business."

"Sure it does," Victor said without hesitation.

"How do you know?" Shaw gave him a wry smile.

He *did* know. Everything he'd learned about himself so far said he was a development consultant. Shaw was trying to show him he still knew the business. It was a beginning. He relaxed for the first time since he'd come into Dr. Shaw's office. "Okay, I see your point. I'll work on that awhile. Tell me, have you ever had a patient like me before?"

"Not personally," Shaw admitted. "There are cases reported in the journals from time to time. But the important thing in any kind of amnesia is the patient's reaction and his ability to adjust. Have you learned much about your past?"

Victor smiled ruefully. "The idea is a little scary, but I'm working on it." He thought about Paris's promise to collect all his personal and business papers and deliver them to him.

"I expect none of us would be totally pleased with our pasts if we were forced to review them, but then, neither would we choose to block them out completely. You're in a position to review your relationships and accomplishments and choose the ones you wish to continue. You are basically a free agent."

Unless he discovered a wife and kids he didn't know about. Could he be sure such a family didn't exist any more than he was sure he'd probably been in love with Paris Hamilton? He rubbed his temple.

Dr. Shaw closed the folder and laid his pen atop it. "I think we've covered enough ground for today. Let's talk again in a few days when you've had time to consider these things."

Victor rose and extended his hand. "Thanks." The interview with the chief of psychiatry had been more productive that he had expected. For the first time since he woke up a stranger to himself, he was eager to learn more about the man he used to be.

Victor watched the door expectantly as he heard Paris's high-heeled footsteps in the corridor. They were easily distinguishable from the whispery soft-shoed pace of the nurses or the more hesitant steps of other patients' visitors. He'd spent the afternoon thinking about his visit with Dr. Shaw. Paris had become Victor's anchor, and he found himself impatient to talk to her again, to ask a different set of questions.

She appeared in the doorway and paused just long enough to glance around the room. Was she making sure Shanna wasn't here? The idea pleased Victor.

"Hi," Paris said cheerfully. "Did you have a good day?"

He smiled and shrugged. "I sat in a tub of hot water and flexed my muscles, and I chatted with a psychiatrist. I'm sure not going to exhaust myself by overworking."

She laughed softly and he enjoyed watching the shifting hues of her eyes. She hefted an attaché case to the table. "Before you get too lazy, I brought everything from your desk except the paper clips. It's a formidable pile. You may be sorry you asked for it."

"I don't think so," he said honestly. "My session with Dr. Shaw made me eager to find out a few things." She looked surprised but pleased. He pointed to the case. "Did you go through it all?"

She hesitated, then laughed. "You always were direct. Yes, I did. I felt a bit guilty, but I had to know if you'd come to a decision."

"Did I?" he asked, still watching her beautiful eyes.

"No. If the answer's there, I couldn't unravel it. There was no final report." He was different today, and she found it easy to admit the truth despite the torture she'd put herself through the previous night. He had an animal magnetism as he lay back, his hair slightly ruffled and his terry-cloth robe open enough to reveal a fine matting of hair.

"Maybe I put the final report someplace else. Did you search the whole apartment?" he asked, unaware of his effect. That elicited a wry smile from her as she shook her head. He grinned. "You don't have the makings of a top-grade spy."

She laughed. The chiming sound pleased him more than he'd imagined possible, and he knew he must have enjoyed her company very much. It would have been easy to fall in love with her, he was sure.

"So you found nothing of interest in three months of my work?" he said, wanting to hear more of her soft, musical voice.

"Oh, a great deal of interest, but nothing that solves the question of what's going to happen to the Oceanside Hotel."

She sat across from him in the blue chair, looking somewhat tense in her pale, cream-colored suit that framed her slim figure to perfection but didn't detract from the image of a competent executive. He supposed she should be tense, with whatever had weighed heavily on both of their shoulders. He tried to imagine her fighting the city council or meeting with department heads to get a construction project off the ground. It was much easier to see her dancing in his arms or sitting across a candlelit table.

"Why is the hotel so important to you?" he asked.

"Because it's important to my grandmother, and she's important to me. The Oceanside has been her whole life. It would kill her to let it go. And it happens I believe the Upfield plan for redevelopment is the best one for Ocean Beach. The Oceanside has been a landmark for more than fifty years. It would be a crime to tear it down and replace it with condominiums."

"Would it have to be torn down? Maybe the building could be converted to condominium apartments." He hoped the papers she'd brought had detailed blueprints of the old building. He wanted to know everything about it.

Paris shook her head decisively. "Rachel would never consider letting Fantazia have it for any reason. She and Josh Fantazia have been bitter rivals much too long."

"Personal or business?"

"Both. It goes back a long way." She thought about Josh visiting Rachel yesterday. She still had no clue to what had transpired, but she didn't trust Josh. Rachel had completely avoided the subject today, as if it had never happened, but Paris hadn't missed the bright gleam in her eyes. Rachel was up to something. And if it had anything to do with the Fantazias, Paris had to find out what it was.

"What are you thinking?" Victor asked gently.

Startled, Paris brought her thoughts back. "Nothing important."

"For a moment you looked like I feel most of the time: like you suddenly found yourself in a maze or on the other side of a looking glass where nothing is quite what it seems."

"Oh, Victor, I'm sorry." How difficult this had to be for him. She didn't want to add to his pain, even unwittingly.

"Nothing to be sorry about," he said with a smile. "It made me feel not quite so alone for a moment."

She relaxed and smiled. "Then I'm not sorry at all. I don't want you to feel alone." The intensity of his gaze made her look away.

He studied her averted face. She loved him, he was sure. He'd seen the warm glow in her eyes before she turned away. She was as concerned with his problem as she was with the one that he'd been hired to solve. If he'd been in love with her, did it influence the decision he had to make about the hotel? Had he been able to separate love and business? Would he be able to now? It was too soon for him to handle that. He had a lot of things to learn first. He changed the subject.

Lifting his terry-clothed arm, he pointed again to the attaché case. "That stuff is apt to make less sense to me than it did to you. I think you should go back and search my apartment for a final report. If you don't turn it up, the city council may be out of luck." He tried to envision her going through his home, but he couldn't summon any images of his apartment.

Paris looked at him earnestly. "Why?" she demanded. "The city paid for the work, they deserve the results. You can still write the report."

He hesitated. Dr. Shaw had been leading him toward the same reasoning, showing him his analytical and evaluative capabilities were still intact.

Paris leaned forward eagerly, her face animated. "You can do it, Victor. The council doesn't want to start over again. They'll give you a chance, I know they will." She'd talk to

Burt Douglas again. She'd call every council member if she had to.

"I'm not sure—"

"The old Victor wouldn't hesitate," Paris declared.

The sudden fire in her eyes made Victor smile. Her enthusiasm was contagious. "Well," he said, "if you're so sure, I suppose I can try."

"Not try," she insisted. "Do it!" She put her hand on his reassuringly.

The warmth of her touch made it impossible for him to refuse. "Okay, but I don't guarantee anything." He closed his hand around hers with gentle pressure. Her eyes responded instantly with a glow that had nothing to do with the report they'd been discussing. After a moment she drew away in embarrassment. He breached the awkward moment. "Can you think of anything I should know before I plunge in?"

She thought a moment, using the time to quiet the rapid beating of her heart his touch had created. Dr. Forest's words reeled in her mind. *He'll like the same kind of people he did before*. . . . Could he love her again?

"One thing's come up," she told him, her musical voice revealing only a hint of the inner turmoil that lingered there. "Remember the body that was found at the Oceanside a few days ago? Does the name Theodore Reno mean anything to you?"

"No, should it?"

"I'm not sure. It was the dead man's name. Lieutenant Chambers came to see me. They found an old deed and a bill of sale for the Oceanside among his things. They were never recorded, but my grandfather had signed them. The strange part is, they were dated 1927 and the hotel was already in Rachel's name then. From all I've heard, my grandfather wasn't much of a businessman. The hotel was in financial trouble before he signed it over to her. Rachel put the hotel on its feet. Then the original building was destroyed in the earthquake of 1933. Rachel built this one soon after that, bigger, grander than the first. But her husband died in the earthquake. Why would this man Reno hang on to those useless documents all this time?"

It was an interesting question, and Victor paused to think. "Teddy Reno . . . I'll keep him in mind."

She gave him a puzzled frown. "You called him Teddy."

"I guess I did. A natural assumption."

Paris couldn't hide her excitement. "A grown man would be called Ted. Is it possible you came across the name before?"

"One of those facts I don't know how I know?" Dr. Forest had said there would be a lot of them. "It's possible. I haven't heard the name since I've been here, but that nickname somehow rings true in my crazy, mixed-up head. After my hour with the resident Dr. Freud, I'm not sure of anything."

She put her hand on his again, and this time she didn't pull away when he squeezed it. "You will be. Give it time."

Her voice was so full of emotion, it made his pulse quicken. Or maybe it was her touch. He'd never noticed the tiny mole at the corner of her left eye. *Or had he?*

"Given the frustration I feel now, I must have been a man who had purpose and direction in his life," he said.

"You were," she said gently. "And you still are. It will come back, believe that." Her eyes misted and she blinked rapidly, aching with love and pain for him. She forced a cheerful tone again. "Good old Victor loved martinis. What do you say I talk to Dr. Forest and see if we can't sneak in a shaker when I come tomorrow."

He looked at her as if she'd just pulled a rabbit out of a hat. "Have you got that kind of pull?"

Laughing, she told him, "My grandmother endowed an entire pavilion upstairs. She's been on the hospital board for twenty years, has sponsored fund raisers, laid cornerstones, and cut ribbons. She has her sherry every evening, so no one can argue that alcohol is against hospital policy. Let me see what I can do."

He walked with her to the elevator. When the doors closed on her encouraging wave and electric presence, Victor felt halfway normal for the first time since he'd wakened in this nightmare. Paris Hamilton was very good medicine. And she was a totally desirable woman.

❧ *Eighteen* ❧

PARIS LET HERSELF into Victor's apartment, glancing around as she wondered where he might have put the final report if he'd written it. She was excited at his willingness to let her pick up his work on the project, but she really didn't believe the report existed. She'd promised to hunt for it more to please him than anything else. He needed something to latch on to, to feel something was recoverable. For the first time since his stroke, she'd seen a glimmer of the real Victor today, the Victor she loved.

Standing in the warm, masculine apartment, she tried to put herself in Victor's place. Where would he keep the most important part of his work? She started with the desk, leafing through the files and drawers carefully to make sure she hadn't missed anything. Then she went through the cabinets, the credenza, the bookcases. When she'd fine-tooth combed the office and living room, she went into the bedroom. There she sifted through the dresser, nightstands, and closet, terribly aware of Victor's presence as she touched his clothes and personal possessions. She had to fight memories of their lovemaking here, feeling his touch and sharing his intimacy. Determinedly, she moved on to the linen closet in the hall, then to the kitchen cabinets. She even went through Victor's neat collection of cookbooks on the shelf over a counter. No report. If there had ever been one, it was no longer here. Had Victor had another visitor after she'd departed that night? Someone to whom he'd given the report or who had taken it without permission? The only other person with a major stake in the outcome of Victor's work was Shanna Fantazia. Much as she hated Shanna, Paris couldn't envision her breaking and entering to steal the report. And she didn't want to consider the possibility that Victor had invited Shanna here to give her the report. Besides, if Shanna had the report and hadn't produced it so far, it had to mean Victor favored the Upfield plan. Why else would a Fantazia hide it? Feeling some weight off her shoulders, Paris locked up the apartment and left.

The Upfield Building was deserted except for the night watchman and the cleaning crews that came every night to keep the halls and offices immaculate. Paris liked the feel of the building at night and found the quiet emptiness refreshing after a hectic day. She had adopted Rachel's habit of frequently returning to the office after everyone else had gone to work or to sit quietly in a womb of music and solve problems without distraction. Rachel used to bring her here as a child. During Paris's school years, Rachel arranged her schedule so she was at home when Paris returned from school. Afternoons and evenings were theirs to share, and if Rachel had work to do, Paris was allowed to accompany her here.

Paris knew she was loved and she loved freely in return. Her grandmother was an imposing figure to be respected, admired, and emulated. Rachel always treated her as an adult but was tolerant of the ways of childhood. She discussed business matters freely so that Paris grew into the affairs of Upfield Land Management effortlessly. By the time she was in junior high school, she worked part-time in the office, filing, typing, bookkeeping. Rachel insisted she work in every department in order to learn fundamentals that would serve her well in management. By the time Paris graduated from public high school, she was more competent than many Upfield employees and was eager to join the firm, but Rachel insisted she obtain a business degree first. The years Paris was away at Stanford and Harvard were lonely for Rachel, but she accepted them stoically until Paris returned, ready to step into Rachel's shoes.

Unlocking the glass doors that sealed the Upfield empire, Paris flipped a switch that controlled a string of lamps as she crossed the front office. Glancing into Fran Markham's office, she was glad to see nothing in the tray flagged for her attention. Fran had been with Rachel fifteen years. At the end of every day she separated routine from important matters so Rachel, and now Paris, would be able to identify them if they chose to work at night.

In Rachel's sumptuous office Paris turned on only the desk lamp, leaving the rest of the room in gentle shadows. Instead of settling behind the desk, she sat in the high-backed leather armchair which she'd always commandeered as a child when Rachel worked late. Remembering how she watched her grandmother study a contract or estimate a bid, Paris wondered again about the two documents Lieutenant Chambers had shown her. Did Rachel know her husband tried to sell the Oceanside to someone else? Rachel had never liked loose ends. She was methodical and precise, some said fanatical. *Never acquire the habit of putting things off, Paris. You can't run a business without clear records. Put everything in its place. If it doesn't have one, make one.*

Paris glanced around the office that had been Rachel's for so long. If Rachel knew about the proposed sale, there'd be a record or note of it somewhere, but Paris hadn't come across any when she'd sifted through everything before moving into Rachel's office three months before. Did Rachel know Theodore—Teddy—Reno? Searching her memory, Paris was sure she'd never heard the name before Chambers's visit. Still, she couldn't shake the feeling it was important. Important enough to ask Rachel about him? She'd feel on safer ground if she knew more about Reno before she did. So far Banyon hadn't uncovered anything, but he hadn't had enough time to make a thorough search. Who else might know? A name from the past . . . unfinished business . . .

Paris straightened. Josh had used the term in his note. Unfinished business. And Rachel had trumpeted the fact she'd been friends with Josh long ago. Pushing herself from the depths of the warm leather, Paris crossed to the desk and flipped through Rachel's personal Rolodex to find Josh Fantazia's number.

Josh sat in the dimly lit study of the penthouse surrounded by silence, the books he'd accumulated over a lifetime, the warm leather furniture, and walnut-paneled walls. Sometimes he missed the house on Darien Hill and the immense rambling Rancho del Cielo. The Hill house had been torn down as oil wells cut a path across the Hill, and he'd never returned to the sprawling Rancho after Collette died. Too many memories haunted the huge rooms and empty halls. When he came back to Ocean Beach, he took a penthouse apartment in one of the high rises on Ocean Boulevard. He enjoyed being in the center of town, and memories were easier to banish in these scaled-down surroundings. The apartment was kept immaculate by a maid and valet whom he paid more than he did some company employees. He was comfortable here, except when ghost memories crowded him and made him feel as if he were in a stark prison cell.

Seeing Rachel had unlocked doors of the past. It has also reminded him of how fragile life was, how the years sped by until they released you from their tyrannical grip. Why hadn't he begun seeing Rachel again when he had come back? With Hillary and Collette both gone, they could have married. The thought made him smile. Much as he adored Rachel, he doubted a marriage between them would have lasted a year. He loved and admired her acute mind, her coolness under stress, her ability to see to the heart of a matter, then act to accomplish her purpose swiftly. But they needed competition in order to love. They needed the thrill of winning or the impetus of losing to drive them on. It had made their affair a vital, vigorous thrill ride that endured all those years when he'd had Collette and Ruth to balance the need of someone to adore him totally, to accept his decisions unquestioningly, to feed his masculine ego without challenging it. He sighed, thinking of Rachel's beautiful body when they'd been lovers, her quick smile and the sparkle in her violet eyes. He'd loved her, with their special brand of love. It was easier to see her as she'd been then than as the invalid he visited yesterday. Where had the years sped to?

He fingered the mail Edwards had placed on the desk, sorting it without much interest. All business mail went to the office, most directed to Judson these days. Maybe it was time to let go of the reins completely. He paused to stare at a cheap drugstore envelope with his name and address printed in penciled block letters. His hand shook as he tore it open and pulled out the single sheet of tablet paper.

Does Rachel know about the Minot Corporation?

He dropped the paper as if it had burst into flames, staring at it in disbelief. Who—? He slammed his fist on the Dakota chair arm. Damn it, he'd been ready to accept Rachel's theory about the son-in-law she'd sent packing, but how the devil could Drew Hamilton have gotten wind of the Minot thing?! Had Rachel gotten another note? He wiped away the sheen of sweat on his upper lip and reached for the brandy decanter.

Maybe he'd been too quick in discounting Perkins and Collingswood. Could they have cooked up a scheme between them? Perkins was the only one who knew about the Minot thing except him, and he sure as hell hadn't been careless. He'd taken great pains to cover his tracks from start to finish.

It didn't seem possible. It was almost fifty years ago. He closed his eyes and leaned back in the soft leather chair. Fifty years, but he could still recall the wondrous warmth of Rachel's silky, naked body against his, the passion with which she'd welcomed him so eagerly. They should have been in the Minot thing together . . . Josh wanted it that way, but she had protested, hesitated. Maybe he'd have talked her into it if it hadn't been for that damned earthquake.

Rachel had rushed out of the hotel suite. He learned later that she'd driven most of the night to get home, slipping past roadblocks and devastation with single-minded purpose. Josh had taken a more cautious course. After listening to the scanty details offered by newscasts, Josh had phoned the mayor of Los Angeles. In minutes he'd been put through on police lines to the Rancho. Collette was hysterical, but she and the children had been safe and the house had escaped damage. He calmed her and assured her he'd be home as soon as the roads were cleared. That wasn't until the next day. He'd motored casually home, certain in the knowledge his family was safe.

Given Rachel's attitude, Josh felt justified in setting up the Minot Corporation without her. Fielding had done well for both of them. He had no regrets about sharing its profits with her, but she had not contributed to the new holding corporation. Her information on drilling sites had been utilized long ago. Minot was a separate entity. Josh had seen Perkins alone the following morning. Within weeks, the Minot Corporation owned stock in several companies that later merged into a powerful and profitable oil development bloc. Over the years it had brought him as much or more income than Fielding. Rachel had missed her chance. He had simply used Collette's name and signature instead. Collette had signed dutifully on the line he pointed to. He doubted she even realized she was a stockholder in a very private corporation. And no matter how many times he'd seen Rachel later, he had never mentioned the matter.

Josh thought about the horribly painful years after Ruth's death. Even now, grief weighed on him heavily like a mudslide when he thought of the winsome, fragile daughter he had loved so much. He and Collette had tried to escape the painful memories by running from Ocean Beach, but even distance had not cushioned the pain. Something had died in Josh, never to be reborn. Something had died in Collette as well. She seemed to fade away gradually, bit by bit, until finally she was gone, too.

Josh had returned to Ocean Beach and discovered Rachel had pushed Upfield ahead of Fantazia in every area. Too late, his interest in his own affairs had been rekindled by her triumph. He threw himself into a fight to win back the ground his son had ceded. He succeeded in drawing even but never quite pulling ahead with any clear lead.

He sighed, opening his eyes and rereading the blackmail note. What price was he going to pay for the folly of greed? So far, no demand had been made, but it would come unless he and Rachel found the culprit behind the torment. Right after his visit with Rachel, Josh had called Willis Fermin, a discreet investigator, to find Drew Hamilton. Any report on Hamilton's activities would take days. Josh had no choice but to wait. In the meantime, he'd have Fermin check out Collingswood and Perkins just to be on the safe side.

As he reached for the brandy decanter, the phone startled him. Frowning, he poured his drink before answering it. Few people had his private number, and he wasn't in the mood for family problems right now.

"Josh, this is Paris Hamilton."

"Has something happened to Rachel?" he asked quickly.

Paris was surprised by the note of genuineness in his voice. Some of the natural hostility she had felt for any Fantazia gave a little. "She's fine. Dr. Forest says she came through your visit with flying colors."

Josh breathed more easily. "That's wonderful. Rachel's

always been a spunky fighter. She may pull through this better than you or I expected."

Amazed by his gentle tone, Paris continued. "The doctor says she may be able to come home soon."

"Wonderful! Now, what prompts this call?"

That sounded more like the Josh she knew. Paris asked her question brusquely. "Does the name Theodore Reno mean anything to you?"

A band tightened around Josh's chest and his breath caught. The phone shook in his hand, and he looked at it as if it had come alive and struck like a rattler. *Teddy Reno?!*

"Josh?"

He faltered. "Give me a minute, Paris. It sounds vaguely familiar." Teddy Reno was dead. Josh wiped moisture from his lip. "Why do you ask?"

"I'm sure you read about the body that was found in the Oceanside. It's been identified as a drifter from Texas named Theodore Reno."

Josh's heartbeat raced in a fitful rhythm. He struggled to keep his voice even. "I can't place the name offhand."

"The fall down the elevator shaft broke his neck, but he'd been stabbed first. The police think someone was with him before the accident."

"Who identified the body?" Josh asked, raising the brandy glass to his mouth. Some of the liquor sloshed over the rim and ran down the side of the glass toward his silk-robed lap. He fished out the handkerchief from his monogrammed pocket and checked the flow.

"A hotel clerk. Reno registered the day before he died. The police found something among his things that connects him to the Oceanside. I'm damned curious to know who he was, but I don't want to ask Rachel if there's a chance it might upset her. I'm hoping there's a simple explanation."

A simple explanation. Fear gnawed at Josh's guts. Reno's name might be enough to precipitate Rachel's last stroke. It had almost given Josh one. Teddy Reno . . . he and Rachel had killed him thirty-five years ago. The night before he'd found his own darling Ruth. . . . Josh swallowed hard. "Let me give it some thought," he told Paris. "My memory isn't what it used to be, and there's something familiar about the name." *Something familiar* . . . It was a name he'd erased from his memory file a long time ago.

"I'd appreciate anything you come up with. Lieutenant Chambers is pushing, and I don't want him to get a court order to talk to Rachel."

"I'll call you tomorrow."

Josh stared at the phone a long time after he hung up. Teddy Reno. He closed his eyes and conjured up a picture of that dark night on Darien Hill. Both he and Rachel had been badly frightened. Did they examine Reno carefully? No, Rachel had felt for his heartbeat, listened for his breathing. Josh had accepted her word that Reno was dead; he'd never checked for himself. Reno had almost pounded his head to a pulp. Josh was lucky to have escaped permanent damage that would have crippled his family and business. But if Reno hadn't died that night, where the hell had he been all this time? Why hadn't he raised a stink and come after them? He would have had more reason than ever to blackmail them.

Blackmail. Josh glanced at the open letter fluttering on the desk. Reno had blackmailed them once before. The bastard would relish the chance to do it again. It was just his style. And Reno had known about the Fielding Corporation thirty-five years ago! It was one of the things he'd threatened to expose. Could he have stumbled onto the Minot deal as well?

Josh gulped down the rest of the brandy and dialed Willis Fermin's private number. When the detective answered, Josh demanded a copy of the police report on the dead man found at the Oceanside and a picture of the corpse. There was to be no hint of Josh's name in connection with this request, and the report was to be in his office by ten in the morning.

Teddy Reno . . .

Josh switched off the light and opened the drapes. Beyond the curve of the beach the offshore-well lights danced in the black harbor. Teddy Reno had been lured back by the smell of offshore oil once before. What had brought him out of hiding now? Josh wondered who had done him the favor of putting a knife into Reno and shoving him down an elevator shaft. It didn't really matter so long as Reno stayed dead this time.

Victor spent the day studying the papers Paris had lugged over. Intrigued by the personal letters, he read them first and was disappointed by the sparse information in them. Several were from someone who signed himself Harry but were only breezy accounts of the man's business and personal affairs in

Minneapolis. They offered no clues to Victor's past except that he had apparently lived in Minneapolis at one time. Victor laid them aside and concentrated on sorting the papers that dealt with the Ocean Beach redevelopment project. He found an interesting item among some handwritten notes: the name Bascomb Dorn and a local telephone number. There was also a stub in Victor's checkbook of a check made out to Dorn for five hundred dollars and dated only two weeks ago. Victor thumbed through the local phone directory in the booth at the end of the hospital corridor and was surprised to find that Dorn was a private detective. A call elicited the fact that Victor had hired Dorn, but the detective cautiously refused to answer any more questions over the phone. He said he would stop by the hospital to talk to Victor in person.

"Mr. Sands?" The man in the doorway was short, thin, and clean-shaven. He wore a lightweight sportcoat and a green shirt open at the neck. "I'm Bascomb Dorn. You were in my office two weeks ago."

"Thanks for coming. Sit down." When the man settled into one of the visitor's chairs, Victor asked. "You recognize me?"

Dorn nodded. "I did some checking after you called. Hospitals don't hang loose when it comes to giving out information on patients, but I got enough to verify what you told me about losing your memory."

"I'm reacquainting myself with the work I was doing before this happened," Victor said. "My guess is that whatever I hired you to do had some connection with it." He watched Dorn hopefully.

The detective drew an envelope from his pocket. Opening it, he pulled out two pieces of paper and handed them to Victor. "You wanted these checked out."

Victor looked at them. One was a xerox copy of the deed to the Oceanside Hotel. The other was a name and address: Stanton Fields, Seafront Apartments, Ocean Beach. "Did I tell you why I wanted them checked?" he asked.

"You wanted me to trace the hotel deed any way possible. You wanted to find anyone who remembered it being filed or had information of any kind."

"Did you come up with anything?" Victor felt a stir of excitement through the confusing haze of obscurity.

"I came up with the names of four women who worked in the recorder's office in 1927. Two are dead, one's living in

Arizona. I haven't turned up the last one yet."

Victor studied the photostat, trying to summon some spark of memory from his mind. A grant deed, property of Rachel Upfield. Paris had told him that much. But something must have made him curious or suspicious. Unless it was a quirk of his personality to meticulously check everything. He realized Dorn watched him.

"What about Stanton Fields?" Victor recognized the name from clippings and notes in his file on Shanna Fantazia.

"He's a real estate packager out of Phoenix," Dorn said. "He's put together deals in every state from here to Maine. His reputation is tops, credit rating the same. His office in Phoenix won't give out any information. They claim he's in New York, but that's a standard dodge on Fields's level. If he's got something going here, they sure as hell aren't going to admit it."

"What about his movements here?"

"He hasn't made any secret of his activities since he moved into the Seafront. He's been looking at property all over town with a realtor named Shanna Fantazia, granddaughter of Joshua Fantazia, Ocean Beach's leading citizen and one of the principals in the fight for the redevelopment project."

"Has Fields contacted him?"

"Not that I can find, but he's trying to put together a condo project and wants the Oceanside Hotel site. That's what Shanna's working on. One other thing," Dorn said, cocking his head as he watched Victor. "Fields is seeing a lot of Irena Hamilton."

Frowning, Victor asked, "Who is she?"

"Rachel Upfield's daughter."

Paris's mother? Victor tried to fill in gaps. "Is she part of the Upfield Company?"

Dorn snorted. "The old lady barely talks to her. Irena is a black sheep. Her escapades used to send Hearst reporters running for their typewriters. The old lady spent a fortune covering up her capers. She settled down some as she got older, but the family breathes easier when she's out of town."

"Where did she meet Fields?"

"At one of those posh spas in Scottsdale."

An image of an elegant resort flashed through Victor's mind. *You'll remember places and not know why. . . .*

"Did they come to Ocean Beach together?"

"I don't know."

"Find out."

Dorn made a note on a small spiral pad.

"Can you get me pictures of these people?" Victor asked.

"Sure. Anything else?"

Dorn had already given him a lot to think about. The problem was finding the connections. He considered giving Dorn Harry's letters and letting him trace the past, but he was still uneasy with his hidden personal life. He wasn't ready yet to turn over every rock. "That's all I can think of now," he said. "I'll call you if anything else comes up. How long do you think this will take?" He handed back the papers Dorn had given him.

"I should have something to report in a week or so. They going to keep you here that long?" He glanced around the hospital room as if it were a cage.

"A few days anyhow," Victor said. He was already getting restless to escape the boring monotony of the days broken only by Paris's evening visits.

Dorn rose and walked to the door, then turned. "Sitting here I've been trying to figure how I'd feel in your shoes. Know what? I can't. It blows my mind. You got a hell of a lot of courage, Mr. Sands." Dorn gave a quick salute as he walked out.

Victor was strangely touched by the detective's remark. There was no pretense or pity in Dorn's manner, only encouragement. It was a breath of refreshing air that blew away some of the fog Victor had been trapped in these past few days.

❧ Nineteen ❧

PARIS FINISHED THE last of the morning's correspondence and glanced at the clock. For the first time since Victor's stroke, she was ahead of schedule. Knowing she was going to escape from the office for most of the afternoon gave her a euphoric sense of freedom she hadn't enjoyed in a long time. She looked forward to the drive down to La Jolla, even though it was for business. She wondered if Josh Fantazia would call. He'd been so damned evasive last night, she couldn't make up her mind if he knew more than he admitted. Paris wasn't sure why she had hesitated asking Rachel about the mysterious Teddy Reno, but Josh's reaction last night put her more on guard than ever. She had the feeling she was rattling doors that had to be opened, yet she was in dread of what lurked there.

Looking out at the sun glinting on the blue Pacific, Paris realized it was a perfect day for being outdoors. Against the silvered rolling waves, several tiny sailboats seemed painted in the distance. With a pang, she thought of sailing to Catalina with Victor that glorious July day. Victor had called her at seven that morning, coaxing her to forget work and run away with him to enjoy the day. Laughing like kids playing hooky, they drove to the marina and rented a sailboat, which Victor assured her he knew how to sail. With a picnic lunch basket bought at Jurgensen's, they sailed off with the fresh morning breeze, two people filled with childlike glee and very adult emotions. They stood together at the tiller, lifting their faces to the salty spray and the hot sun. They laughed with the pure joy of being alive, and they kissed with the taste of heat and salt on their lips. They made love with the bright sun pouring over the thickly padded lounge on the forward deck. And Paris knew that she loved Victor.

She rubbed her temple as she watched a gull idle on an air current and drift lazily in a circle. Smiling, Paris tapped the intercom and asked Fran to get her Dr. Forest. When he came on the line, Paris requested permission to take Victor away from the hospital for the afternoon.

"A change of scenery will be good for him. I'll see there's a pass waiting at the nurses' station."

Lighthearted, Paris instructed Fran to order a picnic basket and champagne from Jurgensen's to be delivered as soon as possible. Then she cleared her desk methodically, putting the papers she needed for her meeting with Zachary in La Jolla in her briefcase and checking her calendar to be sure nothing remained undone. It bore only her small penciled notation about Josh's call.

Paris put through an interoffice call to Ted Banyon, knowing she was rushing him but impatient to settle the mystery of Teddy Reno. Banyon had covered a lot of ground to produce negative results. There were no company records of any kind that mentioned Theodore Reno; he had never been involved in any real estate dealings or with the hotel. Banyon had assigned one of the paralegals to search old newspaper files for the year 1927 and see if Reno's name was mentioned in connection with any happening that might have peripherally affected the Oceanside. He'd have a report on that shortly.

Paris was relieved that Reno had no direct connection with the hotel, even though she had never doubted the spurious nature of the deed and bill of sale. She didn't like loose ends, and Reno was a particularly bothersome one. She glanced at the note on her calendar again, then asked Fran to get her Josh Fantazia.

"I was just about to call you," Josh boomed, a bit too heartily, Paris thought. "The pieces finally fell in place this morning. It's been a very long time. Frankly, I wouldn't bother Rachel with any of this if I were you. Teddy Reno wasn't someone she'd want to be reminded of."

Curiosity piqued, Paris asked, "Who was he?" She was suspicious of Josh's bold assurances.

"A friend of your grandfather's. Lord, it had to be back in '20 or '21 right after Rachel and Hillary were married that Reno first came to town. Mind, I'm a bit hazy on details, but as I remember, it was right around the time of the first oil strike. Reno came out for a visit and stayed on. He had some background in the fields, at least to hear him tell it. He got involved in a few things, but he was overly fond of women, booze, and cards. He got into a number of scrapes with men on the rigs or with laborers down in the tent camps. One day he disappeared as quietly as he came, but there were rumors he was involved in a bogus oil stock scam." Josh paused for breath almost as if he were listening for a reply. Paris said nothing. "It was hard on Rachel," Josh went on in a more subdued tone. "Hillary was Reno's friend and the man had been staying at the hotel. There were some nasty inferences made. Rachel was glad to see the last of Reno. I doubt there was anyone in town who wasn't, unless it was his creditors. I have a vague recollection that he turned up once after that when the gambling ships were anchored out beyond the three-mile limit, but I don't remember any details. I know he wasn't welcome at the Oceanside anymore. Rachel put her foot down."

Paris digested the information. She was glad she hadn't stirred any dusty memories for Rachel. Reno was better left dead and forgotten.

Josh's voice was brusque again. "I took the liberty of getting a copy of the police report. I don't want to butt into your affairs, Paris, but it isn't going to be good for Rachel to dredge any of this up now. I'll have a word with Chief Trent and see that this whole matter is dropped."

Josh Fantazia offering to help her and Rachel? Paris wasn't going to accept any favor he might construe as a debt. "That won't be necessary," she told him. "Our legal department assures me Reno's claim is garbage. The matter will die on its own."

When she'd hung up, Paris realized Josh hadn't asked any questions about Reno's claim, which she had neglected to mention the previous night.

*   *   *

Josh hung up the phone and picked up the photographs that had come with the police report. Two had been taken where the body was found. Debris had been pushed aside for a clear shot of the corpse, but the dirt-streaked face was only a grotesque mask. The others were morgue shots, stark and ugly but clearly showing several angles of the face and body, including the stab wound in the chest. The flesh looked hard and waxy, the features unnatural.

A man changed in thirty-five years. Teddy wore a full beard back then, and his hair coloring had been dark, not wispy white. But there were the high cheekbones and the general shape of the face. The man had also been carrying Reno's identification. Which meant Rachel was wrong. Reno had been the blackmailer, not Drew Hamilton. Whoever had knifed Teddy and pushed him into that elevator shaft had done Josh and Rachel a hell of a big favor.

Josh reached into his pocket for the two blackmail notes, then dropped them into an onyx ashtray and held a match to them. He felt an enormous sense of relief and satisfaction as he watched them burn.

Paris held out a pair of sunglasses to Victor. "I've got the top down on the convertible."

He shook his head, grinning. "You're serious about this."

"I've got a picnic basket so we can stop along the beach. The ride will do you good. Come on."

Smiling, Victor followed her toward the hospital elevator which whisked them down to street level. When the nurse in charge informed him he wasn't getting a lunch tray because he had a "date," he expected some new test the doctors had dreamed up. Instead, here he was escaping the hospital for an afternoon outing with Paris. She'd told him she had two appointments that had to be kept, but the rest of the afternoon could be enjoyed in the sun and a long drive south.

In the parking lot she headed for a silver Mercedes 450SL, the top rolled down as she had promised. He held the door for her as she slid behind the wheel, then climbed in beside her. She flipped her sunglasses down from her golden hair.

"Ready?"

He nodded, enjoying the view of her delicate profile as she backed the car out and began to motor down the street. She was wearing a pale yellow dress with a brief jacket that set off her golden tan. He wondered what it would be like to caress her smooth skin. Her blond hair was loose and the breeze caught it and fanned it around her shoulders. She looked more relaxed than she had the past few days, and her smile never quite vanished. When she caught him looking at her, the smile ripened fully.

"How about some music?" She indicated the radio. He switched it on, fiddled with the dial, and bypassed two rock stations and a plaintive country and western song in favor of soft classical music. Paris grinned.

"Did I do something wrong?" Victor asked.

"Something right. That's your favorite station."

"I should have suspected you were testing me," he said in mock anger.

"Do you mind?"

He wished he could see her eyes behind the dark glasses. "No. When *you* do it, I don't feel like a guinea pig."

Her smile faded and a small crease appeared between her eyes, hidden behind the tinted glasses. "Is it pretty awful?" she asked soberly.

He considered his answer. "No. It's just that there's never any point of comparison. What did I go through before? Was everything always flowers and music in my life? I keep struggling to get a handle on things."

"You will. It takes time. Actually I think you've done marvelously for such a short time. You're collecting bits and pieces every day without even trying. Like the music."

She sounded so sincere, he smiled. "Okay. I promise not to worry about it today." Still watching her, he asked, "Where are we headed?"

She relaxed against the warm leather upholstery, elated by the prospect of an afternoon with Victor. "I have to stop in San Pedro first. We have a construction job underway there. It's a routine check and won't take long. Then we'll head down the coast to La Jolla. I have a meeting at three."

Her face was animated as she talked about her work. Victor turned sideways in the seat so he could get a full view of her. "You enjoy your work, don't you."

She glanced at him. "Yes, very much."

"I assume you're good at it. Upfield Land Management has

an excellent record and reputation, from what I've learned."

"We're the best in the business," she answered without false modesty. "My grandmother built the company. She started with a few pieces of property and an interest in real estate. The construction business was a natural progression after a while. Rachel doesn't do things in half measure."

"Was her husband part of it?"

Paris shook her head, and roared over the wind. "Only the original hotel that was destroyed in the earthquake. He died in it. He was trying to rescue my mother. She wasn't hurt." It felt strange talking about things she rarely thought about anymore. Paris had heard the story long ago and could review it now unemotionally.

"Was Rachel there?" Victor asked, not sure what prompted his curiosity.

Again Paris shook her head. "She was in L.A. on business. She heard the news on the radio. Afterward she decided to tear down what was left of the hotel. It had left too many memories." She winced inwardly at her thoughtless reference to memories, and glanced at Victor. He gave her a quick grin.

"If you're going to feel bad every time the word *memory* pops up, I'll develop a guilt complex. I suspect I'm going to meet a lot of people who don't have your tact. I might as well get used to it." He let his hand steal across the maroon leather and brush a gold strand from her cheek. She didn't pull away from his touch but relaxed again.

"All right. I won't worry about every word if you promise to tell me to shut up if I get into something you don't want to talk about. Is it a deal?" She flashed him another warm smile that made her face glow.

"It's a deal." He was so drawn to her, he had to physically pull back to steady himself. He glanced at the acres of industrial sites and pumping oil wells, as if they were incredibly picturesque. "Where are we?" he finally asked.

Paris felt the quick alteration of mood and geared her own pace down. Their verbal parrying and his touch had sent trembles through her. She had to give him time, she knew, but the knowledge didn't abate her desire. "Terminal Island," she told him. "That's the naval station. We'll be crossing into San Pedro in a few minutes."

"San Pedro's the Port of Los Angeles, isn't it?"

She flashed him a delighted smile. "That's right. Am I telling you things you already know?"

"God, I hope so," he said emphatically. "I'm tired of being a rutabaga."

She threw back her head and laughed so joyously, he stared at her. With an unselfconscious gesture, she reached over and squeezed his knee. "That expression has delighted me from the first time I heard you use it."

Gently he put his hand over hers, letting himself savor their closeness. "Have I been a rutabaga before?"

She didn't draw her hand away. "It was your pet term for the dolts of the world. It came from your background in the Midwest. No one out here's ever heard of a rutabaga."

He thought about the letters from Minneapolis he'd set aside. Without realizing it, he started to withdraw his hand, but she clasped it so he couldn't pull away. Her gentle look was filled with compassion.

"We don't have to talk about it, but you're going to have to face it someday."

He was silent a moment, then said, "Did I talk about my past?"

She returned her hand to the wheel and made a sharp turn as they came off a bridge. "Not much. I know you lived in Minneapolis before you came here. You were born in Chicago, graduated from Northwestern, then got an MBA from Harvard. You worked several years in corporate management, then went into city planning and opened a consultant firm in 1978."

It gave Victor a strange feeling that she knew more about him than he knew about himself. "And?" he prompted.

She shook her head, glancing at him for a moment before returning her attention to the traffic. "I got all that from the city council's questionnaire when you were hired. You didn't talk about your personal life."

"Didn't you pry? I thought women were supposed to be curious."

How much she'd wanted to know about him! And how reluctant she'd been to ask because of his reticence and her fear that she'd learn about some other woman in his past for whom he might still carry a torch.

"It wasn't any of my business," she said, braking gently for a traffic light. "I asked a million questions about the redevelopment project."

"Did you try to influence my opinion?"

She smiled without looking at him. "Of course. My grandmother considers you a scab doing Josh Fantazia's dirty work. You are the enemy. Rachel told me to use any tactics that got results."

"Your grandmother sounds like a fighter."

Paris's chin lifted proudly. "She is. I occasionally disagree with her methods, but she gets things done."

"Did you do what she wanted?" Victor studied the delicate, well-carved profile, wanting to run his fingertip along the firm set of her jaw.

She looked at him. Behind the dark glasses, her green-amber gaze was steady. "Yes, but I fell in love with you against my better judgment."

He was silent a moment, surprised at her candor but pleased with her admission. "Thanks for saying that. I've asked myself a hundred times if we were in love. Not being sure is worse than not remembering. Was I in love with you?"

"You didn't commit yourself."

"Were we lovers?" That brought a faint blush to her cheeks, but he knew it was tenderness, not embarrassment. He laid his arm across the seat again and let his hand rest on her shoulder. Her warmth radiated through the thin cotton jacket. When she didn't answer, he said, "I've wondered if I was a cold bastard who had no emotions. I hope I didn't hurt you— and that I never do. Right now, I'm not sure how I feel about a lot of things, but I'm glad we had what we did." He saw a tear roll from under her glasses. Very gently, he said, "If I can handle what our past was together, I'll be able to think about the future."

Her voice was tight and low, almost lost in the traffic sounds. "What about your past in Minneapolis?"

He sighed. "I need a lot more confidence before I can tackle that. I'm going to do that report first. Then I'll think about the rest."

She looked at him quickly. "I'm glad you're going to do it." She'd known he would, known he had to for his own sake more than anything. And she was glad he hadn't told her the decision before she arranged this outing. Somehow it was important to her he didn't think she was interested only in the results of his report.

The Mercedes hummed up a long, steep hill. At the top Paris turned onto a street where a construction site was protected by a chain-link fence. Paris parked near the shack and beckoned Victor to follow. She trailed around the car, glancing back to see his tall, dark figure following, hesitantly. At the gate she called the foreman, a bluff, burly man named Darcy, who grinned widely and shook hands with Victor when Paris introduced them. He handed them hard hats and the three began to pick their way through the construction area. Upfield was building a small business park where a shopping center had once stood. Victor listened as Paris and Darcy discussed footings, stress factors, and the specifications for concrete. His own understanding of it all made him keenly aware that Paris was building his self-confidence, and he wondered if it was by design. Whatever her reason for planning the outing, Victor relished it fully.

By the time they were on the Pacific Coast Highway headed for La Jolla, Victor was relaxed and content. He and Paris alternately burst into chatter, then turned quiet as they enjoyed the scenery and each other's company. Once out of the cluster of beach towns that crowded the coast south of Ocean Beach, they rode with the glittering Pacific on one side and sun-baked hills on the other. Victor realized that the day touched off vague feelings, mostly pleasant, and that he was creating a "memory." He liked the water, he was sure, and felt confident he could swim. He had no trouble envisioning himself at the tiller of one of the sailboats that dotted the silvery waves offshore. He'd like to take Paris sailing. Perhaps he would when he'd finished the report.

Near San Clemente, Paris turned off on a rutted beach road that meandered among palms and scrub oak. When she came to a small clearing, she parked the car and directed him to remove the picnic basket while she grabbed a folded blanket, then led the way to a narrow path across the sand dunes. She ran ahead like a sea sprite, lifting her face to the breeze that curled her hair like drifting smoke. Laughing, she stopped and pulled off her sandals and ran barefoot through the hot, dry sand. Topping a rise, she turned, dropped the blanket, and spread her arms to welcome the sea. Victor set down the bas-

ket and watched her, relishing the carefree spirit that had been
hidden so well inside the astute businesswoman.

"Like it?" she asked, her eyes dancing. She shoved up her
sunglasses as though she wanted nothing to cloud the gorgeous day. She was so desirable, Victor had trouble seeing the
scenery.

"It's perfect," he said. As she was. . . .

"We'll have our picnic here." She anchored two corners of
the blanket with her shoes. When Victor set the basket down,
Paris sank to her knees and began unpacking the contents. The
first thing she came up with was a dewy, chilled bottle of Dom
Pérignon.

"Good Lord, do you always do this?" Victor said in astonishment as he sat beside her.

She laughed, and her sparkling white even teeth gleamed in
the sun. "As a matter of fact, good old Victor was far more
likely to pull off this kind of trick. You are something of a
gourmet cook. You are a true connoisseur of food and a wine
expert to boot." She unearthed two tulip glasses from the basket and tossed Victor a white linen towel. "Let's see if you
remember how to open a bottle."

Pretending concentration, he unfastened the wire and an-
gled to the bottle expertly. A moment later the cork popped
and the champagne bubbled to the bottle rim. He winked as
Paris grinned. He filled the glasses and they raised them in a
toast.

"To good old Victor," he said.

Paris shook her head in mild reproach. "To a magnificent
blend of the old and new Victor Sands." She clinked her glass
to his and watched him as she sipped.

He took her hand. "You're very good for me, Paris. You
always seem to know the right thing to say or do when I'm
floundering. Until now I've been angry at the world out there
that still has a memory when mine's gone. These past few
days were so confusing I didn't really believe I'd ever pull out
of it. I'm not sure I even wanted to. But you've put things
back in perspective. Thank you." He pressed her warm hand
to his lips, then held it comfortably as he watched her.

Paris's eyes misted and she wished she'd left her sunglasses on. Victor drew her close, slipping a hand to her
shoulder, then caressing her neck as he put his lips to hers.
Paris surrendered, knowing she wanted Victor more than ever

before. He felt so right in her arms. . . .

He brushed a wisp of hair from her cheek. "Thank you for giving me back myself," he said softly. "I must have loved you." His gaze held her, and for a moment Paris was lost in their warm brown depths. He touched her cheek, then raised his champagne glass for a new toast. "To a beautiful afternoon with a beautiful woman."

Paris felt a pleasant glow as she sipped the champagne. For a moment they had almost recaptured the mood of intimacy they'd shared so easily before his stroke. It's almost the way it was when we first met, she thought, the undeniable attraction, the mysterious chemistry more powerful than words. But then Victor had been confident and unhesitant, a man accustomed to going after and getting what he wanted. She had loved that in him, yet she found his new tenderness appealing as well. Victor's new manner didn't soften his powerful magnetism in the least.

The intimate moment ebbed away unmourned because they knew there would be more quiet moments.

Paris unpacked plates, silverware and an array of food Jurgensen's was famous for. There were marinated mushrooms, caviar topped with chopped onions, pate, dark bread, and packed in ice, a platter filled with oysters on the half shell, crab claws and jumbo shrimp. They ate and talked and laughed, and when they were surfeited, they walked along the damp, cool sand where the waves lapped onto the beach. And when they finally locked themselves in the car, and drove on they shifted from companionable silence to easy conversation somehow as intimate as their lingering kiss.

In La Jolla, Paris gave Victor his choice of exploring the city on his own or sitting in on her meeting with Hugh Zachary. To her surprise and delight, he opted to go to the meeting with her. She warned him that the discussion of costs and projections on the office project might bore him, but Victor smiled and said he'd take the risk. Actually he enjoyed watching Paris so much, he didn't want to let her out of his sight, and it also provided a good opportunity to test the skills and knowledge he was slowly excavating from his past.

The meeting lasted two hours. When they walked back to the car, Victor offered to drive. Paris handed him the keys without hesitation.

"You pulled off quite a deal in there," he said with admiration. He pulled out of the business parking lot and eased into the growing afternoon traffic.

"I haven't got it yet," Paris said. "One thing I've learned in this business is not to count on anything until the contract is signed." She leaned back on the headrest and turned to watch Victor drive. He commanded the steering wheel, as he always had.

"You presented a clear picture of what you could do. Zachary was impressed." Victor had studied the man closely, reading his expressions as Paris presented figures. Never once had there been any sign that Zachary wavered in his decision.

"Thanks for the vote of confidence. He likes our pro forma. I know his committee will like it, too. They're sitting on a gold mine, and if they're smart enough to move before the rush gets underway, they can call the shots. Once this complex is operating, there'll be a new one for every spurt in population growth. We're thinking of opening an office down here before long." San Diego County was enjoying a growth boom similar to the one in Ocean Beach fifty years ago. A branch office had been Paris's idea, and Rachel had enthusiastically agreed, seeing the challenge and potential in extending the Upfield reach.

Paris propped her head on her raised arm. "The only problem is that Zachary's partner is a chauvinist who doesn't like the idea of working with a woman." Unless it's a purring cat-panther like Shanna Fantazia, Paris thought. Zachary's partner, Jess Phillips, had begun his business career with an Ocean Beach firm, and he and Shanna had been a hot item for several months. Paris suspected that his attitude now was being fed by Shanna's spite and vindictiveness, but she couldn't prove it.

Victor glanced at her. "Do you run into a lot of that?"

Paris shrugged. "Some, and it irritates me when I do. They're going to have to accept the fact that women in business are here to stay whether they like it or not."

"Are you a militant feminist?"

"I'm a woman," Paris countered. "I'm good at being female and I'm also good at running a huge business. If wanting to crack any male who doesn't believe the two can be harmonious is militant, I guess I am."

He smiled. "I have the feeling I never doubted your ability in dual roles."

She was silent a moment, remembering how exciting and wonderful their lovemaking had been and how direct and efficiently they'd conducted business.

Traffic began to thicken as they neared Newport Beach. Paris offered to take the wheel, but Victor was enjoying the pilot seat too much. "You navigate and I'll get us there," he said.

It was almost seven when they pulled into the hospital parking lot. He stood with her a moment when she climbed out of the car. "Thank you for today, Paris. It was very special—in many ways." He bent and kissed her, resisted taking her into the circle of his arms despite his urgency. Her eyelids whispered shut as she savored this warm intimate moment. Smiling, he waved as she walked briskly toward the Upfield Pavilion entrance.

Bascomb Dorn was waiting in Victor's room, lounging comfortably in the plastic organic armchair, smoking a cigarette which he crushed out as Victor entered.

"Hope you don't mind my waiting," Dorn said. "The nurse said you'd be back soon."

"Not at all. I'm surprised to see you so soon. Have you got something?" Victor felt a renewed excitement about getting back to work.

Dorn shrugged his shoulders. For a private detective he was dressed well, in a seersucker suit and wing-tip shoes. "We struck out in Phoenix. That former clerk is in a nursing home down there, but if she's the one who recorded the deed, you're out of luck. She's got Alzheimer's, and they have all they can do to keep her from wandering off into the desert. She doesn't know her own family, let alone something that happened fifty years ago."

"What about the other one?" Dorn had said there were four possibles.

"I'm still checking. I'm pretty sure she's still in this area. I should have an address before long." Dorn reached into the inner pocket of his seersucker jacket, then handed Victor a typed report. "This is the report I put together on Stanton Fields. I thought you might like to look it over." He got to his feet. "I'll stop by again as soon as I have anything else."

"Do I owe you another check?" Victor asked as they shook hands.

Dorn grinned. "I'll bring the bill when I finish with Esther

Massie, the elusive clerk. It'll give me an excuse to stop by and shoot the bull. Nice talking to you, Sands."

When he'd gone, Victor settled in the armchair to read the report on Stanton Fields.

❧ *Twenty* ❧

SHANNA ADJUSTED HER thoughts to accommodate the unexpected request from Stanton Fields. Glancing at her desk
calendar, she decided her two o'clock appointment could be
rescheduled. She smiled at Fields sitting across from her as
though it were perfectly acceptable for him to arrive unan-
nounced and ask for second showings on property they'd already reveiwed last week.

"I can get away for an hour," she said. He'd offered to wait
if she had something pressing, but his deeply drawn brows
indicated he would unwillingly make the sacrifice. Now she
was rewarded with his easy smile.

"That's very good of you. I realize this secondary purchase
is negligible compared to the Oceanside, but I would like to
finalize it as quickly as possible."

"It's really no problem at all," she assured him. She'd
show him half the city to keep him happy if she had to. Bigger
deals than the Oceanside sometimes fell through when clients
got impatient. Fields's newest plan involved a smaller condo-

minium complex a few blocks back from the beach. He theorized that with the downtown redevelopment, surrounding properties would go up sharply in price as the population once more gravitated toward the central city rather than outlying areas. And condominiums were the wave of the eighties as well as any large city's future.

Shanna paused in the outer office to instruct her secretary to reschedule her calendar, then stepped out into the early October heat as Fields held the door open. To her surprise, he insisted on driving, a first in all the time she'd squired him around. He led her to a white Cadillac in the small private lot beside the building. Shanna noticed the discreet rental decal on the windshield. The car engine was running, and there was a woman sitting in the front seat. Fields opened the back door for Shanna and leaned in to make introductions.

"Irena, this is Shanna Fantazia, the realtor who's been so helpful. Shanna, this is Irena Hamilton."

Shanna's smile withered as Irena acknowledged the introduction with a faint nod but didn't turn to face her. *Irena Hamilton? Paris Hamilton's mother and Rachel Upfield's daughter!* What the hell was Fields up to? Shanna, with her senses alert, settled into the soft gray leather cushions and studied Irena's haughty profile. She was still a beautiful woman except for the hard lines around her eyes and mouth. Shanna had heard about her since childhood but seen her ony rarely and then from a distance. Irena preferred the glitter of Los Angeles, Palm Desert, or Scottsdale to Ocean Beach. What was she doing here now—and with Stanton Fields? Was this some trick Paris had dreamed up to steer Fields away from Fantazia Realty?

Shanna crossed her arms over her thin, curve-hugging yellow linen suit and braced for battle. The air-conditioning was five degrees colder than normal. For Irena's comfort no doubt. She wore a dramatic turquoise silk suit, Italian stilettos, and an aura as cool as the Pacific Ocean. She was a striking woman for her age, bearing a faint resemblance to pictures of Rachel as a young woman in bone structure and general face shape. Her coloring was more like Paris's, but the similarity stopped there. Where Paris had a wholesome California outdoor look, Irena was a mannequin displaying professional makeup and hairstyling. Shanna was willing to bet a face-lift accounted for the smooth, near-perfection of the other woman's skin, and her deftly styled and sprayed coif disguised the scars.

"I really didn't expect this project to move with such speed," Fields said, glancing in the rearview mirror to meet Shanna's gaze. He smiled disarmingly. "I know this is an imposition."

"Not at all." She returned his smile. "Which places did you want to see?" He'd said only "two of the properties" during a lapse in the conversation a few minutes ago, something not unexpected with Irena in the car. Shanna had shown him five, and she was curious which ones he'd focused on.

"The one on California and the one on Fourth."

He hadn't told her much about the proposed project, but she'd researched answers to any questions that might crop up. Judging by other projects Fields had sponsored, the property on California Avenue might present problems. "The lots on California are on the redevelopment boundary," she said. "The city council is considering restricting buildings for a five-block radius to no more than three stories." She'd heard it only yesterday from one of the lawyers at Fantazia Enterprises that she'd been sleeping with off and on since she left her grandfather's company.

In the mirror she saw Fields's white brows crease together. "It's out of the question, then. I won't tie my client up with that kind of deal. What about the other one?" His piercing gaze sought hers again in the mirror.

Shanna knew Irena was aware of the interchange, and she met Fields's eyes with a flash of provocativeness that was purely female. "There's no problem at all," she said.

Irena's purse snapped loudly in the ensuing silence. She put a cigarette between her carmine lips and snapped a lighter, then puffed smoke that was quickly dispelled by the cold air blowing through the vents. She had a bored look, but Shanna knew she was totally aware, like a cat under a rosebush waiting for an unwary sparrow. Shanna still hadn't figured out what Irena was doing here. Irena wasn't in the Upfield Corporation and never had been, but she was part of the family. Did Fields think she could somehow influence Paris or Rachel to sell the Oceanside? Shanna made a mental note to find out if

Irena had a vested interest in the old hotel. If Fields thought
she was worth cultivating, maybe Irena wouldn't be shocked
by an offer of a "finder's fee" when Shanna closed the deal.

She brought her attention back as the car slowed. She was
surprised that Fields remembered the address without asking
directions, but he found a parking space only two doors from
the small apartment complex on a block that would double in
value when the redevelopment was finished. Fields climbed
out and walked around to open Shanna's door and help her
out. Then he opened the door beside Irena and took her arm
possessively.

"This will only take a few minutes, darling. We'll be back
in plenty of time for our evening plans, don't worry."

As Irena slid from the seat, she swung out sleek, nyloned
thighs that poked through her high-slitted skirt and slipped her
arm through Fields's. Shanna hadn't missed the *darling*. So
they were a cozy little twosome. Interesting. Was he trying to
seduce her by showing the property? Surely he didn't believe
Irena Hamilton knew two cents' worth about real estate
values. Shanna walked briskly in with Fields's step.

"The entire block is zoned for condos," she reminded him.
"None of the other buildings are on the market yet, but it
won't take long after the first one sells." The street was a
mixture of small apartment houses and old frame single dwell-
ings that were worth far less than the land they stood on. If
Fields moved fast, he could pluck up prime property and sit
on it until the right client came along.

Fields looked along the street speculatively without slow-
ing his pace. Irena Hamilton was taking quick little steps to
keep up, darting glances as though she found the neighborhood depressing. It certainly wasn't an area the Upfield clan
was accustomed to. Some of the buildings were seedy, but
Shanna knew Fields was estimating their potential.

"As I mentioned before, the owner's anxious," Shanna
prompted. "He's asking top dollar for the place as it stands
now, but I think he'll come down for the right financing. What
kind of down payment are you considering?"

"Fifty thousand," Fields said, steering Irena through the
California archway that had been so popular back in the thir-
ties.

Shanna hid her disappointment. The seller had already

turned down an offer with a minimum down. "You could walk away with it for seventy-five down," she ventured.

Fields gave a slight shrug and smiled. "We'll see."

The apartment complex was built around a courtyard which was encircled by a small garden with a fountain. The flowerbeds had gone to weeds, and the concrete Neptune had a chipped nose and was holding ony a fragment of the original conch shell with his broken hand. His trident had vanished. Fields didn't even look around the court. Shanna tried to figure how his mind was running. The first time she'd shown him the property, he asked dozens of questions. She was tempted to push him now, but she forced herself to be guided by his silence. From time to time he glanced sidelong at Irena, who was definitely ill at ease in the shabby surroundings. Her bored expression had been replaced by distinct nervousness, which Fields chose to ignore.

"Does the building have steel beams?" he wanted to know.

"Yes. It was built after the earthquake and meets all codes. Actually it would be feasible to renovate, but the utility for this block is close to a hundred units and there are less than forty."

"Let's have another look inside," he said.

Irena held back, shuddering suddenly as if she'd caught a chill. "I—I really don't care to, Stanton. Places like this depress me. I'll wait here."

There was a hint of annoyance in Fields's tone. "Aren't you feeling well?"

Irena said, "I'm fine. It's just that—"

"I would really like you to join us," he said firmly, holding her arm when she tried to draw away. "It will only take a few minutes. Be a dear and do it for me." He was watching her closely, and when Irena's chin quivered, Fields's hand moved along her arm solicitously.

Irena gave him a weak smile. "All right." She let herself be drawn toward the door.

Shanna followed them into the musty hall, wondering what the hell was going on. Despite his assurances to Irena, Fields took his sweet time looking at everything. He wanted to see all four floors, and he inspected the halls and fire exits as though he worked for Building and Safety. At one point Shanna thought Irena was going to bolt, but Fields kept her arm tucked through his so she would have to disengage herself physically. Irena made no pretense of relishing the tour.

Shanna answered questions she'd already covered the first time she showcased the property, and when Fields said he wanted to see one of the apartments, Shanna rang the caretaker's bell and waited impatiently as the concierge grumbled about her not calling first. He finally found his keyring and lumbered upstairs to unlock a vacant apartment on the third floor. Irena stopped just inside the door while Shanna and Fields walked through the rooms. When they came back, Irena was gone. Fields said he'd seen enough and left Shanna to thank the caretaker and hurry after him to the car. Annoyed, she climbed into the backseat, damning Irena Hamilton silently but vehemently.

Irena was smoking in short, nervous puffs. The car was filled with blue smoke until Fields got the air-conditioning going. Irena's eyes darted and the hand holding the cigarette shook. Fields's jaw clenched and there was a small tic at the corner of his mouth. Shanna was furious. If Irena Hamilton screwed up this deal or anything else . . . She clenched her fist. Damn it, it was bad enough fighting constantly with Paris without having her goddam mother in the picture. Damn Irena Hamilton. Damn all the Upfields and Hamiltons! She had a lot of time invested in Fields, and by God, she expected it to pay off.

The city council granted Victor more time to complete his report. They gave him until the end of the month because they knew it would take them longer to replace Sands. Their risk was little, but Burt Douglas warned Paris that several council members had grudgingly agreed and were already reviewing other applications.

Victor was pleased when Paris shared the news. He'd already immersed himself in the information he'd collected before the stroke, and a clearer picture of the redevelopment project was emerging. One of the nurses brought him a small table so he could spread his work in neatly sorted piles, and he had fallen into a comfortable pattern of work. He wondered if it was part of his past.

Paris's visits were still the highlight of his days. The day after the picnic, he looked forward to five-thirty with anticipation. When Paris arrived, she was followed by an aide carrying a tray and an insulated Thermos filled with icy martinis. They drank from water tumblers and shared a new intimacy that was enjoyable for them both.

Despite her curiosity about Victor's progress, Paris refrained from questioning him. At times Victor found her looking at him with open curiosity, but he wasn't ready to divulge the direction his work was leading. At times he was frustrated by the slowness of his progress, but he was encouraged when some small point leaped at him from the pages like a waving banner. When he traced its course through the work he'd already done and saw its significance, his confidence would soar. But there were also times when huge gaps appeared and he couldn't be sure if they were in the data itself or his memory.

Weighing the Upfield and Fantazia plans, he found they both had merit. The Upfield plan promised a majestic, grand hotel in the city to which tourists, conventions, and the cream of Southern California society would flock. It would be a landmark, the city's pride, which would help give Ocean Beach the kind of glamour usually reserved for New York, Chicago, and Los Angeles. On the other hand, the Fantazia plan would add much-needed luxury housing to the heart of the city to guarantee that the revitalized downtown was here to stay. More importantly, it would keep the elite from moving to the suburbs and reinforce the city's tax base substantially. A toss of a coin could have settled the matter. Both Upfield and Fantazia were multimillion-dollar businesses with extraordinary designs for the Oceanside site, despite their history of sometimes tempestuous feuding.

Within days of renewing his work on the redevelopment project, Victor was impatient to leave the hospital. Dr. Forest agreed, provided Victor continued his physical therapy on an outpatient basis.

Paris raised her martini in a toast when he told her. "Dr. Forest is getting soft-hearted, " she said. "He's letting Rachel out the end of the week, too."

"Wonderful!" Victor exclaimed. He was delighted to see the lines in her face relaxing. He listened distractedly, watching her dancing eyes and her animated smile, as she told him she was interviewing nurse-companions to supervise Rachel's recovery at home. The nurse would have her work cut out for her, Paris said. Rachel was already protesting that the servants were sufficient for her needs. Rachel had a birthday at the end of the month; if she was strong enough, she would have a party to celebrate the event and her recovery. Paris was to make the arrangements. Paris laughed. If Rachel was giving orders, she was rapidly recovering.

When Paris offered to drive Victor to his apartment after his release, he accepted without reservation. He relished the idea of seeing more of Paris outside the sterile hospital sur-roundings, even though he was reluctant to become more deeply involved without first exploring the riddle of his past.

Drew Hamilton pocketed the bills and pushed the change across the bar. "See you, Ed."

Outside, night had brought only minor relief from the unrelenting Texas fall heat. Drew stood a moment inhaling the muggy air, to clear his lungs of the smoke and the odor of stale spirits, sweaty men, and oil fields. He cupped his hands around a match as he lit a cigarette. Glancing both ways along the quiet street, he got his bearings, then walked toward the corner.

He moved with the light step of a man who knew how to stay alert for his own survival. To an observer, he was good-looking but just another middle-aged oil man on the way home after a few drinks at the local hangout. His light brown hair was streaked with gray and he was now an oil-field manager, not a rigger, but he'd lost none of the well-muscled physique of his younger years, and he moved with gracefulness few young men possessed. If anything, the heavy work on the rigs had broadened his shoulders and thickened his chest. He seemed totally relaxed as he walked, but he was keenly aware of the muted sounds around him: snatches of music from the bar jukebox as the door opened, a swell of voices from an open window, a woman's soft laughter. As he passed a store-front, his glance swept the glass reflecting a murky image of the sidewalk behind him. He turned the corner quickly, stepped into the sheltered doorway, and pressed into the shadows.

The man had emerged from the Happy Hour behind him, a dark blob in the dull neon glow of the bar sign, but there was no mistaking the squat, muscular figure. It was the guy who'd been following him for two days, asking questions on the rig and in places like the Happy Hour. Drew pulled back into the shadows as the man quickened his stride to keep track of his quarry. When he came abreast of the doorway, Drew slid out behind him and grabbed him with a hammer-lock. The man sputtered and tried to claw Drew's arm around his throat.

"Why are you so interested in my business, mister?" Drew demanded.

When the man tried to turn, Drew tightened the armlock enough to make him gasp.

"Why are you following me?" Drew demanded, holding the pressure to show he meant business.

"I—I don't know what you mean—" The words came out like rattling palm fronds.

"Don't give me that crap. You've been asking about me all over town. Why?" Drew underlined his question with a pain-ful shove on the man's arm.

"You're wrong—Agghh!"

"Talk!"

The pain brought the squat man to his tiptoes. "You're breaking my arm—"

"Talk!"

"Okay—okay—let me go—"

"Talk!" Drew released the hold enough so the guy came back down on his heels, but the grip was still tight.

"I'm a private investigator. Jake Farrell. My license is in my pocket. Jeez—you're hurting me—"

"Take it out."

Farrell's hand snaked inside his coat and came out with a flat leather folder. He flipped it open one-handed and held it up. Drew couldn't make it out in the dim light. A goddam private eye?

"Who are you working for?" he demanded.

"A guy in L.A."

Los Angeles? What the hell—? Drew hadn't been there for twenty years, but the name still produced a sour taste in his mouth. He eased the pressure on Farrell's arm slightly and the detective let his breath out with relief. "What's his name?"

The detective moved so fast it took Drew by surprise. As

soon as there was no danger of his arm snapping, Farrell twisted and came out of the hold expertly. At the same time his knee jammed upward toward Drew's groin. Drew let Farrell's wrist slip from his hand as he shoved hard to put Farrell off balance. The knee caught Drew mostly on the thigh, but he sucked air painfully. He doubled as he shot a hard right to the detective's gut. Farrell staggered back. Recovering, Drew hit him with a quick left to the jaw. Farrell fell against the building, making the window rattle dangerously. Drew grabbed his shirtfront and backed Farrell against the plate glass, pinning him with a forearm across the chest.

"Now tell me who hired you before I shove you through the goddam window!"

The detective wheezed. "Willis Fermin."

"Who the hell is he?"

"A detective."

"Private?"

Farrell nodded as he sucked air into his lungs.

"Who's he working for?"

"I don't know."

Drew pressed his arm on Farrell's windpipe. The little man gagged.

"I don't know. I swear! We work that way—"

"Why is he interested in me?"

Farrell hesitated a fraction, and when he said, "I don't know," Drew knew he was lying. He put some more weight behind the arm.

"What are you supposed to find out about me?" A detective in L.A. putting someone on his tail.

Farrell was cooperative again. "Where you go, what you do."

"I lead a pretty dull life," Drew said, leaning hard enough so Farrell's eyes bulged.

"Aagghh—Okay—jeez—He thinks you're sending blackmail letters."

"What?!" Drew didn't know what he'd expected, but he couldn't hide his surprise.

"I'm supposed to see if you go to the post office or drop letters in mailboxes."

Drew snorted. "Hell, there are a hundred ways I could mail a letter and you wouldn't know a damn thing about it."

"I know, I know. I told Fermin, but he's paying the freight, so it's his ballgame."

And someone was paying Fermin, Drew thought. Who? He studied Farrell's face in the deep shadow of the doorway. Too scared to lie. A subcontract for a private eye in Los Angeles . . . Christ, the only one in L.A. who had any stake in whether Drew Hamilton was alive or dead was Rachel Upfield. What the hell was she up to now? What had rattled her cage after all this time? He'd figured her to have kicked off after her well-publicized stroke, until he saw the story in *Time* two months ago about the Oceanside. It took a moment for his cold rage to ease.

"Have you filed any reports?" he asked Farrell.

Farrell tried to shake his head. "Nothing goes on paper. He calls me."

"When?"

"Every two days."

"When was the last time?"

"Yesterday."

"What'd you tell him?"

"Where you live, the job you work, the Happy Hour—routine stuff, that's all I've got."

"What'd Fermin say?" When Farrell hesitated, Drew shook him. "For crissake, don't make me squeeze it out of you again!" He pushed the detective hard against the glass.

"He wants me to get a sample of your handwriting."

Drew burst out laughing. Farrell wasn't kidding about the blackmail. Rachel really believed it enough to hire someone to find him. Was it possible the mighty Rachel Upfield was running scared? Hell, she was close to eighty. It would be the first time. The idea amused him.

"What am I supposed to be blackmailing someone about?" he asked.

"I don't know. I swear, I'm just doing a job. . . ."

Drew took a half step back, stiff-arming Farrell so he stayed pinned to the glass. "Okay, pal, save yourself some aggravation. Go home and get a good night's sleep. And when your buddy Fermin calls, tell him I went to the bus station and bought a ticket for L.A."

"You didn't."

"But I'm going to first thing in the morning." He let go of

Farrell and stepped back. "Make it easy on yourself. Don't bother to see me off." Drew strode off into the darkness, his bulky figure swallowed by shadows and the sounds of celebration at the local corner tavern.

❧ *Twenty-One* ❧

DREW LOOKED DOWN the wide vista of Ocean Boulevard.
The city had changed a lot in twenty years. The downtown
looked gray and bleak, trafficked by few pedestrians and cars.
Some of the buildings he remembered were gone or had
changed enough to be unrecognizable, but the Oceanside
Hotel with its fifteen floors, turrets, high windows facing the
sea, and multi-terraces, still dominated the skyline. Even
boarded up, it stood over its lowly neighbors like a queen
surveying her realm. He remembered the night Irena had
dragged him there while Rachel's big bash was in progress. It
made him smile now, thinking how much more comfortable he
was with its changed appearance.

Farther uptown, he noticed that the Upfield Building had
undergone a face-lift. Its granite facade sparkled in the sun
dancing off the harbor. He walked slowly toward the entrance
and crossed the threshold. Somehow the lobby, though vir-
tually the same as in his recollection of it, seemed less imposing than it had when he'd to beg for Rachel's help. It was hard
to believe she was still sitting up in her aerie ruling her world.
He drew several curious glances as he rode to the top floor.
Christ, some things never changed.

The receptionist lifted her perfectly plucked eyebrows
when he asked to see Mrs. Upfield.

"She hasn't returned to work since her stroke, sir. Can someone else help you?"

That had hardly stopped her long reach. Controlling himself, he asked who was in charge.

"Miss Hamilton, but she's busy at the moment. Would you like to make an appointment?"

Drew shook his head. Paris. His daughter. He thought about the golden-haired cherub beauty solemnly waving goodbye as he drove away from the Ladera Street manor. Paris all grown up and supervising her grandmother's empire. Had Rachel managed to turn her into a replica of herself—hard, cold and brutal? He knew she'd sent Paris to Stanford, then Harvard. Could the Grant in her be bred out of her? He wasn't sure he wanted to find out. He thanked the receptionist and whirled to head for the glass-encased and oak-carved entrance.

He found a bar two blocks away and nursed a bourbon. Maybe it was a mistake to come back. Paris probably didn't want to see a father she couldn't remember. A father who let Rachel win by default because he couldn't find a way to beat her. Hell, he hadn't even put up a good fight, not the kind of battle Rachel would understand. She'd always had everything her way. Still did, probably. What in the world was she up to now, putting an investigator on his heels?

He glanced at his watch. It was the middle of the working afternoon. Paris was no doubt neatly ensconced in her fancy office, making million-dollar deals. The idea of his little girl handling something that size was hard to grasp. She had to take after Rachel, not Irena. Irena never could have done it. Funny, but when he tried to summon a picture of his ex-wife to mind, it wouldn't come.

He should have asked that cool number upstairs if Rachel still lived on Ladera Street. She'd be alone except for the servants and maybe a nurse. Just as he couldn't visualize Irena, he couldn't imagine Rachel weak or ill. So okay, he thought, I beard the lioness in her den. He downed the rest of his drink, then hurried to the parking lot where he'd left the rental car.

Motoring farther uptown, he had to check his maps because he didn't recognize Darien Hill. He double-checked the street signs to make sure he was in the right place. He knew the wooden derricks would have been dismantled long ago.

But he expected grasshopper pumps to lace the Hill. Not here. They'd gone underground. The Hill was bare except for scruffy grass and a few curved streets lined with condos near the top. Circling low on the hill, Ladera Street was a green oasis in the hot autumn dust. Palms and eucalyptus rustled like money. Two vacant lots next to Rachel's were planted in low-maintenance Korean grass and ice plant, the rather magnificent old houses he remembered gone without a trace. Had Rachel bought them out to keep neighbors at a distance, or had the mansions succumbed to the same progress that would eventually squeeze out Rachel, too?

He slowed as he drove up the long curving driveway that vanished among the towering Italian cypresses. His first glimpse of the house made him whistle softly in astonishment. It was as perfect and pristine as it had been when he first saw it. The white siding glistened in the sun and the landscaping was a triumph of symmetry and color. The huge four-story house was platformed up the hill, with terraces and brick walls counterpointing each other and the house. Flowerbeds and hedges, carefully pruned trees, not a damned blade of grass out of place. The white graveled driveway hadn't had any oil-dripping clunkers parked on it, that was for sure. With a shrug, he pulled up in front of the door.

A middle-aged woman in a gray uniform and white apron answered his ring. Drew thought he saw a flicker of surprise in her eyes when she heard his name. She asked him to wait, closing the door and leaving him on the step. She was back in a few minutes.

"Mrs. Upfield's nurse will be down in a moment," she told him as she ushered him into the large sunken living room off the hall.

The parlor, Irena used to call it. Drew glanced around, seeing Rachel sitting ramrod straight the night he'd packed Irena out of here that first time. Through the French doors to the sun room, he saw the funny little sofa where Rachel sat the afternoon she told him he couldn't have his own kid. He blew his breath. None of his memories of this house were pleasant. When he heard someone coming, he turned.

It wasn't the maid but a nurse in a white uniform and starched cap. "Mr. Hamilton? I am Eloise Jury, Mrs. Upfield's nurse. Please sit down." She sat in one of the chintz-covered chairs and waited for him to comply. When he did, she said,

"Are you aware that Mrs. Upfield suffered a serious stroke several months ago?"

"Yes, I've read about it here and there." Serious enough to still need a nurse, yet recovered enough to keep tabs on her business—and Drew.

"She's made a remarkable recovery, but she's not completely out of danger," the nurse said. "She's been home from the hospital only a short time." She tilted her head with a professional air. "As you undoubtedly know, she's a woman of considerable determination and energy. It's difficult for her to accept the role of semi-invalid."

Drew gave her a polite nod, not sure what his reaction was supposed to be. Semi-invalid meant not helpless. Was he glad? Would he have been able to face Rachel down otherwise?

Miss Jury continued. "My duties go beyond Mrs. Upfield's medical needs in the strictest sense of the word. Part of my job is to anticipate potential problems."

He flashed her a wry smile "Like me?"

"I don't mean to be presumptuous, but please try to understand my position," she said. "Excitement is not good for my patient, nor is trauma of any kind."

It was the kind of speech Rachel would make, cut and dried and infinitely polite but to the point. Drew said, "You're saying you won't let me see her?"

The nurse made a small sound that might have been a sigh. "It's not quite that simple, Mr. Hamilton. Believe me, I would if it were left to me, but Martha announced your arrival in Mrs. Upfield's hearing. She *wants* to see you. I am asking you to temper your conversation to take into consideration her precarious state of health."

Drew studied the woman's earnest face She knew who he was. "What has Rachel said about me?"

"She hasn't said anything. I am presuming a great deal based on public knowledge of the family background. There seem to be many people who can create unadvisable sparks for my patient. I suspect you may be one of them."

Drew's wide lips stretched into a smile. So Rachel was still a fireball and a demon. "Okay, I get it. You'll let me see her but I don't start anything, right?"

Getting to her feet, Miss Jury smiled. "Yes. Thank you. Now if you'll follow me." She led the way up the curving, carpeted staircase to Rachel's wing across the hall from the one he and Irena had shared. She opened the door and stood back for him to enter, then withdrew, closing the door behind him. He knew she wouldn't go far.

Rachel was sitting in a mauve velvet chair in the big sitting room adjoining her bedroom. He walked toward her slowly, adjusting his eyes to the sunlight backdropping the figure in the chair. Her hair was white and thin, combed into a neat bun that gave her an imposing look despite the ravages of time. It was obvious she'd been a beautiful woman at one time. Her jaw was still cast in iron, but he detected sagging flesh and an eyelid that slackened slightly over the piercing amethyst gaze he remembered so well. Her cheekbones were prominent under flesh that had wrinkled like cheap silk.

"Hello, Rachel."

Her gaze appraised him as it had when he stood beside Irena on the terrace of the Oceanside. And again it found him lacking. Rachel's chin lifted. "What brings you here?" she asked. Her voice was more fragile but still imperative and melodic.

Drew took a straight-backed chair and straddled it, facing her. "You shouldn't have to ask."

One side of her mouth twitched almost imperceptibly. "You were never one to talk in riddles. Do me the courtesy of not starting now."

"Why did you hire a detective to follow me?"

"I hired no one," she answered, almost too quickly. No surprise. He knew she was lying.

"After all these years, what the hell makes you think I'd try to blackmail you?"

There was a tiny flicker in her eyes. "Wouldn't you?"

Unreasonably, anger began to churn in his gut. Rachel could get to him without half trying. Their gazes locked. "No," he said. "It may surprise you to know I don't even think about you anymore. I let go of the past long ago. It was the only way I could survive."

"I don't believe you."

"I don't give a damn," he answered without hesitation. The anger was subsiding, leaving him emotionless. "You got everything you wanted from me. For a long time I hated you. I didn't sleep nights, thinking of ways to get revenge. I even considered killing you." He laughed harshly. "The trouble with that was I didn't want to spend the rest of my life in prison for it. I have this thing about being locked up. So blackmail you now? Don't you remember the feeble stab I made at it once? You sent me running with my tail between my legs so fast I didn't know what happened." His gaze found hers and held it. Even the pain of that long-ago memory had faded.

Rachel leaned slightly. "Do you deny that you've been sending cryptic notes that can be interpreted as threats?"

She really meant it. Puzzled, he said, "Why the hell would I do that?"

She studied him as though weighing his words with what she read in his face. Finally she sat back with a fluttering sigh. "I find myself inclined to believe you."

"You always did find the truth a little tough to swallow. I never pretended to be anything I wasn't. Maybe I wasn't the polished Mr. Bucks you would have picked for Irena, but I loved her and really tried to make a go of it. For a long time I blamed you and told myself if we hadn't come back here, things would have been different. But people don't change because they move from one place to another. I had as much chance of changing Irena as I did of you welcoming me with open ar.ns."

"I was prepared to like you."

"No, you weren't. You only like people who do what *you* want. You couldn't stomach me, or Irena for that matter."

"That's not true!" Her pale cheeks flushed as her voice climbed.

Drew glanced toward the door, expecting the nurse to scuttle in on the run. When she didn't, he looked back at Rachel but didn't bother to argue. He sure as hell was never going to change *her*.

After a moment she said again, "Why did you come?"

"I caught your detective skulking after me every place I went and shoving his nose into my business. I may not be something you want dragged into your life, but I like what I've got. I don't want any goddam snoops bothering me or my friends."

"I told you I did not hire anyone to spy on you."

"Then you know who did and probably put him up to it." On target. Guilt flickered across her face before she could hide it. He shook his head. "Why, Rachel? What the hell are hell are you afraid of after all these years?"

Her skeletal fingers plucked at the afghan over her legs. He thought about the nurse's warning and wondered if he was pushing too hard. What was Rachel scared of? She'd had everything her own way for so long, been so totally in charge, that she was having a hell of a time handling this. He wanted to gloat but felt only pity. When she finally looked up, her gaze was glacial.

"I will do whatever I must to protect Paris."

"Paris?! Christ, do you think I'd hurt her?" The idea stabbed him with pain and made his breath catch. He stared at Rachel in angry amazement. *Paris* . . . He loved her enough to give her up rather than let Rachel make her a pawn in a protracted dirty custody fight—

"I will not have her hurt or embarrassed in any way, believe that, Drew. I'll do whatever I must to ensure it."

"What do you think I am?" he demanded. "Do you think I walked out of here twenty years ago because I was worried about myself? I wouldn't hurt Paris then, and I won't hurt her now. Whatever you think, I love that girl as much now as I did when you stole her from me. You've had her all these years, but I'd bet there's some Hamilton in her somewhere. Maybe it's time the Grant and Upfield lines had a little tempering. I'm proud of her in a way you'll never understand, Rachel."

He didn't realize his voice had risen until he saw Rachel's startled glance at the door. He turned, expecting to be collared by Miss Jury, but a beautiful young woman in an exquisite gray suit stood there. Drew unwound himself from the chair and got to his feet awkwardly. It was Paris. It couldn't be anyone else with that oval face, high cheekbones like Rachel's, and regal manner. The golden baby curls had turned the color of warm honey and were combed in soft waves around her face. She was taller than Irena or Rachel, and her eyes were a color that came from tossing a lot of family genes in a pot. She was staring at him with an expression he couldn't fathom.

"Is anything wrong, Paris?" Rachel asked. It wasn't like Paris to come in the middle of the afternoon.

Paris shook her head, still staring at Drew. "I better be going," he mumbled, feeling tongue-tied and awkward facing her. All those years, and he wanted to run.

"This is very awkward," Rachel said softly, looking at

Paris, who finally turned to her. Something passed between them silently. Drew sensed it as clearly as he felt Paris's strength. Rachel said, "My visitor arrived unexpectedly. Paris, this is—"

Drew interrupted. "That's not necessary—"

"I will not lie to her," Rachel said with a pained look. "Paris, this is your father."

Paris's gaze moved back to Drew, but she was silent. Her father. She tried to summon some kind of feeling, but there was only a hollow core where it should be. The man in front of her was not the smiling giant of her childish memories. He was average-sized, dark, and bore rough features that somehow managed to be handsome. His hair had a liberal amount of gray among the dozen shades streaked by constant exposure to the sun. He was tanned and muscular, and his hands were calloused and rough. Her father . . .

Drew wondered if she'd heard any of the little speech he'd made to Rachel. Maybe she only caught his angry tone. It would account for the way she was staring at him. He felt like a specimen under a microscope, waiting to be classified. Paris was definitely challenging his right to upset Rachel.

"I'll be going," he said. "Good-bye, Rachel." He walked to the door and Paris stepped aside. "Good-bye, Paris."

He heard the door close as he started down the stairs. He let himself out and stood a moment on the porticoed steps looking at the Mercedes convertible parked behind his jalopy. When he finally climbed behind the wheel, he regretted coming. He didn't know any more now about why Rachel thought he was blackmailing her than he had before. And seeing Paris had reopened a wound he'd thought healed forever.

"Do you want to tell me about it?" Paris asked.

Rachel stared out the window until the car disappeared from view. Without turning, she said, "I misjudged him. He did not come back to make trouble." She sighed heavily and looked at Paris. "Your father is a good man."

Paris looked at her incredulously. "That's it? That's your explanation? What did he say? What did he want? Where has he been all these years?" She was angry and not sure why.

Rachel closed her eyes. "I'm very tired. Please ask Miss Jury to help me to bed."

"Rachel—" Paris's voice shook with frustration.

"How did you happen to come at just this time?" Rachel asked wearily.

Paris conceded defeat, sighing with exasperation. "Miss Jury called me. She was worried about the visitor you insisted on seeing."

Rachel's eyes opened, accusing. "So you knew all along. Well, what do you think of him?"

Paris shrugged. "I can hardly form an opinion after such a brief encounter." Or undo an old one, she thought. What did she think of the man as opposed to the image she'd created of him in his absence? She honestly didn't know.

Rachel studied her granddaughter's face. There was no guile in it, no anger or resentment. Would that be true if she knew the whole story? Rachel prayed it would never have to be told. It was much too late to make amends for the past.

"I really don't want to talk to her." Irena stabbed out her cigarette and fell back against the satin pillows. The sheet slid to her waist, exposing her naked breasts. In spite of her constant exercising, they sagged slightly. Scowling, she tugged the sheet over them.

Stanton Fields drew it down. "You know I love looking at you," he chided. He bent over her and took a nipple in his mouth, tonguing and biting it until it was a perfect pearl. Irena shivered, relishing his touch, then sighed when he stopped, disappointed. "You're being foolish, my dear. I'm not asking you to do anything unreasonable." His hand caressed and cupped her breast.

"You don't know Rachel," she said. She wanted to please him but the thought of talking to Rachel filled her with familiar dread. Her mother still had the capacity to drive her to fury, or nervous incompetence—or both.

Stanton pushed the sheet to Irena's sleek thighs and stroked her body in long sensuous patterns. Irena let out her breath languorously. Her body began to tingle under his expert arousal. With so many men, sex had become boring, but Stanton was an artist at foreplay and at bringing her to orgasm without coitus. It had been a very long time since she had enjoyed such physical pleasure. When he did enter her, he usually sloshed around ineffectually—he, half-limp, she less than tight after a child, innumerable marriages, and affairs.

She watched as he kissed her flesh with warm, moist lips. The brushing of his beard sent an erotic charge through her. He lifted his head, smiling as he spread her thighs and brushed his fingers across her golden hair. Irena's breath quickened as he began to explore the hidden crevices he knew so well.

"Your body is the most exciting I have ever known," he murmured.

"Stanton—"

His tongue teased her. *Oh, God, I'll do whatever he wants . . . anything. . . .* She savored the erotic tingles that made her feel as if she were plunging into a deep, warm pit. She moaned and twisted in delicious torment as his tongue entered her, quickly brought her to a peak of excitement, then tossed her into heady waves of orgasm that left her panting against the tangled sheets.

Stanton got up and padded to the kitchen of the small apartment he'd rented a month before. Not the least self-conscious about his nudity, he came back carrying a bottle of champagne and two glasses. Irena saw he had no sign of an erection. He uncorked the bottle with a satisfying pop, then poured and propped himself beside her.

"I drink to your beauty and the pleasure you give me," he said, touching his glass to hers.

Irena smiled and sipped the bubbly wine. He was a strange man, thanking her when nine times out of ten he gave all the pleasure and asked nothing in return. Except that she talk to Rachel.

"This project means a great deal to me, Irena. I wouldn't ask you otherwise. You'll talk to her, won't you?"

Irena gnawed her lip. She knew she couldn't refuse, but still she hedged. "Paris guards her like a shipment of diamonds. I can't batter down the door."

"Rachel's home now, not in the hospital. Paris is at the office."

Irena shrugged, her pale complexion and creased skin tugging downward in a frown. She looked younger than her years, and still beautiful, but morally corrupt. "There's a nurse. Paris may have left orders," she said.

Very patiently he traced lines on her body. "I don't think so. See if I'm not right. Be sweet and charming. The nurse will let you see your own mother." He leaned to kiss her breast. His lips were cool from champagne. "You can be very charming, you know. I was unable to resist you from the first time you smiled at me."

She sighed. "All right. I'll try."

"That's my girl." He nuzzled her neck, then reached for the bottle to refill their glasses. Some of the cold champagne spattered on her abdomen. Irena giggled as Stanton licked it off.

The second glass of champagne and a leisurely cigarette went a long way toward calming Irena's nerves, but she was torn between wanting to please Stanton and regretting her promise. She glanced sidelong at his strong profile as he relaxed beside her. He was older, by maybe twenty years, but wise in the ways of the world—and sly. He was the only man who catered to her every whim and high lifestyle, but still kept her hanging. He'd asked her to marry him. Even though she hadn't give him an answer, she knew she'd say yes. Not that she was all that eager to marry again, but Stanton was the first person who'd ever shown her a way to get even with Rachel. Scared or not, she'd have the little chat with her mother that he proposed.

He poured the remaining champagne over her stomach— this time purposefully. Irene shrieked at the coldness, then laughed at the way the froth danced over her belly to ooze down to her crotch. Stanton, pleased with her reaction and the effect, pinned down her arms as she giggled, and began lapping up the remaining liquid, his tongue exploring her ever more deeply as he drove her to new heights of ecstasy.

Miss Jury showed Irena in with as much reluctance as she had Drew. Rachel Upfield paid her salary. It wasn't her place to argue. She drew the door shut behind her as she left Rachel's suite.

Irena fixed a bright smile and tried to quell the butterflies in her stomach. "Hello, Mother. You look marvelous." She bent toward the chair and grazed Rachel's cheek with a kiss. She was sure she felt her mother stiffen. Irena sat in the matching mauve armchair across from her mother's. "I hope Paris told you I came to the hospital, but they turned me away. I understand how important it was for you to rest, but I was terribly disappointed."

Rachel's expression didn't change. She'd been surprised

when Martha announced Irena's presence. Rachel's first impulse was to have her sent away, but curiosity impelled her to have her daughter shown in. Rachel studied the empty, pretty face, wondering if Irena was clever or stupid enough to send threatening notes.

"I'm overwhelmed at your concern," Rachel said coolly.

Irena gave a nervous titter. "Now, Mother, don't be a grouch. I have tried to see you. I didn't like having to abide by Paris's ultimatums, but your health was more important than my feelings."

Rachel said nothing. Irena's saccharin concern didn't fool her a bit. Irena wanted something or she wouldn't be there. The silence stretched until Irena squirmed restlessly.

"Has Paris told you about Stanton Fields's offer on the Oceanside?"

So that was it. Rachel nodded.

Irena zipped open her purse and took out her cigarette case, then seeing her mother's frown, dropped it back. She zipped the purse shut.

"I met Mr. Fields in Scottsdale." She was handling it badly, but Rachel made her so damned nervous sitting there staring like that. "I'm sure you've heard of his work. There was a fabulous story in *Business Week* last year—you must have seen it."

"Get on with it, child," Rachel said impatiently.

Irena clutched her purse and tried to smile. "He's in Ocean Beach and would like very much to meet you."

Rachel sniffed. "I do not wish to meet him. His proposal has been reviewed and the decision made that we will not consider it. He has been informed of this. It will do him no good to send you to plead his cause."

"That isn't why I've come!" It burst out before Irena could rein in her anger.

Rachel regarded her coldly. "Why have you come, then? I presume you have a reason for this sudden recognition of filial duty."

"Damn it, Mother—!" Irena clamped her lips and stared at her lap. Her crimson fingernails dug into the soft leather purse. She had to stay in control. Rachel was doing it purposely to aggravate her, Irena knew. "I'm sorry," she lied. "We never have been very well suited to family discussions, have we? It used to bother me that I couldn't talk to you, but

I've gotten used to it over the years. Under the circumstances, I have no choice but to state my 'reason,' as you put it so nicely. I'm in love with Stanton Fields. He's asked me to marry him."

Rachel's brows lifted. "Surely you haven't come for my blessing? You never sought it for any of your other brief voyages into matrimony."

Irena steeled herself and plunged on. "Stanton has looked into my financial affairs and raised some questions."

"Such as?" Rachel held her anger in check, but prodded her daughter on. To come here with such twaddle!

"My father's estate." There, she'd gotten it out. She saw a flash of surprise cross her mother's face. Stanton was right, she had to take the offensive.

Rachel narrowed her eyes, watching Irena closely. "Your father died penniless."

"Grandfather Grant gave him the hotel!"

Rachel straightened her spine against the cushion. "I do not know where you get your information, but you are wrong. My father cosigned the loan. Your father ran what should have been a profitable business into the ground. He was in danger of losing everything to his creditors and of defaulting on the loan and leaving my father to foot the bill. *I* paid off your father's debts. All of them! And in exchange the hotel was signed over to me." She glared at her daughter.

Irena moistened her lips nervously. "Stanton wonders why the hotel wasn't put in trust in my name."

"You weren't born—" Rachel stopped, remembering. Irena had been only a few hours old . . . born on a gambling ship while her father payed poker in a smoky back barroom. . . . It had been a long time since she thought of Hillary's folly. And of all the people to bring it back to mind, Irena. "Your father had already made too many foolish decisions. This matter was mine to decide."

Irena's courage was flagging. "Stanton says a good lawyer might get at least half the property declared mine."

Rachel scoffed, "I cannot stop you from wasting your time and energy on such foolishness if you're determined to pursue this fanciful conjecture. I trust Mr. Fields is prepared to finance this misadventure in madness? Because you will not use one penny of my money to do so! The allowance that provides your extravagant lifestyle is a revokable trust, my dear Irena. I can change it at any time, and on my death, it continues only if Paris chooses. She and I have discussed it fully. Like me, she recognizes your inability to curb reckless spending. A trust such as this is the only reasonable way to provide for your needs."

"You're going to make millions on the Oceanside! It's mine!" Irena blinked furiously as tears blurred her vision. Damn it, she wouldn't cry!

"It is not yours," Rachel said evenly. "Not now, not ever!" Her heartbeat was much too fast. She heard it thundering in her ears. She must not get excited over Irena's outlandish ideas. Foolish, silly child! Listening to promises of sugar-plums beyond her reach. The trust was foolproof, Rachel had seen to that. Neither Irena nor Stanton Fields could do a thing about it. Rachel watched Irena, whose expression had gone ugly, her blue gaze diamond hard.

"Has anyone ever inspected your deed closely?" Irena asked in a brittle voice.

Rachel's breath caught. First the mysterious note, now Irena's question out of the blue. Irena? How? "What are you talking about?" she demanded shakily.

"Hasn't Paris told you?" Irena taunted, bolder now that she had shaken her mother.

"Told me what? Speak coherently or leave." Rachel struggled with her curiosity and fear.

"A man's body was found in the Oceanside Hotel two weeks ago."

Rachel was caught off-guard again. "I know that."

"He was identified."

Irena looked so pleased with herself, Rachel longed for the strength to strike her. She said nothing.

"It was very peculiar that the police found a deed to the Oceanside among his things. Where do you suppose he got it?" Irena smiled cruelly, then taunted again. "Aren't you going to ask me who he was, Mother?"

The room was silent except for the ticking of the ogee clock that had been Rachel's since girlhood. Each faint sound pierced the dark veil of memory, fluttering a curtain that Rachel did not want opened. She impaled her daughter with a hard violet gaze.

"His name was Teddy Reno," Irena said. "You remember him—Daddy's friend."

Teddy Reno was already dead! Long ago! Rachel's pulse raced and each breath raked her lungs painfully. Her chin quivered and her voice was barely a whisper. "Who told you this?"

Irena tossed her head. "The police. They wanted to know if I'd ever heard of him." Irena was enjoying herself now. It was time she had an upper hand with Rachel!

"You were just a child—"

"He came to the hotel to visit Daddy when you weren't there. Daddy talked about him a lot."

Irena was not quite six when Hillary died. How much of what she was saying was true and how much fancy? A deed to the Oceanside? When? How? Memories crowded Rachel's mind, twisting and tangling with each other in a confused jumble. Teddy Reno had died on the night after V-J day. She had murdered him. No, his body had never been found. *Because she hadn't killed him!* She and Josh had left him for dead, but they were mistaken. But now, after thirty-five years, he was dead at last. *Teddy Reno was dead.*

Rachel brought her attention back to Irena with effort. "You told the police that?"

"As a matter of fact, I haven't." Irena gave a sly smile. "Not yet."

Rachel looked at the daughter she had borne amid tribulations and a marriage that was already dead. The daughter who had caused nothing but trouble all her life. The daughter who bluffed, lied, and cheated her way through life with never a care for anyone but herself. Gifted, yes. But a girl who squandered her God-given talents. Paris. Paris would save them both.

"Perhaps you should," she said evenly. She had never cowered before Irena and she would not now. At Irena's startled expression, Rachel said, "Do you think after all these years that I would tremble at the rattling of old bones? My dear, you do not know me very well. Yes, Teddy Reno was your father's friend. A pity he chose to come back and die in *my* hotel, but the world will not mourn his loss. Teddy Reno was a liar, a cheat, and the worst kind of thief. Your father would have done well to cut his ties with him, but I could never convince him. Perhaps they were too much alike."

Irena's calm shattered. Her face mottled with rage. "He

had a bill of sale for the hotel! Daddy sold it to him!"

Rachel gave Irena a pitying look. "It was never registered. And if by some fluke, the deed and bill of sale you say this man had could be proved genuine, where would it put you? I have supported you handsomely on income made from that hotel as well as my other investments. Would you feel morally obligated to turn it over to Mr. Reno's estate? Perhaps he has a daughter who could spend it as readily as you. Don't be a fool, Irena." Rachel was breathing rapidly, spent by her burst of anger. "The deed and bill of sale are fakes. If your father ever signed such documents, he had no intention of carrying the sale through. *None at all*, do you hear! Now go!" She waved Irena away and tapped the bell that would summon Miss Jury.

Irena stumbled to her feet, still trembling with rage. "I don't think you and Paris will like the publicity this is going to make!"

Rachel sighed wearily. "Don't be a fool, Irena. I'll see to it you never get another penny. I guarantee that is no idle threat. I can do it, and I will if you begin raking over dead coals. *Leave it be!*"

Miss Jury came in, rushing to Rachel when she saw how pale and exhausted she was. Rachel waved toward the bedroom. Miss Jury put her hands to Irena's shoulders and propelled her from the room. The idea—upsetting her mother like that, making her ill! What kind of a daughter was she? Tight-lipped, she returned to her patient and helped her out of the chair. Poor thing, so tired she could hardly walk into the next room. Miss Jury pulled back the flowered satin spread and helped Rachel into bed. Poor thing was so tired, she didn't want to undress. Miss Jury took Rachel's shoes off and covered her with a light quilt. She drew the shade and pulled the drapes, leaving the room in soft dimness. Tiptoeing, she returned to the sitting room and sat where she could see the bed. What had that daughter said to upset Rachel so much?

Rachel was aware of the nurse's presence as she drifted in presleep. Teddy Reno . . . why had he come back? And why had he died in the Oceanside Hotel? All these years she'd carried the terrible burden of guilt, thinking she'd killed him long ago. She shuddered, and a long sigh escaped her lips. She heard the quick rustle of Miss Jury's starched uniform.

But Teddy Reno was dead now. At last she could be certain. After a long time, Rachel slept.

Irena drove furiously, slewing the car around corners and taking the hill much too fast so she had to slam on the brakes at an intersection when another car shot out of nowhere.

She let her mother order her around like a child. Stanton would be furious. *She* was furious! Irena's breath heaved and her knuckles formed white beads on the wheel. God how she hated that woman. What was she going to tell Stanton? She'd barely gotten a rise out of Rachel after flinging accusations and innuendos at her. Damn it, Rachel had practically laughed at her.

Irena caught a glimpse of herself in the rearview mirror: face pale, eyes wild, her mouth set in a hard, ugly line. She couldn't go back to Stanton and admit defeat. She slowed the car, then turned on Ocean Boulevard toward the Upfield Building. By the time she reached the top-floor offices, her anger had become cold, hard rage. She marched past the protesting secretary and into Paris's office.

"I want to talk to you!" she demanded. She heard the shrillness in her voice but couldn't control it.

With infinite patience, Paris set aside the papers she was reading and clasped her hands as she peered up at her mother. "What is it, Irena? I'm busy."

Irena leaned on the edge of the desk, glaring at her daughter. "I've just come from the house and a very unsatisfactory talk with Rachel. Damn it, I won't be shoved aside anymore. You'll listen to me this time!"

Exasperated and on the edge of anger, Paris sighed. "I am listening, but so far you haven't said anything. Now will you please get to the point!"

Irena straightened, started to retort angrily, then backstepped to the blue leather chair and sat down. She had to keep cool; it was the only way to deal with this impossible child. Irena lifted her chin and looked at the wall behind Paris so she wouldn't be unnerved by Paris's green-gold gaze. "I informed Rachel I intend to fight her about the hotel." It wasn't strictly the truth, but it's what she intended to say before Rachel managed to turn the tables. Irena felt her daughter's cool appraisal.

"On what grounds?" Paris asked. Something had upset her

mother, something more than her usual irrational and childish attitude about money.

"It's mine!" Irena snapped.

Paris measured her words. "What proof do you have of that?"

Irena's gaze fell to her daugher's face, then slid away nervously. She opened her purse and took out the monogrammed gold cigarette case, extracted a cigarette, and held a lighter to it. Puffing nervously, she finally answered. "A deed."

Paris recoiled, astonished at her mother's bold lie. What in the world was Irena trying to do other than make a fool of herself? "Let me see it."

Irena dragged deeply on the cigarette trying to stay calm. "I don't have it with me."

"I'll be in the office all day. Bring it in anytime."

She'd been a fool to mention a deed, but she couldn't back down now. "I can't do that," she said.

Paris leaned on the desk, crossing her arms in front of her as though warding off a pestilence. "Of course you can't, Mother. Because there is no deed. I happen to know that for a fact because I had our legal department check very carefully. Spurious claims on the Oceanside are suddenly very popular." Paris sat back. What did Irena hope to accomplish with this nonsense? Where was it going to end?

Irena's energy flagged. Paris had always been able to see right through her. It was impossible to bluff her. Of course she would have put her legal dogs on it when the police found a deed among Teddy Reno's things. "It was meant to be mine. My father wanted me to have it. He always wanted me to have it, not her." Her anger was returning, though badly chipped along the edges by Paris's keenness.

"You hardly remember him. You were five when he died." Paris pitied her mother's delusions.

"I remember!" Irena knew she was losing but went on desperately. "He always said it would be mine, no one could change that!"

"It's Rachel's," Paris said firmly. "It has been for fifty years. It may eventually be yours. But not now. It's a little late to make any grandstand plays." Hinting at Rachel's death sickened her, but Paris had to appease her mother—something Rachel wouldn't attempt. But someone in the family had to fill the appeaser role.

Irena lost control. "It's mine! I want it!" Nothing was working out right. She shouldn't have come. Stanton would be furious.

Paris's patience snapped. "Just what do you expect me to do?" she demanded. "You have no proof, no legal claim. Talk to a lawyer if you don't believe me. You'll find out you're wasting your time."

Irena's eyes blazed and her lip quivered. "You don't know the things she's done! You believe everything she says, don't you! Well, she's not the paragon you think she is! I may not be the most loving daughter, but it's her fault. She never wanted me. She never had time for me. Oh, no, let the servants take care of Irena. Let someone else be surrogate mother while she was off having her filthy little affair with Josh Fantazia. Or off building the best hotel, the most successful business! The great Rachel Upfield, too busy to love a child who was only in the way! Too busy to be a wife or mother. Rachel Upfield, the empire builder!" Irena stubbed out her cigarette viciously.

Paris recoiled under the force of her mother's rage, shaken by the venomous words and image she conveyed. An affair with a Fantazia? She stood, leaning on the desk, not trusting herself to get any closer to Irena. "Get out," she said angrily. "Get out now, Mother!'

Irena sprang up, backing away from the desk nervously. She had never seen such naked fury in Paris's face. Suddenly Irena was as frightened of her daughter as she had always been of Rachel. Her breath came in tiny gasps as she scurried toward the door, darting frightened glances at Paris. She groped for the doorknob, yanked it open, and fled.

Tears stung Paris's eyes as she paced in front of her desk, reviewing her past—her father, her mother's moral degeneracy and her suggestion of Rachel's affair with a Fantazia . . . Having much to absorb, she buzzed her secretary and told her not to let anyone interrupt her for the remainder of the day. She had a lot of work to complete and couldn't spare a free moment.

❧ Twenty-Two ❧

THE MORNING AFTER Irena's visit, Rachel struggled against weariness and impatience. She had slept fitfully, forcing herself to lie quietly so that the night nurse did not hover nearby. In the morning Miss Jury's too-bright smile and constant attendance told Rachel she looked as tired as she felt. But she refused to stay in bed. Miss Jury was maddeningly efficient with "our bath" and helping Rachel dress. Finally, when the woman considered her "settled" and went downstairs to prepare a tea tray, Rachel picked up the phone, cursing her weakened left side as she had to put the receiver down in order to dial.

"Fantazia Enterprises . . ."

"I wish to speak to Josh Fantazia."

"Who's calling, please?"

"Rachel Upfield."

"Yes, Mrs. Upfield—one moment please," an agitated voice said.

Once again in her hour of need, she was turning to Josh. How strange it seemed after the long chasm of years spent as strangers. He had once again become her strength. Rachel gazed out the window, studying the low bank of clouds on the horizon. Catalina, which she'd been able to see so clearly yesterday, was swallowed in thick, gray mist. Rain, she thought. The long summer was over. She eased her aching bones as the phone hummed to life.

"Rachel?" Josh's greeting was hearty. "How are you?"

His warm greeting brought a smile to Rachel's lips. "I'm fine, Josh. Can you come by the house sometime today?"

He paused. "Is something wrong?" Concern laced his still-deep voice.

She sighed sadly. "Wrong—right—I find it difficult to distinguish these days. I would like to talk to you and prefer not to do it on the telephone."

"Of course. I have nothing pressing. Would now be as good a time as any?"

"Yes. Thank you, Josh."

He arrived within the half hour. His chauffeur waited outside as Miss Jury reluctantly showed him in. Rachel's angry insistence had cowed her into submission. She brought a second tray of hot tea and freshly baked cinnamon buns. Rachel shooed her out impatiently.

"They will kill me with kindness," Rachel complained.

Josh clamped her frail hand between his strong warm ones. "Just be glad you're here to enjoy it." She looked more fragile than she had in the hospital, and he wondered if she was overdoing it.

Rachel sighed deeply. "I suppose I should be, but at times I wish the stroke had killed me on the spot."

"Don't say that," he chided. "You have many good years left."

"Have I? I don't delude myself, Josh," she said, smiling at him tenderly. How comfortable and right it felt having him hold her hand. "I'm old, and I haven't led an exemplary life that increases my chances of survival much longer. Marshall Forest is fond of reminding me that as I have sown, I now reap. He compares my blood pressure to a wildcat well." She smiled when Josh squeezed her hand gently. With a twinkle in her eyes, she added, "I regret none of it, and I make no excuses for my life."

"Nor should you." She was beautiful when her eyes sparkled that way. Six decades since he'd first been captivated by them in the railroad station as he went off to war. Sixty years, and he loved her differently but as fiercely as he ever had.

Rachel looked at Josh tenderly, wondering if she would change anything of the past were it in her power. Perhaps the estrangement from Josh . . . the wasted years . . . "For my own peace of mind, I must apologize on several accounts," she said.

"When have we ever needed apologies between us?" he asked softly.

Rachel persisted. "I was wrong about Drew Hamilton. He came to see me."

"Here?" Willis Fermin had reported locating Hamilton in Texas and that Hamilton had boarded a bus headed for Los Angeles. Josh told Fermin to continue the tail, even though he was convinced the blackmailing would cease with Teddy Reno's death. It had been almost two weeks since the last cryptic note. Perhaps he should have told Rachel about Teddy, but he'd been worried that dredging up the ugly past would be too much of a shock. Besides, he wanted to be sure about Hamilton before fixing blame.

"The investigator in Texas bungled the matter," Rachel said. "Drew realized he was being followed and forced the man to admit who had hired him. Though our names weren't mentioned, Drew came at once to accuse me." She shook her head sadly, remembering the genuine shock on Drew's face when she vowed to protect Paris from him. "I realize now I never took the time to know my son-in-law. He's a strong person. An ethical and loyal one as well. I did him a great injustice. He knows nothing about the blackmail letters. He has no quarrel with either of us."

Josh studied the weary lines in Rachel's face, the remnants of beauty still present enough to stir him. He wondered if he should tell her about Reno, but couldn't find a way to soften the shock.

"It was Teddy Reno," she said flatly.

Josh looked up in astonishment. "You know?"

"My dear daughter Irena was eager to thrust the news upon me in the hope of forcing my hand. I suspect there has been a conspiracy of silence surrounding me these past weeks." And Josh was part of it as well as Paris. He cared that much. . . . Rachel was touched. "Irena told me about the dead man's bill of sale and deed for the Oceanside. How like Teddy to complicate our lives even after his death. The guilt I've carried all these years thinking I'd killed him."

Josh stroked her hand, pressing it to his lips. *"We* carried, Rachel. I shared it as much as you. When I found out about the dead man, I knew it had to be Reno who sent the blackmail notes. I was going to tell you, but I had to be sure there were no more letters."

"I don't know what he hoped to gain by destroying us now. Revenge? Satisfaction for his hatred of me?" She sighed. "Thank God it's over."

Josh studied her hand. "The trouble with reaching our age is that one accumulates too many things to regret. We can't change the past, but it's never too late to mend some personal fences." It was suddenly important to unburden his conscience about forming the Minot Corporation without her. He had to know that Rachel forgave him. "I lied to you a long time ago. Not in words but in deed."

"Don't say it, Josh, don't tell me now. I don't want to know," she said quickly. It was too late for confessions; time was too short to bring each other pain that would sadden their lives at the end. She raised her hand to cover his lips. "We have suffered enough," she said very softly, gazing into the warm, brown depths of his eyes. "There are things better left unsaid now." Even now she couldn't bear to see him hurt if she confessed about Ruth. She could never bring herself to speak of it.

"All right," he said with a gentle smile. "But tell me you forgive me for my unspoken sin."

"I forgive," she said, stroking the quivering line of his jaw, slackened with age, but still firm with the resolve reminiscent of his youth. It was easy to forgive when she had so many sins to be forgiven. She lay her head back. "What would we change if we had our lives to relive?" she asked quietly.

"Many things."

Rachel smiled. "Perhaps, but it would not surprise me if we did the same things again. They were right for us at the time."

She was right, of course. "At least we can strike murder from our list of guilt," he said. "Teddy Reno is dead now."

Rachel scowled faintly. "It always puzzled me that there was no mention of his body being found." She stopped abruptly as she recalled how Ruth's death had driven the problem from Josh's mind and left her alone with her worry and guilt. So long ago . . .

"We'll never know the whole story, but it doesn't matter. It's strange how perspective changes with age. We've come full circle, haven't we? Do you think your doctor would approve of my kissing you, Rachel?"

He mocked a wry smile. Rachel's eyes misted. "Not nearly as much as I would disapprove of your not doing so," she said.

Her left arm lay useless between them as he embraced her and lifted her chin. Her lips were dry and warm, but welcoming as they kissed. Bittersweet memories rose as they sealed their renewed pact. They would work together again. When after a long time Josh released her, Rachel sank back against the cushions smiling.

"I have always loved you, Josh. I always will," she said with a sigh.

"Ditto," he said, and squeezed her hand.

Paris studied the report from the detective who'd been following Irena and Stanton Fields. She'd read it over twice, searching for some clue that would tell her what her mother was up to with these last few visits to Rachel and herself. She was convinced there was far more behind them than her mother had indicated, but for the life of her, Paris couldn't weave together the tenuous threads that tied Irena's demands to the redevelopment project. Rachel refused to discuss her father's appearance, yet Drew Hamilton had to tie into the entire picture. Paris was already putting her pain and anguish into perspective. At the moment her curiosity more than anything else was aroused.

According to the detective's report, Irena was currently staying with Fields in an apartment he'd rented in Ocean Beach. They were together constantly, but there seemed nothing out of the ordinary about their activities. Miss Jury dutifully reported Irena's visit to Rachel, clucking professionally as she recounted the angry quarrel that had upset her patient. But when Paris called Rachel that night, her grandmother had said nothing at all about it. Miss Jury's latest call this morning was to tell Paris about Rachel's latest visitor: Josh Fantazia. Frankly, Paris was baffled.

And if all that wasn't enough, she was certain she'd seen Drew Hamilton, her father—the words were foreign to her mind—parked a few yards down the street, watching her, this morning when she'd arrived at the office. Her encounter with him in Rachel's house still rankled. The resentment and hatred

she'd felt so long were hard to reconcile with the quiet, unde-
manding person who'd reappeared in her life so unexpectedly.
She'd taken time to absorb it all. Was he, too, part of this
insistent, clamoring voice of the past?

Sighing, she turned her thoughts to Victor, whom she
hadn't seen for three days. He was engrossed in wrapping up
the report for the city council. In the first days after he'd left
the hospital, she had stopped by his apartment regularly, discussing the report to help bolster his confidence and to show
him the revised concept she'd developed just before his
stroke. He studied it with interest and asked if she would leave
it with him but had given her no indication of his intentions.
His report had to be in in four days. She had done all she
could to weight his decision in favor of the Upfield proposal.

Four days. The report would be handed to the council on
Rachel's birthday. She prayed that Victor's decision and the
council's would be a pleasant birthday gift.

Victor looked up from his work with a frown of annoyance
as the doorbell rang. He rose and crossed the apartment in
quick strides, more from impatience with his own lack of
progress than at the interruption. When he opened the door,
Donovan, the doorman, handed him a letter.

"This just came by special delivery, Mr. Sands."

"Thanks," he said, accepting it, then straightening his
terry-cloth robe. He examined the letter as he returned to the
desk. No return address, but it was postmarked locally. He slit
it open with a brass letter opener embossed with a medallion:
Souvenir of Catalina. Paris said they'd bought it on a sailing
trip to Catalina. Putting aside thoughts of the beautiful woman
who haunted him, he pulled the photocopies from the envelope. Frowning, he read the two copies of legal documents.
One was the deed to the Oceanside Hotel. No, not the same
one he'd had in his files. This one deeded the property to
Theodore Reno. The other page was a copy of the bill of sale
in the amount of one hundred thousand dollars.

The deed and note found in the effects of the man who died
in the Oceanside. Theodore Reno. Teddy Reno. Who sent
them? More intriguing, had they been copied before or after
the man's death? And by whom? Paris insisted both documents were fakes, that her grandfather had never intended to
sell the hotel. But now someone wanted to make sure Victor

saw these before he finished his report.

He reread the documents. Why were they important? The sale had never been recorded, so the property never belonged to Reno. *Teddy.* Victor's mind echoed the nickname. It was still a puzzle, but he accepted the fact he must have learned about the man somewhere in order to remember his name. *Learned fact, not personal memory.* If he'd met Reno, he would never know where or why.

Sitting at the desk once more, he took a clean sheet of paper and began to make notes. *KNOWNS: Reno knew Hillary Upfield. Hillary Upfield signed a bill of sale and a deed to Reno. Deed in Reno's name was never recorded. UN-KNOWNS: Did Upfield intend to record the deed? Did Reno pay the hundred thousand dollars? What happened to the money if he did?*

Victor glanced at the date on the two documents. *June 8, 1927.* Quickly he found the file with the Oceanside's financial statements for the year 1928. He reviewed the figures, even though he was certain there had never been any infusion of a hundred thousand dollars into the faltering business. When Rachel took over the finances, a number of months passed until the hotel once again showed a profit and the ledgers were in the black. That fitted with Paris's contention that her grandfather hadn't been a good businessman and had turned the hotel over to Rachel to avoid losing it.

He turned to a copy of Rachel's deed. The date caught his eye. June 8, 1927. The same day as Reno's documents. Victor sat back, his mind racing. Was this the clue to answer why he'd hired Bascomb Dorn to find the clerk who'd recorded Rachel's deed? Two deeds and a bill of sale signed the same day. It couldn't be coincidence. He laid the two deeds side by side. Both standard legal forms. What happened to abort one deal in favor of the other?

He saw it then. Unmistakably. The signatures weren't the same. They were close enough to pass casual scrutiny, but he'd stake his life that they hadn't been penned by the same hand. Excited, he realized this must have been what he'd un-covered before his stroke and the reason he'd hired Dorn to trace the clerk. He'd seen Hillary Upfield's signature in a hundred places in his files. He opened one at random and took out a tax form, then held Hillary's signature beside the two deeds. Rachel's deed was a forgery.

He whistled softly. Had he hired a handwriting expert to prove what he'd found? Did Paris know? Paris with her earnest green-gold gaze, her warm smile, her sensuous beauty, and quick wit. Was she playing him for a fool to win the redevelopment contract for Upfield? He started to close the file, then let it fall open again. Something else nagged at him. Something he'd seen, something he'd learned. The date— June 8, 1927. He flipped through the file rapidly, scanning documents. Ten minutes later he found what he was looking for in the personal data he'd amassed on Rachel Upfield.

On June 8, 1927, Rachel had been in Oceanside Hospital. Irena Upfield had been born at 11:30 the previous night.

Deeds were recorded first thing in the morning. The procedure hadn't been changed since it was instituted. Anything brought in or received by messenger later than 9:00 a.m. was recorded the following day. *Learned information* . . .

For the first time since his stroke, he was jubilant. He was making progress. He'd have the report finished by the time of Rachel's party. His report would meet the council's deadline, and it would restore what he'd lost before he was stricken.

❧ *Twenty-Three* ❧

PARIS INSISTED RACHEL nap before the birthday party. Rachel had been in good spirits and seemed recovered from the upsets of the past week, but Paris knew the evening would provide an unneeded strain. To her amazement, Rachel had insisted on inviting Irena and Josh. And she had not objected when Paris told her she'd invited Victor. There was no telling what would happen with such a volatile mix of guests. Victor's report was in, and the city council would take its final vote on the redevelopment project the following day. It was almost as if Rachel felt the need to have all her adversaries present in the final moments of the contest.

Paris spent the entire day at the house on Ladera Street. She'd engaged caterers, waiters, and bartenders, overseeing the final preparations herself and insisting Rachel do nothing but relish the birthday party. She tucked Rachel in solicitously after lunch, drawing the shades on her bedroom French windows and leaving her to rest in the cool, sumptuous room, away from the bustle downstairs. But Rachel couldn't sleep. She lay in the darkened bedroom, slave to memories. Memories of Hillary, who had slept in the big four-poster bed beside her, memories of Josh in the lush suite of rooms his company rented in L. A., entangled in her arms and legs.

She tried to recapture the joy and love she'd felt for Hillary when they'd first wed. So long ago . . . When had it begun to erode? Perhaps it lacked substance from the start, like fog rolling in from the sea. Joy and love were much easier to connect to Josh. She sighed, wondering what she would wish changed of the past. That she had understood Hillary better? That she'd been less ambitious? That she had not maneuvered to take Paris away from Drew and Irena?

The thought made her smile. No, she could never wish that. Paris was too dear to her, too much a part of her, so much like her. Yet like a new and improved model. . . .

She closed her eyes, wooing sleep that would not come. Paris had not spoken of her father since the day she found him at the house. No questions, no accusations. Knowing her, she probably suffered in silence—a Grant trait. Drew had probably already returned to Texas or gone on to another oil field. He was still a man without roots, but he was honest. She wished now she'd encouraged him to stay and get to know Paris better. She'd been a fool to think him capable of blackmail. But how could she ever have imagined that Teddy Reno had not died that night on Darien Hill? She'd paid a thousand times over for that horrible night when she believed she'd slain him. She felt no grief at his death now, nor surprise that he'd died at the hands of another. He was a man who attracted violence. The wonder was that he'd managed to live so long.

Josh had told her the whole story about the deed and the bill of sale, assuring her he'd persuaded the police to drop the matter. She had been right about Carbello and right to act so quickly that morning after Irena was born. If Josh hadn't helped her, she would have lost the Oceanside. Now at long last, it was all coming to an end. The council's decision to-morrow would close that chapter forever.

So many closed doors. Let them stay closed. Let me die in peace, she thought.

The house was a triumph of color, festooned with ribbons and studded with flowers and lush, green plants. For a nostalgic moment Rachel was transported back to her wedding day when her father had filled the house and yard with fresh blooms. How long it had been since she thought of how he had cheered on and financed her start in business?

Paris looked stunning in a gown the color of autumn leaves in the sunlight. Over it, she wore a sequined jacket and spare jewelry. Rachel had never seen her more radiant, and her heart swelled with pride. Rachel was glad she had invited Victor Sands, no matter what his recommendation was to the council. Paris needed romance and love in her life; every woman did. She'd been too devoted to the office and hospital the past few months, too worried about an old woman who loved her fiercely. Rachel admired Paris's spirit in defying her in regard to Sands. What would she have done if her father had forbidden her to love Josh? The thought made her smile as she watched the guests arrive.

Rachel was seated on the Regency sofa, a glass of sherry within easy reach on the rosewood table of French origin beside her. Paris had surprised her with a lovely new gown as a birthday gift. It was a regal purple affair, striking with her white hair, and it was cut along simple lines that were very becoming to her frail figure. She felt like a reigning monarch. Paris had moved chairs away from the sofa so people would not be inclined to linger and tire Rachel. If she chose, she could invite special friends to sit, but Paris warned her not to encourage anyone to talk too long. "You watch over me the way I did you when you were a child," Rachel protested, but secretly her granddaughter's concern pleased her.

Rachel smiled as the police commissioner took her hand and wished her many happy returns. The mayor was more reserved; Rachel took pains to assure him that their friendship was in no danger no matter which way the city council's decision went. He looked relieved, and Rachel wondered if he knew which way the vote would go. The president of Farmers and Merchants Bank . . . the symphony conductor . . . president of the Women's Club . . . commodore of the Yacht Club . . . Rachel blessed her excellent memory for names and faces. She hadn't seen some of the guests for years. No one would fault an old woman for any lapse of memory, but it was a matter of pride to welcome everyone by name before Paris introduced them.

The guest list numbered close to fifty, and after they arrived they scattered over the living room, sun room, dining room, and patios. It had been overcast all day, but the dark clouds had held offshore. With luck, the rain would not fall until after the party. Wind screens had been erected along the fence so guests could take advantage of the garden and the cool breeze that had sprung up at dusk. A second bar had been set up on a side patio, but Paris had decided to keep the buffet tables indoors.

In a momentary lull in the arrivals, Paris came to kiss her grandmother's cheek. "How are you doing, darling?"

"I couldn't be better," Rachel said honestly, clasping Paris's hand warmly. In her modest purple gown, Rachel had a wool lace shawl draped over her legs. "I saw you talking to Clarence van Ault. Did he give an indication of how the council's vote would go tomorrow?"

Paris gave her a mock scowl. "This is a party. I won't discuss business and neither will you!"

Rachel offered a smile. "All right, dear. Not another word. I promise."

"That's better. You really are incorrigible, you know." Glancing toward the hum of voices at the door, Paris saw Josh Fantazia arrive. Despite her efforts, she still found it hard to accept the change in attitude between Rachel and Josh. Or Irena's accusation that the two had once been lovers. Paris struggled with old animosities that were difficult to appease. In a tone more churlish than she intended, she said, "Here's your special guest. I was hoping he'd decline."

Rachel glanced at Josh, unable to still the warm glow that filled her. "It's my birthday, Paris. For my sake, put aside your differences with Josh for tonight."

Paris gave her grandmother a keen look. Rachel was watching Josh with a warmth Paris had never seen between them before. She patted Rachel's shoulder. "All right, darling. I guess I can do that for you."

Rachel touched her hand gratefully. Paris returned to the door as Josh approached the sofa, smiling when Josh greeted her in passing.

"Happy birthday, Rachel." Josh sat beside her without waiting for an invitation and took her hand. He looked years younger in his black tails, the ivory-knobbed cane the only hint of age. "You are as beautiful as the day I met you."

"You are a charming liar, but you always were and I have always lapped up your compliments like a kitten at spilled cream."

He shook his head. "You have always been beautiful to me. Where have the years gone, Rachel? It's hard to believe there'll soon be a third generation behind us. My grandson

Phillip and his wife are expecting their first child. I'm going to be a great-grandfather next year."

Someone to carry on the Fantazia name, she thought. How sad it was that a woman's name died with her. There was no one to carry on the Grant or Upfield name. And the Hamilton name would end with Paris. A dynasty of daughters. Perhaps it was better that way. It forced each generation to strike out on its own.

"A penny for your thoughts," Josh chided.

Rachel smiled. "Wool gathering. A prerogative of old age."

"You'll never be old, Rachel. You are one of those remarkable people who cannot be cataloged by years."

"By what, then?" she asked, looking into the dark eyes that had mirrored her love for so long.

"Achievements, victories, perhaps an occasional defeat to spur you on. No, it's more than that. I'd call it character, your ability to roll with the punches." He stroked her hand. "It's a very special woman who can forgive the distance I've put between us for so many years. Do you ever wonder what our lives would have been if I had asked you to marry me after Collette died?" he asked softly.

She looked away from his gaze, recalling the aching nights of longing, the pain of knowing he was back in Ocean Beach and unable to see her. *The past that never could be undone.* Looking at him again, she said with a twinkle, "I imagine that would have depended on whether my answer was yes or no."

He chuckled and pressed her hand gently. "All right, we won't mention it again, though I shouldn't promise so glibly. As ravishing as you are tonight, you give an old man ideas. I'm tempted to carry you upstairs and make us both forget we are octogenarians."

"I believe you could," she said tenderly. Then, with another twinkle, she added, "If we honeymoon at Memorial, we might survive our fling."

He laughed aloud, a rich, deep sound she hadn't heard for years. "I love you, Rachel."

"Enough to withdraw your bid on the redevelopment project?" she teased.

"No," he said, still laughing. "Not that much."

From the archway Paris watched the intimate conversation.

How happy they both looked. She'd never seen Rachel sparkle so much. They did love each other and had undoubtedly enjoyed the affair Irena had disclosed. More power to them. It pleased Paris to know that Rachel had not always been alone. Perhaps Josh and his granddaughter, Shanna, were the separate entities that they were rumored to be. She'd heard about their arguments, but had always chalked them up to the gossip spread by jealous cohorts. Maybe Josh supported his granddaughter out of family loyalty, rather than shared philosophy.

"Hello, Paris."

She turned to see Victor smiling at her, and her heart quickened. He sported a navy cashmere jacket and blue slacks, very sexy on his handsome frame. She had missed him terribly the past week but had steeled herself to the separation while he finished his report. And now it was in, and she dared not ask about it. Not tonight. She gave him a bright, warm smile. "I thought you'd changed your mind about coming. I'm glad you didn't."

"And miss my chance to meet Rachel at long last? Not on your life." He held out an envelope. "Are you collecting the birthday greetings for the guest of honor?"

Paris laid it on the engraved silver tray with the others. At Rachel's insistence, the invitations had specified no gifts, but the mound of cards was heartwarming.

"She's looking forward to it as much as you are," Paris said. "I once told you that business wasn't a spectator sport for Rachel. She likes to shake hands with her opponents over the net."

Victor glanced at the elderly couple on one of the sofas. "So I see, though lovers might be more accurate than opponents in that case."

Paris gave him a surprised look, and he smiled.

"It's one of the talents a man without a memory develops. When I meet people, there's nothing to prejudice my observations and objective opinion."

His tone was light and Paris could not gauge his mood from it. She forced herself to put his report from her mind. As she saw Josh rise and take his leave of Rachel, she led Victor across the room.

"Rachel, this is Victor Sands."

"I'm delighted to meet you, Rachel," Victor said comfortably. "It's a cliché to say I've heard so much about you."

"Not all good, I daresay." Rachel offered her hand. He took it as he might a fragile piece of porcelain, firmly but respectfully. She liked that.

His smile was genuinely warm. "If it were all good, you'd be very dull. Actually, I've been poking around in your past so much, I wanted to see if the picture I formed is anything like the real woman."

"Is it?" She regarded him frankly with her lavender gaze.

"More charming in the flesh," he said, still smiling.

Rachel gave him an appraising look. "Old ladies are excused from the niceties of tact, Mr. Sands. Before my granddaughter finds a way to shush me, I want to tell you how much I admire the adjustment you've made to your predicament. Only those who have suffered strokes can fully appreciate the feeling of helplessness they create. I consider myself fortunate that mine caused only physical damage, but I understand and empathize with your trauma. I also applaud your courage in completing the job you were hired to do."

"Thank you," Victor said, with a touch of surprise. He hadn't expected Rachel Upfield to be quite so forthright and charming. Coming from her, the words were the highest compliment.

Rachel gave him a waggish smile. "I felt I should say that before the council announces its decision tomorrow. My opinion may differ then."

Victor laughed good-naturedly. "I suspect mine can never be changed," he said. She was a remarkable woman, and he understood better now why Paris was devoted to her.

Rachel glanced toward the doorway, and her smile vanished like a magician's illusion. As Victor and Paris turned to see the cause, Rachel demanded sharply, "Who is that?"

In the doorway, Irena, resplendent in a pink sequined gown that clung to her like a shimmering skin, stood with a tall, bearded, white-haired man wearing a ruffled shirt and tuxedo, whose glance slid around the room and came to rest arrogantly on Rachel. Paris scowled at the unfamiliar figure, then realized she'd seen the man's picture among Victor's papers.

"Stanton Fields." She couldn't believe her mother had brought the man! Beside her, Victor stared at the newcomer curiously.

Rachel bristled. "She dares bring him here?! This is not some neighborhood block party to which she can drag her latest paramour." Rachel moved as though she might rise and cast out the intruder.

Paris put a hand on her shoulder, restraining the frail body and reassuring Rachel. "I'll take care of it, dear." She went toward the door to head off her mother. Irena smiled nervously and quickly hooked her arm through Fields's, detouring him toward the patio before Paris could intercept them.

Rachel scrutinized the retreating figure. So that was Stanton Fields. She'd pictured him more the milktoast type since he hid behind a woman's skirt and sent Irena forth to do battle for him. Woman? Bah! Irena was a sniveling crybaby and the defiant child she had always been. As they vanished outside, she turned her attention back to her invited guests, smiling pleasantly as the president of Sperry Oil came toward her.

Victor moved away to relinquish Rachel to her new guest. Irena Hamilton, the family black sheep. Curious that she'd bring so unwelcome a guest to her mother's party, but quite in keeping with all he'd learned about her the past weeks. She was a striking woman who had not bowed to her years, but she had a hard look of selfishness. There were photos of Fields in the dossier Dorn had compiled from newspaper and magazine articles about the developer. Surprisingly, Fields was less dynamic in the flesh.

At the mahogany bar set up in one corner of the dining room, Victor ordered a drink. Beside him, a heavyset man looked at him, then clapped him on the shoulder.

"Victor! How are you?"

Victor realized he was looking at someone he should know and didn't. For a moment the terrible confusion he'd suffered those first few days in the hospital assailed him with typhoon force. He'd feared this situation and known it would happen, and now it was here. He managed to smile and grasp the hand extended to him.

"We just got back from Hong Kong," the big man said. "I really owe you one for tipping us off to what Rogers was after. We got the deal."

Good old Victor . . . "I'm glad things worked out," Victor said.

The man grinned. "An eight-million-dollar deal, old

buddy. That's the kind of work we like to get." He clapped Victor's shoulder again. "You must be just about finished with your job here. Are you heading back to Minneapolis or hanging around awhile?"

"I haven't decided," Victor said. It was something he'd delayed thinking about while he finished the redevelopment report, but he couldn't put it off any longer now.

"Let's get together for lunch soon," the man said, clapping his shoulder again, then moving off to greet a couple who hailed him.

Victor carried his drink out to the patio, relieved that he'd gotten through the first ordeal. It hadn't been as bad as he had expected. He felt confident now that he'd be able to tackle the unknown as it came. And he knew he'd go back to Minneapolis and unravel all the questions it held, now that he had finished the report and could take a brief vacation. He leaned against the stone parapet and inhaled the cool, misty air. Fog and dampness were rolling in from the ocean, portending rain.

Victor became aware of someone watching him and turned to find Irena Hamilton and Stanton Fields a few feet away. Irena wore a low-cut pink-sequined gown—too low for her age; her escort wore a black loose-fitting suit, and a beard, and a cigarette dangled from his thin lips. Fields tossed the cigarette over the balustrade and came toward Victor with his hand extended.

"Good to see you again, Sands."

So they had met. Curious, Victor smiled and shook hands. He'd let Fields do the talking and see where it led.

"Frankly," Fields said, his smile ebbing, "I've been expecting you to call. You promised to get back to me. Have you verified the information I gave you?"

Victor studied the bearded face and gray eyes. So Fields had told or given him something. Connected with the redevelopment project, it had to be. But what? Had Fields sent the special delivery copies of Teddy Reno's deed and bill of sale? If he'd expected Victor to call, he also must have sent something *before* that as well.

"I'm afraid you'll have to refresh my memory," Victor answered. Before he could give an explanation, Fields's face clouded like a sudden squall.

"You said you'd get right on it!" Fields's eyes blazed and

his fists clenched. Stepping closer to Victor, he snarled at Irena. "Go get yourself a drink, Irena. I want to talk to Sands alone!"

She scurried off meekly, glad to escape from the rage she saw building in Stanton. If only he hadn't insisted on coming here tonight. . . .

Fields glared at Victor. "What the hell are you trying to pull, Sands? If you think you can double-cross me—"

Victor's anger snapped. "I'm not double-crossing anyone. I don't think I ever made you any promises—"

Fields moved astonishingly fast for an old man. He closed in, snarling and throwing a quick right to Victor's jaw. Victor staggered back, his drink splashing over the parapet and his glass shattering. He reacted instinctively, blocking Fields's second punch that was marked by a wide swing of his arm. The fist grazed Victor's shoulder as Fields stumbled. He exploded into profanity and barged in like a street fighter.

He was fast. He barreled a punch past Victor's guard that crashed Victor against the stone wall. Before he could recover, Fields was on him like a madman, raining blows wherever he could land them. Victor sidestepped and threw a hard left. Fields staggered back with a grunt, looking dazed for a moment. Blood trickled from the corner of his mouth and he wiped it gingerly, leaving his beard streaked with blood. Victor braced for another attack, but Fields wheeled and strode back into the crowded dining room where Irena had vanished.

Victor rubbed his jaw and felt his swollen lip. His second encounter with the past hadn't gone well. What the hell was wrong with Fields? Tempted to follow and demand an explanation, Victor hesitated. In his present mood Fields was capable of disrupting the party. Better to let it go until he could unravel Fields's mysterious comments. Turning toward the garden, he walked down the path toward the front of the house. He'd call Paris in the morning and explain. Right now he needed time to think.

Paris became aware of a commotion in the dining room and looked up. Rachel heard it, too.

"What is going on over there?" she demanded.

"I'll find out." Paris patted her grandmother's shoulder and hurried toward the dining room. People near the patio doors parted like a curtain as Stanton Fields barged through. His beard was smeared with blood and his face was contorted in an angry mask. At the bar Irena gasped and downed the glass of champagne she was holding. Paris blocked Fields's path.

"What's the meaning of this?" she demanded.

Hissing, he shoved her aside brutally and strode to the sofa, taking a stand in front of Rachel.

"Hello, Rachel. It's been a long time."

She gave him a contemptuous look, raising a hand to halt Paris's approach. She studied Fields's disheveled appearance. "You are an uninvited guest, Mr. Fields. Please leave or I'll have you thrown out."

He snorted. "You would, wouldn't you? You haven't changed any." He reached into his coat pocket and drew out an envelope. "Before I go, do me the honor of accepting these birthday greetings. You have no idea how much I've looked foward to giving them to you." He shoved the card at her.

Rachel's glance didn't waver as she accepted the envelope and wedged it under her left hand as she extracted the card. Opening it, she looked down to read it. Her face went ashen and her lip quivered. She looked up at Fields.

Her pained whisper was barely audible. "Who are you?"

The room had fallen still, and Fields's sardonic laugh raked the quiet. "Why, Rachel, how could you forget me?"

Rachel shook her head and her hand went to her breast. "It—it can't be—"

Frightened by the look on her grandmother's face, Paris tried to step between the two. "It's time for you to leave," she told Fields, her musical voice suddenly stern. Her mother was a fool to bring this man here. *I should have thrown him out as soon as he arrived.*

Fields spun around and shoved Paris violently. The force of the blow reeled her into Josh, who quickly closed his arms around her to keep her from falling. A ripple of astonishment eddied through the room. Before anyone could react, Fields sprang behind the sofa and grabbed Rachel's thin shoulders.

"Stay where you are, all of you!"

Paris freed herself from Josh's arms and took a step forward, but Fields froze her in her tracks by tightening his grip on Rachel and shaking her. The blood had drained from her face and her lips had a slight blue cast. Her eyes were fixed on the greeting card Fields had given her.

"Read it aloud!" Fields commanded. When she didn't

comply, he shook her so her head snapped back.

"Stop it!" Paris screamed. She took a step but halted quickly when Fields began to shake Rachel again.

"Read it!" he ordered.

Rachel lifted her chin defiantly. Her voice quavered like a breeze rustling dry grass. "I will not. Kill me if you must, but I will have no part in your drama."

"Rachel, please—" Paris implored. Whatever this madman wanted, he should get it, so he would depart. Why had Irena brought him? Paris's gaze swept the bar but couldn't pick out her mother.

"Read it!" Fields screamed

A rustle of motion ran through the gathering. Several men moved as if to corner Fields. As he looked around quickly, his hold on Rachel loosened. Paris threw herself at him, hitting him off guard and shoving him away from the sofa and Rachel. He fell backward, his arms flailing as he tried to fight off Paris. She clawed and kicked and beat at him, her fury outmatching his strength. The room was galvanized into action, and the sudden swell of noise roared in Paris's ears. She closed her eyes as Fields tried to gouge them.

Suddenly Paris felt strong hands pull her away from Fields, who lay supine on the floor. A man straddled Fields and punched him, while someone restrained Paris, who was ready to enter the melee with more force than before, and much less fanfare. She had a glimpse of Irena's frightened face, hands pressed to her mouth. At that moment Paris hated her mother with a fury beyond belief. Voices swelled.

"Call the police!"

"Stop them—somebody stop them!"

"My God—Rachel—!"

Josh sprang as Rachel slumped. Paris ran to them, bending to her grandmother. Rachel's eyes were closed and her breathing raspy and shallow. Her face was bloodless, her lips blue. Paris sprang up and raced for the phone, ignoring the startled cries around her. She dialed emergency, and a sob caught in her throat as she gave the address and asked that Dr. Forest meet the ambulance at the hospital. Dropping the phone, she ran back to her grandmother. She was only dimly aware that the man who had subdued Fields was standing behind the sofa. Drew Hamilton, her father.

Josh laid Rachel down and put a small pillow under her

head. There were unashamed tears in his eyes as he bent over her.

Paris knelt beside him. *Dear God, let her be all right. Another stroke . . . The excitement had been too much for her. How could Irena have brought that madman here?* Tears ran down her cheeks as she held her grandmother's limp hand. *Let her live. Let her be all right.*

The faint cry of a siren wailed in the distance, echoed by the wind which had sprung to life. A few minutes later two paramedics rushed in. Paris watched their quick, sure motions with a terrible feeling of *déjà vu*. Rachel had to be all right. She had to be. The paramedics were using the same heroic methods as when Rachel suffered her first stroke. Paris tried to convince herself it was a good sign. Rachel was alive.

Someone lifted Paris to her feet gently. She let out her breath, realizing she'd been holding it. Drew Hamilton put his arm around her.

"It's going to be okay." His face was incredibly sad, his dark eyes filled with concern.

When Paris looked at him, the sobs she'd been swallowing erupted in racking sounds. For the first time in too long, she let her father draw her into his arms, welcoming his warmth even though the bitterness was still in her heart. He pressed her to his shoulder and let her cry. The paramedics put Rachel on a gurney and wheeled her out. Josh walked beside the stretcher still holding Rachel's hand. Drew led Paris outside after them. The wind was whipping the trees with an anguished sound as the storm neared. Paris shivered in the cold, damp air. Drew pulled his coat off and hung it around her shoulders, then helped her into the ambulance. Josh signaled his chauffeur to follow, and climbed in beside her. As the doors closed, the two of them bent over Rachel, their faces taut. Moments later the ambulance rolled down the drive, its siren screaming. Guests got into their cars and followed it down the hill like a funeral cortege.

Drew hurried inside to where he'd left Rachel's assailant unconscious on the floor. To his amazement the man was gone. In the excitement no one had stood guard over him. Drew ran through the empty dining room and out onto the patio. Irena was leaning against the parapet weeping hysterically. He grabbed her.

"Where did he go?" he demanded.

Irena looked up in confused misery. "Drew?" Her makeup was smeared by tears. Black streaks of mascara creased her face like a hag's wrinkles. There was a nasty red blotch on one cheek. She clutched Drew's arm. "Is it really you?" she sobbed.

"Where did that guy go?" Drew demanded. He'd heard someone in the crowd around Paris and the struggling man say Irena had brought him. "Answer me, Irena!"

Frightened, she began to cry again. Drew grabbed her shoulders and shook her. "Stop it!" Irena hiccupped. "Where is he?" Drew demanded again.

She sniffled. "He hit me." When Drew shook her again, she pointed toward the path. "He's gone."

Drew leaped down the steps and raced along the path, but there was no sign of the man. He'd slipped into the crowd and driven off. Damn it! Drew hurried back. Irena had gone inside and was leaning on the bar, draining champagne from glasses that stood there. She gave Drew a frightened look and tried unsuccessfully to smile.

"They said you brought him," Drew accused. "Who is he?"

"I didn't know he was going to—" She cowered under Drew's angry glare. "He said the hotel was mine. He was going to get it for me." She knocked over an empty glass as she reached for a full one. Drew struck it from her hand.

"Who is he?"

"St-Stanton Fields—a friend—" She was crying again.

"Friend?! He tried to kill your mother!" He gave Irena a pitying look, resisting the impulse to strike her. She richly deserved some form of punishment—maybe Rachel's condition was enough.

"I didn't mean for this to happen, I swear. You've got to believe me, Drew. Tell Paris—" She buried her face in her hands and the sobs erupted in spasms.

Drew shook his head. *Irena . . . poor little Irena. She still couldn't face up to the truth about herself.*

After a while, Irena looked up, her face swollen and her eyes red. "I didn't want to hurt Rachel. Not that way. Please believe me, Drew."

Poor mixed-up, pathetic Irena.

"He lied to me all along. About his name, about wanting to marry me—"

"His name?" Drew said, peering at her.

Irena wiped her nose on a cocktail napkin as she searched for another champagne glass. "He fooled everyone."

The little lost Ice Princess. "Who is he, Irena?"

She sounded like a frightened child. "He knew Daddy a long time ago. I was only a little girl." She bit her lip, struggling with tears again as she looked imploringly at Drew. Someone had to understand it wasn't her fault. "He used me. All he wanted was to get even with Rachel. He—" She sniffled. "He never wants to see me again." She covered her face and wept.

Drew left her for a minute and went into the living room. Under the ice-blue chintz sofa, the greeting card Rachel had been holding lay on the floor. He picked it up and read it. Beside the printed greeting a spidery hand had written:

> *"What's past and what's to come is strewn with husks and formless ruin of oblivion."* You were reading Shakespeare the first time I met you. It's fitting you should read it one last time. Your last, dear Rachel, but before you die, speak aloud the truth. You and Irena were with Ruth Fantazia the night she died. I saw you. It's time you tell Josh, or I will.

There was no signature. Drew shoved the card in his pocket, remembering the day Rachel had silenced him by telling him the story of Ruth Fantazia's death. Rachel had buried it carefully, and he'd all but forgotten it in the intervening years, but now it had arisen from the past like a ghost. He went back to Irena.

"What's his real name?"

She blinked and wiped her eyes with the back of her hand. "Teddy Reno. I didn't know until tonight, I swear. I believed he was Stanton Fields. He's insane."

"Where is he now?"'

"The Oceanside Hotel." Irena trembled and hugged her arms across the sequined bodice of her gown.

Drew turned and strode out. He knew Reno had told Irena his destination either with orders or the hope she would blurt it out and force Rachel to follow. Only he'd made one major miscalculation: he'd incapacitated Rachel. Now Drew had the information, and there was no way he was going to ignore the bait.

❧ Twenty-Four ❧

THE FURY OF the crashing surf and howling wind thundered through the high-vaulted lobby like a drumroll. The walls wept and the air felt damp and unpleasant. Drew had found the side door open, an obvious invitation from Reno. Why would Reno come here, of all places? Drew recoiled at the cloying air, remembering the hotel in its heyday. It was hard to believe these rooms had once been alive with gaiety and music and voices. It was only a dim ghost of the past. Rachel's past come back to haunt them all.

He let his eyes adjust to the gloomy darkness. Above the stone stairway that led to the upper lobby, a glow of light formed a hazy fog. Reno was up there. Drew moved softly on the balls of his feet. He didn't know what to expect, and he didn't want Reno to take him by surprise. If Reno was expecting Rachel, there was no telling what kind of trap he'd laid.

The light was coming from the mezzanine. At the head of the grand staircase, Teddy Reno cast a giant shadow. Drew stopped, squinting at the figure. Did he have a gun? Very slowly Drew moved closer, but halfway to the staircase, his foot hit some unseen object that clattered across the floor.

Reno's voice boomed like a cannon through the tomblike room. "Rachel? I knew you'd come!"

Drew moved into the spill of light, his hands spread to

show he was unarmed. "It's not Rachel."

"Who are you?" The angry words rolled down the stairs.

"Drew Hamilton. Irena's first husband."

Reno hunched, peering down. "Where's Rachel? I told that stupid bitch to send her!"

Drew inched closer to the stairs without taking his gaze off Reno. But the dark shadow leaped instantly. A shot blazed and roared. Drew jumped from the wood that splintered a few feet away.

"I'll kill you if you don't get out of here. I want Rachel!"

Drew stood very still. "Rachel isn't coming."

"She'll come! This time I hold all the cards! She tried to kill me once, now I'm going to kill her!"

He was crazy, and he was dangerous. Drew's stomach knotted as he forced himself to speak calmly. "Why? What good will it do? You're an old man. Do you want to spend the rest of your life in some stinking prison? That's where you'll wind up."

"It will be worth it!" Reno screamed. "I've waited a long time for this."

Drew eased toward the step again, but Reno brought up the gun. The light behind him cast a long shadow down the stairs. "Stay where you are, Hamilton!"

Drew backed off. "Let's talk—"

"I'll talk to Rachel! Oh, I have a lot to say to her!"

"They took her to the hospital. She can't come."

Reno's breath hissed. "You're lying! Irena will make her come."

Drew shook his head, still watching the gun in Reno's hand. "Rachel is a sick old lady. She may not get out of the hospital this time." He spoke quietly as he would to a spooked horse.

Reno hunched forward, backlighted by the yellow glow. "She'll come. She has to come. She'll come." He wasn't screaming now but talking quietly to himself. His face was an ugly mask shadowed with hatred, and he looked demonic in this light.

Suddenly Reno darted out of sight. His shadow danced grotesquely on the wall of the mezzanine. Drew flung himself up the stairs, but Reno was back before he hit the first landing.

"Stop right there!" Reno raised his arm and light splashed

across the darkness. He was holding a lantern. Not an electric torch but an old-fashioned kerosene lantern. Drew stopped in his tracks, realizing suddenly that the pungent odor in his nostrils was more than dampness and mold. Kerosene. He saw the wet trails where Reno had poured it down the steps. He put his hands up placatingly.

"All right. I'm not moving."

The lantern wavered. Reno was crazy, the kind of crazy that didn't care if he killed himself as long as he got what he wanted. Drew gauged his chances of outrunning a lantern and a gun.

"Rachel tried to kill me," Reno said. "Her and her boyfriend Fantazia. Two of a kind, goddam greedy bastards. They cheated me from the start! Rachel cheated everyone, even her own husband and daughter. Well, she won't get away with it this time." The lantern swung crazily as Reno gestured.

Drew tried to buy time. "How did she cheat her husband and daughter?" In spite of the danger he was fascinated by Reno's ravings. Irena had always claimed the hotel was hers, but he'd discounted it as one of her childish fantasies. If Reno's accusations were true, he was surprised not at Rachel's cupidity but at his own failure to catch on to the truth before this. Strangely, he felt no anger. Rachel was what she was. It was Paris that Drew cared about. He couldn't stand by and let her be hurt, no matter what Rachel had done.

Reno laughed bitterly. "What's forgery to a woman who'd kill for what she wants? She stole the hotel from her own husband. Ain't that a bitch? I've waited and planned a long time for this. Now I'm going to destroy her!" He raised his arms, and the light splashed across his face. His expression was maniacal.

Drew spoke quietly. "Rachel's in the hospital."

"She'll come! She has to come!" He swung the lantern in a dangerous arc.

"Wait! Reno!" Drew's mouth was brassy. If Reno let that lantern go, the hotel would go up like a tinderbox.

"Get her! Do you hear me? I want Rachel!" The cry vibrated in the cavernous lobby. As it faded slowly there was a sound behind Drew.

From the shadows, a voice said, "I'm here, Teddy."

Drew whirled. Paris was standing near the foot of the

stairs. For a moment in the deceptive gloom, it could have been Rachel. Paris looked at him. "What are you doing here?" he whispered fiercely. "Get out. He's crazy. There's no telling what he'll do."

She whispered back. "Irena came to the hospital and told me you were here. I can't let you fight Rachel's last battle."

Terrified of the danger she was in, he said savagely, "Better me than you. Now get out of here!"

"What are you two whispering about?" Reno demanded loudly. "Is that you, Rachel? Is Josh with you or are you brave enough to face me alone this time?" He laughed mirthlessly.

Paris stepped into the light.

"Rachel?"

"No, it's Paris. Rachel is dead." Pain squeezed Paris's chest as she uttered the truth that was so hard to accept. She saw Drew's agonized expression and Reno's baffled one.

"She can't be," Reno shouted. "She has to die in agony!"

Paris took a deep breath and climbed the first step toward her father and the madman on the mezzanine.

"She died in her own private hell. Let her rest in peace."

Drew knew Paris was speaking not only to Reno but to him, and herself as well. But Teddy wasn't buying it.

"Why should I? The world has to know what a thieving, lying bitch she is. She can't buy or bully her way out this time!"

Paris took another step up. "Let her be, Teddy. It's over." She sounded incredibly weary, and Drew's heart ached for her. No matter what Rachel had done, Paris loved her, just as he had always loved Paris. He had to get her way from here, and the maniac Reno. He started down the steps.

"Stay where you are—both of you!" Reno screamed. The shadows along the wall leaped erratically. Drew turned back quickly, but it was too late. The lantern flew from Reno's grasp in a wide arc. Drew ducked instinctively as it sailed past, fanning the air so remnants of the chandelier tinkled overhead. It crashed in a burst of flame at Paris's feet. Drew dived as she screamed.

A trail of flame exploded around him as the fuel Reno had poured down the stairs ignited. Blinded, Drew skidded off the side of the railingless steps and landed with a bone-jarring thud. He staggered to his feet in pain. The flames spread rapidly through the trash that littered the huge room. He couldn't see Paris anymore. He lurched forward through the black smoke.

"Paris?! Where are you?" Drew groped blindly.

Above him Reno cursed and screamed Rachel's name. For a moment he was outlined in the flames, a madman swinging a fuel can. Before he could release it, the top of the stairs roared in a ball of fire, engulfing him. Drew plunged toward the spot where he'd last seen Paris.

Coughing and choking, he shouted her name into the inferno. "Paris?! Paris?!"

He heard a faint cough. She was on the floor. He fell to his hands and knees and crawled toward the sound. He found her and quickly began swatting her clothes where the flames had caught. Heaving and gasping, he picked her up and stumbled to his feet. She buried her face in his coat. The stench of burning hair and clothing filled his nostrils.

He'd lost all sense of direction in the holocaust. Veering to avoid new flames snaking toward him, he slammed against a wall and, using it as a guide, he plunged ahead desperately. Just as his lungs were about to burst, he stumbled into a hallway filled with drifting smoke but no fire. He set Paris on her feet, keeping a protective arm around her as he tried to catch his breath.

Paris rubbed her stinging eyes and gulped with relief as she huddled against the wall.

"Are you all right?" Drew asked, peering at her from swollen, bloodshot eyes.

She nodded, blinking and glancing at the fire that moved toward them steadily, cutting off any retreat.

"Let's go," Drew ordered. "We can't stay here." He tried to propel her down the hall.

Paris pulled back. "We can't get out this way. The windows are barred." The hall led to the dining room where workmen had covered the tall windows with wire mesh before boarding them over. She glanced in the direction of the serving room, but the flames had already gobbled up the air current coming from the kitchen. They were trapped.

"Is there another door?" Drew shouted. They'd be roasted alive if they stayed here much longer.

Paris summoned a picture of the hotel layout from memory and recalled a branch in the corridor that forked down to the hotel offices. Rachel's had been at the end, and an exit door led to the outside. She pointed. Drew pulled her along as fire belched behind them. Wood crackled and a shower of sparks sprayed as a section of wall collapsed.

Touching her hand to the hot wall, Paris groped for the side hall, then pulled on her father's shirt to lead him down it. She could feel the heat through her thin sandals. How many offices? How many doors? Had she made a mistake? Then suddenly they were at the end of the hall. She pulled Drew back and shouted.

"Office. An outside door—"

Drew threw himself against the panel. Behind them, the flames jumped suddenly, lighting the hallway and showing them the heavy boards that had been nailed across the door in a crisscross pattern. Drew swore angrily and threw his weight against it again. The fire edged closer rapidly. The entire front of the hotel was engulfed. There was no going back. He heaved his weight against the barricade again as the noise of the flames and the surf and storm outside roared in his head. A board cracked, and he attacked it again with frenzy. Finally the door splintered inward. Drew tumbled into the darkness. Under him the floor was cool. The room was built on a solid foundation. It would buy them a few minutes. He heard Paris shout as he got to his feet and reached for her hand. She dragged him across the room to another door, then exclaimed in a cry of despair. In the flickering light from the burning hall, he saw that the outside door had been nailed shut by spikes driven into the molding.

Drew battered at the wood with his powerful shoulders, ignoring the pain that seared his bones. The hard wood didn't budge. Behind them, a beam gave way with a thunderous roar as it fell across the doorway to the hall.

Drew attacked the door with new fury. His shoulder was dislocated, he was sure, and his chest ached with raw throbs. The room grew hotter as the fire ate along the baseboards facing the hall. Paris tugged at his sleeve insistently, then pointed at something. In the eerie glow, he could make out several planks in the pile of rubble that blocked the hall. They ran and quickly salvaged one from the smoldering heap. It blistered their hands as they positioned it between them and made a run at the outside door. The wood cracked. They backed and battered it again; They followed with a third at-

tempt and the door splintered. Cool air bathed their faces as
they made two more strikes at the broken panel. They dropped
the plank and clawed at the hole. When the opening was big
enough, Drew shoved Paris through.

The outside steps had broken away and she plunged several
feet onto the cold, wet sand. Rain drenched her mercifully as
the wind screamed in her ears. She turned, searching for her
father. Drew was outlined in the flaming doorway as the fire
fed itself on the new supply of oxygen. His clothes flared like
a human torch.

"Daddy!" The cry came from some deep well of memory,
anguished and pained.

Drew fell, his arms outstretched as though reaching for her.
He hit the sand with a sizzling thud. Crying, Paris tried to
crawl toward him but suddenly encountered a looming shadow
that blocked her way.

Victor yanked off his coat and wrapped it around the burning man, rolling him in the wet sand and slapping out the little
blazes. When only smoke remained, he lifted Drew up gently
and led him out of danger. For the first time Paris became
aware of the screaming sirens and flashing lights of fire trucks
on Ocean Boulevard. Then Victor returned for her and carried
her to where her father lay stretched out, moaning in pain.
Despite the agony of his burns, he managed to smile up at his
daughter, who hovered overhead in worry and concern.
"Don't worry, babe," he said in a husky voice. "Even an old
oil rigger-turned manager has a thick hide."

✜ *Twenty-Five* ✜

PARIS GAZED OUT the hospital window at the purple sea and the dark mound of Catalina Island. The storm had passed with the night, leaving the landscape sparkling in crystal air like dew-laden flowers opening to the morning sun. Some of the horror of the previous night began to blur in her thoughts as she accepted the events, realizing what was gone could never be recovered. She remembered Victor appearing miraculously, carrying her away from the fire and sitting beside her in the ambulance. She remembered crying, not in pain as Victor feared, but for the terrible loss she felt, the emptiness.

Rachel was dead. Her father was in intensive care with burns over thirty percent of his body. He'd risked his life to save her. In spite of everything Rachel had done in the past and Paris's blind acceptance of the gulf that separated her from her father, Drew loved her enough to risk his life for her. He had always loved her, she knew that now. When Dr. Forest stopped by to see her in the morning, she asked him to make sure Drew had the finest care available. And she was praying for a miracle.

She heard footsteps and turned from the window as Victor entered the hospital room. He held out a small bouquet of violets wrapped in white lace.

369

"I don't know if these are what good old Victor would choose, but I couldn't resist them."

He smiled so tenderly, Paris's heart ached with love for him. "They're beautiful."

He drew up a chair and sat close to her. "How are you today?" He'd stayed at the hospital most of the night, pacing the corridor until the doctors assured him Paris's burns were not serious and she would recover from the ordeal without complications. Even then he didn't leave until a friendly nurse took pity on him and let him peek in as Paris slept.

"I'm fine," Paris said. "The doctor says I can go home in a day or two." She raised her bandaged hand. "Did I thank you properly last night? You probably saved my father's life."

"I was in the right place at the right moment," he said. "If I'd caught on sooner, maybe I could have prevented the whole episode."

"Caught on to what?"

"Stanton Fields, Teddy Reno, the whole thing. When I met Fields last night, he didn't give me time to recognize that something was wrong. When he attacked me, I figured it was something I'd done. I left the party so I wouldn't cause any more scenes, but by the time I got home, I knew something else bothered me about Fields. I couldn't put my finger on it until I got out the file I had on him. The man claiming to be Stanton Fields was an imposter. I'd been looking at Fields's picture on company brochures and in *Business Week* and reading enough about him to know him like a favorite uncle. Fields the developer and Fields the attacker were two different people. There was a resemblance, but there were significant differences, too. Fields doesn't smoke. Fields has a scar on the back of his hand. Most of all, Fields is in New York. I'd been told that but I didn't believe it because he was here. By the time I figured it out last night, I knew the imposter was a dangerous man." He'd gone back to the house on Ladera Street, but it was too late. The servants told him what had occurred and that Rachel had been taken to the hospital. By the time he got there, Rachel was dead and Paris was gone. Weeping and shaken, Irena told him about Reno and the hotel and that Paris had gone there.

"How did you know about the side door?" Paris asked.

"Some of that learned information Dr. Forest talks about, I suppose. The hotel was an inferno by the time I got there. No one could get in or out the other doors." He took her bandaged hand gently. "Learned information or luck, I'm glad I was there."

"So am I," she said with deep feeling. "For me, and for Drew. My father wouldn't have a chance if you hadn't acted so quickly. He's going to make it, I know he will. He's got to. I have a lot to make up to him." She sighed and looked at Victor with tears in her eyes. "I saw only what I wanted to see in Rachel. I never disturbed the shadows of the past. I wanted her to be perfect and to take the place of the mother and father I didn't have."

"Don't judge her too harshly, Paris," Victor said tenderly. "She loved you very much."

"I can't judge her at all, Victor. She was a wonderful person. Nothing will ever change that. But she wasn't God and she shouldn't have tried to be." She thought about her father facing down Teddy Reno in Rachel's place the previous night. The extent of Reno's hatred or Rachel's sins of the past would never be known. It was better that way. Bury the past with those who were buried.

"What will you do now?" Victor asked.

"Carry on for Rachel. Run the company."

"Will the redevelopment project tie you down totally?"

She looked at him keenly. "The council—You recommended the Upfield plan?"

"Yes. The council voted this morning. You've got the job." The forged deed had caused some doubts, but Victor hadn't been hired to pass judgment on Rachel's ethics or the way she built her fortune. He suspected a certain amount of ruthlessness had been necessary for a woman of her era.

Paris's new concept for additional wings had been the decisive factor. It proved that the old could blend with the new to great benefit. Restoring the Oceanside Hotel would serve the community better than condominiums which could be built in districts adjacent to the downtown.

"But the fire—?"

"It gutted the hotel completely, but the shell is as sound as a fortress, just as you and Rachel have been saying all along. Right now it's the muckiest quagmire you ever saw, but that fire saved you a couple of hundred thousand dollars in demolition costs." Victor smiled at the relieved look on Paris's face. Her eyes lost their haunted look and were once again the beautiful sea-green he found so enticing. Framed against the window, her hair was spun gold, and her complexion a silky light brown. She was beautiful. He wanted very much to kiss her. He was sure that he had loved her before, and he was sure he did now.

"Thank you, Victor," she said. "Upfield will do the job. I owe Rachel that."

"You and Rachel fought a good fight and won fairly."

The telephone in the console chattered softly, and Paris reached for it. She put her bandaged hand over Victor's when he would have stepped outside.

It was Josh Fantazia. "Congratulations, Paris. Your grandmother would be very proud of you." He sounded very old and tired.

"Thank you, Josh." Coming from Josh Fantazia, it was a high compliment. She thought about him sitting beside Rachel the previous night sharing those last sad minutes. "I hope we can be friends now, Josh."

"Rachel would like hearing you say that. She and I were rivals much too long. We wasted so many years." His voice caught and he cleared his throat. "One area in which I couldn't hold a candle to Rachel was granddaughters. I regret the part Shanna played with Fields, but she was taken in like everyone else."

"It's over, Josh," Paris said gently. "I'm glad you and Rachel patched up your differences before it was too late."

He sighed, considering how fragile life was and how recklessly people wasted time. "The police are closing the file on the bum Reno killed in the Oceanside. We'll never know what Teddy's full scheme was, but I guess it doesn't matter."

"No, it doesn't matter," Paris said.

Josh cleared his throat again. "Have the funeral arrangements been made?"

"Not yet, but I'll call you as soon as they are."

"Thank you, my dear. And if there's anything you need, please call me. Anything at all."

As she hung up, Victor studied her pensive face. "Can the president of the Upfield Company take some time off?"

"I won't be going back until after the funeral."

"You need more rest than that."

"The redevelopment proj—"

"One of the things I learned about the Upfield Land Management Company is that it has top-notch people on every level who work as a team. It's permissible for the head coach to organize the plays but miss the game."

"And what will I do instead?" She hoped he was leading to what she wanted to hear. She smiled and folded her silky fingers gently over his hand. He looked down at her from his immense height, through those gentle brown eyes. His corduroy slacks were slightly loose from the weight he'd lost while ill, and he pulled the knees up as he sat on her bed.

"I was thinking of a few weeks in Cabo San Lucas, where there's nothing to do but lie in the sun and fish."

"You hate to fish—!"

Victor laughed, delighted with the spontaneous burst that relieved the tired lines of her face. "I don't know that for a learned fact," he said. "Maybe I never took time to relax and enjoy it. I owe it to myself to make an honest judgment." He learned toward her, holding her green gaze. "Will you go with me, Paris? I'm leaving for Minneapolis tomorrow to pull together the pieces of my elusive past. I have the feeling it won't take long. Whatever's there didn't hold me before. I don't think it will entice me back now. I belong in Ocean Beach. With you."

"I'd love to go fishing," she said softly.

He lifted a finger and swept back a blond strand of hair, then leaned over and kissed her nose. "A few weeks should be enough time for you to decide if the new Victor is someone you'd like to spend the rest of your life with." He stood and drew her into his arms, being very careful of her bandaged burns. "I think good old Victor loved you very much. If he didn't, he was a fool. But I'm talking now for the new Victor who's only one month and four days old. Is that too young to get married? I love you, Paris."

She'd waited so long to hear those words. She gathered them to her heart as he kissed her. She returned the kiss eagerly, sealing the promise of their rediscovered love. The past was gone forever and the future was theirs.

❧ Epilogue ❧

THE SAILBOAT DRIFTED lazily, its sails slack under the heat of the noonday sun. Over the stern, a fishing line dragged gently through the blue water, its red float bobbing. Suddenly the ball disappeared, surfaced, dived again. The line went taut as it began to feed out of the reel with a humming noise. Paris stirred lazily, shading her eyes with her hand.

"You've got one!" She poked Victor awake. "Hey, fisherman, pull him in!"

Victor rolled and captured her in his arms, pulling her back to the cushions they'd spread on the deck for sunning. Laughing, she tried to escape.

"Not me, the fish, silly!"

He nuzzled his square, handsome face against her sunwarmed flesh that was perfumed by suntan oil and saltwater. "I'd rather have you."

"He'll get away—"

"As long as you never do." Victor pulled her close and claimed her lips as his hands roamed her sleek naked curves unhampered by a suit. "Any regrets, Mrs. Sands?" he murmured.

"None at all, darling. I told you you hated to fish." They came together in desire and love. Eventually the humming line went slack again, but by then they didn't notice.

Bestselling Books
from Berkley